nothing
ABOVE

A. MARIE

Editing: My Notes in the Margin
Proofreading: Judy Zweifel, Judy's Proofreading
Cover Design: Samantha Lovelock at Honey + Sin Designs
Formatting: Champagne Book Design

You can find the full playlist on Spotify

Playground—Bea Miller, Arcane, League of Legends
Grind With Me—Pretty Ricky
… Don't Save Me—Chxrlotte
Na Na—Trey Songz
Holy Water—Zayde Wølf
Sex Metal Barbie—In This Moment
Roots—In This Moment
Cold As Ice—Ava Max
Liar—Mood Monroe
White Lie—Lenii
Play Nice—Jules LeBlanc
Numb—Carlie Hanson
Nothing Is As It Seems—Hidden Citizens, Ruelle
Killer—Valerie Broussard
Don't Tell Anyone—Story & Blue
Mental Funeral—EHLE
Wait—Jay Warren
In The End - Acoustic Version—Beth Crowley
If Looks Could Kill—Jeremy Shada
Chaos Control—Daktyl, Lily Kershaw
Hard To Kill—Beth Crowley
like that—Bea Miller

Figure You Out—VOILÀ
good—Wrabel
ALONE—XYLØ
Waiting Game—BANKS
Play—David Banner
Hurt Me—Suriel Hess
Kill The Lights—Hidden Citizens, Lush Machine
Never Be Like You—Flume, kai
No Good—UNSECRET, Ruelle
Destroy Destroy Destroy—Transviolet
Dark Side—Bishop Briggs
could you love me while i hate myself—Zeph
No Good—Th3rdstream, Nefertiti
I Scare Myself—Beth Crowley
Serial Killer—Moncrieff, JUDGE
Love The Way You Lie—Eminem, Rihanna
If I Killed Someone For You—Alec Benjamin
Alpha—Little Destroyer
Smother Me—Kelaska
I Would Die for You—In This Moment
Hayloft II—Mother Mother
The Blood Legion—In This Moment
killer queen—Mad Tsai
Unlearn—benny blanco, Gracie Abrams
Little Girl Gone—CHINCHILLA

This book is a 145k-word dark romance standalone intended for audiences 18+.

It contains content that may be triggering and/or disturbing to some readers, such as, but not limited to: foul language, graphic violence, explicit sexual situations, anxiety, cheating, stalking, chronic illness, spousal abuse, drug and alcohol use, grooming, murder, talk of suicide/attempted suicide, kidnapping, drugging, theft, involuntary sex work/sex acts, talk of sexual assault/rape, attempted sexual assault, spit play, blood play, breeding, masochism, auralism, orgasm control, swallowing/exchanging of bodily fluids, public play, raw sex/ sex without a condom.

While this book does feature cheating, it is <u>not</u> between the main characters.

Any on-page sex between the main characters is consensual.

If you've read any of my previously published books, i.e., romantic dramedies, and are going into this one with the same expectations, I strongly suggest you leave those here before you turn the page. These characters are morally gray and their story is gritty and unconventional.

With all that said…enjoy.

To anyone that's sick and tired, literally and/or metaphorically.
You're not alone.

"With freedom, flowers, books, and the moon, who could not be perfectly happy?" –Oscar Wilde

nothing ABOVE

One

Reece

STEP THROUGH THE ROW OF PINE TREES, THEIR THICK BOUGHS keeping me cloaked in shadows from the glare of the round, orange moon overhead. After a glance in both directions, I take off up the long driveway, my shoes soundless against the black asphalt as I stick close to the edge.

At least this driveway's paved. Last job's was gravel, which made me have to go a hell of a lot slower in order to remain silent. I felt like a motherfucking sloth, half-expecting moss to be forming on my skin by the time I reached the house.

This job will be easier, faster, and smoother.

Should be.

Better fucking be.

I've been casing this place for a few days, and the security is non-existent. With no front gate, no fencing, no dog, no cameras, no security system, there's nothing to ward off intruders at all, not even an exterior motion-activated spotlight.

This mark's definitely cocky. Stupid too. Kinda explains why someone made the order on him. He probably deserves what's coming to him.

Cresting the hill, the massive white Colonial comes into view, so I pull my balaclava down over my face until only my eyes are visible.

Approaching the three-car garage, I slow my steps along the

window to confirm both the hundred-thousand-dollar ebony Range Rover Sport and three-hundred-thousand-dollar pearl Porsche 911 GT2 RS are inside. Parked side by side, the two look like total opposites. Not only is this garage also lacking a single measure of security, but it's got glass windows practically begging to be broken. *So motherfucking cocky.*

Shit like this tells me this mark's never had to work hard for what he has. Work? Yeah, I'm sure he works a lot, but not hard. There's no way he works *hard*. If he did, he'd value what he has a little more. I've seen places that cost a tenth of what one of these cars is worth that had more safeguards than this entire house does.

Thanks to both vehicles having blacked-out windows, I wasn't able to see who drives either, but based off the intel given to me, one's for the mark, while the other's for the wife I was instructed not to go anywhere near.

I'm not sure why my boss would have any information regarding the mark's wife and I didn't make the mistake of asking. When given my next assignment, I usually get an address and a timeframe to have the goods to him by; that's it. The rest is up to me to figure out.

Whoever hired Cyrus for this job though, knows the mark well because he had a couple more details for me. Along with the warning about the wife, he also told me which door to use as well as a general route to the laptop I'm here to steal.

Shit, the mark himself could've hired Cyrus. Or the mark's wife. This is Fox Hollow; crazier shit happens here. Daily.

Crouching down in front of the door by the garage, I set my lock-picking kit on the ground and unroll it.

I wasn't always this prepared, this…professional. Back when I was somehow getting by on sheer dumb luck rather than skill, I used to break locks to get into places. But that was before I knew anything about this world.

Before it became mine.

It's not that I chose this life in particular, it's that I didn't have any other choice. I was a delinquent as a teenager, but I didn't get in trouble for the petty crimes I committed. Mostly because I never got caught.

My dad, on the other hand… While he didn't get caught for his bad deeds either, they did catch up to him. And instead of facing up to his mistakes, he took his own life, putting the full weight of his sins on the rest of our family's shoulders.

Unbeknownst to me, my mom, and my twin sisters, Silvino Souza had a huge gambling problem, the kind that ruins lives. His secret gambling addiction ruined our fucking lives, and now I'm stuck working for the man who took on every bet my father made, even the one for the deed to our family's business, Silvy's Flower Shop. My dad had used his life's work, my parents' only source of income, as collateral on a bet, and lost. He lost it to Fox Hollow's crime lord, Cyrus Andeno, who wasted no time coming to collect. The day Cyrus showed up at Silvy's was the day I lost my father, along with any respect I ever had for him. Promising Cyrus he'd make things right, my dad ran to the back office, shut and locked the door, then blew his brains out using a handgun none of us knew he had.

Sometimes, when I'm in Silvy's, I swear I can still hear the gunshot followed by the thud of my father's lifeless body hitting the floor. They were the last sounds I heard from my old life.

My mother's piercing scream cut off by Cyrus's obnoxious fucking cackle were the first sounds marking this life—my current life.

Those days I was made up of two-thirds stupidity and one-third arrogance. At nineteen, I was young, dumb, and reckless as all hell. Cyrus was perceptive and calculated, his men strapped and ruthless. I didn't stand a chance against any of them and I definitely didn't have money to hand over. I barely made anything working part-time for my parents. It's one of the reasons I stole shit. The other being I love the thrill of it. But I was small time and so was everybody I ran with. Nobody I knew back then had the kind of change Cyrus expected. That's why when he turned to me and my mom, wanting what he was owed, I stepped forward before she could. I know exactly how Cyrus would have my mom—or worse, my younger sisters—pay it off.

I volunteered, thinking it'd be a short-term situation, but I quickly learned it was more of a life sentence. While I was scrubbing pieces of my dad's head off every inch of his office, I found bank statements that were red long before his blood ever spattered them, so when Cyrus took ownership of Silvy's Flower Shop, he also took on the debt. He paid it off, adding it to my newly acquired tab, and started shaving a hefty fee off the top of my mom's monthly earnings, calling it "rent." I've been pulling jobs like tonight's for Cyrus ever since. That was six years ago, and so far, the debt still isn't cleared.

With it being late October, the cold's already settled in, eliminating the wildlife's summertime lullabies, so it's quiet out here except for what I'm assuming is a squirrel making its way up a nearby tree. I hold my position until the rodent stops, blanketing the night in silence once again, then press my ear to the door, listening for any movement inside.

Nothing.

Using the two towels draped on the back of my neck, I wrap each around a shoe, making sure the soles are completely covered before securing the tops in place with a couple pieces of cord. After determining which size lock pick I need, I set my lock wrench by my feet and return my ear to the door, this time right next to the knob. I work the lock pick in the keyhole until I hear each tumbler click, then slide in the lock wrench to hold them in place while twisting the knob. Holding my breath, I slowly crack open the door. Whether Cyrus's client is inside or not, I'm not risking getting caught. I've never been to jail and I'm not about to get sent there over a fucking laptop.

I may not be triggering an alarm right now, but that doesn't mean everyone inside is asleep, so I keep my hearing sharp, listening for any noise as I carefully replace my tools in my kit and wrap it back up. It's two o'clock in the morning, so everybody should be knocked out, but...you never know. So many people get up several times a night either because they're thirsty or they have bladders the size of hamsters.

There's always the horny yet boring fuckers, too. Some couples only have sex under the covers of their warm beds in the dead of night where no one will ever hear or see them. Luckily, those sessions don't last long. Cowards never do.

One strategic step inside puts me in the mudroom. After closing the door behind me, I hug the walls, walking so soft I'm practically skating across the tiles as I enter the kitchen. It's huge and open and so white it hurts my eyes, even in the dark. Since I'm wearing black from head to toe, I duck down behind the impressive island, walking the length of it while bent over.

Light from a hallway has all my joints locking up.

Blue. It's blue light. And it's moving.

Fish tank.

Cyrus said the laptop would be past the fish tank.

Another couple minutes in the same spot, then I'm on the move again, checking all directions as I dart for the hall's opening. Gliding along the same wall the eye-level fish tank is on, I stop next to it, studying the sea life inside. The tank's gotta be at least six-hundred gallons, obviously salt water, and full of almost-glowing fish and anemones and coral and…a shark? A real fucking shark swims directly at the glass, turning at the last second to show the side of his long brown body.

Watching it disappear under a cove of rocks in the bottom corner, I notice the back of the tank isn't a solid background; it's clear glass just like the front. The tank isn't just *in* part of the wall, it *is* the fucking wall, making it visible from both sides.

Cyrus said the laptop was past a fish tank but didn't specify what exactly "past it" meant. Is it further down the hall or in whatever room's on the other side of it?

Seems like his client doesn't know the mark as well as I thought.

Ducking low again, below the tank, I make it to the open doorway and peek my head around to take stock of the space. *Primary bedroom.* Inside are three doors leading to other rooms, most likely a bathroom and two closets—his and hers—as well as various other pieces of decorative furniture. The bed taking up the middle of the wall perpendicular to the tank is occupied but completely still.

With my breath held, I venture inside to do a quick sweep of the room, keeping my footsteps along the walls and close to heavy furniture. All I need is a fucking floor creak to wake someone up right now. The entire bedroom is white, too, and the tank is giving off a good amount of light, so I'd be spotted instantly.

No sign of a laptop, I let myself exhale before taking another large inhale to hold. Right as I turn toward the bed to check the night-stands, the body closest to the tank kicks a leg into the air, freezing me in my tracks. They're just out of view from me with the bulky com-forter blocking most of their body, but I can clearly see the smooth thigh as white as the bedding it's currently trying to get free of.

A huff—a soft, feminine huff—fills the air, then the room is si-lent again. The body next to her doesn't react at all, so after a full two minutes of barely breathing, I continue on.

My body feels like it's on autopilot as it leads me over to her side. Not only am I closer to the mark, but I was explicitly told to stay away from the wife. None of that stops me from approaching her first.

I need to know if she's awake anyway.

Lying on her side, facing the fish tank, the woman has a gel-filled face mask covering her eyes and most of her nose, forcing me to look her over for other clues. Her lips are parted as her bottom jaw hangs loose and relaxed. Long hair so blonde it's white is slightly wavy by her hairline from sweat, which explains her sticking a foot out from under the covers to cool off. The ceiling fan above the bed is on full blast, yet she's sweating? She's not wearing much clothing either, only a midnight silk tank and matching shorts that make her porcelain skin look even paler. Beneath the tank, the ribs above her small tits expand with each steady breath.

Everything about her says she's sleeping except for her being over-heated. She shouldn't be. This room is fucking frigid, she's got ice on her face, and she's barely dressed. Did she just get in here? Was she just riding her husband's cock?

Another glance in the mark's direction gives nothing away. Some guys pass out seconds after a good nut. Him sleeping like a baby snug-gled under their comforter right now tells me jack shit.

It's her I need to worry about.

I reach a hand out to feel her eye mask, remembering my gloves a second before I make contact. The Velcro keeping the fabric tight around my wrist will make too much noise if I undo it, and the only other skin showing is around my eyes.

My mask doesn't have any Velcro.

Lifting my balaclava over my chin, up to my nose, I lean down and touch my lips to her mask, expecting the plastic to be freezing and stiff. It's not though. It's room temp and pliant. She didn't just go to bed; she's been here a while. *She's asleep.*

This close, I allow myself the smallest of inhales through my exposed nose, just to see what she smells like. Sweet vanilla with a hint of Jasmine, but there's also an earthiness like being outdoors on a cold day. She smells fucking good.

She also looks good. I don't need to see her eyes to know that. Everything about her, from her light skin to her even lighter hair, reminds me of the Snow White Hibiscus. Despite having white hair, she can only be in her twenties or thirties, so I'm assuming she dyes it that color. Probably to match the rest of this goddamn house. Other than the fish tank, there's no color in here whatsoever except the pitch-black sleep set she's wearing.

Why is she even wearing clothes? If she were mine, I'd make her sleep naked every night, giving me round-the-clock access to her pussy.

This further proves her husband doesn't appreciate what he's got. If he's not careful, his wife'll get swiped out from under him, too. I'd do it myself if I wasn't working for Cyrus.

But I am. And I have my orders.

It's a shame she's not one of them.

Although, I wouldn't hand her over to Cyrus. No, I'd keep her all to myself. She smells sweet, looks innocent, and probably feels soft—the exact opposite of my lifestyle.

Prying my eyes off her, I send another glance over to his side, and—

What the *fuck?*

Where her husband's head should be, lying on the pillow next to hers, there's another fucking pillow. He, or whoever else is here, purposely angled the pillow so it looks like a body.

Who's he trying to fool? His wife?

Or me?

Fuck.

The back of my neck tingles as I withdraw several inches to tug my balaclava back in place.

Almost instantly, the eyebrows above her mask pucker.

Can she sense me?

My right ear picks up a moan and I stand fully. It's a quiet moan but it's definitely a moan...coming from somewhere else in the house.

What the fuck is going on?

After one last look at the sleeping woman, I follow the sound out of the bedroom and down the hall, stopping next to another open doorway. From my viewpoint, I can only see a wall of shelves lined with books—books wrapped in blank white paper.

Somewhere further in the room, a chair creaks in time with heavy panting.

One hand behind me, gripping the Glock tucked into my waistband, I risk a peek around the doorjamb. Inside, a man's sitting at an antique white desk, masturbating.

He snuck out of bed, a bed currently occupied by his sexy wife, to jerk it to dimly lit, amateur porn...on the laptop I'm here to take.

Fuuuuck. What am I supposed to do now?

I could wait him out and steal the laptop once he's done. Chances are this won't take long. But then what? If it was the wife who hired Cyrus, he'll just be handing over the same thing I could give her right now.

And if it wasn't the wife...when will she figure out her husband's not the man she thinks he is? When it's too late like it was for my mom?

With his back hunched over as he hastily tugs his cock, the mark moans deeply. "That's it, baby. Keep fucking yourself just like that. Show me how much you can take."

He's talking dirty to a fucking screen when his wife is in the other goddamn room.

Removing my gun, I enter the office.

The woman thrusting a dildo in and out of her pussy uses her free hand to point directly at the camera—at *me*—and says, "Daddy?" but the mark's so wrapped up in getting himself off he doesn't notice.

So this isn't a low-budget film? It's happening in real time?

I lift my left hand, and the woman on the screen automatically mirrors the move.

This guy's not just busting a nut to some internet porn behind his wife's back, he's motherfucking cheating.

On God, this bitch better just have a daddy kink. If she's underage…

With a low groan, the man comes into a hand towel, resting his forehead on his desk.

"Daddy, who's that?"

Finally, the mark notices something other than his own pleasure, and whips his head my way to spit, "Who the fuck are you?"

When he stands, his dick droops like it's tired.

He definitely passes out after nutting.

Deepening my voice to say, "Get up," I gesture to him with my gun. Not making the same mistake as him, I toss a glance over each of my shoulders, ensuring we're alone.

"What do you think you're doing? Do you have any idea who I am?"

I put a gloved finger to my lips even though he can't see them, and tell him, "Don't wanna wake your wife." That's the whole reason behind him positioning a pillow as his stand-in, isn't it?

"My wife?" the man repeats all confused, probably more for his sidepiece's sake than mine.

Motherfucker, I already got your number.

I won't hurt his wife, but he doesn't know that.

"Get up," I repeat, keeping the gun trained on his chest as I advance toward him.

Clearly not put off by her virtual fuck buddy being married, the woman continues fucking herself, the dildo in her hold practically disappearing into her pussy.

"Who's your friend, Kordin?" is all she says before her gaze shifts to me, her pace down below increasing.

She's not underage at all. She's at least several years older than the woman down the hall, probably closer to the mark's age than his own wife is. She's attractive. Not someone I'd jeopardize a marriage for, but then again, I don't cheat.

I keep her eyes for a beat before dropping to watch her work her pussy over. Shiny lips without a trace of stubble tighten around the twisted glass wand coated with her pussy milk. Her moans kick up, filling the office, and maybe under different circumstances, I'd be fighting a hard-on of my own, but all I feel is disgust.

I'm no good either but I'm not a cheating piece of shit. There are very few lines I won't cross, cheating being one of them.

"Fucking skanks," Kordin says. "All of them."

All of them? This isn't a one-time, one-sidepiece situation?

Kordin shoots a hand toward the screen, but I swat his wrist away before he can close it, telling him, "Don't move. Just watch."

"Who are you? Why are you here? What do you—"

"Shut up and watch."

As soon as he returns his focus to the laptop, he murmurs, "You can have her."

I shake my head before my brain's even finished processing his words. I don't want her.

Then he says, "My wife," making my eyes narrow under drawn-tight eyebrows. *That's the her he's referring to? His fucking wife?*

"Whatever you're here for, I'll let you have her instead."

Have her? What the fuck is he saying?

His head swivels in my direction. "You saw her, didn't you?"

My throat bobs with a swallow and I feel a stirring beneath my pants' zipper. I fucking saw her all right.

Truthfully, I don't think I'll ever be able to unsee her.

"You want her," he states confidently. Cockily. So fucking cocky. "You want to cram your cock in her."

More blood rushes below my waist as I squeeze my fist around the gun so tight my knuckles throb. He's not offering to let me have his wife, he's offering to let me fuck her.

And I would. I would fuck her raw, but only if *she* wanted me to. His blessing means less than nothing to me.

"I know you do. Everyone that meets her wants to. But you actually can. You can fuck her, then walk away from here no questions asked. Only if you leave everything else alone."

Everything else…

He doesn't care about his possessions. He means himself. I can fuck her only if I leave *him* alone.

He's willing to sacrifice his wife to save himself. Just like my father did.

Without another word, I move out of the shot and push a few buttons on the laptop to take a screenshot.

"Not that—"

Flipping my gun around so I'm holding the barrel, I knock his stomach with the handle, causing him to double over, looking just as pathetic as his limp dick still dangling over the waistband of his silk pajama pants.

"Shut the fuck up," I grumble while taking more screenshots. Him being red-faced and hunched over gives me exactly what I need.

Satisfied with the amount of images taken, I end the video call and the squelching noises all at once.

"I only fuck my wife from the back."

What the fuck? Why is he telling me this? And why would he do it in the first place? Backshots are great every now and then, but not every fucking time. There're so many other positions.

Something's wrong with him. Not her. She's got a nice body with perfect tits for palming, not to mention lips that look like they could suck a dick like a vacuum hose. Without seeing under that mask, I was still able to piece together that she's gorgeous.

"Ass up, face down on the mattress. She wouldn't even know it was you. She'd think it was me."

He's dead fucking serious right now. He'd let another man fuck his woman. No, not even fuck her, but rape her. If another man so much as touched my girl, whether she wanted it or not, I'd break whatever hand he used.

And bullshit she wouldn't know the difference. I don't fuck like this guy—*that* I can guarantee. I'm not wasteful like him. Even doggy style, I'd put more of that woman to use than just her pussy.

"You'll have to wear a condom because I'm not raising a fucking defect."

Defect? Because I'm not rich like him? Typical hollow prick.

"Or would you rather watch instead?" Kordin's wheeze turns into a dark chuckle. "That's why you took the pictures. You like to watch."

Watch?

"She wouldn't know that either. I could fuck her while you watch and nobody would know. It'd be like you were never here."

The spots filling my vision almost keep me from seeing Kordin straighten to his full height.

"Is that good enough for you? Will that keep your filthy hands off the rest of my things, you bottom-feeder?"

My empty fist collides with the spot between his eyes, knocking him backward, then my body's on top of his as I cut my elbow across his face again and again and again. I have to force myself to ease up and not kill him. He needs to be conscious so he can see the consequences of his actions without being able to do a goddamn thing about it.

His wife deserves to know who she's living with. *Anyone* could get into this house, and if her husband's offering her up to me, he'd offer her up to them, too.

These types of men disgust me. My father disgusted me. All they think about is themselves. They could never, ever put someone else's needs, someone else's *life*, before theirs.

I should have her. I should take her out of here and burn this place to the ground with this fucker still inside. I'd be doing her a fucking favor. I'd be doing the world a fucking favor.

The problem is I don't have anything to offer her. I won't be her monster but I can't be her savior either. I'm too busy trying to be my own family's to be anyone else's.

So this will have to do. I'm supposed to make it look like a typical break-in after the laptop's in my possession, but I'm not taking the laptop. I'm leaving it all right here, out in the open, where secrets wither and die.

I push to standing and reach for the hand towel on the desk.

Coherent but just barely, Kordin lifts a finger at me, gritting out, "Not…that…"

There's a pool of blood under his head and he's worried about a fucking hand towel? He said the same thing about the laptop. He doesn't want me touching dumb shit but is fine with the idea of me raping his wife.

Who's defective? Me?

"You'll pay."

Instead of telling him I already am, I snatch the spunk-covered towel and jam it into his mouth. Since I'm not worried about being caught anymore, I unwrap the towel around my right shoe, returning it to the back of my neck.

"Bite down," I say, giving Kordin one small courtesy before I stomp on his right elbow, breaking the arm in at least two places.

Predictably, he thrashes, trying to scream, but thankfully only gurgling sounds make it past the expensive damp cotton filling his mouth. I don't waste time, immediately doing the same exact thing to his right knee, too, that way he can't drive himself anywhere. He will be right here, in this exact spot, until his wife finds him. It's up to her from there. I wouldn't help him if I was her. I'd stuff his face in a pillow like he does to her and wait for him to suffocate.

For that reason alone, I'll stick to one part of the original plan by making it look like there was an actual break-in. If she decides to off her husband, it'll look like an invasion gone wrong and she'll be in the clear.

Without warning, I rip the towel from Kordin's mouth and place it next to the laptop again. There's more blood than jizz on it now but hopefully she gets the point.

I bring up the screenshots, enlarging the worst one so it takes up the entire screen.

"No. Don't…" Kordin's left leg kicks out at me, missing my own by several inches but giving me my first smile of the night.

His labored breathing provides a soundtrack for the next few minutes as I rush around the room, knocking over pieces of decor and pulling random books off the shelves, a trail of crinkled white paper in my wake. I'll do the same in another room, then I'll break a window just before I leave out the same door I came through.

But first…

Towering over the broken, bleeding, and now whimpering man, I tell him what I wish I could tell my dad, "You did this."

On my way past, he gets one final word out, asking, "Why?" but I don't stop to answer.

Why am I here? Because I don't have a choice.

Why am I doing this? Because his wife does. She can get out still.

I couldn't.

I can't.

Two

Lex

THUMP!

The cold compress prevents my lids from so much as lifting, so I push the now-lukewarm mask up my clammy forehead, blinking several times until the aquarium isn't as blinding. The clown fish I recently bought hunkers down into the anemone it seems to have made its home in, keeping only its orange head out of the fluorescent-pink tentacles gently undulating in the salt water.

Scanning the rest of the aquarium, I check for anything strange to explain the sound that woke me. Everything appears normal except my husband's ugly bamboo shark, who must be in his hiding spot. If he wasn't, I'd assume he was responsible for waking me up. Just like every other male who overestimates himself, that hard-headed asshole will run face-first into the glass without thought. I've seen him do it.

But if it wasn't him, what was the noise?

It sounded like… I don't know. I thought I heard something, but it could've been a dream. Even when I'm not on edge, bedtime hours blur together for me. Some I'm awake pretending I'm not, while others I'm asleep wondering if I actually am. I can't always tell what's real and what's not at night.

Dreams, I question.

Nightmares, I don't. I know all too well just how real those are.

I turn my face to the ceiling, regarding the blur of blades as I contemplate popping a sleeping pill. I probably already should've.

On an inhale, I sit up before immediately freezing.

What is that?

Tilting my head left, then right, I lift my nose just slightly until the scent intensifies enough for me to identify. Rum, tobacco, and… citrus? Orange, not lime or lemon, and the rum and tobacco weren't consumed, they're notes in a cologne. A man's cologne. A man with good taste but not the kind of money to afford the best.

The man of this house can afford the best.

Somebody else was in here.

The unmistakable sound of glass breaking and raining down onto the floor hits me right in the midsection, making my stomach cramp worse than it did before I went to bed.

Somebody was *just* in here.

My first instinct is to react, but is that wise?

Kordin. He should be the one to handle this.

Shaking the mattress, I whisper, "Kordin, wake up. I think somebody's in the house." *Hopefully out of it now.* I can only assume that's why the intruder broke a window. If he's already been through the house—including my fucking bedroom—then he should be done.

When Kordin doesn't respond, I tug the comforter down, hissing, "Kordin—"

Gone. He's gone. Again. And in his place is a pillow. *Also again.*

Why does he even bother? It's not like I'm some out-of-touch mother who'd actually fall for the old pillow-as-a-body trick while my rebellious teen sneaks out to go fuck around. I'm his wife of eight years, and I'm so tired of this shit I could fucking scream.

I don't though. I never do.

If Kordin's not in bed, did he actually leave or is he still in the house somewhere?

Did he see the intruder? Engage with him? Them? Because it's possible there are multiple intruders. I'm only picking up one man's scent but that doesn't mean he's acting alone. Only that he's stupid enough to wear cologne while breaking and entering.

nothing **ABOVE** | 17

God, what kind of animals am I dealing with here?

After removing the compress from my head, I quickly but quietly kneel down beside the foot of the bed, and watching the doorway, stick my arm between the mattress and frame to grab my .32 along with the magazine beside it. At only eight ounces, the lightweight pistol still feels heavy in my palm as I load it and consider my next move.

I don't want to shoot anybody, but I will if I have to, especially if I'm outnumbered.

With numb legs, I get to my feet and leave the safety of my bedroom, the pistol pressed to the back of my thigh, my index finger alongside its trigger.

Once I'm in the hall, I hear footsteps in the kitchen. They're light but still audible if I hold my breath.

One, pause, two, pause, three, pause, four, pause.

Maybe only some of them are audible. They're definitely getting further away like the person is leaving…while hobbling? *Are they hobbling?*

"Lenox," Kordin groans from the other end of the hall, near, if not in, his office.

His office.

The kitchen goes silent, making my chest constrict. Why aren't they leaving? They got what they needed, didn't they?

I glance where Kordin's voice came from, only seeing a vase in the foyer on its side.

Did they get what they needed?

Shivers rack my body so hard my teeth chatter. In bed, I was burning up, but now, I'm freezing. It could be from my period or… I don't even want to think about what else it could mean. Not right now.

Regardless of the cause, I know I'm weaker than I used to be. Physically.

Mentally, I'm the same, and mental strength is what counts most. A strong person can only defeat weaker opponents, but a wise person can defeat anybody.

That's what I choose to focus on because I have to be smart here.

Suddenly, another series of steps and pauses, this time much faster, grows louder, bringing the intruder closer to my location.

No, no, no. Please go. Just go.

Keeping the gun hidden, I tuck my free arm under my breasts, my left hand between my rib cage and right armpit. It controls some of my convulsing as well as gives me somewhere to prop my elbow in case I need to aim and shoot.

Eyes trained on the French doors at the back of the house, I catch the reflection of a lone masked figure as he approaches the end of the hall. Now that he's on carpet, I can't hear his footsteps but I see him linger just past the corner. Judging by his body language, he's uncertain. He doesn't want to hurt me—it's why he didn't while I was asleep—but he's willing to. Asleep I was vulnerable.

Now I'm not.

But he doesn't need to know that. At least not yet.

I force out a quiet sob, saying loud enough for both men to hear, "Kordin, I'm scared. What's going on? What do I do?"

The intruder spins around, putting his back to the wall, too, and at first, his masked face is trained on the corner as he listens, but when I whimper again, he turns his head until his gaze finds mine in the glass's reflection.

Easing my hold on my torso, I let my shivering take over my body so it looks like it's fear I'm shaking from, not chills.

"Please," I half-mouth, half-whisper to really sell it. I even put a bend in my knees like they're giving out. If anything, it just puts me closer to the floor to dodge his bullets should they come flying my way.

The hand holding his gun goes limp at his side a moment before disappearing behind his back. When it reappears, it's empty.

He put his gun away. He's buying it.

I'm not. There could still be others. I haven't smelled them, heard them, or seen them, but that could be part of the strategy. This guy might be the decoy.

Decoy for what exactly? I'm not sure. About any of this.

I keep my senses alert, not letting my guard down an inch, but slump forward.

"Go," the deep, unfamiliar voice commands, raising the hairs on my arms.

Go?

"Where?"

"To your husband."

To Kordin? Does that mean he's letting me go?

My eyes don't stray from his as I inch down the hallway, my shoulder blades scraping the wall the entire time. He doesn't make any moves, just watches my retreat. There's something about his stare. It's assessing, but there's something else in it, too. Something that warms me up just enough to counteract the cold. It's not the mask. I've encountered too many masked figures to be affected by the sight anymore. It's what's under the mask. I can't even make out the color of his eyes, yet I can *feel* the depth in them.

Only when I reach Kordin's office do I remove my gaze from the intruder's to push off the wall and stand just outside the threshold. Among all the books and décor littering the floor is my husband attempting to drag himself through what appears to be a lake of his own blood. He's only in a pair of what were white pajama pants but are now splashed in red. For some reason, maybe from the altercation, his cock must've sprung free and is just…sagging as he scoots forward.

My husband has never looked as powerless as he does in this moment. He's never *been* as powerless as he is in this moment.

"Don't move, Kordin," I say while sending a glimpse sideways. Filling the other end of the hall now, the intruder's observing me directly instead of through a reflection. He's more imposing to regard head-on, and strangely harder to look away from.

"Safe," Kordin gasps.

Tearing my eyes away, I turn back to my husband, his left arm extended in front of him, his whole body visibly shaking.

"Shh. I'm safe," I tell him.

"Help…"

"We'll get help. Just stay still until I can…"

Kordin's outstretched hand latches on to the edge of his desk, finally pulling my attention up from the floor. I barely even register the towel there as I zero in on the laptop next to it. An image of Kordin and some woman, clearly fucking themselves to each other, fills the screen.

"What's happening?" I ask, my voice rising as I feel that scream claw its way to the top of my throat. "What is this?"

Movement has me whipping my head to the side, the hand with the gun already midair, but the hall's empty. Where'd he go? Why'd he do this?

Not a second later, I hear Kordin tap a series of buttons and look over just in time to see his screen go black before he slams the laptop shut.

"In…the…safe."

In the corner, his safe sits, almost expectant. I glance from it to him as I start to back up.

"Kordin, I don't know what's going on, but you need an ambulance. I have to call the—"

"No! Not until…you help…put it…in safe."

It wasn't my safety he was concerned with, it was his.

Tremors rock my frame, these ones different from the others.

Three

Reece

AS SOON AS ONE BOUNCER FINISHES PATTING ME DOWN, his fucking lookalike opens the steel door and nods me in. The only person allowed to carry here is the man who owns the club—Cyrus.

"Welcome back, Reece," Adie addresses me from the greeter's stand. "Will you be venturing upstairs tonight?"

While The Playground, the strip club and main draw, makes up the entire underground level of the building, The Head Office is just a room in the top floor. In that room is where all the gambling happens, so I don't go up there unless I absolutely fucking have to.

"Is Cyrus up there?"

"No, Boss is currently making his rounds downstairs."

"Then that's where I'll be."

"Enjoy your evening."

I try not to snort as I turn for the stairs. Nothing about my visit tonight will be enjoyable.

The black stairwell swallows me whole as I descend, the song "Playground" by Bea Miller, Arcane, and League of Legends pulsing through the hidden speakers needling its way in my ears, around my neck, and down my spine like a living, breathing thing. When I hit the last step, neon lighting replaces the dark, turning my white button-up under my black suit the same color as a Mallow Flower, the one mauve was named after. Following along the hallway that leads to the main space, I walk under flashing signs featuring sayings everyone's used at least once in their lives.

Tag, you're it.

Ready or not, here I come.

Catch me if you can.

Can you keep a secret?

What are the rules?

I dare you.

By the time the club comes into view, you're fucking ready—patrons, for the good time awaiting them; me, to face the consequences awaiting me.

It's been two days since I walked out of that hollow's house, leaving his fate up to his wife, and I still don't have a good explanation for why I did what I did. Not for myself, and especially not for Cyrus.

Hooking a left, I bypass the wall of dancers swinging back and forth on swings hanging from the ceiling and go straight to the bar. Different bottles of liquor fill the shelves behind the bartenders, most of them empty with LED lights inside. Everything down here has a purple glow, giving the whole club even more of an underground feel.

"What'll it be, handsome?" my favorite bartender, Oksana, asks when she makes it over to me.

"Let me get a snakebite."

She pours a finger of Canadian whiskey into a shot glass, then adds a dash of lime juice before sliding it across the granite countertop into my waiting hand. I toss it back.

"Another. Double this time."

Oksana's eyebrows lift but she doesn't say anything, just pours.

Glass in hand, I do a small circle, taking in the club. For a Friday night, it's not too packed. It's definitely busy, but nothing crazy. Dancers are spread out around the large space, treating the clientele to shows either on the smaller side stages, the swings, or right in their chairs with tame lap dances meant to induce blue balls. This is the only place blue balls are a good thing because they lead to larger purchases, larger tips, larger deposits directly into Cyrus's pockets.

In the middle is the main attraction, a circular stage called the Merry-Go-Round. It's a revolving stage with five poles on it, one in the center that reaches the ceiling while the other four surrounding it are free-standing.

Right now, it's just Pearl up there by herself, and she's spinning around upside down on the floor-to-ceiling pole with only a teal bra and matching G-string. Hundreds of dollar bills litter the stage inches below her long mermaid-colored hair as she twirls to "Na Na" by Trey Songz. Pearl gives a hell of a lap dance and an even better blow job, so the mountains of cash piling up for her aren't surprising in the least. I'd add to it if I thought she'd actually get to keep it. Without breaking speed, she pulls herself up to stretch a leg out under her, hooking the other knee around the pole to continue spinning with her head thrown back and her hands massaging the tits threatening to spill out of her push-up bra.

The girls who work here, work *hard*. They're the female versions of Cyrus's men, meaning they do whatever the fuck he tells them to. It took me a while to understand that, but once I did, I stopped sticking my dick in anyone on his payroll. If I pay for a BJ, I wanna know the money goes to the mouth sucking me, not Cyrus's. He's gotten enough out of me already.

Pearl slides down the pole, her platform heels landing on the stage with an audible *clack* that gets everybody's undivided attention, including mine. Bending over, her ass cheeks spread wide in my direct line of vision, that little string tight in her crack covering exactly nothing.

Damn. A backshot sounds pretty fucking good right about now.

Upside down, she spots me from between her knees and gives me a *come-hither* smile, and since it's been a long motherfucking while, I obey. One foot steps forward, only to move right back to avoid a body breezing by. I don't even look, just wait for them to pass as I keep my gaze locked on Pearl running two fingers—middle and ring, none of that trigger-finger bullshit—back and forth between her pussy and ass, and *goddamn*, I need to get my dick wet.

I finally break my stare, checking around me for any unfamiliar faces. There's gotta be at least one woman in here that doesn't work for the same motherfucker I do.

Immediately, my eyes snag on the person who just cut me off. Their hair? It's white. And their body? It's young. She's dressed in a black lace gown—it's more than a dress, it's a gown—with no back whatsoever except for a long train of see-through fabric starting at the bottom of her spine and billowing out behind her like a bride walking down the aisle at a goth wedding. Loud clicks from her high heels announce her every step as she strolls confidently through the most infamous building in Fox Hollow like she's been here before. Like she's comfortable. Like she's home. But the way she's dressed… it's not her home. There's no way it could be. This place isn't for her or people like her. Fox Hollow isn't just the town's name, it's a classification. Here, you're either a fox or a hollow, and if you're not sure which one you are, you're a hollow.

This woman, she's got hollow written all over her, from her gown to red-bottom shoes to her walk like she could own this place and everyone in it if she wanted to.

Her man probably talked her into coming here to spice things up in the bedroom. I see it all the time. What I don't see all the time is that hair color.

Two women with the same white hair in the same week. What a fucking coincidence. It must be a new trend among the hollows or something. With all the money they spend trying to hide their age, I would've assumed having their hair white is the last thing they'd want.

But what the fuck do I know? I'm a fox.

I'm just about to tear my gaze away when she twists her head to the side, revealing her profile.

It's her. It's *her*. Kordin's wife, Lenox.

What's she doing here? I've been coming to The Playground since I started working for Cyrus and I've never seen her.

After a quick scan of the club to make sure her husband isn't here, too, I'm back to watching her. *Is she here for me?*

No. No, that's wishful thinking coming straight from my own blue balls. She couldn't have known it was me that night in her house.

She couldn't. I'm good at what I do. Really fucking good. I've never left a single shred of evidence behind before, and even though I spoke to both her and her husband, I disguised my voice. I kept my mask on the entire time and I was too far away for her to see my eyes, so there's no chance of her being able to identify me. None.

All the blood that was heading toward my groin goes cold as she faces forward again. *Why the fuck is she here?*

"Where's Cyrus?" I ask Oksana, setting my full shot glass on the bar while keeping my attention on Lenox.

"Did you check Lost and Found?"

Lost and Found…exactly where Lenox appears to be heading. Fuck.

"You done with that?" I hear Oksana ask with a heavy dose of annoyance.

"It's not the drink," I assure her. "I just…"

Lenox disappears into the hallway leading to the private rooms and I leave without finishing my sentence, except instead of following the white-haired hollow, I beeline for the employees-only door, choosing to cut through the dressing room.

"Reece!" several of the dancers screech when they see me, but I don't stop to apologize, I just make my way through the half-naked women as quickly as possible before pushing out the door on the opposite side, into the same hall Lost and Found is located.

I catch the tail of her train fluttering into one of the Lost rooms before the door closes shut, leaving only me and a dancer turned key girl named Promiscuous.

Lost and Found is made up of a dozen private rooms—six are "Lost" and six are "Found." Each Lost room has a loveseat, a table with a box of tissues, lube, condoms, some frilly shit to make it feel homey like a candle or a vase of fake flowers, individual audio systems, as well as a large clock the dancers inside rarely take their eyes off of. Every Lost room shares a wall containing a large piece of smart glass with a smaller, darker Found room where others can watch what's happening. It's up to whoever's paying to be in a Lost room if they want to be watched—found—or not. They don't get a say in who watches, but they can choose if they want to see who watches by flicking a button on their side to make the normally opaque glass transparent.

Since no one's around, I use her real name. "Hey, Promise, who wants to be found?"

"Who's asking?" Promise asks without looking up from her romance novel. I know it's romance because there's a shirtless man on the front.

"Me."

"Really?" She gives me a once-over, then stands from her stool, setting her book down. "Since when?"

"Since I'm fucking looking for someone."

She rears back and I have to remind myself to calm the fuck down.

I change my tone to lie, saying, "Oksana said Cia was back here somewhere."

Six months ago, I went on one date with another dancer here, Cia, or Stacia when she's working. It was terrible—the conversation, the chemistry, the everything—and not even a full date considering I ended it early using a fake excuse. She's a nice girl, but... I don't know what it was exactly. She just wasn't for me. Unfortunately, because I didn't tell her that myself, everybody, including Cia, is under the impression that I have a hard-on for her. As much as I hate to continue the rumor, it helps my case if I make it seem like I do in this instance.

Someone who actually does have a hard-on for her though, is Cyrus, and he takes her to Lost and Found a lot.

Promise regards me for a beat before asking, "What do you want with Cia?"

"What do you think?"

"I think I can give you what you're looking for instead." I'm about to turn her down when she whispers, "For cheaper," stepping into me with deft hands that unbutton my shirt so fast my chest and abs are exposed before I push her away, shaking my head at her. And myself. Mostly myself. *Fucking focus.*

Promise's eyes roll toward the ceiling as she retrieves her book. "I heard your dick ain't that good anyway."

"Fuck you."

"Fuck *you*," she spits right back, sitting down and burying her nose in the pages again.

My hands burn with the urge to snatch the book out of her grip and tear it in half.

I'm running out of patience and this bitch is pissing me off the longer she holds me up with her bullshit. I don't know who Lenox is in a Lost room with right now but I saw her go into one.

She could be with a dancer.

She could be.

Or she could be with Cyrus. He uses these rooms for business as much as pleasure, and he never, ever wants to be found.

"Who wants to be found?" I repeat.

"Right now?"

I jerk out a nod even though she's fully engrossed in whatever she's reading.

"No one."

"None of the rooms want to be found?"

She shakes her head.

"How the fuck is that even possible?"

Silence is my answer.

I count the doors. "Give me room five."

"Lost?"

"Yes, fucking Lost," I snap again, making her look at me.

"I thought you were wanting to watch…"

We stare at each other silently until a smirk splits her lips.

"Here comes Cia now," she says.

Cia rounds the corner, the same one Lenox came from, and beams when she sees us.

Me. She beams when she sees me.

Fuck.

But…

"How did you know she was coming?" I ask Promise because she's not even facing that direction.

Dropping the smirk, Promise deadpans, "None of your business," then hands me the key to five Lost, asking how much time I need Cia for.

I pay her for five minutes, long enough for one song.

"Wanna be found?"

"No."

"Phone," she says with her hand out, and I place it in her palm because if you want to go in a room, you have to do it without your phone. It's not for privacy. It's so footage can't end up on some website where Cyrus isn't earning a direct profit.

Only halfway down the hall, I hear Promise mutter, "Knew his dick wasn't shit," and I don't have to guess who she's talking about. Fuck her and fuck whoever said that about my dick. My dick works fine. And lasts longer than five minutes.

"Want me to clean up first?" Cia asks.

I'm quick to shake my head and guide her inside the room.

"Just a dance."

"Oh. Got it." Her face falls. "Do you have a song in mind?" she asks, recovering with a forced perk to her tone.

"You pick."

While she takes care of the music, I drop down onto the loveseat, all the way to one side so she can't straddle me.

In a pink strappy bralette, a G-string, and garters that attach to lace thigh-high stockings, Cia's a sexy sight any guy would be lucky to have all to himself. She's too nice for this place, but like a lot of us foxes, she was dealt a shitty hand, and now at only twenty-one years old, she's stuck here at The Playground, working off whatever debt she owes Cyrus.

"Don't Save Me" by Chxrlotte comes on, then Cia starts moving, never once meeting my eyes as she watches the clock.

My face hardens listening to the lyrics, my chest tight thinking about what Cyrus makes her do, what he makes all of us do. I can't save Cia. I did what I could the other night for Lenox, but that was a mistake. One I could lose my life for.

When the song ends, Cia gives me her back as she hides a sniffle. I don't move for her and I don't offer any words of encouragement. I just sit here with her until a knock on the door exactly a minute later spurs us into motion.

I spring from the loveseat, telling her, "I'll let Promise know you're not feeling well."

Cia shakes her head and wipes under her eyes, the chunky mascara coating her fingers. "She'll come to check on me. Or worse, she'll send Cyrus to."

"I'll pay for more time. Is thirty minutes enough?" I wait for her to nod, then tell her to stay put.

Back out in the hall, Promise instantly says, "Cyrus wants to see you," making me stop to glance around.

How the fuck did she... She didn't even look up from her book.

"He's not here anymore though. You just missed him."

Anymore. Just missed him.

"But he was here? In Lost and Found?" I ask carefully.

"Yep, just got done."

"Which room?"

Promise glares at me over the cover model's penetrating ocean-blue eyes.

I send another glimpse down both ends of the hall.

"Got a room that wants to be found."

That pulls my attention right back to her.

"Which one?"

"Four."

Lenox went into four Lost. But I told Cia I'd give her more time to collect herself in five Lost.

I can't.

I could.

I shouldn't.

I...have to.

If Lenox was in the same room as Cyrus, I have to know if she's okay. As hard as it was to walk away from her that night, it's been even worse not knowing what happened to her or what's going to happen to her.

Swallowing every ounce of ego I can, I mumble, "I, uh," and point down at my crotch. "I lost it."

"Lost it?" Promise questions.

"I lost my, uh…"

"Yes?"

"Fuck. I went limp, okay?"

Promise bursts out laughing, the sound echoing down the corridor.

I ignore her and pull out my wallet. "I told Cia she could stay in there a little longer and finish herself off."

"Finish herself off? Oh Lord, he actually believes it," she murmurs to the ceiling.

"Believe what?"

Pointing at a Lost room, she says, "We don't come in there. Not with clients. It's all an act."

I know that's the case.

I assumed that was the case.

I mean, I thought…

Every time? Goddamn.

"Regardless, any woman that fucks with me gets off," I tell her, pulling out a few bills.

"Apparently not," she sneers but takes the money anyway. "So thirty more minutes for five Lost. How long for four Found?"

"How much time is left?"

She checks her watch. "Fifteen minutes, but Cyrus said to give her more if she needs it."

So he was in there. With Lenox. And she might need more time…for what? To recover?

"Put me down for thirty."

I hand over more cash before collecting the key for four Found from her.

As I spin to leave, Promise says, "Reece?"

"Yeah?" I ask without turning around.

Almost in a whisper, she tells me, "I'll make sure Cyrus leaves Cia alone for the full thirty."

She knows Cia needs a break. These women are like a family to each other; to most of them, it's the only family they got.

"And me?"

"You're still in five Lost with her, aren't you?"

When I look back at the key girl, her face is pressed to her book, even more so than before.

While she's blatantly ignoring me, I head to room four, looking between both the Lost and Found doors. This is my only shot to come face to face with her. I'm taking it.

I twist the handle to four Lost.

Four

Lex

CAT JUMPS UP FROM HER PERCH ON THE LOVESEAT'S armrest, asking whoever just interrupted, "Do you need something?"

With my back to the door as I sit against the loveseat's armrest, I can't see the person, but one inhale through my nose and I know exactly who it is. I smelled him on my way back here, when I unknowingly passed him by the Merry-Go-Round, but I never imagined he'd have the balls to actually approach me.

I was wanting to get the hell out of here as quickly as possible, but now I think I'll stay a little…bit…longer.

"Kitty?" I hear him say, his voice softer than it was at my house. It's still very deep, just nowhere near as deep as when he was purposely deepening it. "No, it's nothing like that."

"Cyrus didn't send you in here?"

He must shake his head because she blows out a breath, relaxing her posture to ask, "Then what the fuck you want, Reece? I'm working."

Reece. Sweet name for a sweet guy that likes sweet girls. If I still had a gag reflex, I'd make myself puke right now.

"Shit, sorry. I was looking for four Found and picked the wrong room."

Cat's frown confirms my suspicion. He's lying. Working for Cyrus, this man, Reece, would have to know his way around The Playground. Not only does he know which doors lead to which rooms, he knows what goes on behind them. He was aiming for four Found…to watch four Lost. To watch this room specifically.

"It's okay," I finally break my silence to say.

When the door doesn't close immediately, I turn my head over my right shoulder and meet the intruder's eyes once again, this time with no mask blocking their color. Or depth.

God, a girl could fall into those without ever worrying about how she'll get back out.

Even without the mask, they look black. Are they black? Or just dark brown? From here they look like bottomless pits of obsidian.

A couple pieces of his raven hair fall over his forehead as he lowers his head to stare directly at me. Below a prominent nose is a thin, almost nonexistent top lip compared to the plump bottom lip just under it. I could bite that lip all the way into my mouth and suck on it like a lollipop.

The thought has me licking my own.

Reece's throat bobs with a swallow.

He's too easy.

Dressed in a form-fitting black suit, his jacket's lapels hang open, showcasing a white button-up, except it's missing a few buttons, so his chest and the top of his chiseled abs are visible. Reece is one gorgeous specimen. He should be walking runways, not stalking around in a ski mask, ruining people's lives.

"You can come in," I rasp. "If you want."

I can feel Cat's gaze on the side of my face, but my oldest friend only tells our voyeur, "Yeah, come keep Lexi company for me."

"Where're you going, Kitty?" Reece steps inside and closes the door behind him, lingering there for a second. "I thought you were working."

With his hands in his pockets but his chin lifted, he strolls over to the middle of the small, warm room. My eyes track his every move while his stay glued to mine.

"I am working," she protests.

Tearing my gaze from Reece's, I ask Cat, "Is four hundred okay?"

"Five would be better."

"Can you grab my wallet?"

"I got you, baby." Bending at the hips, Cat braces her palms flat on the coffee table, walks them across the surface a hand at a time to where my purse is, then lifts a platform heel behind her in a sexy pose.

Reece scans Cat's body, focusing on her cheeky panties. I wait until he looks my way to pretend to blush from catching him in his perusal.

Cat stands up again to hand me my clutch, and I give her five crisp hundred-dollar bills.

"What'd you do to earn that?"

While any other person in this club would've asked that with suspicion and jealousy, Reece's tone only holds curiosity.

"Wanna see?" Cat asks him, and after a brief hesitation, he shakes his head.

With my left elbow propped on the back of the loveseat, I stick my middle finger between my teeth, rubbing both knuckles along the jagged edges to hide the smile trying to take shape.

"Good, 'cause I'm never having another kid again. Them little rats are expensive."

Reece's dark eyebrows furrow. "Kid?"

"Yeah, my kid's doing a fundraiser for his school. Some kind of run he needs sponsors for. Lexi just donated five hundred dollars."

She grins at Reece, but when all he offers is a deeper frown, she matches his expression.

He looks from her to me, then back again before rolling his eyes and pulling out his own wallet.

"Sixty?" Cat scoffs, staring at the cash he forks over. "His teacher can drop that in one trip to the craft store."

Reece's eyes meet mine again, so I shrug a shoulder. Teachers everywhere are grossly underpaid; Fox Hollow's are no exception.

"Fucking shakedown," he murmurs.

He passes over more bills, making Cat's smile reappear as she singsongs, "Thank you."

"Grind With Me" by Pretty Ricky starts playing quietly and I almost get up and change it. This song's been in Lost and Found's rotation for so long.

"Now, I gotta go round up more donations from the girls and I only have about ten minutes before Cyrus comes back here and notices I'm off the floor. Can I trust you to take good care of my girl here?"

That bottom lip of his glistening from his tongue swiping left and right across it, Reece hesitates before giving a stiff nod.

Cat and I say bye to each other and she gives me a silent *I hope you know what you're doing* look before she leaves.

I open my lips to speak, but Reece cuts me off, asking, "Your name's Lexi?"

He doesn't recognize it? Is he brand new?

"To some," I answer carefully.

"You and Kitty know each other."

I nod even though he didn't pose it as a question.

Suddenly feeling flushed, I arrange my dress's skirt so the thigh-high slit falls down both sides of my right leg.

Reece zeroes in on the movement, studying the newly exposed skin as well as the gold chain decorating my thigh.

"You're Reece?"

Instead of answering, he asks, "Why'd you wanna be found?" His eyes rise to mine again. "If nothing was happening in here, why'd you agree to be found?"

"I guess I was hopeful." I dip my face, going for sheepish as I peek up through my lashes at him. "Do you work here?"

From his spot on the other side of the coffee table, he seems to consider his answer before saying, "Yeah."

I bend both knees and drag my stilettos up the leather upholstery until there's just enough room for one more. "Do you…want to sit?"

He barely glances at the empty space at my feet.

"What were you hoping for?"

"Oh, you know…" I trail off.

"No, I don't. What would a hollow like you want in a place like this?" He nods at my wedding ring. "A *married* hollow."

"Hollow?" I feign ignorance.

"Fox Hollow is made up of foxes or hollows and you're no fox."

"How can you tell?"

His laugh is just as condescending as his tone when he says, "The way you…"

I arch an eyebrow. *Don't slip. Not yet.*

"The way I what?"

Taking a hand from his pocket, he waves at my body. "Dress. You're dressed like a hollow."

I remove one leg at a time from the loveseat, rotating so I'm sitting normally with my feet on the floor, then hang my head. "I see. I don't fit in. Maybe I was wrong coming here. I just… It's been a really rough week."

Rustling from Reece's direction grows closer.

"What were you hoping for?" he repeats directly above me.

Craning my neck back, I gaze up at him and force an exaggerated swallow.

"A little…"

"A little…what?"

"Distraction. Excitement. My husband—"

"He knows you're here?"

"No," I burst, shaking my head. "He wouldn't approve of me coming here."

Neither of us speaks for a moment, then Reece says, "Excitement… You mean a dance? Or more?"

"A dance would be nice."

"I can go get—"

"Oh."

He frowns. "What?"

"I was just… I mean, you're here. I thought… You know, because you said you work here."

"You want *me* to dance for you?"

For an answer, I bite my top teeth into my bottom lip.

"I'm not a dancer."

"I'm sorry. I've made a mess of everything. I think it's best if I leave."

I begin to gather my clutch only to freeze at Reece's demanding voice, rough like cheap wool, telling me, "Sit back."

Okay, so he does have some balls.

Now I want to see how big they are and if he has the foggiest idea how to use them.

My head touches the backrest just as "Holy Water" by Zayde Wølf comes on.

Reece curses and shifts on his feet.

"Please," I plead, exactly like I did in my house, except I keep my lips parted after the word passes between them.

Slowly, he removes his jacket and drops it on the table. Next, he undoes the remaining buttons on his shirt, untucking it and sliding the sleeves off one sculpted arm at a time before adding it to the rest of his outfit.

A few dark tattoos break up the otherwise pristine canvas that is Reece's trim, yet muscular body. His lats stick out enough for me to appreciate them without even seeing his back. Abs that look carved from stone lead the way to a sexy Adonis belt that makes a very prominent V disappearing below his waistband. I contemplate making him lose the pants right now just so I can find out where it leads, but decide not to…yet, because we will get there.

Sinking down to a knee, he wraps an arm under one of mine, and drags me forward until my ass cheeks kiss the edge of the loveseat. He hikes my knee up his bare shoulder, causing the slit in my dress to gape wide open, then runs his nose up my thigh, the tip cold against my skin.

I suck in a breath and lift my chest in the air, my nipples tightening to hard points. The movement automatically has my leg drawing Reece's body closer, so when he drags his nose up my stomach, over my breasts to my chin, his bottom half matches up perfectly with mine. I spread my thighs wider, allowing his semi-hard length to settle against my tingling pussy. I'm so desperate, the crotch of my bodysuit is already smeared with my pussy's cream.

Other than the floor-length train, there's not much to my dress. It's a backless, lacy, halter-top bodysuit with a thin skirt attached to the waist, so each time Reece rolls his body along mine, making sure to thrust into me on every drawn-out wave, sensation spreads through my body like a wildfire consuming a field of sagebrush.

Reece, however… Either his cock isn't that big or he isn't enjoying this—enjoying me—at all because he's still not fully erect.

I've never been on the receiving end of this before. I was always the one giving the lap dances, and they never turned me on. Even if the client was attractive, or kind, or generous, I still hated my job, hated my life.

Is that how Reece feels? Does he hate this moment as much as I used to?

At least I was competent in my tasks. This lap dance is just as half-cocked as his work the other night.

I'm going to have to hurry this along. I've already been here longer than I planned to be.

On one of his lazy hip rolls, I pretend to grimace.

"What's wrong?" he's quick to ask.

"I think it's your pants. Something's scraping me. The button maybe."

"I can take them off…"

"Is that allowed? I don't want to get anybody in trouble."

The next instant he's on his feet, taking both shoes and socks off, along with his dress pants.

Down to only a pair of jet-black boxer briefs and a matte-black watch, he returns to me, repeating the same moves as before, still half-assed and half-mast, but at least now completely unarmed. If he even was to begin with.

As the song winds down, his movements slow. With his mouth hovering inches above mine, he looks in my eyes to ask, "You know Cyrus?"

Hypnotized, I half-moan, half-answer, "Mm."

"Why was he in here earlier?"

Reece's incompetence.

Why was I in here? Because Cyrus insisted we discuss said incompetence in person. As much as I loathe setting foot in this club again, this is the smartest place for us to meet because the alternatives…

There are no alternatives.

Those obsidian pools flick to my lips so quick I almost miss it, and now his are all I can focus on, that bottom one specifically. What would it feel like on mine? What would it feel like on any part of me?

"What was Cyrus doing in here? With you?"

"Not this."

"Holy Water" transitions into something a little more my speed, "Sex Metal Barbie" by In This Moment, and I close my eyes, remembering my goal. Without my vision, my sense of smell heightens even more, and in addition to Reece's musk, I pick up something else.

No, not something else. Someone else.

It's a perfect lead-in really.

Opening my eyes, I ask, "Did Stacia treat you well?" It'd explain why he can't get hard.

Unless it really is me.

Is it me?

"How'd you—"

Reece tries to lift up, but I tense my thighs around his torso, stopping him.

"I can smell her."

"*Smell* her?"

"Stacia overcompensates for her cheap perfume by spraying too much of it all over her body."

"What does her body have to do with mine?"

Is he saying they didn't just fuck?

It doesn't matter. That's not the important part here.

It's not a part at all.

"Yours must've been close enough to hers to pick up some of the notes of her perfume because I can smell her…on you."

He doesn't respond right away, his face closed off as he turns something over in his head.

Come on, rookie. You gotta wise up working for Cyrus.

Thankfully, I did, which is why I'm the one getting a lap dance right now instead of giving one. Reece might be stuck here permanently if he can't think outside the box his boss keeps him in.

Pity.

I decide to throw out another clue by telling him, "Your cologne isn't as cheap but it isn't expensive either. It lasts just long enough to hang in the air for a few minutes after you leave a room."

Again, he attempts to get up, but I swing my other leg around his back, hooking my ankles and locking him in place. One quick tug breaks my thigh chain at the clasp, and I dangle it over our heads.

"I may look like a hollow now." Draping the chain around the back of his neck, I grasp the other end with my free hand, then twist until both ends overlap the front of Reece's throat, my knuckles digging into his Adam's apple. "But I was brought up a fox."

"What the fuck?"

"A fox who's never totally defenseless." I pull on the chain. "Which unless you're hiding a gun up your ass, you currently are. Just like you made the mistake of thinking I was when you broke into my house. Did you touch me?"

"What? When?"

"When you came into my bedroom. Did you touch me while I was asleep?"

"No!"

I squeeze until my nails cut into my palms.

"I don't believe you. Foxes like their prey vulnerable, weak, incoherent."

"Not. Me," he sputters through reddening lips and an even redder face.

"I should've shot you when I had the chance, because I wasn't unarmed. I had a gun and enough bullets to—"

Reece's lips press against mine, his full weight dropping on me as his arms shift from holding himself up to snaking under my back. One of his hands finds my hair, grabs a chunk, and pulls roughly, making me grateful I didn't hide a blade in there. My head's forced backward, but Reece follows right after, keeping our lips together. Considering he's on the verge of suffocating, it's not exactly a kiss, but it's as close to a kiss as I've had in years.

Without thinking, I nip that bottom lip I've had my eye on since he walked in, biting it until I taste that delicious coppery tang I miss *so* fucking much.

Reece groans as his cock doubles in size against my pussy.

He's responding to me.

He's responding to me.

I give in again by rolling my hips up into his thick cock, both of us moaning loudly.

Oh my God, that feels good. Better than anything I remember.

I just want to…

The thought hits me mid hip rotation. Releasing both my hold on the chain and my bite on Reece's lip, I shove at him, but with my hair still in his grasp as he rolls to the side, he takes me with until he's on his back and I'm straddling him.

"You fucked me," I say, venom lacing my voice, blood coating my lips.

Palming his throat through a cough, he glares up at me.

"What are you talking about? I didn't touch you and I sure as hell didn't fuck you. I fucking could've, but I didn't. If it was up to your husband, I would've."

What? Kordin wanted Reece to fuck me?

That man continually surprises me with how low he's willing to stoop. If I didn't hate my husband so much, I might actually respect him.

I shake my head, feeling Reece's fingertips burrowing through my strands to get a better grip.

Asshole.

"You still fucked me."

"How?"

"Because you didn't take the fucking laptop like you were supposed to!"

"Your husband was fucking cheating on you!" he roars while lifting his head off the loveseat.

I react instantly, butting my elbow right up under his chin so hard I hear his teeth clack together.

"Goddamn it," he grits out before he knocks my elbow away, then we're rolling again, back to where we were originally, except with his hold on my hair tighter and much more threatening.

It's not half bad actually. If only he'd—

Ow.

Did he just pull pieces *out*?

This fox has a lot to learn.

I jolt my head straight up, losing more hair but also making Reece jerk his back to avoid collision. Thanks to our bottom halves already hanging off the cushion, the momentum causes us to sag even lower. Reece catches my ass with his free hand, and keeping us connected in the same position, relocates us to the floor between the table and loveseat.

My skin starting to prickle, I rip the flimsy skirt off my bodysuit, then buck up to free the material out from under me.

Reece drives me back down with his hips, pinning me to the floor, then drops his forehead to mine on a strangled exhale.

"Fuck. Your pussy—"

I stuff a wad of skirt in his mouth, muffling the rest of his sentence.

"Save your sweet nothings, rookie. This is business," I make myself say. It feels good to me, too—the front of his body against mine, his body's *reaction* to mine. There's no denying he'd make a really, really good hate fuck, but I'm here for one reason only and he's not it.

Whipping his head to the side, Reece tries to empty his mouth but winds up gagging instead, his body heaving violently on top of mine.

There was a lot of material balled in my fist.

Unable to roll us again, I do the next best thing by rocking us to the side, banging Reece's head into the table's leg. Reece's choke turns into a groan, and something about the change allows the skirt to free-fall from his mouth.

Damn it.

"Stop fighting!" he yells in my face.

"I can't!" I shout back, digging my nails into his flexed traps and earning myself a growl from his chest so thunderous it rumbles mine.

Calmer, Reece says, "I'm getting up. Don't hit me."

As soon as there's enough room between our bodies, I bring a leg up and knee his side.

He falls back down on top of me. "Fucking liar."

"I didn't agree to anything. And that wasn't a hit. This is a—"

"Don't," he warns, already sensing my plan.

My hands remain on the tight muscles between his shoulders, my acrylic nails embedding themselves under his skin.

It's been a minute since I've wrestled with a man this size. I almost forgot what it was like.

Almost.

"On God, if you keep trying to kill me—"

"If I keep trying to kill you, eventually I will succeed. Then you'll be dead and there'll be nothing you can do about it, so stop wasting your energy on empty threats and focus on trying to kill me first."

What kind of training is Cyrus giving his men these days? This is fucking sad. Even Tommy put up a better fight than this and I caught him from behind.

"What the fuck is wrong with you? I don't want to kill you. I don't even want to hurt you."

"Tell that to my scalp."

His hand slips under my head again, but instead of his fingers tangling in my hair, they cradle my skull, gently massaging the scalp.

My body goes rigid in anticipation of the impending blow.

Except…nothing comes.

What the fuck is this? It can't be actual tenderness. It never is.

"Get off." I drive my palms up into Reece's shoulders, pushing, but he doesn't so much as budge. "Get off. Get off me!"

My heartbeat stutters, making it hard to breathe.

"Chill the fuck out. I'm not gonna hurt you."

I'd prefer if he did though. Pain, I know. Pain, I can handle. Pain, I can reciprocate. It's anything else—

No, it's *everything* else I can't do.

Feeling like I'm the one choking, my jaw trembles as I pant, "Get the fuck off me."

"Not until you calm down."

"Is this your kink? Being fatherly?"

He lifts my head so our faces are only an inch apart. "Is that what you're used to?"

"Excuse me?" I bite out, acid churning in my stomach. Did someone tell him about me? Did *he*?

"Your husband's sidepiece kept calling him Daddy during their video fuck."

Oh.

I fill my chest with a full breath, feeling the tightness ebb, then exhale through my nose.

That's all this is—a good-cop routine. Reece expects me to cry and fall apart over my husband's infidelity, his subsequent coddling act putting his dick first in line for me to jump on in retaliation.

Unfortunately for him, I don't trust any cops, especially the nice ones.

"My husband's preferences and mine don't always align. It's why he keeps his girlfriends at his beck and call," I lie.

"You knew he was cheating?"

"Why do you think we don't have an alarm on our house?"

"Because your husband's a cocky hollow—"

"Security systems track everything. The alarm being activated, the alarm being deactivated. Doors opening, doors closing. Same with windows. Every time Kordin would sneak out of the house, or even go into another room if we used sensors, there'd be a notification. There'd be a trail."

Reece looks at me blankly.

"Of evidence."

Still nothing.

"That can be used in court."

"For?"

"How long have you been working here?"

"Six years. Why?"

"Because in the eight years I've been gone, it appears Cyrus has resorted to scraping the bottom of the barrel to find employees."

"Fuck you." He goes quiet for a minute, mulling over everything I said. "Gone from where? You still live in Fox Hollow."

I remain silent, wandering through eyes as dark as shadows.

"You used to dance here?"

I scoff. *Dance.* He and I both know The Playground girls do a lot more than dance. We're in one of the rooms that proves it. Private dances do happen back here, but they rarely stay dances.

Lowering his voice, he asks, "How'd you get out?"

"The only way there is. I paid."

"By marrying a rich hollow," he spits like an accusation that I don't take offense to in the slightest. Correcting other people's opinions on my life is not worth the energy, so I don't even try.

"I married Kordin for his money and now I'm going to divorce him for the same reason." The lies flow off my tongue like warm honey.

The truth is it was never about the money and always about freedom. Not even mine, but hers. Eight years ago I was willing to do whatever it took to ensure her freedom, her safety, and tying my life to Kordin Debrosse's seemed like the lesser of two evils. At the time, maybe it was. But unfortunately, it's not anymore, and paying to get out is no longer an option.

Money dictates the poor, but secrets rule the rich. If I'm right and Kordin's laptop holds enough secrets to sink a cargo ship, then I need it without him having any idea I'm the one who took it.

"Because he cheats on you?"

I give Reece a slow nod. He seems really hung up on Kordin's cheating. If I had to guess, it's because he got his heart broken by someone that cheated on him. I heard heartbreak packs a nasty one-two.

Heard, because I've never experienced it myself. The heart can't be trusted and neither can anyone in this town.

"His laptop has the proof you need?"

"Yes."

Kordin's failure to keep his dick in his pants is not why, after all these years, I came back to this hellhole and trusted the devil himself with stealing my husband's laptop for me under the guise of a common burglary. The reality of the situation is much, much more complicated than a gold-digging wife looking for any reason to take her wealthy husband to the cleaners.

But I can't tell Reece the truth. I can't tell anyone the truth.

My plan was to pay an old contact to get the data off the hard drive but Kordin made me help him lock the entire laptop in his safe before calling an ambulance, and I can't get in there. Nobody but Kordin can.

I take another grounding inhale, and shut my eyes, whispering, "You fucked me."

A cold vacuum suddenly replaces Reece's warm bulk, and I open my eyes to see him pushing to his knees, then feet. The column of his throat looks inflamed with a line of tiny angry divots from my chain, his temple is already developing a lump, both sides of his torso are scraped raw, and when he bends down to grab his pants, eight angry half-moon imprints of my nails bloom with fresh crimson blood.

He'll be feeling me for a while.

His stiff cock strains against his boxer briefs, the thin material stretched to near translucence. Everything about him is beautiful.

"You fucked yourself by marrying that piece of shit."

I fuck myself a lot I could tell him and still be lying. A lot doesn't even cover it. Whether metaphorically or literally, I'm always fucking myself. Instead, I stand, too, packing both the ruined skirt and chain into my clutch.

At least I'm trying to fix my biggest mistake. Reece is pussyfooting around his. If he wasn't, he would've fessed up to Cyrus already.

"What will you do now?" Reece asks as he rolls up the sleeves of his unbuttoned shirt.

"What I always do…fight."

"Dressed like that?"

He's talking about right now? I thought he meant in general.

"I just fought you dressed like this."

"I went easy on you."

Reece didn't *go* easy on me, he *is* easy. His offense was nonexistent and his defense was laughable. Or it would've been if I actually let myself laugh.

"The men out there." He points at the door. "They won't."

"You think what I'm wearing will make a difference? Sexual assault is not a reaction, it's an action." One every woman has to be on the lookout for all the time, regardless of what she's wearing. I turn for the door, adding over my shoulder, "And I'm not your concern."

"Fuck. At least take my jacket."

At the door, I pause, saying, "How about you take my advice instead? Figure out a way to make yourself useful, and quick. Incompetence gets more people killed in Fox Hollow than revealing outfits ever did." Then I leave the room, Reece, and the jacket still in his outstretched hand. Covering up my body never protected it, but defending myself did.

Five

Reece

PROMISE'S SCOWL MORPHS INTO A SMUG SMIRK AS SOON AS she sees my face.

"I was gonna kick your ass for sneaking into four Lost but it looks like Lexi already did."

"You know Lexi, too?" Lexi must've been her stage name.

"Yeah, I know Lexi. She's practically famous around here." Promise says it with an edge, like she's not particularly happy about it.

"For what?"

She eyes me for a minute before saying, "She left, didn't she?"

"Others have left," I tell her even though I'm not entirely sure how accurate the words are. Some people have gotten out, mostly in body bags, but there've been a few that made it out of here alive. I have to find a way to add my name to that list.

"Not like her. Lexi was Cyrus's favorite. She made him that good-good money. Nobody thought he'd let her go."

"Why did he? Because she paid him?"

"That and…" Her eyes get all glazy. "Some crazy shit went down between them."

"Like what?"

"Like personal shit. Family shit."

Family shit? The Playground family or blood family?

"Lexi almost choked Cyrus out."

"Shit."

"Yeah." Promise chuckles, her shoulders shaking.

"How?"

"With Cyrus's cane. She stole it while he was being ridden in three Lost, just as he was blissed out, his eyes rolling in the back of his head, then shoved it up to his throat."

On our date, Cia told me Cyrus always requires two women at a time. One to fuck or suck him, and one to blow in his ear when he's about to come. It's not hard to guess which one Lenox was, especially if she was Cyrus's favorite.

"And what happened?"

"She made him swear that he'd let her go."

"It worked?"

Promise shakes her head. "No, Tommy got ahold of Lexi and kicked the shit out of her. Three Lost had to get a new door because he put her head through it. Made a nasty cut on her forehead," she says matter-of-factly.

I work to keep my voice even to ask, "Tommy who?"

"He's long gone." With her closed fists up to her throat, she stares at mine while whispering ominously, "Strangled out back."

"With a necklace?"

Promise drops her hands and lets out another chuckle. "No. A bike chain. Tommy's bike chain actually. He had to ride a bicycle around after losing his license from too many DUIs. Somebody took the greasy chain right off his bike's frame and used it to strangle him to death."

"When was that?"

"Coincidentally, right after Lexi's shift ended."

It's not a coincidence. Promise knows as well as I do Lenox killed Tommy herself.

Shame she didn't finish off Cyrus, too.

"You should rub your throat, by the way. Get rid of those notches before Boss sees."

I do as she says, massaging my neck with small circles over the impressions left from Lenox's thigh necklace. I already wiped the blood off my bottom lip but my back is a different story. Her nails bit me good and I can't reach everywhere she could. Thankfully, my jacket covers up any blood seeping through my shirt underneath.

"What do you mean 'after Lexi's shift'?" I ask Promise. "Which shift?"

"The shift from that same night. Cyrus made Lexi finish it. Blood running down her face, bruises everywhere, possible concussion, she should've gone to the hospital, but you know Cyrus. Said Lexi needed to be taught a lesson. Had her clean up, then sent her back out to the Merry-Go-Round."

"Did she still perform?"

"That's the thing about Lexi, she's always performing."

No shit. She gave the performance of a lifetime in her hallway. Had me convinced she was a typical jumpy hollow, when really, she's anything but.

"So how'd she get Cyrus to finally agree to let her leave?"

"As long as I live, I'll never fucking forget how it all went down. From the day Lexi showed up, she was detached. I'm not saying she didn't have good reason to be, but it was more than just being closed off. She was emotionless, like a machine. That night, something snapped, and after facing off with Cyrus, then Tommy, she channeled all her emotions up on that stage. She danced everything out to "Roots" by In This Moment and ended up snagging the eye of the biggest bankroll in the club. The catch of a literal fucking lifetime. Some hollow in a three-piece fell in love with her at first sight and reserved a Lost room for them for the rest of her shift. About a week later, Lexi showed up with some serious bling on her ring finger and enough cash to persuade Cyrus to actually let her go. She ran off with her new man without so much as a glance behind her, and nobody's seen her since. Until tonight."

She keeps using Lenox's stage name, so is it just her stage name or does she go by Lexi, too? A few dancers do that.

After a pause, Promise shrugs, muttering, "It looks good on her."

"The hollow life?" I question, because there's no way Lenox is in love with Kordin. I might've believed she was before tonight, but not after seeing her shed the innocent-suburban-housewife act with my own eyes.

My cock twitches at the reminder.

Cutting my thoughts short, Promise surprises me by saying, "Freedom."

I frown. Is Lenox free? It didn't sound like it to me. How could she be free while being shackled to a man who comes and goes as he pleases with nothing and no one to hold him accountable for the shit he does outside his marriage?

Unless she… Does she cheat on him, too? She could've with me just now—easily. I would've torn that gown apart the second she gave me the okay. Fuck smelling me. I wanted to bury my cock in her so deep she'd be *tasting* me. But she didn't give in. Although her pussy was slick the entire time I was between her thighs, she kept it to grappling.

Grappling that got me harder than I've ever been in my fucking life.

"Cyrus is coming."

Promise's whisper hits my ears a second before Cyrus's voice booms, "Reece, there you are," so I drop my hands just in time. Does she pick up people's scents like Lenox?

"I heard you were skulking around here somewhere."

Rolling my shoulders back, I turn around to face my boss, telling him, "I was looking around for you, but it seems you're in high demand tonight."

Promise makes some sort of noise I can't decipher, so I don't try, only focusing on our boss.

Cyrus walks right up to me, the use of his cane making his gait slow and uneven but no less threatening, then stops when the toes of our shoes are touching.

His graying hair's pulled back in a short ponytail, the sheen of the thin strands either from sweat or product, I'm not sure, but his scalp is starting to show beneath, making the entire hairstyle look desperate, depressing, and ugly as fuck. He has enough money for hair plugs but because he has pussy on tap, I guess he thinks he doesn't need to invest in them. He should anyway. He looks like a Clematis seed head.

"You a hollow now, Reece?"

Promise sold me out. That's why she's making strange sounds. Did she give up Cia, too?

I start to tell him, "I didn't—" when he cuts me off.

"Hollows seek, foxes find."

Cyrus cups the back of my neck and closes the distance until we're nose to nose.

"So which is it? Are you a hollow now? Or are you still a fox?"

Promise speaks up, her voice all professional courtesy, nothing like it is when she's talking to me when I'm by myself. "Boss? I have a—"

"Does it look like I'm talking to you, bitch? Unless you're sucking or selling, your trap should be shut so tight an ant couldn't piss between those cock suckers of yours."

Air flows through my nostrils loudly, louder than my heart pounding against my ribs.

"You a hollow?" he repeats to me, both his silver canines glinting as he bares his teeth.

I try to shake my head, but Cyrus jerks me forward, our noses bumping together.

"I asked you a question. Are you a fucking hollow?"

"No," I grit between clenched teeth.

He moves his other hand up to my temple and presses his thumb into the newly formed bump there.

Blinding sparks of pain burst in front of my eyes like fireworks on the Fourth of July, blurring Cyrus's face. After another moment, he pushes me away from him, sending me backward.

"Put me in a room before I get this twat's blood everywhere," he tells Promise, wiping his thumb on his slacks.

"Five Lost is open," she rushes to say, eager to get back on our boss's good side.

I shoot her a glare, but she avoids my eyes completely. Two-faced bitch turned on me, which isn't surprising, but Cia? That's her family.

Just before I follow Cyrus into five Lost, Promise gives a subtle headshake from behind her paperback.

What's that supposed to mean?

One scan of the empty room and I have my answer. Promise didn't give up anyone.

Cyrus doesn't know I met Lenox.

"Who gave you the mouse?" he asks, referring to my temple, before dropping down on the loveseat, his cane still in his grasp. "It looks new."

Lenox's advice runs through my throbbing head. *Make yourself useful.* Cyrus could kill me right now for not completing a job he sent me on. I have to convince him I can still finish it.

"Some drunk out front hassling one of the girls coming in for her shift."

"One of my girls?" He sits forward, his knuckles white around his cane. "Right in front of my business?"

Cyrus will treat his employees like utter dog shit but nobody else gets to.

"I took care of it before anything could happen."

"You took care of it?"

I nod, hoping to God he doesn't ask which girl so he can check with her.

He lowers his chin along with his voice to ask, "You took care of *him?*"

I nod again.

There's a long stretch of strained silence before he sits back. "Congratulations. You just bought yourself another day on this earth. Tell me why I should grant you any more than that."

Fuck.

"I can still get the laptop for you," I say, cutting to the chase.

Cyrus lifts a thick eyebrow. "You couldn't get the laptop the first time."

"The mark was awake, working on it when I got there. If I would've tried to take it from him, it would've looked suspicious."

"You beat him pretty good, no? Why didn't you take it then? You could've grabbed other valuables on the way out. That'd be far more forgivable than not taking anything at all."

"That was my plan…until the wife woke up, screaming about calling the police."

"The wife? You saw her?"

There's something in his gaze, something unidentifiable, that keeps me from telling the truth. Is Lenox still his favorite?

I shake my head. "She was in another room."

The corner of Cyrus's mouth quirks. "Her bedroom?"

What should I say here? If I admit to knowing it was her bedroom, that'd mean I saw it, and her. If I say I don't know, I'll look like an amateur. Cyrus knows I'm not an amateur.

"Yes, her bedroom."

"How do you know it was her bedroom?"

"I searched it before moving on."

Spreading his knees wide, Cyrus secures his cane in his armpit, then sticks a hand down the front of his pants, completely unconcerned that I'm right fucking here staring at him.

"So, you did see her. Was she in bed? What was she wearing? A nightie? Fucking sweatpants and a hoodie again?" He snorts.

What the fuck?

"I'm not sure."

"Get sure." His voice scrapes my ears as he pulls on his cock, his fist inside his pants pressing against the zipper from underneath, pushing it to its limits.

"She was buried under a heavy comforter. I couldn't even see her body."

"Her body? Was she naked?" He quirks his head, murmuring, "Fascinating," low enough I have to read his dampened lips.

"No," I say too quickly, my own body feeling stiff and underused, like I need to hit something. "She was covered up. All I could make out was a mound in the middle of the mattress."

"Was the mound moving? Was she riding her hand? Tell me what she looked like. What she sounded like. What she *felt* like."

He shuts his eyes, giving me the opportunity to picture it myself—finding Lenox alone in bed again, this time awake and riding her hand. White-blonde hair fanned out around her as she fucks herself furiously, panting, moaning. Her tongue wetting her bottom lip as she finds me at the doorway, just like tonight when our eyes first met in four Lost.

My own cock aches for release, so I stroke myself through my pants before I even realize what I'm doing.

Keeping my steps slow, I approach her, taking in her sweat-slicked body glowing blue from the fish tank. Then I just. Fucking. Watch. Only after she makes herself come, both her pussy and my cock leaking, do I drag her ass to the end of the mattress and spread her thighs as far apart as they go. Teasing her quivering slit with my cock's head, I drag the fat tip through her wetness, coating myself enough to slip inside without any added pressure. She tries to squirm, her eyes closing on a moan, but I seize her hips with a threatening growl, keeping her full gaze on me instead as I pull out, then slam back into her until my thighs hit her ass cheeks with a clap. I pump in and out of her just like that, driving her crazy, so crazy her long fake nails shred everywhere she can reach—my forearms taut from holding her in place, my shuddering abs trying to keep from blowing too soon, the back of my neck when I bend to snatch her lips to taste the absolute fuck out of her.

Cyrus's stuttered breath brings me back.

Ripping my hand away from my cock, I shake my head. What the fuck am I doing? What the fuck is Cyrus doing?

Is this the effect Lenox has on people?

It's no wonder she did well here. Holy fuck, I'm about to explode in my pants from a fucking fantasy. With another man in the room. A man who's admitted to wanting to kill me.

Concentrate, motherfucker.

"I didn't touch her."

"But you wanted to," Cyrus states confidently.

He's the kind of fox Lenox was referring to, the kind okay with molesting women in their sleep. But like I told her, I'm not that kind of fox.

Seeing Lenox in her bed, I did want to touch her, but nothing like Cyrus is thinking. I wanted to preserve her. Innocence is hard to come by anymore, and it's even harder to keep intact. I wanted to keep her exactly how she appeared in that moment—soft. Not because I get off on it but because I don't. My mom is soft. My sisters are soft. I did for Lenox what I would've done for them. I wish my dad had been exposed for what he was doing behind our family's back long before it got to this point.

I didn't know Lenox was already past this point, has been past this point for years, and is now trying to come out the other side.

"I didn't see her. I didn't hear her. I didn't touch her," I say, willing my blood to return to the rest of my body before Cyrus opens his eyes and sees the evidence of my lies for himself.

It was only when Lenox showed me her rough edges that I really wanted her. I wasn't turned on by her fighting me, I was turned on by the fact that she had fight, period.

"She was sleeping soundly until I stomped on her husband's arm."

The movements in Cyrus's pants grow fast, erratic, *loud*.

"What did that sound like?"

"His arm breaking?"

"Yes," he hisses like a goddamn snake. "Describe breaking his arm to me. How did it feel to know he wouldn't be able to touch her with it?"

Touch her with it? Does he mean just sexually? Or physically, too? Does Kordin *hit* Lenox? She didn't give any indication either way. Promise's words echo through my head. *"She's always performing."*

He could. Kordin could abuse his wife. He definitely seemed the type the way he spoke about her.

I should've broken both his arms.

Then I remember what Lenox said. *"I'm not your concern."*

She's right. She's not my concern. But my mom and sisters are, and I'm no good to them if I'm dead.

I need to fix this, for my mom and sisters, for myself, and in the process, hopefully Lenox, too, because I did fuck her over.

I just have to get Cyrus's trust first so he'll let me try. To earn his trust, I'm going to need to play along because this is all a performance.

One I'm so fucking unfamiliar with. I've never gotten anyone off using my voice alone, especially not a man.

Taking a step toward the loveseat, I lower my voice to say, "It felt good," then cringe at myself.

Cyrus drops his head back on a groan though, his Adam's apple to the ceiling. Staring at it, at the way his heartbeat pulses in his throat, I drag my eyes to the cane tucked against his ribs. She's the reason he does that, I bet.

"I broke his right arm at the elbow," I tell him. "Snapped the bones in multiple places. I could feel the crunches under my foot."

"Was he right-handed?"

I nod, then force myself to say, "Yes," out loud.

The laugh that leaves Cyrus could extinguish fire.

"More. Tell me more," he says, practically frothing at the mouth.

Lying through my teeth, I create a gruesome tale of events that never happened, full of details twisted enough to entertain the sickest person I've ever met. No, not just entertain. Pleasure. I'm pleasuring Cyrus, the king of deception, with deceit itself.

Right when I'm getting to the part where the mark's wife begs for her life from the other room, Cyrus's left hand shoots out to the side, and he orders, "Blow in my ear. Hurry."

A knot in my stomach, I lean over the loveseat, trying to keep enough distance between us that we're not touching, but my shirt grazes his open hand and his fingers react automatically, closing around the material to yank me closer. I have to reach out with both hands to keep from falling on top of him.

"Blow!" Cyrus demands, his tight fist against my sternum.

I have no choice but to obey, blowing in his ear.

Gurgling noises build in his throat, finally erupting out of his gaping mouth the same time the crotch of his pants darkens from the growing wetness of his cum.

Fuck. I did it.

"I've got a job for you," Cyrus says as he shoves me away from him, all business once again.

Straightening, I ask hesitantly, "Who's the mark?"

"Same mark. We need all the information on him we can get our hands on."

"From the laptop?"

"Forget the laptop."

"Then how—"

"By getting yourself hired at the mark's firm and finding out everything you can on him."

It's so fucking risky, showing my face like that. I have zero experience working undercover and even less time to dedicate to learning how.

"What am I supposed to do about my regular job?"

Cyrus pulls out his gun, examining it, and without him needing to say a word, I ask, "When do I start?" because it's this or get a bullet in my brain.

"Immediately."

"What information am I looking for?"

"Any and all."

That sounds a lot different than just his extramarital affairs.

"Boss, if I don't know what to look for, it'll be like searching for a needle in a goddamn haystack."

He stops to regard me, repeating, "Any. And. All."

"The mark… Who is he? What if he recognizes me?"

"He's a hollow cunt named Kordin Debrosse. He runs Debrosse Investment Properties Group. If you roughed him up as good as you say you did…"

He pauses, only resuming after I nod my head.

"…he shouldn't even be able to work for a while."

"What about your client?"

"What about them?"

I swallow.

"Are they aware of the new plan?"

Cyrus's lips spread in a terrifying sort of smile before they thin back out. "Do I need to remind you what's at stake if you fail again?"

My own face hardens. "I won't fail."

"Good." Grabbing several tissues, he wipes at the hand that was just around his cock, getting between each and every finger before moving on to his cuticles and under his nails.

"How old are your sisters now? Ripe for the picking, huh?"

I don't answer him either. I just spin on my heel, giving him my back as I stroll from the room, Cyrus's laugh following me all the way out. Fucking bastard knows I'll do anything to make sure my sisters never work here. It's bad enough both sisters and my mom technically work for him at the flower shop.

It's up to me to protect them the way my father failed to.

I can't fuck up again.

Six

Lex

I'M JUST ENTERING THE LOCKER ROOM OF OUR TOWN'S MOST affluent wellness center when a trio of women cut me off, intrigue in their expressions and determination in their exaggerated hip sways. Forming a semicircle around me, effectively blocking my path forward, the three make a show of examining my appearance. My overpriced yoga pants and snug-fitting tank must meet their standards because they give each other self-righteous head tilts.

"Hello," I greet with a pleasant tone, despite my building irritation at being approached so ridiculously. What is this, middle school?

The leader steps forward first, her astringent designer perfume nearly knocking me over.

"We wondered if we'd ever get to see you. In all the times Kordin's been in, he's always alone."

I keep my expression flat. My husband is a lifetime member here—according to him, only for the status—except I wasn't aware he actually used it. Kordin and I have been using our home gym for as long as we've been together, preferring to actually work out instead of pretending to while getting the gossip on everybody… Or so I thought.

This is my first time visiting the local high-tech gym, and I'm only here because of its full-service spa. After my Graves' disease diagnosis two years ago, massage became a regular part of my treatment plan.

Kordin jumped on the opportunity to send me away by "gifting" me weekend trips to different spa retreats all over the tri-state area, and because I genuinely wanted to get better, I went on them all, knowing my husband would be spending the time fucking other women whose bodies hadn't failed them. Despite being in remission for the last year, we've continued the ritual. I get more out of a massage from a stranger than I ever have being fucked by Kordin, so I cherish the weekends I can get out of town, if only for my mental health.

Unfortunately, my physical health seems to have taken a dive as of late, and I was hoping a massage might help. With Kordin in the hospital, I remembered his membership and thought I'd brave the hollows in their natural habitat to get one. Because my name wasn't on his list of approved guests, I assumed the last time he personally stepped foot in here was before our wedding.

Much like most things with my husband, I assumed wrong.

Now that it looks like I won't be escaping without a brush with some of the hollows' idle-born tentacles of meddling first, I give a recycled version of the line I gave Reece, telling them, "Sadly, our schedules don't always align."

"I thought he said you two worked together."

"We do, but very different positions. As CEO, Kordin has a lot more freedom than I do." I consider that for a second before adding, "Without anyone to answer to, he can get away with doing whatever he wants, whenever he wants."

"Perks of being the boss," she says with a haughty tone, missing my insinuation completely.

"Mm."

"Anyhoo, I'm Reagan Hull."

Hull. Why does that sound vaguely familiar?

At my lack of recognition, her eyebrows dip minutely. "Matthew's wife. Kordin's a good friend of ours."

Maybe Kordin mentioned them before.

"Nice to meet you," I lie before giving them all the same once-over they just subjected me to. They appear to be in the same uniform, just different patterns of too-bright colors mixed with animal prints.

Between the three pairs of identical running shoes in front of me, there's not a single scuff to be found, meaning they're all coincidentally brand new or these women don't run. I'm betting on the latter. On my way in here, none of the exercise machines I passed were being used.

"I'm Yelena, Greghory Sykes's wife," the beta of the pack says, but the name Sykes doesn't ring any bells and she doesn't offer up any further explanation, so we just stare at each other blankly until the last woman cuts in with her own lackluster introduction.

"And I'm Suri Blanc-Shulle. David's wife."

"I'm Lenox," I state, purposely leaving out any mention of Kordin's ownership of me.

"We're so sorry to hear about what happened," Reagan says.

Ah. This confrontation makes sense now. They heard about the break-in.

Before I can get a word out, the circle tightens, closing the gap uncomfortably, then I'm peppered with more questions and generally useless commentary.

"Was it really a home invasion?"

"You must've been so terrified."

"What all was taken?"

"Nothing insurance can't cover, I hope."

I nod and say, "Yeah," quietly, not really referring to any one comment in particular. Reece didn't take anything, but even if he had, Kordin has insurance on everything down to his electric toothbrush. It's *all* covered. The damaged items, including the one broken window, have already been replaced.

"Kordin's so brave to sacrifice himself like that," Reagan says with another perusal of my appearance, this one intended for my more intimate parts. "Who knows what those miscreants could've done to you if he hadn't stepped in."

Yes. Kordin Debrosse, a courageous hero. And in the face of multiple assailants? Even better.

Sometime between surgeries, my husband's found a way to control the narrative.

I should've been coming here all along. I wouldn't be playing catch-up right now.

Pressing both hands to my face, I sniffle behind my fingers as I bounce my shoulders.

"It was so awful. I thought they were going to kill us. I didn't know what to do. In that moment, I shut down, picturing my entire life, everything right up until kissing Kordin goodnight that night." I pause to dab my dry eyes. "It wasn't until he tried to fight them off that I snapped out of the shock."

"Kordin was *fighting?*" The women share a look. "Was it something he learned here?"

I almost snort. Here? The wellness center with rows of unused equipment gathering dust? The only moves I've seen made here so far are from older, richer men on the younger, poorer employees.

My hands fall limp by my sides as I tilt my head. "I don't know where he learned those moves, or even when. One minute Kordin was the same man I've loved for eight years, the next he was fighting like a trained hit man." If this lie makes it back to Kordin, at least I know he won't refute it. It paints him in a positive light after all. We haven't discussed what all happened in that office, so it shouldn't raise any flags that I'm going along with his fabricated account. How could I possibly know what took place before I got there? "It just goes to show no matter how well you think you know someone, everybody has their own hidden parts." *No, not good enough.* "Secrets," I amend, my gaze touching on each of theirs.

"Not my Greghory." Yelena snickers. "He's too pure of heart to ever keep a secret."

The other women's eyes drop to the floor while their eyebrows lift as high as their frozen foreheads allow.

"You'd be surprised," is all I say, nudging the seed a little deeper into the soil so it can take root. *How well do we know our husbands really? What are they capable of?*

If I can't even answer those questions, then I can't imagine them trying to because while love is blind, money is downright stupefying.

Both are incredibly effective weapons when used correctly. Separately, they're dangerous. Together, they have the potential to be lethal.

I'd probably be dead if I ever loved Kordin. Maybe. I don't know.

That's just it, I don't fucking know.

My mouth as dry as my eyes, I tell the trio, "I appreciate your concern…" What was their concern for? Certainly not me. "But if you'll excuse me, I've got some contracts I need to read over."

A chorus of gasps erupts. If pearls went with athleisurewear, these women would be clutching them in their over-moisturized palms right now.

If I told them what I'm really going home to read, they'd be clutching rosaries.

"They don't seriously expect you to work right now, do they?"

"Especially on a Saturday."

"They" might not. But I do. There's not a single person at Kordin's firm I trust to cover for me, and I've already been out of the office, working remotely from the hospital for the past two days just to make sure I don't fall behind.

"As much as I'd rather stay by Kordin's side day and night right now…" I conjure genuine sadness at that scenario. "…it just isn't feasible. As a portfolio manager, I don't have the same freedom my husband does. I need to get back into the office."

"Maybe Matthew should assign you security, too."

"Security?"

"Yeah, in case those lowlifes come back to finish the job." Reagan leans in to whisper, "You know, tie up loose ends," before straightening again. "After Matthew visited Kordin last night, he put one of his men on him. Didn't he tell you?"

My head moves noncommittally. That's where I heard her last name. Matthew Hull, as in Chief Hull, as in chief of the fucking police department. Kordin didn't mention so much as knowing Chief Hull, let alone that he'd be getting a personal visit from him. While I was meeting with Fox Hollow's biggest criminal, my husband met with Fox Hollow's police chief.

Not only that but now he's got a cop stationed outside his hospital room.

Double fucking damn it.

"Kordin's a good friend of ours." I bet he is. The best connections are the ones your enemy knows nothing about.

Reagan insists, "I'll call Matthew. See if he has someone he can put up at your house at least. It'd give us all a little peace of mind knowing you're still safe in Kordin's absence."

A scream bubbles in my throat, ready to spew at high volume. Kordin does not keep me safe. No man has, does, or ever will. *I* keep me safe. Me. No one else.

And if Kordin was able to keep this big of a secret from me, then I'm currently fucking failing because the more steps I fall behind my husband, the less safe I am. The less safe *she* is.

After untangling myself from the women, I grab my belongings and head home.

Seven

Lex

MONDAY MORNING, I'M WALKING TO MY OFFICE WHEN PHIL, the COO, stops me to ask, "How's he holding up?"

I'm taken aback at first that he's even talking to me until I remember he sort of has to. His boss is incapacitated and I'm the closest one to him.

"Oh, you know Kordin. Stubborn as always."

Phil chuckles before putting his hand on my shoulder, causing me to flinch. Now he's touching me?

"How are *you* holding up?"

As much as I want to believe Phil's asking because he cares, the bulge in his pants has me questioning his sincerity.

With a badly done combover and a nose marred by too many unchecked growths, Phil reminds me of the clients at The Playground that would come in complaining about their wives and how "she just doesn't understand me." *Getting your dick sucked by someone who understands you even less doesn't fix a crack, it only enlarges it,* I always wanted to tell them but couldn't.

Just like I can't tell Phil to remove his fucking hand from my person.

"I'm okay. Just a little shaken up," I say, lifting both shoulders, one more than the other.

Phil doesn't take the hint, only grasps harder while taking another step toward me, practically drowning me in mint-and-green-apple aftershave as he turns me to face him.

"If you need anything, anything at all, I want you to come straight to me." He grips my other shoulder, too. "I'm a call away, Lenox. Day… or night."

"Thank you, but really, I'm okay."

Despite our differences, I've never cheated on Kordin. For the majority of our marriage, I couldn't have even if I wanted to because he was fucking insatiable. He wanted to fuck me all the time, from the moment he woke up. He believed empty balls improved his performance at work.

But that was before he stopped caring. No, not caring. Caring isn't the right word. It's too strong. Too selfless. It implies he ever gave an actual shit about me and I'm not sure he did. If he did, how could he quit so quickly? And so completely?

I could've been cheating on him for the past two years. Once we received the diagnosis for my health issues, I suddenly lost all physical appeal to Kordin, giving me the time, the desire, and the motivation to cheat. But still, I didn't.

It's not like I need to. Just because Kordin wanted sex often, doesn't mean he was ever any good at it, so I've been seeing to my own needs all along. With my romance novel collection and an entire drawer of sex toys at my disposal, I'm not only more efficient at getting myself off, but imaginative in ways to do it, too.

"Lenox," echoes from down the hall, and we both turn toward the voice, Phil's hands finally falling away.

Kaisin, Kordin's younger brother, as well as the CFO here, is strutting toward us with one hand in his pocket and a flock of people behind him. During his approach, my brother-in-law's eyes trail my body from head to toe before moving to Phil, asking him, "How is she?"

I bite the tip of my tongue between my molars to keep from shrieking. I know it's unusual for Kaisin to go out of his way to address me directly as well, but why the fuck wouldn't he ask me how I'm doing when I'm right here?

"She says she's okay—"

"And I am," I cut Phil off with a savage side-eye.

He turns a dark shade of red, his face resembling a too-ripe Bing cherry that's already started to wrinkle.

"Is there something in particular I can help you with, Kaisin?"

"Yeah. You can actually. Go home."

I turn my narrowed gaze on him. "Excuse me?"

Physically, the Debrosse brothers are similar in a lot of ways. Their eyes are the same murky blue, and their noses are nearly identical, but where Kordin's hair is dirty blond and kept at a tight one and a half, Kaisin's is a touch lighter and fluctuates between a scruffy two and a sloppy three. It's their behavior that really sets them apart. One brother conducts himself like the owner of a successful company while the other behaves like the result of a faulty condom. Right now, Kaisin's trying to pass as his big brother by letting his superiority complex run uninhibited so he can pull rank. Rank he doesn't have over me when the CEO, my husband, is here.

"You just suffered a very traumatic life event." Kaisin waves a hand down my body like he's presenting evidence to the jury. "Work is the last thing you should be worried about. Take some time off and come back when you're thinking clearly."

Thinking clearly? How does he know what I'm thinking? How does anybody? Nobody has bothered to ask.

Kaisin pulls me into a hug that has my whole body tensing up. We're not those kinds of in-laws. We're not even those kinds of colleagues. Aside from the occasional greeting around the office, we rarely speak to each other, inside or outside of this building.

Between Phil and now Kaisin, it's too much contact all at once. I wasn't prepared to go from practically nothing, no physical touch whatsoever, to two different men's hands on me in one morning.

Even though their touch pales in comparison to Reece's, theirs is somehow more jarring.

"Go home, Lenox. We got it from here."

We. He means the men at this firm because I am the only female.

I push him off me much nicer than I would if there weren't witnesses.

"Thank you for prioritizing my wellbeing, but I can assure you,

I feel fine." Even if I went home, I'd still be working, just like I did Thursday and Friday. Where's the recognition for not falling behind those days? I must've been thinking clearly enough then, so why is today such a big deal?

Kaisin's smirk looks more like a grimace before he exchanges glances with the men behind him, the ones who "got it from here."

They alternate between looking at my brother-in-law, then me, except they never make it to my face like they do his. You'd think I was Medusa the way they avoid my eyes. In these circles, to give someone direct eye contact is to give that person respect and these men do not respect me. They've resented me ever since Kordin gave me the higher position I was in no way qualified for at the time. I didn't even know what a portfolio manager was, only that I'd have a reliable salary—a salary that started at more than triple the income I'd been earning at The Playground while doing less than half the work and with my clothes on—so I accepted.

Not only was I naïve, I was also desperate.

More than I am now.

Among the group behind Kaisin, a pair of obsidian eyes meets mine head-on, giving me pause, not only because they're the first ones to hold my gaze, but they're unfamiliar. They are familiar, but not familiar *here*. At my place of employment.

Dressed similarly to the last time I saw him, he's in black top to bottom, except for his stark white undershirt. However, he's now got a badge on, indicating he's employed here, too.

This isn't what I meant when I told him to make himself useful.

I scan the small crowd again. They're on their way to the boardroom for the routine Monday meeting. The meeting Kordin typically runs. Without him here, Kaisin will fill in and he could turn them all against me even more. If it goes to a vote, I already know I'm out.

In some cases, desire is more powerful than respect. I can't make these men respect me, but I can get them to desire me. I need to be careful in how I go about doing it though. This isn't The Playground where I can strip down to a thong and grind on top of their laps. I have to be smart.

"Who's the new guy?" I ask no one in particular, a plan quickly taking shape.

Striding forward, Reece says loudly, "Reece Souza," so no one can speak for him.

Souza. Unless he has a squeaky-clean record, he's using a fake last name.

"Is he any good with stains?" I have no idea what Reece was hired for and I don't dare acknowledge him directly, only talk about him like the others would. "My blazer. I spilled creamer on the sleeve on the way here." I remove my blazer before anyone can get a good look.

I make it a point to wear long sleeves at the firm, so without my blazer, every man's attention goes straight to my shoulders exposed by my blouse being held up by only two thin straps. The cold air rushing over my skin causes my nipples to pebble, and since my breasts aren't big enough to warrant wearing a bra with most outfits, including this one, every gaze lowers to my chest.

"So?" I say, drawing my shoulders back. "Can he give me a hand?"

"Stain? You want me to take a look at it?" Kaisin's words come out low and almost pleading despite him being clueless when it comes to stains. I know for a fact he's clueless because all of Kaisin's pants have piss stains to the left of the zipper from him not shaking his dick good enough after pissing. Every. Single. Pair.

That's another similarity between the brothers. Kordin's cock pulls that way, too.

"I got her," Reece says, his voice confident enough to convince me—and the others, because they all move aside to let him through.

I turn to Phil and posing my question as a challenge rather than a request, I ask him, "If I wanted to attend the meeting, do you think you could stall for a few minutes?"

"I could try."

Shocking me again, Kaisin grips my bare elbow. "You don't need to attend the meeting. You need to go home."

If I hadn't been the one to order the break-in myself, I'd wonder if it was Kaisin who did it. He looks a little *too* happy about all this, a little *too* comfortable stepping into the role nobody but his last name gave him.

Before I can react, Reece walks between us, forcing Kaisin to let go.

Looking from Reece's severe side profile to Kaisin, I say softly, "I just want to have a discussion. Let me come. Please."

Several throats get cleared, none as loud as Reece's next to me as he rips the blazer from my hold.

Kaisin gives a terse nod.

With the sexy fox crowding my space, I spin on my heel, ready to teach him another lesson, this one a little less bloody than the last…hopefully.

No promises.

"Come in, Mr. Souza," I say when we reach my office, holding the glass door open and waving Reece inside.

Without a word, he charges past me, eyeing my custom maple-and-walnut executive-style desk as well as everything on it. He acts so much like a fox, it's a wonder he got hired here in the first place.

I turn to watch him while closing the door behind me.

Located on the top floor of the building, my office has two walls of glass, one to the outside, overlooking the cleaner, greener parts of Fox Hollow below, with the cloudy Hudson River in the distance, and one to the hall, allowing anyone walking past to see in here, including one of the several cameras placed all over this floor. At my desk are three chairs—my leather executive chair and two tufted barrel chairs on the opposite side. Neither of which have ever been occupied, nor have the two other chairs, meant for more casual conversations. Both are brown leather armchairs, facing each other in front of the three floor-to-ceiling bookcases full of non-fiction books I've never read and will never read. I prefer fiction to reality any day, but a self-help book discussing the benefits of waking up at five every day looks far more professional than a paranormal why-choose romance featuring four shifters running a train on their fated mate. Or so I've been told countless times by my husband who makes me cover all my books at home with white butcher paper.

I gesture to the untouched sitting area. "Please take a seat."

Crossing the room, Reece starts to lower himself into the arm-chair closest to the bookcases.

"Not there." I tap the one sitting opposite it instead. The one with its back to my interior wall of glass and the camera trained specifically on this room. "Here."

Beside the bookcases is a private bathroom, so once Reece is seated in the correct chair, I excuse myself to it, leaving the door open. The camera doesn't reach the bathroom but I do have to step to the side to avoid being seen by any passersby. At just the right angle inside, I can still make eye contact with Reece as I bend over, dragging my thong down my thighs beneath my pencil skirt. As soon as the panties hit my knees, I release the material and stand back up, letting the black lace fall to the floor on its own. One foot at a time, I step out of them.

Reece's chest expands on a ragged inhale, then his dark eyes lift from the thong at my feet to my eyes. His arms flex as he leans forward.

"Ah," I tut. "There's a camera aimed at your back. Glued to the monitors live-streaming its feed are three security guards, waiting for something to do."

Reece's tongue sneaks out to wet that full bottom lip of his, and I have to take my own irregular breath.

I retrieve the discarded panties before taking the seat across from him, my legs crossed one over the other.

"What are you doing here?" I ask him.

He shakes my blazer with his left hand. "Stain removal."

"For such a dumb fox, you sure have a smart mouth."

"For such a smart fox, you sure like having hollows' hands all over you."

"I'm not a fox."

"You're not a fucking hollow."

No, I most certainly am not.

"Do you know what an apex predator is?"

He shrugs. "Top of the food chain. Nothing above it. Like a lion."

I uncross my legs. "Think bigger."

Reece's gaze turns hungry and predatory as it drops to my skirt, but with my thighs still touching, he can't make out anything exciting. *Yet.*

"Sharks. That's why you have one at your house."

"That's Kordin's shark. He thinks he's a shark. All these men do." I lazily wave a hand around us. "And me, the only woman here, a guppy among them. But it's a common misconception, that sharks are apex predators."

Reece's eyebrows almost collide. "What the fuck hunts sharks?"

"Orcas."

I separate my legs a couple inches.

Those eyes as black as the deepest part of the ocean zero in on my pussy before snapping back to mine.

"Right now your body's blocking me. If you stay exactly where you are, the guards will only be able to see the back of your head and shoulders, not what's in front of you."

Chest heaving, the crotch of Reece's pants grows a nice-sized tent.

"It's called tonic immobility…what killer whales do to sharks."

"What?"

"Not only can orcas swim faster than sharks, but they can maintain top speeds longer. Using that, plus their size, they ram into the shark, stunning it just long enough to flip it over."

"That kills them?"

"No. It only puts them in a trancelike state. Being upside down messes with their breathing."

"Then what happens after that? What does the orca do?"

I let my knees fall open, saying simply, "Feasts."

Reece groans, his fist clenching around my blazer until his knuckles pale.

"Pull out your cock."

"You're joking."

"I don't joke. Pull out your cock."

"What are you gonna do?"

Pushing from the chair, I go over next to Reece and drape the majority of the blazer over the armrest so it's clearly visible.

Both of us stare at the fabric.

"I'm not going to do anything," I whisper. "You are. Pull out your cock and let me see what my pussy does to you." When he doesn't move, I add, "Now."

His eyes crinkle at the corners but he listens, undoing his pants. Thick, long, and beautiful, his cock springs free, standing erect and proud.

"Good boy. Don't let this fall." I finger the blazer. "Hold out your right hand."

Moving behind him, I lean over his head and spit into his open palm.

As I'm returning to my own chair, I hear him mutter, "What the *fuck?*" When I sit down again, he's eyeing the puddle of my saliva with a deep frown.

"Stroke yourself with it, rookie," I tell him through an eye roll.

"To what? Your fucking voice? I'm not—"

Reclining as far as the chair back allows, I spread my legs again. Reece's swallow is audible.

"Not to my voice. To my pussy. Start stroking."

"Fuck," he breathes, his wet hand dropping to his cock. Starting at the tip, he rubs his palm all over his shaft, spreading my spit around evenly, then he strokes himself. Up, down, up, down; his fingers squeezing on each descent like he's pushing into a tight hole.

An ache tugs at my pussy, insisting on attention, and I tighten my inner walls, pretending it's my hole he's driving into. God, I'd take him so well. I'd take him so deep.

"You got a fat pussy," Reece points out.

"What I lack in tits, I more than make up for with pussy lips. They'll swallow your cock to within an inch of your life."

"Yeah?"

My head bobs on a nod, watching his fist expertly work his cock.

"Mine? You want my cock?"

I shrug, telling him honestly, "It'll do."

"Get over here and I'll show you exactly what my cock can do."

My clit begins throbbing at the vision of straddling Reece's lap, then sliding down his cock to show him what my pussy swallowing him whole really looks like. And feels like. I contemplate crossing my legs again and pressing my thighs tightly together just to get some friction, but Reece notices the smallest shift in my knees and growls, so I keep them exactly where they are, spread eagle for his viewing pleasure.

Oh my fucking God. I need to masturbate soon.

"It's not going to happen."

"Maybe I'll come to you then," Reece says, his voice strained. "Bury my face in that fat cunt of yours and do some of my own feasting."

It's been a very long time since I've had someone's lips on me like that. I already know Reece's would feel good on my pussy, especially that bottom lip.

No. I shake the thought away. I have a mission and Reece is merely a tool in executing it.

"Before you could even hike my skirt up enough to get a single lick in, at least two guards would be in here, hauling you out."

"I don't care who showed up. By the time anyone could get me off you, my face would be so covered in your pussy's milk, my pores would be sweating your cum for a week." His strokes slow and he sits forward, looking in my eyes to say, "I can make you feel good. Better than *him*."

A moan escapes my throat before I can stop it, causing Reece to recline again, his hips bucking off the chair as he fucks his hand.

I manage to rasp out, "Keep your hips still," while praying the cameras can't see the movement.

"No." He does it again, this time thrusting upward even harder.

"It may be your hand on your cock, but make no mistake, *I'm* the one fucking *you*. Keep your hips still and picture my pussy sucking your cock without getting fucking greedy like every other man would by pumping up unnecessarily."

"Don't talk about other men right now."

"Then don't act like them," I snap, feeling as crazed as he looks. This is taking too long and he's making me hornier than I planned. I only wanted my inner thighs sticky with simulated desire, not shaking from actual need.

Phil comes into view behind Reece, and nudging my thong out of sight, I say through unmoving lips, "We have company."

"Guards?"

Reece's hand freezes around the base of his cock, and I give him a harsh tsk.

"Keep going. It's just Phil."

Slowly, he pulls on his cock, his fist palming the cut head completely before gliding back down his swollen length.

"The motherfucker that was feeling you up?"

My only response is another roll of my eyes.

"Get rid of him."

I give a tight expression as Phil draws nearer.

"Or I will," Reece adds.

As soon as he begins to turn his head, I rush out, "I wouldn't do that if I were you. He'll see the bead of sweat on your forehead. The glass is soundproof, so he can't hear us right now. It looks like you're just getting a stain out. Keep it that way."

Phil approaches the door, gripping the handle, so I snap my legs together, my knees knocking into each other painfully.

Reece groans and closes his eyes, his speed increasing at whatever his imagination is now conjuring instead. Or whoever.

A hot spark ignites in my stomach, burning through the rest of my body instantly.

Despite Phil opening the door, I say, "Eyes on me," to Reece.

Standing with my door propped half open just past Reece's shoulder, Phil says, "About done? I'm not sure how much longer I can hold them off."

I give him the best wince I can muster. "Sorry about the holdup. The stain's worse than I thought." Meeting Reece's gaze, I ask him, "Think you can finish soon?"

His bottom jaw shifts side to side before he says, "Yes."

I give Phil an expectant look.

"Okayyy," he draws out, glancing between me and the back of Reece's head. His eyes linger on Reece's elbow bowed out to the side, but the blazer under it keeps him from probing any further.

"See you in there."

"That you will," I singsong as he lets the door close before he returns to the boardroom.

Dropping the saccharine charade, I grip the armrests, then tell Reece, "Duty calls." I've got enough cream built up to create a couple sticky strings between my thighs.

"Spread your legs again," he grits. "This time play with your pussy."

"I…" Would like to. I'm planning on it actually, but later. Much later. "I'm short on time."

"It won't take long. You're already dripping for me."

"For you?"

"Yes, me. Touch your pussy. See for yourself what *my* cock does to *you*."

"Would you watch?" I ask, hating the insecurity in my voice. I sound needy.

But I feel even needier. When's the last time my own husband looked at me with hunger? Hunger for *me*, not just his own release? So long I can't even come up with a day. Or month.

Or year.

"Watch?" he questions.

I brace myself for the inevitable. For the rejection. The aversion. My comeback already prepped and awaiting launch, I open my mouth to do what I do best—fight.

Reece continues first though, saying, "I won't fucking blink."

Keeping an eyebrow arched, I close my mouth again but spread my legs as far as my skirt allows before sticking a hand up it.

"Use it. Fuck yourself with it…for me."

Two fingertips on my wet lips, I drag them up to my clit, circling the sensitive nub harder with each rotation until I'm panting and my own lower half is rocking against my hand, trying to find the perfect amount of friction. True to his word, Reece doesn't so much as blink, his black eyes stuck to mine like they're magnetized.

"I'm gonna fucking blow."

"Then blow."

"Only after you do."

"Such a gentleman," I deadpan.

"Come first or I'll make you myself. Fuck the consequences."

His words, his gaze, the precum dotting the plump head of his rigid cock, everything crashes together, making my pussy seize up. I clamp my legs together, trapping my fingers against my clit as I come like a volcano erupting—suddenly and unapologetically.

Reece grunts as his own release tears through him just as quickly. Ropes of semen shoot from his tip and back down onto his fist still milking away.

"The blazer," I say before the cum can run down onto his pants.

He catches the mess, wiping every last bit up with the sleeve of my blazer, then looks at me, spent, but with something else in his expression. Something I don't know and I don't particularly like.

I don't like it at all.

"Well, I've got a meeting to get to."

Ungluing my legs, I smear my cum around on the inside of my thighs, down to the hem of my skirt, then stand, smoothing my dry hand down my outfit.

Reece jerks a thumb over his shoulder. "You're going in there like that? I can smell your cum from here."

My annoyance follows me across the room. Do I have to spell everything out for him?

"And you almost lost your mind because of it," I say. "Imagine what that'll do to an entire room of men."

"Of sharks," he says without blinking.

"Exactly."

"Is that what this was about?" He motions at his lap.

"Tonic immobility. Orcas don't just go for the kill after giving sharks a hard blow, they mutilate them first by eating specific areas. The liver, the stomach, and…the testicles."

His eyes fall to my skirt.

"They'll be so wound up from the scent of my arousal, they won't be able to focus on what comes next."

"What comes next?"

I move away from him, hesitating by the door. "Get yourself

cleaned up, then get the fuck out of my office and out of my life because you're fired."

"Wait." He swivels in the chair. "Don't whales work better together? In pods? I just helped you—"

"Don't flatter yourself, rook. You gave me something semi-interesting to look at while I fingered myself to orgasm. A simple search on my computer could've given me better inspiration with quicker results."

"Sorry I'm not a fucking quickie like you," he says despite him not sounding sorry in the slightest.

"Tell Cyrus our arrangement is over." I thought I made that clear at our meeting. "Find yourself a new way to be useful to him. I'm no longer outsourcing help."

Relying on Cyrus for his got me exactly where it's always gotten me—fucked.

"Lexi."

"Don't call me that. Not here."

"Lenox," he says softer, and oddly enough, I have the same knee-jerk reaction. Here, I am Lenox, but right now, I don't feel like her. I feel torn right down the middle. One foot firmly in my present while one toes my past. Reece isn't from my past but he lives how I did, reminding me of that life just the same. I've become too comfortable in this role, too complacent. I shouldn't have been.

I forgot my roots, but they're still very much a part of me, possibly the most important part if I want to get to the bottom of all this.

But if I don't identify as Lexi and I don't feel like Lenox, who does that make me right now? A new role entirely?

Or one that's been here all along, I just haven't allowed myself to explore her before?

"Let me help you."

"The last man I accepted help from was my husband. The man before that was Cyrus. Both made me their whore with no escape route."

"I wouldn't."

"No, you *couldn't*. Because you're someone's whore, too." I yank the handle and step through the open doorway.

Eight

Reece

FUCK. THIS WAS IT, MY ONE SHOT TO GET BACK IN CYRUS'S good graces. And I just fucking ruined it by...what? What did I do wrong? I did everything Lexi, or Lenox, or who-the-fuck-ever that just was in here, told me to...except insist she come first. But she surprised the hell out of me by actually doing it, which was fucking hot, hotter because she wasn't putting up a front. She couldn't. She just let the fuck go. It was beautiful and intoxicating and—

And distracting. Damn it, what do I do now?

I can't go back to Cyrus fired on the first day. He'll kill me and force my sisters to bury my body...before making them clock in for their new jobs at The Playground. They're not even out of high school yet.

Fuck!

Lenox. Lexi. She was right. She—

A scrap of black amongst the brown of the chair across from me snags my eye. Sticking out from where the cushion meets the armrest are the panties she took off.

She left incriminating evidence behind, something I've never done and would never do. This jacket of hers that's got my spunk all over it now, it's getting burned when I go home, along with any chance of anybody being able to figure out what happened in here today.

I knew before I walked in this morning where every camera on this floor was located as well as which ones were actively running. Lenox—not Lexi?—spoke about the camera pointing at her office like it was, but it's not. It's one of a few decoys I discovered placed around the forty-second level during my recon last night. Either she lied to me or she's legitimately unaware someone's looking out for the Debrosses' privacy because not only is her office going unmonitored but so is both her husband's and his brother's.

If the wrong person were to stumble across those worn panties discarded in a public space while her husband's holed up in the hospital, there'd be questions. Attention. Suspicion. None of which she can afford right now.

She does need help.

Lexi—

Lenox—

What the fuck do I call her? She didn't seem to like either name when I tried them out. I'm not calling her Mrs. Debrosse. Kordin Debrosse doesn't deserve to have that kind of claim on her.

Fuck, I'm calling her Lex. This shit's too confusing.

"Tonic-immobility bullshit," I mutter to myself while tucking my dick back in my pants. I also adjust my phone to stick half out of my pocket, so when I stand and twist, it falls out, skittering across the floor in the direction of Lex's abandoned chair. Keeping the jacket in front of my hand as I bend to pick it up, I grab the panties, too, before pocketing both items and straightening.

I stop by the cubicle assigned to me, hiding Lex's jacket in my bag under the desk, then go to the conference room. I wasn't invited to the meeting but I'm new here. I don't know what all my limitations are yet. At least that's what I'll say if anyone brings it up.

Even if I get kicked out, it'll be worth it just to see the look on Lex's face when she realizes she isn't getting rid of me that quickly.

When I enter the room, everyone's out of their seats, attention on Lex stationed at another wall of windows. Her shoulders are slumped forward, her head bowed, almost touching the glass, and when she turns in a circle, facing the room, her eyes are drowning in tears. What the fuck happened in here? She was away from me for a fucking second.

My first thought is Phil and that touchy-feely shit guys his age always try to pass off as innocent, so I round on him, but someone saying, "What the hell happened?" stops me in my tracks.

The other men tear their focus off Lex to glare at…me.

Me? What the fuck did I do?

Lex makes eye contact with me, her expression hardening.

Oh fuck. What did she tell them?

Lex shakes her head imperceptibly, so I keep my fucking mouth shut, lifting my chin a half inch to silently tell her *lead the fucking way then.*

"Is it your jacket?" Kaisin asks, and all eyes swing back to Lex, taking in her thin frame barely covered by a loose black tank and tight black skirt that stops well above her knees. I thought I saw some kind of markings on her wrists the other night at The Playground, but with both of us in constant motion and at each other's fucking throats, it was a little hard to tell what they were. Then in her office, I was more interested in her pussy. And face.

There's no mistaking the marks now though. They're scars. Raised and pearl-colored, they run up her wrists and are about three or four inches long each. I've seen some of the girls at The Playground with similar scars, but don't know what they're from.

She also has a finely outlined, barely noticeable crescent moon tattooed on her right middle finger.

Lex pins her brother-in-law with an incredulous look before masking it with a sniff.

"It's not my blazer. It's this." She waves a hand out around her. "My work is all that's keeping me going right now." Hanging her head, she murmurs, "It gives me purpose when life feels so pointless and…fragile."

I bite my molars together to keep from smirking. Goddamn is she a good actor. She didn't even need to come beforehand to have these men eating out of her palm.

I'm glad she did though.

Phil shuffles his ass over to Lex, caressing her back, and now I'm biting my molars together for an entirely different reason. This motherfucker and those goddamn hands.

Kaisin is quick to separate the two, taking his sister-in-law into his arms, but Lex is even quicker to pull out of them, putting space between her and both men as she gazes out the window again, her elbows bowed out to the sides from her hands propped on her hips.

"I'm staying." It's quiet but everyone in the room hears her just fine.

"You're *my* sister-in-law. It's my responsibility to look out for you while my brother's unable to."

The way Kaisin says "my," it's like he believes Lex belongs to him, and not just as his brother's wife.

I eye both their backs. Does Lex bounce between brothers? I wouldn't put it past her.

"Your productivity's…"

Lex spins around. "Normal. It's been normal."

"It'd be completely understandable if it wasn't," Kaisin says almost mockingly. "You were robbed at gunpoint."

I didn't pull my gun on her. Did she tell him that?

Or did Kordin?

"It kills me to say it but you're unfit to work right now."

Planting both palms on the table, Lex bends over, and every man in the room, myself included, leans in, trying to catch a peek down her shirt.

I'm the first to realize my mistake and pull back, squaring my shoulders. Everything she does is for show. I gotta stop falling for it.

From this angle, the light beams down on the scar at her hairline, the scar a fucking man put there. Not just a man, a fox. Cyrus's fox. Is that how she got the scars on her wrists, too?

"Do I look unfit?" Lex asks the room.

"Lenox," Kaisin scolds so fast and harsh it snaps, echoing throughout the room like a whip against flesh. Despite the reprimand bordering disturbing territory—fucking prick shouldn't talk to her like that, not alone or publicly—it's also strangely sexy.

While Lex doesn't look unfit bent over the table, she does look like she could use a heavy hand against her ass cheek as she's pounded into from behind.

I must not be the only one to think so because several men settle awkwardly into their chairs, a couple folding their hands over their laps.

Lex's lips twitch and she parks that same ass against the end of the long conference table, one leg still on the floor while she lifts the other, bending it at the knee as she rotates to drape it over the edge. With her thighs open, the scent of sex fills the room, triggering more uncomfortable sounds and movements.

All anyone on this side of the table can see is Lex's skirt stretched over the raised thigh, but I know what lies just on the other side—a finger painting of her own cum.

I lock all my muscles to keep from reacting because even though I saw the artwork for myself, I didn't get to taste it and I want to. Fucking bad.

Still standing, Phil and Kaisin both drop their gazes to Lex's crotch. I doubt they can see anything from their positions, but they're sure acting like they can with the way they're licking their fucking chops all of a sudden.

Kaisin wants Lex, but does Lex want Kaisin? Could she cream all over her fingers while gazing into his eyes?

She worked at The Playground, killed at least one of Cyrus's men, and married a dirty-dick hollow. Lex could do anything she had to… including use me like a motherfucking pawn.

That's what I need to keep in mind, not her dripping pussy.

"I've got more stamina than any other person at this firm. If there was a way I could prove it to each and every one of you, I would."

Her tone, her expression, her everything is innocent, yet her words can be, and are, taken as anything but.

Talk of stamina and Lex proving hers pushes every other thought from my head until all that remains is that same dripping pussy I just tried to forget about as it's put to the test over and over again by my cock.

Phil doubles over, falling into a nearby chair while choking on his own tongue. Beside him, Kaisin turns away, probably to hide the hard-on I just spotted against my will.

Jesus Christ. Every motherfucker in this room is now sporting wood, even me and I *just* fucking blew my load. It usually takes me a few hours to wanna go again, not minutes, but here I am, fully erect, ready to fuck Lex in front of her husband's subordinates… and brother.

Mint-green eyes meet mine as I find my own seat, and I duck my head at her. *Mission accomplished.* She's got all our balls.

"I, for one, am interested in seeing Lenox's stamina," one guy says like Lex isn't sitting right here, and a chorus of agreement follows.

Kaisin doesn't argue, just hurries from the room with a mumbled apology.

Lex watches his back before scanning the conference room in his wake. She states rather than asks, "So it's settled. Business as usual while Kordin recovers from his accident."

I swallow a scoff. It was no accident. I meant to hurt that son of a bitch.

Without further debate, Lex stands, asking, "Who's up next?"

Two men push from their chairs the same time Lex takes her own, every visible inch of her skin pebbling with goose bumps as she tunes in to their presentation.

She's cold. Freezing. I'd offer her my jacket, but she'd probably just ignore it like last time. Or fire me again.

Under the table, Lex's legs start bouncing. Her top half is completely motionless, but both her legs are bobbing furiously and… anxiously? My mom does the same thing. She tries to say it's restless leg syndrome but it's anxiety and it's only gotten worse since my dad's suicide.

Other than that small tic, Lex doesn't seem nervous. She didn't seem nervous finagling a room full of men either.

She's always performing.

And if I want to help her, I'm going to have to put on my own performance.

For the rest of the meeting, I avoid looking at her, even when I feel her eyes on me, roaming my body the same way they did in her office.

"Hey, new kid," I hear behind me and pull up short. *Kid?* Kaisin might be a couple years older than me, a few at most. It's just a power move calling me that. Same way these assholes will talk about people right in front of them like they're invisible.

I fucking hate hollows.

I don't really like foxes either though.

Kaisin hustles over to me, asking, "How'd it go in there?"

He didn't return for the rest of the meeting which speaks to how valuable his presence here is. Lex, however, made moves like a fucking boss in the conference room. Whoever thinks this place is better off without her is a dumbass.

Kaisin leans that way.

So does Kordin.

And Phil.

Speaking of, I catch sight of him and Lex coming out of the conference room, together, and narrow my eyes. His hand's on her again, this time snaking under the curled white hair flowing down her back to rub at her neck.

Lex's shoulders scrunch together like she's a fallen angel about to push her wings out from them and unleash absolute hell, but she doesn't because she isn't. She's Lenox, the professional, the wife, the coworker too "nice" to say anything to the loser pawing at her in their workplace for fear of causing problems.

Lexi would probably charge him for that neck massage. Or cut his hand clear off.

I go to answer Kaisin, but he's watching his sister-in-law, too, envy written all over him.

"She's good," I say.

He nods distractedly, agreeing, "Yeah, she is," before coming to, and glancing at me. "Good how?"

They fucked. If not in real life, then in Kaisin's head.

I gesture to Lex. "You were worried about her, right? Lenox? She seems good to me."

"Oh, yeah. Good." He runs a hand through his already disheveled hair, repeating, "Good." Dropping his hand, he says, "It's just… She didn't seem…like out of it, did she?"

"Because of the robbery you mentioned?"

"Yeah. That would be hard for anybody, but especially her."

"Why especially her?" I ask with genuine curiosity.

"This isn't exactly her element."

He's so fucking clueless he might actually be onto something. "What's her element?"

Lex sure as hell makes this life look like her element. I don't know if she actually did go to college or if she learned along the way, but she makes a convincing portfolio manager to me. Thanks to my knowledge of Fox Hollow, I got hired on as a regional marketing and research coordinator, but the position isn't needed. Not with Lex involved. She *knows* Fox Hollow, probably better than I even do.

She should anyway.

"Well…" Kaisin puffs out a breath that turns into a chuckle. "Let's just say, if it weren't for us, she'd still be on the streets."

One word catches my interest.

"Us? I thought you said she's married to your—"

"My brother. Yeah, Kordin married her, but between you and me…" Leaning in, he lowers his voice. "I found her first. She's supposed to be mine."

"She *was?*" Kaisin could've just as easily meant she *is* supposed to be his.

And the way he wobbles his head noncommittally, I think he did.

"So, what happened?"

It's pretty fucking out of line to be discussing such personal shit, especially on my first day here, but Kaisin either doesn't know that or doesn't care because he just keeps going, telling me about the first time he ever laid eyes on Lex. Although he's careful about not saying where he saw her, it's not hard to guess it was at The Playground.

"Was it mutual?"

"What do you mean?"

"Did she like you, too?"

His face turns serious, losing himself to a memory, then he scoffs, saying, "I think so."

And I think they never actually met. Strippers are supposed to make every person in the room feel special, feel wanted. Stripping's not just about which body parts a dancer can show, it's about which emotions they can provoke from their audience while doing so.

"I got an older brother, too," I lie. "We've fought over plenty of girls through the years. I don't know what I'd do if he actually married one though." I let that linger before putting the blame back on him. "Why'd you tell him?" Since Kaisin doesn't appear to have a filter, I'm assuming that's how Kordin found out about Lex.

"I don't know, man. I'm still kicking myself for it."

Yeah, he is.

"How do you do it?"

"Do what?"

"Work with both of them."

He only laughs, so I make myself, too.

Exactly how obsessed is he with Lex?

"You're better than me. I don't think I could do it, work alongside them day after day, year after year. Work alongside her."

Our gazes wander over to Lex heading into her office, the glass door closing softly behind her.

"You got a girl, Reece?" Kaisin asks out of nowhere.

Feeling the heat of his stare on my cheek, I tear my eyes away and nod. "Yeah. Fiancée. We just got engaged this summer."

"Congrats."

I mumble a thanks, wondering if this lie will make it to Lex, then wondering why I care. She's the one with a husband.

"When's the wedding?"

"Soon." I'm guessing that's how engagements work, otherwise why bother?

"You got any pictures of her?"

If I actually had a girl, Kaisin Debrosse is the last person I'd show her to. Motherfucker's one step away from being delusional. I'm only entertaining this little camaraderie because there's a chance he might have something on his brother. And if Kaisin's as honest as I'm hoping, it's only a matter of time before he spills, with or without meaning to.

"Uh, yeah, I should." As soon as my hand closes around my phone, I feel the panties—Lex's panties—and have to keep my expression neutral as I flick them to the bottom of my pocket, carefully pulling my phone out without taking them with. I swipe through my open tabs, landing on one of the models I pay for exclusive images of. She just joined the subscription service I use, so she's not as well-known yet. Hopefully Kaisin isn't one of her fans, too. Once I find a photo she's actually semi-clothed in, I enlarge it, showing my screen to him.

"That? That's what you're marrying?"

I study the picture, trying to imagine it, not marrying her—a stranger on the internet I jerk off to sometimes—but marrying anybody. I've never really envisioned myself married before. Growing up in a house with three females, the last thing I wanted as a kid was to hang around another woman, much less live with one. Until I got a little older and discovered what pussy felt like, making females the center of my universe again, just in a completely different way. Then Cyrus entered my life and the thought of marriage made me fucking ill. I would never chain someone to this world, not if I loved them, *truly* loved them.

"Shit, dude, you hit the jackpot. She's a twelve."

"Mm," I hum in response. The model is hot but she can't sell a fantasy for shit. She'll pose with a sword next to a pool with a sprinkler in it. As far as commitment to her roles goes, she's lacking. Not like Lex in hers. She's like a goddamn shapeshifter.

Shapeshifter…

"Anyway," I say to Kaisin, jerking a thumb behind me. "I got some paperwork to fill out, then a training webinar I'm supposed to sit through, but, uh, what's there to eat around here?"

"Want to meet up later so I can show you?" he asks, falling for it. The icing on the cake is when he offers, "My treat."

Keeping the majority of my smile to myself, I accept before opening my texts and sending one off. Almost instantly I get a reply containing a single question mark. I don't bother with repeating myself. I don't need to. I know she'll get it.

One last glance in Lex's direction, I tuck my phone back in my pocket, safely on top of her panties, then head to my cubicle, finally letting my smile free.

Nine

Reece

ONCE I FIND A PARKING SPOT DOWN THE STREET FROM THE apartment building my mom lives in, I check the surroundings before getting out and locking up my Alfa Romero.

The five-story red-brick Classical Revival used to be a clothing factory over a hundred years ago but was remodeled into loft-style apartments several years back. The exterior still looks like a factory though, and while the location isn't the worst, it isn't the best either. It's downtown, in a neighborhood that's trying to turn things around but isn't quite there yet, especially during night hours, so there're junkies lingering on every corner as soon as the sun goes down. Luckily, by the time my sisters leave for school in the morning, the streets get reclaimed by the residents with honest jobs, and their two-block walk to school is mostly clear of anyone looking for trouble. I've walked it with them enough times to make sure.

We used to live in the suburbs, in a house small enough to be cozy but big enough to fit our family, in a friendly neighborhood full of other families who knew each other and looked out for one another. We had a backyard we'd catch fireflies in during the summer and build snowmen in during the winter. Now my sisters have to share a room and can't go outside after eight p.m.

After they graduate, I want them to get the fuck out of Fox

Hollow and never look back. Go to college, fall in love, travel, live lives worth fucking living. I was only two years older than they are now when I started working for Cyrus, so I know what awaits them if they don't. If they stay here… They can't stay here. Selfishly, I want them to stay near me, always. They're my baby sisters. I love them and want to watch every step of their journeys. But I need their journeys to lead them away from anything Cyrus can touch and taint and control.

I'm still trying to figure out how to get my mom out from under his thumb. Even with Cyrus taking most of what Silvy's brings in, my mom loves her work. She feels connected to her customers. For most of them, she's done floral arrangements for every milestone their family's celebrated over the years from births and communions to birthdays and proms. She's helped decorate anniversary parties, proposals, weddings. In her mind, her customers are family, too, and she doesn't want to abandon them.

A couple on the sidewalk is fighting when I pass them, curses flying from their mouths like bats escaping their cave for the night. Something about them both cheating on each other…with the same person.

What a fucking predicament.

That no one else needs to hear about.

The guy's wearing a hoodie three sizes too big, with a stiff hood pulled up past his ears, you'd think for warmth since it's so cold out, but his camo cargo shorts paired with socks and sandals contradict that. No, I'm thinking it's more to hide the scabs all over his face.

The woman's in a fur coat I know can't be real otherwise it'd have been stolen off her already, and she's got a pipe in one hand and a lighter in the other, waving them both over her head during her rant about wishing her man's dick would fall off.

"Take it somewhere else," I bark at them.

"Fuck you, you nosey-ass bitch," the man says, thrusting a clenched fist near his suddenly quiet girl, making her recoil. "This is between me and my lady."

I want to snort. Now she's a lady? But not when he fucks around on her? Or when he beats on her? She's not reacting to his raised hand for no reason.

Disgusting.

"Not anymore. Not with the way you're fucking yapping for the world to hear all your fucking business. Get the fuck out of here with that shit."

"You wanna try making us?" he spits, stepping up to me.

I pull my gun on him so fast, the tweaker has a hard time processing the fact that he's staring at a muzzle. I wait for it to sink in, but before he can actually do anything about it, I bust his face with the handle. One hit right between the eyes and his nose is flowing like a fire hydrant being flushed.

"Ah! You—"

"Get him the fuck out of here," I tell his girlfriend.

Under over-plucked eyebrows, her bloodshot, sunken-in eyes widen as she asks, "And go where?"

That's the thing about Fox Hollow. Run-down buildings take precedence over rundown people. This couple needs rehab, but they'll never get it here.

"I don't wanna see either of you around here again." Without pointing the gun directly at her, I angle it so she gets a good look at the barrel glinting in the streetlight. "Got it?"

She audibly gulps and nods before waiting for me to move aside to get her man. Together, they take off running.

After tucking my piece away and getting buzzed in, I take the stairs up to the third floor—low enough to the ground in case of emergency but high enough that nobody can climb in through a window—then knock on the door, framing my hands on the jamb, my forehead an inch from the metal.

Someone skips up to the door on the other side before tearing it open, and I'm already frowning. "You didn't even look through the peephole."

My sister Breckyn rolls her eyes and walks away, saying over her shoulder, "Literally, we *just* buzzed you up."

"So what?" I argue, coming inside and closing the door, passing both bedrooms and the bathroom to enter the kitchen where my mom's cooking dinner—cawl stew from the smell of it. "It could've been someone already in the building."

Breck's twin, Charlie, pops her head up from where it was resting on the back of the sofa, a textbook balanced on one knee and a notebook on the other that's more blue than white. Groggily, she says, "You're paranoid."

Paranoid. They have no idea how evil this world can be.

"Don't open the door again without looking through the peephole," I warn. They both ignore me, so I look at my mom for backup. She gives me none, however, as she stirs the pot on the stovetop, pretending not to hear us.

"Right, Ma?" I cock my head when she doesn't so much as twitch.

"Mom discovered audiobooks," Breckyn tells me.

Looking closer, I see my mom is wearing earbuds, the cord disappearing into the top pocket of her overalls where I'm guessing her phone is.

"What kind of audiobooks?"

Without even looking up from her homework, Charlie laughs, and says, "Spicy ones."

She and Lex would get along, I think, then scowl. *Where the fuck did that come from?* In addition to the romance books I saw at her house, I also found a book in the bottom drawer of Lex's office desk that looked… Yeah, spicy's a good description for it. It had one woman and four lumberjack-type men on the cover, and after my curiosity got the better of me, I cracked it open. The story, the excerpt I read anyway, was intense. Lots of holes being filled in lots of ways.

That doesn't mean my mom and Lex are going to meet though. I don't know why I thought that. Lex is…my boss. My *temporary* boss.

My temporary boss I got something for.

"Hey." I rap my knuckles on the counter, finally gaining my mom's attention.

Pulling the earbuds from her ears, she smiles over at me before putting up a finger, and taking out her phone to hit pause.

Finally hugging her, I steal a look inside the pot, confirming what my nose predicted. Cawl stew, a Welsh dish usually made the day before eating, so Mom's probably just warming it up right now. Full of lamb, leeks, and root vegetables, it's a perfect meal for a chilly fall night like tonight.

I actually felt bad for Lex earlier, having to go out to her car without a jacket on. I left before she did, so I know that walk must've been cold. Maybe I'll stay later tomorrow and watch her leave. I don't like…anybody there. Phil, Kaisin, they all rub me the wrong way. Like little beady motherfuckers just waiting for an opportunity to corner Lex. With Kordin out of the picture, she's prime for the picking, too.

I guess I'm the one to blame for that. Not that I feel guilty for what I did to Kordin, because I fucking don't, but I don't like knowing I possibly put her in danger. After spending one day at her husband's firm, I can tell those men do consider themselves sharks. Thanks to Lex's conference room showdown, they've picked up her scent, and now there's no going back. The blood's in the water. They want her.

I still don't understand why she did it. What was the purpose of stirring all of us up like that? She's planning to divorce Kordin and take all of his money. Is she planning to take his company, too? Motherfucker deserves it.

"You got it?" I ask after my mom and I separate.

She gives me a gauging look, but nods toward the fridge. "Of course I got it. Have you no faith in me?"

"I have faith in you. It's everybody else I don't trust."

Opening the fridge, I spot the South African flower and pull it out, inspecting everything from its bright pink bracts surrounding the white fuzzy center to the leathery leaves and thick stem. It's fucking gorgeous. And wide, easily seven or eight inches in diameter. Not as big as some I've seen of this variety, but bigger than the flowers people usually buy. I'll have to figure out a way to sneak it to her without the real cameras picking it up.

"Why do you need it?" Mom asks over the clinking sound from her gathering bowls.

"No reason," I mumble, setting it on the counter so I don't forget it on my way out.

"Reece has a girlfriend," Breckyn sings several times until Charlie chimes in, too. Getting teased by twin sisters is the fucking worst because everything they do is doubled, like they share a brain but with two mouths still, making them so much fucking louder while being scarily in sync with each other.

"Shut up," I tell them while bumping Breck out of the way to grab spoons.

She's on my back in a flash, asking, "Who is she? When can we meet her?"

While trying to shake her off, I let out a deep chuckle. She's like a fucking koala bear stuck to me.

"I don't have a girlfriend."

"But you want one," Charlie states as she joins us in the kitchen, the space cramped and hot.

Breckyn drops her feet back to the floor, agreeing with her twin with a nod I can practically hear.

"No. I don't," I say with a bite of annoyance I can't hide. Avoiding everyone's eyes, I set the utensils out on the small table. I've already got my hands full with these three, but of course, I can't tell them that.

And I'm not giving the flower to Lex for any reason other than it reminds me of her. Or she reminds me of it. Either way, I thought she'd appreciate the gesture. Maybe even take it as a peace offering. Our first few meetings were not my finest, so hopefully I can change her opinion of me enough that she'll let me keep my new job long enough for me to get my hands on what we're both looking for.

The four of us sit down to eat and everyone falls into easy conversation, nobody bringing up the girlfriend thing again. The twins talk about different kids at school like I personally know them or give a flying fuck who they're beefing with this week. I listen anyway, taking bites off the crusty bread between mouthfuls of chunky stew.

"...and they're really going to the dance together. Can you believe?"

"Dance? Homecoming?" I mumble, my mouth full of lamb.

My mom nods. "Everybody's putting in their orders last minute." With wide eyes, she laughs, because it happens every dance, every year. People always wait until the last minute to place their orders for corsages, boutonnieres, and other arrangements for their dates.

Looking around the table, I swallow my food to ask, "It's this weekend?"

Three head-bobs is my answer.

"Who are you two going with?"

Those same three heads drop.

What the fuck? As much as I don't want anyone taking my sisters out, dancing on them, touching them, maybe even more, I want my sisters happy. Their chins skimming the top of their goddamn stew doesn't seem very happy to me.

"Neither of you got asked?"

Both my sisters are beautiful. Like me, they have our half-Portuguese father's dark hair and even darker eyes, but while we all have our Welsh mother's fair skin, they inherited her kind face. They have just enough difference between them to be able to tell the two apart. They're only annoying to me because I'm their older brother, otherwise they're smart, funny girls. Who wouldn't want to take them to homecoming?

My mom's the first to meet my eyes, saying, "The girls decided to opt out of attending homecoming this year."

I can see the pain it causes her to say it and clutch the spoon in my hold, my thumb rubbing the top of the handle roughly.

"Why?"

Charlie says, "Because it's a stupid tradition born from patriarchy."

"So ask someone. Anyone." My eyes land on Breckyn and she shoots Charlie a look. She's in love with Charlie's best friend but won't do anything about it. "Or go alone. Break tradition and go to your last homecoming however the fuck you want to before you graduate."

"Well, we don't want to," Breckyn says with her nose in the air like that'll make her statement more believable.

"That's not what you both were saying last month when you found out the theme. Roaring twenties? The costumes you were planning to wear? Remember that?"

"No," both twins say in unison, making me scoff and drop my spoon to sit back, arms crossing over my chest.

Charlie screen-mirrored her phone with the TV and made me watch as she scrolled through forty different options, asking my opinion on each one. Forty fucking dresses. And that was just Charlie. Breck took over once she was done and showed me another fifteen or so until she decided dresses weren't the vibe she was going for and started looking at suits. Not normal modern-day suits either; suits with pin stripes and matching fedoras. None of which I'm familiar with but I sat through it all and gave my thoughts on every single piece. And for what? For them to decide they don't want to go anymore? That's their choice but it's a choice I don't approve of, especially without a good reason to back it up.

"Why aren't you going? Really?" I ask Breckyn.

She finally breaks, sighing. "It'd be too much."

"Too much what?"

My mom's leg under the table starts bobbing, the chirp of the floor under her foot giving her away.

"Money?"

Nobody makes a fucking sound.

Goddamn it.

"Why didn't you come to me? Why didn't you ask?" My question isn't directed at anyone in particular. "You all know you can come to me with anything you need and I'll take care of it." It's bad enough my mom won't let me help out with her rent. As long as I work for Cyrus, she doesn't feel comfortable accepting help from me, which I understand…to a point. I make money the legal way, too.

"It's not a need," Charlie cries, splitting my heart in two like one of Lex's fictional lumberjacks chops wood.

"It's a want," Breckyn finishes, her elbows on the table as she holds her chin in her palm.

I look around the table, touching on each woman's face. I let them down. I should've handed over the money as soon as the girls mentioned the dance and told them to get whatever they needed. No, whatever they *wanted*.

In my defense, I assumed they'd ask. They don't know about my involvement with Cyrus. But I'm not very good with this shit. At nineteen, I became a father figure to two girls I'd only ever been a brother to.

I think about what my dad would've done.

Then I do the motherfucking opposite. Just because my mom refuses my money, doesn't mean I can't still give it to my sisters.

Leaning to the side, I remove my wallet from my back pocket and take out everything I have in there, placing it all on the table and double-tapping the seven fifties, one twenty, and a dozen or so ones with my middle finger.

"If that's not enough, let me know and I'll get you whatever you…" I meet Charlie's eyes, Breckyn's, then my mom's. "…want."

"It's too late," Charlie whispers. "Everything'll be picked over by now."

It'd be really fucking great if I had contacts in high places.

I do have one. Kind of. She wouldn't help…would she?

I eye the flower on the counter. *Maybe after a peace treaty.*

Digging back into my meal, I tell the twins, "Let me worry about the clothes. You two figure out the rest. You're going to homecoming."

Smiles surround me, hesitant at first, then bigger and brighter, stretching the faces of my family into the best kind of happiness there is. I'll do anything to keep them like this, even swallow my pride to ask the fakest person I've ever met for a favor.

Ten

Reece

LEX DOES A DOUBLE TAKE AS I ENTER HER OFFICE, THEN FOLDS her hands on top of a file on her desk. The loose white curls framing her face do nothing to soften the deliberate suspicion in her icy blue eyes.

"Do you wear contacts?"

"No."

"What color are your eyes?"

"Depends on the lighting. Why are you here?"

"Scott told me to report to you," I say, name-dropping a random guy I met yesterday during my orientation. "Yesterday your eyes looked—"

"Listen, rookie. I don't have the time, energy, or desire to deal with you right now. Whatever Cyrus is paying you to be here, I'll double it for you to leave and never come back."

"Cyrus isn't paying me. I'm here on my own," I lie, wondering if a small part of me isn't lying.

"On your own? What does that mean? Like out of the goodness of your heart?"

"It means I fucked you over and I'm here to fix my mistake. Anyway, Scott said you'd want to know what I'm working on, so…"

One of her eyebrows lifts. "Considering you're no longer employed here, I'm very interested to know what you're working on."

I ignore that because I don't think she really wanted to fire me.

If she did, she would've had me forcibly removed from the conference room…and now. Since she's just watching me, I push my luck by taking a seat in one of the chairs across from her and give her a rundown of my tasks for the day.

Her eyebrow never levels back out as she listens to me drone on and on. I don't actually have that many tasks and I have even fewer plans to do them, but I find myself wanting to see all of her reactions. Learn them, memorize them. She has to show parts of her real self sometime. I want to capture whatever I can while I can.

If she'll fucking let me.

When I finish, she gives a drawled, "Riveting," so sarcastic my lips quirk.

"As for what else I'm working on… I have a lead."

"A lead?" she asks somehow even more sarcastically than before.

"Kaisin," I say, zeroing in on her expression.

Surprisingly, she nods.

Unsurprisingly, she also sits forward and mocks, "Congratulations." She even does a salute above her frown.

Fucking shit.

"Are we done? Or do you require even more of my time to waste?"

"Kaisin—"

"Kordin wouldn't tell Kaisin if he had cancer, let alone mistresses. Besides the obligatory Thanksgiving, Christmas, and Easter dinners their mother insists we all attend every year, the Debrosse brothers do not interact with each other whatsoever once they leave this building. If it weren't for nepotism, Kaisin would never have been able to land himself the title of CFO at a multimillion-dollar company because, quite frankly, he's a moron."

"He wants you."

"Beginning when I was sixteen, the sole purpose of my entire existence has been to attract any person I encounter with a taste for pussy."

Sixteen? She was working at The Playground when she was sixteen years old? That's too damn young. Even my sisters at seventeen are too young.

"And Kaisin Debrosse? Despite being terrible at it, he definitely has a taste for pussy."

"Terrible at what? Eating pussy?"

She gives me a flat look.

"How the fuck do you know he's terrible at it?"

"Have you looked at Kaisin? Really looked at him? The piss stains on every pair of pants he owns because he's too lazy to shake correctly? Do you think he knows, or cares, how to treat a clit?"

That's true. He probably doesn't even know where it is.

"It's more than attraction," I voice the thoughts I've had since I laid eyes on the motherfucker.

Her lips purse and now I'm the one cocking an eyebrow. I'm not as stupid as she tries to make me out to be. I catch a hell of a lot more than I throw back. Except when it comes to her. Lex is a complete mystery to me.

"Kaisin is in love with you. Has been ever since he saw you at The Playground."

She frowns, her Blue Milkweed gaze falling to her desk as she whispers, "That's…interesting."

"You didn't know?"

As if remembering I'm still here, she shakes her head. "You picked that up in one day?"

She didn't answer my question.

"Uh-huh. It could work in your favor. If you're trying to get the company in the divorce…" She doesn't correct me, so I keep going. "…it'd be good to have him on your side."

"I'll work on him," is all she says.

"*I'll* work on him," I tell her with more growl than words.

"No offense…"

I shrug, already preparing for her next words to be offensive as fuck.

"…but you lack the proper skills. Like I said, I've been at this for a decade."

"I thought you weren't in the business of pleasing men anymore."

"Pleasing men? No. But I'll never stop hustling them. You're just too *easy*," she half-moans, sending an electric current to my cock.

"No offense…" I start.

Dropping the act, she scoffs.

"…but you lack subtlety. Kaisin needs subtle or he might crack too soon."

"Soon works."

"Why the rush?"

Her eyes flick to the side as she thinks. Finally, she whispers, "Kordin won't be in the hospital forever."

I want to ask her what she plans to do when he does get released. Will she leave him? Or will she stay? What'll happen if she stays? Will they go back to normal? What is their normal? Is it what I'm thinking? Because what I'm thinking is a lot like what happened in her office yesterday but with a hell of a lot more touching, and licking, and—

Fuck.

It's none of my business. They're married. She's married.

To a fucking asshole who only fucks her from behind. Now that I've seen Lex's front up close for myself, there's no way I'd let that shit slide. I'd put her in every position imaginable, and ever since facing off with her at The Playground, I've come up with a lot of positions.

A. Lot.

She looks up at me suddenly.

"Is that all?"

I swallow before sliding the hardcover in my hold across her desk, propping it upright to keep the flower behind it hidden from view of anyone walking by. Thanks to the flower's massive size, I had to spring for a hardback edition.

Lex eyes both items like I just handed her a pile of shit, not a thirty-two-dollar book and a flower my mom had to special order from her supplier.

"What is this?" she asks without moving to accept either.

"A book I thought you might want to read."

She studies the couple on the cover. I purposely chose one with one woman and one man, none of that sharing shit everyone around here seems to be doing lately.

"I only read non-fiction."

I bite back my smile to tell her, "The books at your house weren't non-fiction. The book in the bottom drawer of this desk isn't non-fiction."

Eyes a mix of silvery blue-green like the leaves of the Sterling Silver variety of Caryopteris trail up to mine as Lex tilts her head. The lump I just swallowed returns, doubling in size, but I refuse to show it, only ignoring it to tilt my head, too. What does she think about me now?

"And the artichoke?" She glances at the flower.

Clearing my throat, this time I do smile. "It's not an artichoke. It's a flower in the Proteas family called King Proteas, named after the Greek god Proteus. He was a shapeshifter."

Lex's gaze slingshots back to mine.

My smile shrivels up, my elbows coming down to rest on my knees as I lean forward to explain, "The son of Poseidon, Proteus was known for his wisdom. He supposedly knew everything past, present, and future, but he didn't want to share any of it, so he'd change his shape and escape whenever anyone would try to make him."

Like everything else with this woman, the silence that follows confuses me. Does she understand what I'm saying? As soon as someone gets close to something Lex doesn't want known, she changes to a different personality. No, not just a personality. A different *person*. She's a modern-day shapeshifter.

"Consider it an olive branch."

"For?"

"Bad first impressions. And… I need a favor."

"What kind of favor?"

"You have…" Fuck. This is harder than I thought it'd be, especially with the full weight of Lex's attention on me. "You have money."

"You—"

"Money gives you connections," I add quickly. "Connections to places. Stores." Right? Isn't that how that shit works?

"Spit it out, rook."

"I need to get a dress and a suit. Formal ones. By Saturday. Sooner if possible."

Lex is quiet for a minute as she sizes me up, then asks, "For you and your fiancée?"

I try not to give anything away hearing those words. If Kaisin's loose-lipped around me, it makes sense he's loose-lipped around everybody.

I didn't want that lie to reach Lex, but now that it has, I do want to see how she reacts to it—*if* she'll react at all—so I nod.

Nothing moves. Not one fucking tic to give away her thoughts. Not a leg bounce, not a jaw clench, not a—

Lex stretches her hand out next to the gifts before using her entire arm to swipe them both off the desk and into the garbage can below.

My chest expands on a ragged inhale as I sit up straight. Not once does she break the connection and not once do I stop considering jumping across the desk to seal my mouth to hers just to see if I can get something out of her. *Anything.* Goddamn it!

"So that's a..."

Her voice is quiet yet hard as she says, "That's a get out of my office."

"Do you always have to be such a fucking bitch?" I breathe out, both pissed and impressed.

"Yes, I do," she answers unapologetically, then gestures to the door. "Out."

How the fuck does she do it? Sit here without any emotions? I gave her gifts I actually put thought into. Did I want to spend my evening in a fucking bookstore, searching for a book I thought a total stranger might enjoy? Fuck no, I didn't. I felt like an idiot, even more so than I do right now having her clown my ass.

I should've bought her the one with the demon couple on the cover.

As I'm shoving out of her office, she says, "You're fired."

I almost turn back around to tell her to go fuck herself—without me watching this time—but seeing Kaisin keeps my mouth shut.

"Hey, man, what's going on?" he asks.

I run my hand through my hair before dropping it by my side, flexing and unflexing my achy fingers.

"Nothing. Just you know...work."

I join him on his walk to wherever he's headed until he stops, spinning around in front of me to lean in and ask, "How'd you man-age a one-on-one with Lenox?"

"Oh, it's, uh… It's kind of embarrassing. After I couldn't get that stain out yesterday, I guess she's questioning my overall capability, so she wants me to report to her every morning with my tasks, that way she can confirm if I'm actually completing them." She does call me rookie every fucking chance she gets.

Kaisin nods, looking past my shoulder, probably at Lex, and I have to stop myself from moving to block her from view. Even want-ing to choke the shit out of her, I still have the urge to protect her.

"You want me to give you the name of my dry cleaners? If the professionals can work their magic, it might get Lenox off your back."

I eyeball the dark dots all over the front of Kaisin's slacks, the words "fuck" and "no" on the tip of my tongue. Not only are the dry cleaners Kaisin's using not what I would consider professional, I don't actually want Lex off my back. I do—*sort of*—but I don't want any-one else thinking she's off my back. I need to have a reason to meet with her regularly without raising suspicion.

But I also need to get close to Kaisin.

"It's worth a shot," I say, already plotting a story about the dry clean-ers fucking up my order. It'll prolong my excuse to come and go from Lex's office, plus Kaisin will owe me for a terrible recommendation.

"I think I have their card in my office."

I jut a hand out, telling him, "Lead the way."

We bullshit in his office for a few, mainly about the virtual-reality headset Kaisin bought recently, and when I'm headed back to my cu-bicle, I take a corner too fast, running right into someone. Not just someone. Lex.

She clutches one of my biceps like she's trying to right me even though I've got at least seventy pounds on her.

Automatically, I try to apologize, but she beats me to it, saying, "Forgive me, Mr. Souza."

Forgive her? For what? Trying to suffocate me numerous times? Getting me to jerk off in her office on my first day here? Firing me twice? Throwing away my gifts right in front of my face without so much as a thank-you first? Immediately saying no to the first and only favor I've ever asked anyone in my entire fucking life? Or plowing into me just now?

The grin she gives reaches her cheeks, then her eyes—that are now green—transforming her entire face. Her hand squeezes my already flexed arm briefly before releasing the muscle altogether.

And just like that, Lex's slate is wiped completely clean. One goddamn smile and all's fucking forgiven.

"Once I'm on a mission, I put blinders on to everything else around me."

We stare at each other as I try to decide if her words have a double meaning.

"It's okay."

That grin disappears without a trace, like it was never there to begin with, then Lex spins on her heel, leaving me to watch her long curls sway side to side down her black dress cinched at the waist with an oversized belt.

Was it there?

Later, at my cubicle, I reach into my pocket for the business card Kaisin gave me, and a black square sticky note comes with it. Written in white marker is an address I've never been to before. One quick search on my phone tells me exactly what it is though—a high-end boutique.

Lex did it. She got me in.

But how did the note—

The hallway collision, the arm squeeze, the grin I couldn't take my eyes off of. She was distracting me, and probably anyone watching, as she slipped the note into my pocket. She did a reverse-pickpocket... subtly.

Damn. Lex can deny it all she wants, but she's still got a hell of a lot of fox in her.

Eleven

Lex

THE ELEVATOR DOORS SLIDE APART, THE CLOYING SCENT OF disinfectant threatening to knock me back ten years.

The police officer assigned to Kordin's room stands at the sound of my heels clicking against the vinyl flooring, his crossword puzzle dropping behind him to his chair in his haste.

"Mrs. Debrosse."

Already wearing the concerned expression I practiced on the drive over here, I press my free hand to my chest, openly staring down at the four empty cups lined with dried tan splotches of what I discovered yesterday is French vanilla coffee that he gets from the cafeteria downstairs.

"Officer Tyler, please tell me you were able to go home for a decent night's sleep?"

"No, ma'am. I mean, yes, ma'am," he stammers.

"Well, which is it?"

"There's another officer for the night shift, so I did get to go home."

"Thank heavens." I drop my hand, tucking this new bit of info away. I knew there had to be at least one other guard, but I didn't have solid confirmation it was just the two providing Kordin with round-the-clock security. Any time I've visited, only Officer Tyler's been here.

"It's just…you asked if I got a decent night's sleep, but I didn't."

"Oh." I give him an appraising look that colors his cheeks. Even though there aren't any rings on his fingers, I lower my voice to ask breathily, "Did the wife keep you up?"

Reece doesn't wear a ring either and he's engaged, about to be married. To a "twelve." At least that's the rumor swirling around the firm.

Reece could have a family as well. Or just starting one. That'd explain why he's in a rush to get wedding attire, if he had to move the date up suddenly.

My own cheeks heat.

The cop misreads the blush and smiles, revealing a chipped front tooth.

"No, ma'am. I'm currently unattached."

I hold his gaze too long to be considered common friendliness. I've been doing this—working men—for so long, it's almost involuntary at this point. I wasn't exaggerating when I told Reece they make it easy. They really, *really* do. More times than not, in their constant and desperate quests to find a hole to penetrate, they set themselves up for retaliatory invasion.

So while I do still regularly fuck men, I just leave out the pleasure now. *Theirs.*

Dropping my eyes, I immediately feign surprise at what I find in my hand. "I almost forgot. I got you this. I figured you deserved something a little tastier than…" I glance around us conspiratorially. "…hospital coffee."

He chuckles as he accepts the to-go cup from me. "That's very thoughtful."

I shrug shyly, telling him, "I like to show my appreciation through gifts." The officer stationed at my house every night also receives tokens of gratitude, only a different kind.

"Thank you, but you really don't have to go out of your way." Using his other hand, he hooks his thumb in his vest and puffs up his chest. "This is all standard protocol when a crime of this nature has been committed."

Is that what Chief Hull is calling this? Standard protocol? Since when?

"It was nothing," I assure him.

"Is that my wife? Lenox?" Kordin shouts from the other side of the curtain blocking the majority of his room from view. "Send her in here," he orders Officer Tyler…who apparently has authority over me now.

I lift my eyebrows, saying, "Excuse me," before he can actually try telling me what to do.

Pushing past the heavy curtain, the rings on the overhead bar pinging together noisily, I pull it closed behind me as I step inside Kordin's private room. With three fractured ribs, one punctured lung, a broken arm and leg, he's bruised, swollen, and heavily bandaged. Both his right arm and leg are in casts, and he has an IV in the crook of his left elbow. He's been in here for almost a full week, and I'm hoping he still has at least another.

This morning his doctor called me to say he thought Kordin could be discharged sooner than expected, so he can finish recovering at home. I had to go full hollow on him, voicing my concerns regarding the second-rate care my husband's so obviously receiving. Luckily, he backtracked fairly quickly, promising not to make any decisions without our input.

"There she is, the love of my life."

Settling back into my full-time role of Kordin Debrosse's wife, I side-eye the curtain as if I'm flustered by his compliment.

"Hello to you, too."

"Would it kill you to smile, dear?"

I don't answer and I certainly don't smile.

Denim-colored eyes study me long and hard. "Humor me. Try it. I want to see if it will."

Honestly, once upon a time, it felt like I would die from smiling on command. Every man I've lived with has demanded the act from me, none of them bothering to actually earn a real one.

Not that I remember what that feels like.

"Do it." My husband's voice crosses that thin, nearly invisible line between casual and stern. "Smile."

I force my lips to stretch, making Kordin's curl.

"You know? I think you look better with a stick up your ass."

I smooth out my features and approach his bedside. "How are you feeling today? You seem more energetic."

"I feel like I could use a nurse."

"You've got several just down the hall."

"They don't care for me the way you could."

"I'm here now, so what can I help you with?" I motion to the untouched tray of food on the table hovering above his lap. "Are you hungry?"

"I'm too nauseous to eat anything. I can't even drink."

His left hand strikes the table, sending it out of my reach.

"It's normal to feel nauseous after everything you've been through," I try to soothe, some of those past memories resurfacing. "The pain medication alone can suppress your appetite. When's the last time you had a dose?"

He shakes his head. "I can't remember. They knock me out, then make me groggy when I wake up. The best pain medicine is my wife. You should stay the night with me."

"Overnights aren't allowed. You know that." He's only asked a dozen times.

"They'll make an exception for me. Then tomorrow—"

"Tomorrow I have work."

"You can miss a day."

"I've already missed two."

"I don't like us being apart."

Every time he says something like this, all I can think about is what Reece told me. How did Reece fucking me even come up? Was it Reece's suggestion? Or Kordin's?

I don't trust either of them.

"If that's true, what were you doing out of bed?" I ask, unable to hold back any longer. We haven't had the time or privacy to have this conversation, and I was waiting until he was feeling better, but since he seems to be just *full* of piss and vinegar today, I guess now's as good a time as any.

Besides, it'd look worse if I didn't bring it up at all. Lenox Debrosse is meek but not that meek.

"Are you talking about when I was stressed and needed to decompress?"

"That's what you call decompressing?"

"Lenox, honey." He smacks his lips. "That was nothing. What you saw, it wasn't what it looked like. Those porn sites are designed to look realistic."

I hold his stare. He doesn't deserve forgiveness, especially not after such a weak defense. I'm not an idiot. I know exactly what I saw and it wasn't a porn site.

But this is a mere battle, one he can have, because I'm focused on winning the war.

"Why didn't you come to me? I could've helped you."

"You can help me right now." The sheet over his crotch begins rising.

"Kordin... They just removed your chest tube yesterday."

"I've been stuck in here for a week. I have needs."

I take in my battered husband in his hospital bed.

Considering it's been over a month since he even pretended to care about my needs—longer since he met them—I really don't have any sympathy to spare him for his recent orgasm drought.

Boo.

Fucking.

Hoo.

"There's a guard right outside," I say like that'd ever actually stop me. I've fucked in front of an audience before and didn't feel embarrassed. That was for money though.

Even if it wasn't for money, I still don't think I'd be ashamed. Not if I was fucking someone I wanted to fuck. What Reece and I did in my office yesterday was fairly public and I didn't feel an ounce of shame.

Maybe Reece feels ashamed. He is engaged after all. To a possibly pregnant "twelve."

"He's paid to protect me, not cock-block me," Kordin says while pulling the thin sheet down his beat-up body, revealing the tented gown beneath.

The bed's remote slides off the blanket, so I lean over Kordin, diverting his attention as I catch it out of view.

Kordin flinches, but the distinct scent of dirty scalp overwhelms me, forcing me to pull back as well. Even with a few inches of space, I switch to breathing through my mouth. I'm not sure when my husband's last sponge bath was, but if this is how bad his head smells, I can't imagine the odor coming from his balls.

I don't even want to try.

"Help me with this thing," he grits, tugging at his gown.

Lifting the thin, patterned material up high enough to unveil Kordin's stiff dick with one hand, I use the other to push the *pain* button on the remote enough times to make my thumb ache. One of the nurses went over all its functions with me, and unfortunately, no matter how many times I press that particular button, the IV machine will only dispense one dose of medication at predetermined intervals. She also cautioned that it isn't always responsive immediately, and since I need Kordin to get his meds *now*, I hit it a couple more times.

Kordin lifts his uninjured hand, closing it around the hair by my ear, and the thought of him about to bring me in for a kiss rouses a small butterfly in my stomach.

"I miss you. I'm counting down the minutes until I'm back home with you. Do you miss me?"

"Of course I do," I lie.

I go in for a kiss, but he turns his face away, saying, "Show me how much. Show me how much you miss me."

I lick from palm up to my middle fingertip, then wrap my hand around the base of his cock, grasping as I pull upward.

"For fuck's sake, Lenox," Kordin half-groans as I stroke.

Having Kordin's cock in my hold again, I'm realizing how thin and short it actually is. Compared to Reece's, it's quite inadequate-looking.

Sadly, it's just as disappointing in every other way.

His fist full of my hair tightens before pushing, causing my head to swivel on my neck until I'm facing the other direction. He wasn't holding me to him, he was preparing to turn me away from him...so he doesn't have to look at me.

Back when Kordin still thought I'd make a good breeder, he used to love to watch me work his cock. Now, he avoids my face during any sexual interaction whatsoever.

I squeeze my eyes shut, keeping the building moisture safely behind my eyelids, then send a shot of unfiltered hatred down toward that lone butterfly, vaporizing it with seething acid.

Thankfully, it doesn't take long for Kordin to grunt his release, the top of my fist warm from his cum. I wipe it up using napkins. As I'm throwing them away, I hear a series of squeaks in the hallway, and I tilt my head, training my ear toward the door.

Hasty footsteps lead away from Kordin's room. *Finally*. The laxative I put in that pig's coffee must've kicked in. I added just enough to loosen things up for the man, without making him shit out all of his organs. I need him away from his post for a little while, not be chained to the toilet for the next several hours. That'd be too obvious.

"What news do you have for me today, my love?"

"The only thing you should be worried about is resting," I tell him with a gentle tone before adding, "But if it bothers you that much being out of the loop, I could always bring you your laptop."

"That's what you're for."

"Bringing you your laptop?"

There's the tiniest of flutters in my stomach's lining as I wait for Kordin to tell me if there's a way to bypass the fingerprint authentication on his safe.

"Keeping me in the loop," he says, grinding my stomach's butterfly resurrection to a screeching halt.

After I give Kordin a brief rundown of my workday—the parts I want him to know—he yawns and asks, "How's the newest addition coming along?"

"Reece Souza?" I debated on whether or not I should tell Kordin about Reece but ultimately decided it'd be better if he hears about our new hire from me rather than someone else later on, leading him to question why I didn't say anything. "He's getting married this weekend."

"This weekend?"

Watching his mouth open on another yawn, I nod. Why else would Reece need an expensive suit and dress on such short notice?

I didn't want to help Cyrus's pet at first. Since he asked for the favor immediately after giving me a thoughtful gift—*Is it really thoughtful if it was only given in hopes of gaining something in return?*—I wasn't going to at all. But after thinking about it, I saw an advantage to fulfilling his request—indebting him to me. I'm well aware Cyrus holds his leash, but a second set of ears around the firm could be beneficial. Those men don't share things with me like they would with Reece. I'm not one of them, and I never will be. Not only am I a woman, but I'm the CEO's wife. In their eyes, I'm also still the unqualified portfolio manager. I've worked my ass off the last eight years to become not only qualified, but overqualified, for my position at that company, but it hasn't made a difference. When I walk into rooms there, it doesn't go unnoticed. That little bit of gossip I picked up today about Reece's fiancée was a fluke. If those two assistants had spotted me walking behind them, I don't know if they would've spoken as freely.

And truthfully, it's good Reece is getting married. While Kordin's staff doesn't appreciate my presence—apart from their lascivious looks in my direction—they might Reece's in my office every morning. In all the time I've worked at the Debrosse Group, I've never had anyone report to me, so if the fox is going to continue the charade—I know he lied about Scott because Scott isn't even in our department—then our daily meetings will be noted by others, if they haven't been already. The meetings themselves need to appear as professional as possible and both of us having spouses helps reinforce that image.

If he happens to be a family man, too, that's...even better.

"Make sure you get him something expensive," Kordin says, his words drawn out. "Something that'll make a splash. I have a reputation to uphold."

Kordin gives notoriously generous gifts. They're generous in that they cost a lot of money. He doesn't actually put any thought into what the recipient might want, only how good the gift will make him look.

For Reece, I think I might be able to accomplish both.

"I have the perfect gift in mind."

"Put both our names on it," Kordin reminds me just before his eyes close.

"Of course." I wait thirty seconds to ask, "Anything else?"

His jaw goes slack and his head rolls to one side.

"Kordin? Anything else?"

A quiet snore is my only answer.

I'm balancing on the platforms of my stilettos to dart over to close the door. Officer Tyler's current whereabouts may be accounted for but the nurses' aren't.

Back by Kordin's bed, I retrieve the clear tape from my purse, and use it to tape his eyelids open, then hold his phone up to his face. The facial recognition works, letting me right in. I go straight to the internet browser and search his history. An online bank appears multiple times, so I click on the link, absolutely praying that Kordin is dumb enough to auto-save his passwords. Somewhere on his desktop, Kordin has a folder with all his passwords, so maybe…

No. No luck. The website login pops up empty and doesn't offer any suggestions when I start typing his email.

I take a picture of the web address with my own phone before clearing the browser and tab. Next, I skim his messages, instantly finding the woman from the video chat Reece crashed. I thumb through all photos sent between the two, but don't find anything useful. It's mostly just tits. So many tits. Kordin is a self-proclaimed tits-man.

I don't know what he saw in me because I have none.

The thread below hers though, that's where I find something.

While it became obvious after my diagnosis that Kordin was cheating on me, I'd never seen any of his mistresses in person…until last month when a speeding ticket came in the mail from a traffic camera, this one in a school zone. My name and address were on the envelope, but when I opened it, the vehicle pictured wasn't my Range Rover. It wasn't even Kordin's Porsche. It was a Mustang Mach-E, a car I'd never even seen before, let alone driven or purchased. And yet, it was registered to me, so I had to have bought it.

Unless someone else did.

In addition to having the make, model, color, and license plate number, I also had the exact time and location the photo was taken. Every day at eight thirty in the morning, I waited at the same spot. Two days later I caught sight of the Mustang SUV and followed it to see just who the fuck had stolen my identity. The driver was a woman, a well-endowed woman with a son. A son she dropped off at school before speeding back home to meet with none other than Kordin Debrosse.

The person who stole my identity…was my husband, and he used it to make a large purchase, possibly more than one purchase, for another woman, possibly more than one woman.

In the traffic cam images, the license plate frame was an after-market one Kordin's girlfriend clearly bought. But in one of these sexts she sent Kordin of her naked on the hood, underneath her visibly unmaintained asshole, is the original frame with the name of an online car company.

So he used an online car company. The bank we use for our joint account is local and I'd know if he was making payments on another vehicle, or bought one outright, which means he's definitely got a separate account through the online bank.

I take a picture of the spread-eagle photo, too.

If I had his laptop, or even just the hard drive, I could access that account and possibly whatever else Kordin might be up to.

I hear someone ask Officer Tyler if he's feeling all right, telling me he's finished exhuming his digestive tract already, so I hurry to return Kordin's phone. Before I can remove the tape though, the door behind me opens. Without thought, I touch my lips to Kordin's as I let out a throaty moan.

"Oh geez. I'm so sorry. I just…" Officer Tyler stammers, chuckles, then shuts the door.

I open my eyes to study my husband's. For the briefest of moments, I pretend they're not being held open, and pursing my lips, I kiss his lifeless mouth. Is this really too unbearable? Kissing me? Looking at me?

I'm looked at all the fucking time, but as an object, a hole, a means to an end, not as a person, not as myself. Never myself.

But whoever I am, I'm not this.

Revulsion rolls through me like a tidal wave—revulsion with Kordin, but mainly with myself for stooping to this level—and I break it off, my forehead dropping to his chin as a single tear drips onto his neckline.

I should be relieved he doesn't kiss me anymore. Even willing and conscious, Kordin's kisses were lackluster.

I peel the tape off Kordin's eyelids, turn, and leave.

While my juicer works on extracting juice from the produce I just dropped in it, I flip over the book Reece gave me and read the back. With the embracing couple on the cover, it's definitely a romance, but the word sweet in its description jumps out at me like an ax murderer in a thriller. The only thing in my life I like sweet is revenge. This book probably has less sex in it than my own life does. *I should've left it in the trash.*

My dinner of cold-pressed juice in hand, I pad over to the living room. On the coffee table, that king flower I also made the mistake of bringing home gives a much-needed pop of color to the room, breaking up the minimalist style Kordin prefers. It's so big and so ugly. I don't know what Reece was thinking buying it for me … Other than what he said.

A shapeshifter…

Instead of grabbing my laptop next to me and getting a head start on tomorrow's workload, I bring my phone up to confirm if the story

Reece gave me is true, not only about the flower but also the Greek god it's supposedly named after.

An hour and a half later, the legend of Hera's birth comes up in one of the many rabbit holes I have no choice but to follow at this point in my investigation, giving me an even better idea than the one I had earlier at the hospital. Tomorrow, Reece is getting a *very* personal wedding gift.

Twelve

Reece

"**A**RE YOU READY?" CHARLIE ASKS FROM BEHIND THE dressing room's curtain.

Next to me, Breckyn claps her hands, saying, "Yes," just as enthusiastically as the first time we did this whole routine. And because people who shop regularly in this price point apparently can't dress themselves, the saleslady comes out first, followed closely by my sister, wearing a shimmery gold dress with cutouts on the sides.

"Damn," I breathe. Charlie doesn't look like the same little girl that made me sleep on her and Breck's floor every Halloween growing up because she was scared of costumes. She looks like a woman. A beautiful woman.

Standing from her spot on the sofa, Breckyn praises, "A vision."

My mom comes in from the sales floor, arms loaded with other dresses. "I found some—" Her eyes widen at Charlie before clouding over with tears. "It's perfect."

"*She's* perfect," Breckyn stresses while circling her twin. "The dress doesn't make the woman; the woman makes the dress."

"Or suit," I add, causing both sisters to grin my way.

"So this is the one?" Charlie asks with a hint of hesitation in her voice.

"Yes," I say with none in mine.

"You didn't even look at the price tag yet."

"I don't need to. Whatever it costs, it's worth seeing the look on your face while you're in it."

"How do I look?" She spins to face the mirrors, inspecting her appearance from each angle.

"Happy."

Our eyes meet in the reflection before hers shoot to our mom's.

"You look very happy, Charlie," she says in agreement.

Blushing, Charlie turns for the dressing room, mumbling, "Breck's turn."

"You're sure you don't want to at least try on a dress?" my mom asks Breckyn, arms still full.

Breckyn sends me an unsure look, so I give her a headshake and take over.

"Ma, she wants a pinstripe suit. She's getting a fucking pinstripe suit."

"Okay, okay. I just thought I'd check before I put all these back."

"Allow me." Another saleslady appears suddenly and takes the pile from my mom.

Lex not only gave me the address for her high-end clothing store connection, she must've called ahead and told them to shut the entire store down for me...and my fake fiancée, because that's exactly what they did.

I eye the impeccably dressed saleswoman, wondering what all Lex can get her to do. Report back on everything that's happening here tonight? If so, Lex is gonna know I lied to her about who the outfits are for. She'll know I lied, but not why I lied—to make her jealous. To see *if* I could make her jealous. If Lex wasn't jealous, why'd she throw away my gifts? But if she was jealous, why'd she give me the store's address?

I don't understand her. No one seems to. Which is exactly Lex's goal I'm fucking sure.

So maybe she was jealous and that's why she gave me the address, to throw me off. Too bad it's not gonna work. I'm no hollow. I don't just seek. I find.

Which reminds me...

"Ma? You got it?"

My mom sighs. "Of course I do. I left it in the car to keep it cold, so be sure to grab it when we're done." She takes Breckyn's vacated seat beside me and pins me with a serious expression. "I wish you'd tell me who she is."

"Who?" I play dumb.

"Whoever the flowers are for."

I push out my bottom lip.

"Fine." She laughs, throwing her hands up. "At least tell me something about your life. You keep too much to yourself."

We sit in a long silence, neither of us wanting to expand on that.

Finally, I tell her, "I got a new job."

"That's all I get?"

"What else do you want to know?"

"How are you liking it so far? Is your boss nice?"

I can't help but chuckle. No, Lex isn't nice. She's a nightmare and an unapologetic one at that. But in case the women working here know who my boss is, all I say is, "It's a job."

"Doing what?" Breckyn questions.

"Why?" I ask right back.

"No reason," she's just as quick to say.

"She hasn't found anyone to shadow," Charlie calls out.

Since Breckyn's ignoring me now, I look to my mom for an explanation.

She shrugs, and says, "Career week. You remember?"

I do. I also remember spending the day I was supposed to shadow someone in a career I was interested in at my girlfriend's apartment instead. She was a year ahead of me and had her own place, so it came down to following some asshole around all day who I'd never turn into or fuck around with my girl. I'm not saying I made the right decision, but I did pick up some lifelong skills that've served me well up to this point. Before that, I'd been eating pussy all wrong because I was always sneaking around with girls, needing to be quick and quiet. With no parents around to catch us though, that girl was vocal...about everything.

"What kind of career are you considering this year?" I ask my sister.

Each year, local high schools require their students to pick a different workforce pathway to research, that way they're exposed to several options by the time they graduate and are more likely to know what they want to do for the rest of their lives. While freshmen, sophomores, and juniors just do reports, seniors actually have to go out into the world and shadow someone, hopefully after weeding out the careers they decided weren't for them based on the previous years' reports. The whole exercise is helpful but I still think seventeen and eighteen is too young to decide something so important. At any time, anything could happen and change the entire course of your life. No amount of research can prevent it or prepare you for it.

"Real estate analyst," Breck says. "But so far nobody's open to letting me shadow them. They're scared to tell me their secrets I guess."

Shit. That's similar to what Lex does. And she's an expert at not giving too much away.

Breckyn flops into a corner chair, huffing, "Shadowing is half the grade."

"For the project or overall?"

Coming out from behind the curtain, Charlie answers me, saying, "For the project, but she's acting like it's for her overall grade."

"It might as well be. I've never gotten anything lower than an A. This could ruin my perfect GPA."

"When's career week?"

"Why?" she asks the same way I did.

"Because I might know someone." Whether she agrees to or not is its own challenge.

Breckyn sits forward, her hands entwined in front of her like she's praying. "It's next month but I can complete the shadowing before then, if needed. Tomorrow even. Whatever fits his schedule."

"I'll see what I can do," I say, leaving out that Lex is a woman.

Next thing I know, Breckyn launches herself onto my lap, and throws her arms around my neck, squeezing so hard I let out another chuckle.

"You're the best brother in the whole world."

"I don't know about that." I jerk my chin at the saleslady watching us with a soft smile and even softer eyes. "Now let's find you a pinstripe suit."

Without bothering to knock, I push my way into Lex's office and set the book down on her desk with the flower hidden behind it just like I did yesterday. The only difference today is I picked out a paperback.

Lex studies the flower first this time but doesn't ask me what it is or what it means. She probably doesn't know different flowers have different meanings. Most people don't.

"It's a Globeflower. It stands for gratitude."

Her eyes meet mine. They're blue again, like Starflower Jessie.

"Thank you. For yesterday."

She doesn't respond at all, just returns her attention to her laptop, clicking her mouse more times than necessary.

"The clothing—"

"How's your lead?"

"Kaisin? He's warming up to me."

"Uh-huh. Why don't you tell me what you have planned for today, so I can get on with my own work. I'm busy, and as usual, you're wasting my time."

I do the same thing as before, making up bullshit tasks I will not be completing. Lex keeps stealing glances at the book until finally, I stop to ask, "What?"

"What is she supposed to be?" she asks, staring at the red-skinned woman with horns and wings.

Not staring. Glaring.

"A succubus."

She levels me with a look just as scrutinizing.

"It's a female demon that fucks sleeping men."

"I know what a succubus is. I'm wondering why one's on my desk."

"I thought it looked…entertaining."

"Entertaining…" Leaning back, Lex props her high heels on her desk, the pointy tips less than an inch from the book's spine. "A bit ironic, isn't it?"

"Why? Is that something you do?"

"Is it something *you* do?" she bites back. "You're the one that came into my room while I was unconscious and—"

"I already told you I didn't touch you while you were sleeping."

"How do I know you're telling the truth?"

I sit forward and tell her, "Because if I touched you, no other man would be allowed to. Not Kaisin, not Phil, not even Kordin fucking Debrosse."

After a stare-off neither of us rushes to break, she lifts a hand nonchalantly and says, "Judging by what happened yesterday, it must be true. You didn't touch me."

"What happened yesterday?" Did someone try something with her? I'm leaving after her from now on.

"I visited my husband, and without the tube in his lung anymore, he was more…himself."

I almost fucking laugh. A tube in his chest. I hope I popped his lung enough to cause long-term damage. I hope I—

"Which led to… Well, I'm sure you can put the pieces together yourself," Lex says, ending my amusement.

"What? Did he fuck you from the back like he always does?" I should've broken both his legs and arms, then he wouldn't have been able to do anything.

If my arms and legs were out of use, I'd have Lex saddle up and ride my cock. Or sit on my face and ride my tongue.

No, not or. *And*. I'd have her sit on my face *and* then my cock. I'd let her do it all.

Shit, I'd let her do it all *with* full use of my limbs.

"How do you know about that?"

"Kordin bragged about his favorite position with you."

Her cheeks get a bit of color to them, not quite red, more of a pinkish tinge like a Cherry Blossom kiss to her milky-white skin. I want to watch as that blush spreads—everywhere—but not from talking about another man.

Ignoring my heavy inhale and even heavier exhale, she nods at the book and flower. "What would your fiancée think about these, rookie?"

Fully fucking riled now, I counter, "What would your husband think about you finger-fucking yourself for me, Snow?"

Shit. The nickname just came out.

"Snow?"

I scramble to think of something other than the inspiration behind it.

"You're as cold as snow, and twice as fucking beautiful," I admit, then lock up my muscles, fucking pissed at myself for complimenting her. The last thing Lex needs is another compliment. All she probably hears are compliments.

She cracks what I'm pretty damn sure is the first real smile I've seen touch her lips.

I'm fucking hypnotized by it, my voice not even sounding like my own as I rasp out, "You should smile more often."

Lex's smile vanishes, and with a quick kick, she sends both items I bought her over the edge of her desk, the crash of them landing in the trash can breaking my fucking stupor.

"What the fuck was that for? I paid—"

"Please. I've used toilet paper more expensive than that shit."

"That shit? They're called fucking gifts."

"They're evidence. Use your head."

"Evidence of what? We're not fucking."

"Do you think your fiancée would believe that? Do you think a judge would?"

"I just thought you—"

"See, rook, that's where you're mistaken. You don't know me. You don't know *anything* about me, especially not my reading preferences. If I wanted to read about rape, I'd pull out one of my own journals."

On God, if my eyebrows sink any lower, I won't be able to see out from under them.

"Are you just talking about old journals? Or current ones, too?"

"Why do you work for Cyrus?"

The subject change out of left field catches me off guard, and I all but stutter out, "I chose to."

"What does he have on you?"

"Nothing."

"I'm not buying that. You're too sweet to willingly work for someone like Cyrus."

"I'm *sweet?*" Now I do laugh. "What the fuck makes you think I'm sweet?"

She gestures to me, saying, "Your overall sweetness."

"Because I don't condone women being raped?"

"Yet you'll buy a book about a woman doing it to men?"

"I don't fucking know what happens in that book. It said on the back she falls for one man. *Falls* for him."

"Do they fuck in it? Consensually?"

I unclench my jaw to spit, "I. Don't. Know."

"You're sweet," she practically purrs, drawing all of my attention to those lips of hers. Fuck, I want to feel them again.

"Nothing about me is sweet."

A buzzing noise like a phone vibrating cuts through the tense silence causing Lex to return her feet to the floor. Gaze locked on her desk as she shuffles papers around, she doesn't so much as glance my way.

I don't have time to ask why the sudden change when Kaisin approaches her door.

She knew he, or someone, was coming. How? With her door closed, there's no way she could smell anyone.

Right as the CFO pokes his head in, I speak up again, starting midsentence so it sounds like I'm finishing up. "Should have those finished by the end of the week."

"Sorry to interrupt, but, Reece? You got a delivery."

I shake my head. That doesn't make any sense. "What is it?"

He looks at Lex who's avoiding eye contact with both of us, her lips tugged to one side, not exactly in a smile but in a way that's just as out of character for her. Mischievous maybe? She is mischievous, but she doesn't let it show. Not like now. What the fuck is going on?

"Honestly, I'm not even sure. You're better off seeing it for yourself."

I'm out of the chair, charging out of Lex's office, already imagining all the different scenarios I'm about to walk into. I didn't leave anything incriminating out. Did Lex?

I smell it before I see it, the unmistakable scent of Sage, and lengthen my strides. The closer I get, the louder voices grow, each of them talking about "him" and "how generous he is." My first thought is Cyrus, except nobody'd ever mistake him for generous. But he's the only person who knows I work here.

I round the corner before coming to a complete stop. Taking in the potted tree in front of my cubicle, I notice hundred dollar bills tied to most of the branches, and among the cash, a lone card. A dozen or more sets of eyes on me, I go over and open it. In looping, delicate script is a generic message wishing me and my fiancée a long marriage full of love and happiness. At the bottom are two printed first names followed by one last name: Kordin and Lenox Debrosse.

"Mr. Souza?"

I spin around at Lex's voice. Was this her idea? Or Kordin's?

"My husband regrets not being here himself, but I hope you'll accept this gift on behalf of us both. Congratulations to you and your bride on your wedding this weekend."

Wedding? She thought that's what the dressy outfits were for?

My gaze bores into hers, but she gives nothing away.

I feel a slap on my back and blink long and hard so I don't break Kaisin's jaw right fucking now. I hate him touching Lex but I'm not a fan of him touching me either.

"Congrats, dude," Kaisin says. "When you said your wedding was soon, I didn't know you meant this soon."

"Kordin's the fucking man," someone says.

"He gives the best gifts," someone else agrees.

Lex crosses her arms but not before I catch her balling her fists.

There's my answer. She bought the tree. But does she know what it is? What it actually is?

"Yeah," Kaisin says, eyeing the tree. "My brother usually does give good gifts, but a shrub… That's a first. What kind is this?"

"It's called a—"

"Pepper Bush," I rush to cut off Lex, citing only one of the names used for the Chaste Tree. Just from the name alone, she has to know. Unless the place she bought it from called it something else.

"It smells like pepper." Kaisin bends down to inspect the cone-shaped flowering spikes. "I guess it could pass as Lavender. Lenox, why'd Kordin pick this one? At least Lavender smells good."

"It has medicinal uses," I tell him while staring at Lex. Other than her eyebrows sinking, nothing else on her moves.

"Really?"

"Yeah, it helps women with hormonal imbalances."

Lex's eyes shoot to mine. "It does?"

I nod slowly, not blinking. Maybe she didn't look up this plant before buying it, she just saw the name and thought it'd be funny.

I might believe that if she hadn't told me she doesn't joke.

"So…pregnancy?"

Because I'm watching Lex like a hawk, I see her wince at Kaisin's question, her shoulders caving in as if someone punched her in the gut.

"Like pregnancy?" Kaisin repeats when I don't answer, and I finally tear my eyes off his sister-in-law to look at him, shaking my head.

"No, not like pregnancy." Does he understand women's hormones change constantly and not just when they're pregnant? Menstrual cycles are pretty much the main topic of conversation anytime I'm within earshot of my sisters. They've both been dealing with PMS symptoms since they were nine years old, well before either of them needed any of the pads or tampons my mom kept our shared bathroom stocked with. I used to think just hearing about it was fucking gross, then I got my first girlfriend and realized periods, hormones, all that shit, are a regular part of females' lives, and since I like females, it's a regular part of mine, too. Now it's like discussing the weather to me. Nothing about that stuff fazes me anymore.

Elbowing me in the side, Kaisin mock-whispers, "It's not a shotgun wedding, is it?" Which earns him a round of laughs from our small audience.

My eyes slingshot back to Lex. I should say yes just to see what she does. I should, but I don't want to. Just like I didn't want her hearing

I was getting married to begin with. I don't want her to think I'd actually do the things I've done with her if I had a fiancée. I'm not like Kordin. I've never cheated and I never would.

Her focus on the floor, Lex says, "You don't have to answer such a personal question, Mr. Souza."

"It's not a shotgun wedding," I say loud enough for everybody to hear.

After an awkward silence, several other people offer me their own well-wishes before fucking off back to their work. Without another word, Lex turns for her office.

I contemplate going after her—our interrupted conversation is far from over—but Kaisin reminds me he's still next to me by saying, "Too bad you didn't get a bachelor party."

"Too bad," I echo because I don't know what else to say. As little thought as I've put into an actual wedding, I've put even less into a bachelor party. I've seen enough take place at The Playground to know what happens at them, and if I'm getting married, the last thing I'd want to see is another woman naked.

"Kaisin?" Not breaking stride as she floats down the hall, Lex just tilts her head slightly over her shoulder to address her husband's brother.

"Me?"

"Can I speak to you in my office?"

"Um, yeah. Sure." Kaisin all but sprints after Lex, his excitement of being alone with her fucking palpable.

Long after he disappears, I force myself to turn away and inspect the Chaste Tree instead. I don't even want to touch it in case its namesake is true.

"How are you going to get that thing home?" some guy asks, but I just shake my head because I'm wondering the same goddamn thing.

She's funny all right. Real fucking funny.

Thirteen

Reece

I T'S FINALLY FRIDAY, AND I'M SITTING IN THE PARKING LOT, waiting until Lex leaves to peel out, too. I was working out of the office all day today but I left early to make it back here in time to watch her walk out to her Range Rover. Kaisin's been up her ass the last couple days. After calling him into her office on Wednesday, they've been spending a lot of time together. Yesterday morning, I barely handed Lex another flower and book before that motherfucker popped up, asking if he could "steal Lex to go over some things." I almost told him to try it, but didn't. Couldn't.

I could've. I chose not to. Because I'm fucking subtle.

Also, Lex isn't mine to keep. She's…

Anyway, I don't know what those two are up to. I do know I don't like that they're doing it together. I told Lex I'd handle Kaisin.

I also told her yesterday's book had consensual sex in it, but that didn't stop her from throwing it away. I understand what it's like not to trust people but she's not even giving me a chance.

She's the biggest bitch I've ever met. I want to fuck that attitude right out of her.

Or let her use it to fuck me.

What a fucking disaster that'd be. A fun, sexy, sweaty, and probably even bloody disaster.

My cock swells in my pants at the thought.

Lex's Range Rover rounds a different corner than she usually takes.

I consider following her just to see where she's going. Is it to someone else's house? Kaisin's? Every other night I've done this, I've gone straight home after watching her head for hers, but not talking to her all day, or even seeing her, I'm…curious.

Before I can stop myself, I take the same turn and follow her all the way to a grocery store, parking near the back when she pulls in. She's only inside for twenty minutes before reappearing, carrying two brown paper bags. We're back out on the road in no time, heading in the opposite direction of her house and through neighborhoods I've never been in before. They're full of smaller houses packed in tightly, with almost no yards or even driveways, only enough parking on the street for one car per house.

Lex goes through a roundabout, taking the exit on the left, which forces me to slow my own approach. The delay causes me to lose her, those bright-red taillights nowhere in sight as I come out of the roundabout.

Not ready to give up yet, I drive around, checking side streets for her black SUV.

I spend more time than I should doing that until a text comes through simultaneously on my phone and car's stereo, interrupting the music pumping out of my speakers.

Cyrus. I'm being beckoned.

He's gonna want an update. An update I wouldn't give him even if I had one to give. Lex didn't approve of me working undercover at her husband's firm. That was all Cyrus, and knowing him, it's all *for* Cyrus. Why would he want information on Kordin Debrosse now? Lex left the fox life behind years ago.

Unless Cyrus knows something I don't, like Kordin abusing Lex. I can't even picture it, but she did make it seem like she was trying to wrap shit up before Kordin was released from the hospital. She also said she fucked him there. Or let him fuck her, she didn't specify. Did she let him? Or did he force her?

I tighten my hold on the steering wheel, my knuckles threatening to burst through the skin.

Lex isn't mine to keep and she's not mine to save; my sisters are. And if I want to keep Cyrus away from them, I'm gonna have to give him something.

Abandoning my search, I head for The Playground, flying past less and less glass on buildings until there's none to be found, everything shuttered up tight to prevent theft. Where there's glass, there's a way inside. I don't rely on glass to get into places I'm not supposed to be in, but I'm not a junkie looking for something to sell for a quick fix either.

Down in The Playground, I find Cyrus at a back booth, his arms spread out on each side of his head with his numerous rings glinting under the overhead chandelier.

"Sit," is all he says, so I do, taking the spot furthest from him. "Speak."

I grit my teeth at the commands. I'm not a fucking dog.

"The mark is still in the hospital."

"Maybe you can get to the point by telling me something useful," he says while scouring his club, both looking and sounding exactly like Lex when she's being a sarcastic little shit.

How close were they?

"His firm isn't as successful as it's said to be."

Cyrus finally looks at me, his bushy eyebrows lifting. "You don't say."

While out scouting today, I stumbled across a few properties the Debrosse Group already manages. They advertise specializing in high-tech buildings, but the ones I saw were regular ol' mom-and-pop type shops like Silvy's, nothing modern or updated at all. If they're any indication who the Debrosse Group takes on as clients, there's no way Kordin's firm is bringing in high-tech-building-worthy numbers on the scale they're pretending to. I don't know how they get away with peddling the lie, or why they even bother.

"Who's running the place right now?"

"His brother." On paper, Kaisin is in charge. In reality, he's exactly like Lex described, a moron.

Cyrus's sigh makes my chest ache.

"And his wife? I assume you've met her by now."

"Yes," I make myself say. "She's there, too." Although she has no real authority. She should, but for some reason I can't seem to pinpoint she doesn't. It's a weird dynamic there.

"She recognize you?"

I shake my head even though he's not looking at me anymore. "She never saw me to begin with."

"She wouldn't need to see you to recognize you."

Examining his profile, I ask, "Do you know her?" He doesn't say anything, so I add, "Lenox Debrosse?"

Despite being in a dim corner, I can make out his expression as it darkens. He's quiet for so long I don't think he's going to answer, but then he says, "Kordin Debrosse took something from me. Something very, very valuable." He rotates his head to meet my stare. "I'm going to get it back."

Now I'm the one staying silent, a million thoughts racing through my mind. While there's not a doubt he's talking about Lex, there are plenty about handing her over to him.

"I could go to the hospital, make the mark tell me where the laptop—"

"The laptop." He huffs a laugh. "Forget the laptop. That got us in the door. Now that we're inside, we're taking everything."

"Everything?"

"Everything."

He had me believing he was going to kill me over that laptop, and now he's using my mistake for his own gain. No, he's making *me* use my mistake for his own gain.

I'm beginning to question if he was even planning on handing it over to Lex in the first place.

Eyeing his highball glass, I imagine breaking it and using a shard to slice his throat wide open. He'd bleed out, gurgling his pathetic last words, but I wouldn't stick around to hear them. I'd…

I'd…

I don't fucking know. I don't even know *where* I'd want to go or *what* I'd want to do. I just know I don't want this life anymore.

"Tell me about the brother. Is he an easy mark?"

"Cake."

"Good."

"The wife—"

"She can't suspect anything. Stay as far away from her as possible."

"But if—"

"I said stay the fuck away from her."

My phone vibrates in my pocket, but I wait until Cyrus blinks first to take it out, glancing at the screen.

"Here he is right now," I say.

"Who?"

"The brother. He wants to get a drink with me tonight."

"Go, go." He lazily shoos me with one hand while waving someone over with the other.

Another dancer takes my seat, then Cia appears beside me, batting her long eyelashes up at me.

"Hi, Reece."

"Hey." Hearing my name come out of Cia's mouth makes me realize Lex has never called me by my name. She always calls me rook, rookie, or Mr. Souza. I wonder what it'd sound like hearing her say my name. I wonder what it'd sound like hearing her scream it.

"What are you doing standing there? You know what to do," Cyrus says to, I assume, me, so I turn to leave, but then I see Cia shudder. With cheeks the color of an Amaryllis, she bends down and crawls underneath the table. The other dancer scoots in closer to Cyrus, her lips already formed into an O by his ear. His head back, our boss starts moaning, both his hands now under the table.

I leave The Playground vowing that whatever happens, however the fuck this shakes out, neither of my sisters will ever set foot in here.

Fourteen

Reece

I walk into The Pen, the nightclub The Playground wishes it was, already on the lookout for Kaisin since I spotted his two-hundred-and-fifty-grand Aston Martin parked outside. I've only been here a couple times because their drinks are twenty bucks a pop, but thankfully, Kaisin offered to cover our drinks tonight. Even if the Debrosse Group isn't pulling in what they claim, the Debrosse brothers are living like they are. Lex, too. There's no way she doesn't know the scam they're running. She knows better than anyone what kind of properties they're investing in.

She's always performing.

"Rook."

My head whips to the side, finding my white-haired boss staring back at me. She's in a skintight, black strapless dress with a single zipper running the length of the front but with two sliders, one at the top and another at the bottom of her hemline. One quick tug in either direction and she'd be fucking bared to me.

And everybody else here.

I swallow as I throw a glance past her shoulder. "What are you doing here?"

Instead of answering, she drops her gaze down my body, openly checking me out. "Follow me." Spinning around, she pushes through the crowd.

I rush after her, quickly getting in step with her to clear the path.

Over the loud music, I hear her say something about sweet and look down to find her side-eyeing me with that same mischievous look she was wearing right before she surprised me with the Chaste Tree.

A random guy runs into her, pushing her away from me, and I instantly shove him hard enough to make him fall to his hands and knees.

Facing each other over his hunched back, I question, "How's that for sweet?"

Without breaking eye contact, she takes my hand in hers and pulls.

Pulls? Does she want to—

Placing a high-heeled foot on the guy's back, she uses my hand to help pull herself up, standing there momentarily, several inches taller than me. Over the guy's curses, she looks down her nose at me, and asks, "How's that?"

A chuckle sneaks out between my lips. No probably about it, there'd definitely be blood if we fucked.

Before I can say anything, the guy's elbows buckle, causing Lex to drop suddenly. I reach out and catch her body with my free arm, pulling her front against mine until I'm holding all of her weight.

"Is this your way of telling me you want to dance?"

"You can't afford my dancing."

"I'd sell my soul trying."

She breaks eye contact, muttering, "You're giving me a cavity, rookie."

"Would you prefer I dropped you instead?"

"Yes."

I scowl, telling her, "No."

"Next time you get the opportunity, don't hesitate. Drop me."

The opportunity to drop her? She *wants* me to drop her?

She slips from my grasp, then sidesteps me to continue on… somewhere.

I follow close behind her, my entire body still buzzing from the contact with hers. *What the fuck am I doing? What the fuck is she doing? Kaisin's here. Isn't he?*

She says something over her shoulder that I miss, so I quicken my steps to catch up with her as she enters a short hallway.

"I thought I was meeting your brother-in-law."

"You are."

I grip her elbow and pull her to a stop.

"Are you here with him?"

"Yes."

Fuck. I didn't expect her to answer that quickly. Or honestly.

What do I do now? She's here with Kaisin, but in what way?

Does it matter?

It does. It matters. But why?

Because…of her dress. It's low cut and short and I want to drag the zipper down with my fucking teeth, then lick my way back up what's underneath starting at that pussy I haven't been able to stop thinking about.

I give her another once-over, biting my lips together so I can't actually try.

Shaking her head, she scans around us. "Don't do that."

"Don't do what?"

"Eye-fuck me."

"Too late."

Our eyes connect and hold.

People coming and going bump us from both sides, so I cage her in against the wall, putting my body between hers and everyone else's.

She peeks up at me with an arched eyebrow, and I shake my head. *Whatever.* If this makes me sweet, then so be it. I'm mother-fucking sweet.

"What's your real last name?"

"Souza."

She scoffs.

"What causes these?" I ask, grazing one of her wrists with my fingertips. Aside from my first day there, Lex always has them covered up at the firm.

"Pressure."

"From the poles?" When Lex just blinks, I explain, "I've seen similar marks on some of The Playground girls."

"Yeah," she finally says.

"So, what are we doing here?"

"Bonding apparently," she deadpans, making me grin.

"What are we doing here?" I repeat with a jerk of my chin.

"You…" One of her hands touches my abs, pressing, not hard enough to make me move, but enough to let me know she'd like me to. "…lack patience."

I lower myself until our faces are only inches apart.

"How's that for patient?"

Despite her lips touching, the smallest hint of laughter somehow hits my ears.

"Do that again."

That mouth dips into a frown before Lex says, "If he asks, you didn't see me."

"Who?"

I follow her gaze to find Kaisin coming out of the men's room.

"Where—"

Pushing off the wall, I scan up and down the hall. She's gone. Completely gone. Out from under me and into thin fucking air.

"You made it," Kaisin says with a clap on my back that makes my skin prickle. He's got a ring of white dust on his right nostril and his pupils are dilated to shit. "I wasn't sure your fiancée was gonna let you out."

I give him a cruel smirk. *Still not a fucking dog.*

We go to the bar where Kaisin gets us a round, then he leads me to another hallway guarded by a stocky bouncer. Kaisin only nods at him as we pass a sign for VIP.

A long time ago, this place used to be a maximum-security prison, but the conditions were so bad, it got condemned. Someone snatched up the building several years back for a fucking steal and gutted the inside, giving it a remodel before eventually turning it into a lucrative dance club. They kept the jail theme going throughout, right down to the name—The Pen, short for penitentiary.

The long hall we walk down is made up of frosted glass walls with floor-to-ceiling bars and colored lights streaming up from the floor to highlight them. Different body parts press up against the glass from the other side as we pass. By the time we reach the end of it, I'm on the verge of becoming hard as a fucking rock...until we walk in on a group of people I wasn't expecting to see again until Monday.

"Surprise!" they all cheer in unison.

Kaisin grips my shoulder, yelling, "It's your bachelor party!"

"You did this?"

"Yeah. I mean, Lenox came up with the idea, and she called in a favor to get the whole VIP section. She also ordered the..."

I tune him out, zeroing in on *her*. She's off to the side, her hands clasped together, her eyes are all mine.

A server steps between us, severing the connection, and when they move aside, she's not looking at me anymore.

"...then, you know, maybe after this her productivity will pick back up."

"Who? Lenox? I've seen her there every day this week, grinding." I quickly add, "Except today while I was off-site. Did she skip work or something?"

Kaisin throws back the rest of his vodka tonic and shrugs. "Numbers don't lie."

What numbers is he talking about?

"This is really nice." I gesture around the private room. "Let me buy you a drink."

He waves me off, telling me, "They're taken care of."

I give him a questioning look while also drawing him over to the bar.

"Lenox is covering the whole thing," he explains. "Probably my brother's doing."

Just like this bachelor party was Kaisin's.

Fucking Debrosse brothers.

I order us both doubles, but when I go to tip the bartender, my wallet's not in the pocket it's usually in. Or any of my other pockets. Or the floor around me.

I know I had it when I entered the club because I had to show my ID.

Someone must've swiped it between then and now. Who the fuck—

Lex catches my eye, the image of perfected innocence.

She pickpocketed me. Again. Except this time, it wasn't a reversal. She straight jacked me. The worst part is I can't even pinpoint when she did it. I was so distracted by her, she could've done it on the dance floor when her body was molded to mine. Or outside the bathrooms. The lightest touch from her had me numb to everything else.

I start across the room, stopping almost immediately when two leasing consultants cut me off, wanting to introduce themselves. As soon as their names leave their mouths, they ask if I'm happy with my current living situation. Neither one waits for me to answer before telling me about some housing options I might like better.

"Tonight's not about work, boys," Lex tsks as she joins us what feels like three hours later, carrying a tray of shots that she damn near knocks into my chest.

"Oh, uh, sorry. Lenox, right?" one asks, earning himself a glare from the other.

And me.

How doesn't he know who she is?

"In the flesh. It's nice to finally meet."

Both men duck their heads, their cheeks practically steaming they're so red.

Lifting the tray higher into our faces, she offers, "Shots?"

They each take the ones on the sides before excusing themselves.

Once we're alone, I grab the glass closest to me and ask, "Where's my wallet, Snow?"

"Safe."

"It was safe in my pocket."

She takes the last shot, dropping the tray by her side.

"It's safer in mine."

"You don't have any pockets."

"Sly fox."

"Didn't you call me a dumb fox before?"

Instead of answering, she clinks my glass with hers.

We knock back our shots at the same time, the alcohol's burn tearing up my throat the entire way down, but Lex doesn't so much as flinch.

I'd really like to know where she's keeping my wallet but doubt she'll tell me.

"When do I get my wallet back?"

"When it's over."

"When what—"

"Reece Souza!" a woman in a sexy prison guard uniform shouts.

All the people closest to me spread out, including Lex, leaving me standing in the middle of the room by myself.

"Right there!" Kaisin yells with a finger jabbed in my direction. "He's right there!"

The "guard" comes right up to me, then cocks her head. In her hold is a black, hopefully plastic, baton. Her voice is all seduction as she breathes, "Are you Reece Souza?"

"Yeah."

"Come with me."

I look her over, head to toe and back. Like every other employee here, she's hot. Short, dark hair styled to look like she just got fucked, a pretty face covered with expertly applied makeup, cleavage on display and pressed together thanks to a few strategically undone buttons, and ass cheeks hanging out the bottom of her short uniform.

"Where?"

"To the yard."

She takes my hand and leads me out the same door Kaisin and I came through earlier.

Cheers fill the room before spilling out into the hall as everybody rushes to follow us.

We snake around the main dance floor, right up to, then on the stage. There's a chain-link fence backdrop, and scattered around the floor are various items that could be used for working out like cinder blocks and overturned milk crates, as well as a pull-up bar, picnic table, and basketball hoop.

"Hands in front of you."

I put my hands out, wrists up, and she secures a pair of handcuffs around them.

Another woman comes up behind me, dipping her hands into my back pockets.

"What the…"

My elbows capture hers against my ribs when she tries moving for the front ones.

"You're going to be moving around a lot," the first woman tells me. "Do you have anything in your pockets you don't want to get broken?"

I nod and release the woman's arms. "My phone. Left pocket."

"It's empty," she says after searching for herself.

What? It was in there.

Lex.

My right pocket gets checked, too.

The woman in front of me wrinkles her nose.

"Don't you have a wallet?"

They were looking for my phone, but she's asking about my wallet.

"Left it at home," I lie.

"You came to a club without any cash on you?"

Now it's about the cash in the wallet.

Lex knew what these women were about.

I shrug my shoulders. "I'm on a budget."

With a lip curl, she shoves me down onto a chair I didn't notice set up behind me.

I curse as I work not to fall backward.

"That watch don't look cheap."

"No, but it's staying with me."

She doesn't return my smug-ass smile, only turns to hype up the club. I take the time to look out at the hundreds of faces focused on the stage. All my new coworkers are front and center, Kaisin right in the middle of the chaos, his gaze locked solely on the MC, Warden Missy. I don't see Lex, but wherever she is, I know she's watching.

She better be fucking watching. This was her doing.

The heat from the spotlight makes me warm and itchy as I test the restraints on my wrists. It's my first time being handcuffed and they must be legit because they're not fucking budging.

Two more women—a brunette and a redhead—join the blonde who dumpster-dove my pockets, all three dressed in white tanks and low-sitting black-and-white-striped drawstring pants, then the three start circling me.

Warden Missy's voice drags my attention away.

"…on the groom's last night of freedom."

All eyes swing my way before the song "Play" by David Banner fills the speakers, making everybody go fucking crazy. Jesus, these lyrics.

I can't even help the grin that sneaks out, but I do stare ahead of me so I can't search for Lex again.

"Let's see what kind of husband he'll make."

I don't know what to make of that statement, and I don't have time to try because hands, lots of hands, begin touching me in all different places—my neck, my shoulders, my thighs—robbing me of my ability to think straight. Someone grabs a handful of my hair and jerks my head back, exposing my throat, while someone else straddles my lap, my fists caught between our stomachs as she dances on my thighs. The weight disappears before reappearing a second later, the body now facing the opposite direction, so my knuckles brush her spine. Leaning back, she grinds on top of my dick, but all I can see is the brunette still holding my hair. My Adam's apple bobs with a violent swallow while my cock begs, motherfucking *begs*, to be released. Fuck.

My hair's freed the same time the one on my lap gets up, then I'm yanked to standing by the handcuffs. The redhead drapes my arms around her shoulders and backs her ass up, dancing against my dick.

My mind wanders out to the side of us again, but I don't actually give in. What does Lex think of this little show? Exactly how much did she orchestrate? The song, too? It's way too fucking close to reality to pass as coincidence.

Spinning us around so we're facing the chair, the redhead bends at the waist, gripping the chair back.

"That makes three positions," Warden Missy says, finally clueing me in on what's actually happening here. We're supposed to act out as many sex positions as possible, but I've just been sitting here like a limp dick because I was too wrapped up in…women.

Finally, I do it, I look over again, scanning the crowd, this time finding her thanks to the higher vantage point. She's sitting on a stool, her elbows behind her on the bar as she faces the stage, eyes glued to mine. Her lips moving have me glancing down to see her mouth the word "Sweet."

Pushing the redhead's back until she's practically bent in half, I leverage a foot on the seat and thrust my hips hard enough for her to lose her footing, stumbling forward a few steps.

I'm quick to grab two handfuls of her shirt though, bringing her right back and lifting her top half so her back's flat against my front, then I pump into her ass again.

The audience loses their minds, but I don't break concentration as I move her into several other positions.

"Nine, ten, eleven!" Missy counts, dramatically fanning her face as well as between her thighs.

"Geez, let someone else get a chance," I hear one of the other women complain, the blonde I think.

Bending the redhead over the chair again, I rasp, "Don't move," then lift my arms, removing them from around her to sit down on the floor with my back to her, my knees bent and spread wide open. "Straddle me," I tell the brunette, and she does all too eagerly, helping guide my arms over her head and down around her waist. One hand held in the other, I crook two fingers and say, "Sit on 'em," to the blonde standing nearby, taking in our every move with unconcealed jealousy. I knew it was her whining about being left out. That's why her greedy ass is only getting my fingers.

Her knees inside of mine, she lowers herself until her pussy hovers just above my fingertips, the heat incredibly fucking evident even without actual contact. I lean back, ducking my head between the redhead's legs to knock both her thighs with my jaw so it's clear for everyone watching—I could finger one, fuck one, and eat out the other right fucking now if I wanted to.

Missy Warden doesn't even bother with a number, just screams into the mic, spurring on the entire club.

The blonde widens her knees, pushing against mine, and lowers her pussy on to my fingers, but I yank my hands out from under her, not giving her the satisfaction. Bitch thought I forgot she just tried jacking me.

I didn't fucking forget.

A few more creative positioning ideas later, the song comes to a close, ending the challenge, and the four of us disentangle ourselves. I don't know what the final tally is and I doubt anyone else does either. Lines got blurred as soon as I brought the other two women into the mix.

After uncuffing me, the redhead leans forward, her lips tickling the shell of my ear as she says, "If you and your fiancée ever want a unicorn, you know where to find me."

With a noncommittal eyebrow raise, I descend the stage's stairs directly into the pit of my colleagues already asking every question filling their drunken heads.

"What'd her pussy feel like?"

"How'd she smell?"

"Think she'd go out with me?"

Laughing them off instead of answering the way I want to—*Like a pussy. Gamey. And, no.*—I give an excuse about needing a drink and push through, heading straight for the bar.

Several people tap my back when I pass, mostly congratulating me, some praising me, and a couple bitter fucks cursing me, but I block it all out, my attention solely on Lex's exposed shoulder blades as she sits with her back to me now. Her white hair's in a complicated-looking bun at her neck, a couple loose curls by her ears.

Posted beside her is Kaisin, leaning over to talk to her.

Since they don't know I'm here yet, I hang back and listen.

"You're gonna get me in trouble."

The only part I make out of Lex's response is "So?"

Draping an arm around her back, Kaisin practically gnaws on one of her ears as he tells her, "It is."

Busy drilling a hole into the side of Kaisin's face, I miss what Lex says, but I decide I've heard enough. Heard enough. Seen enough. Tolerated enough.

"Hey." I clap Kaisin's back harder than he's ever clapped mine, then pull him off Lex one-handed. "I owe you a thank-you."

Baby Debrosse stands on his own, no longer putting his weight on Lex, and accepts the thank-you he definitely doesn't deserve. "You're welcome." Using his beer bottle, he points behind me. "How was it up there? It looked like a lot of fun."

"It was. Greatest night of my life," I lie before making a show of checking over my shoulders.

Now that the show is over, the group is being herded out of the main area and back down the hall we came from.

"Everyone's heading back to the room."

Kaisin hesitates, glancing at Lex's back.

"Looks like you're all set," I tell him with another pat to his shoulder that forces him a couple more feet away from Lex.

"I'm waiting on Lenox."

Lex turns her head to acknowledge her brother-in-law. "I still haven't gotten my drink yet."

"Good idea. I could use one, too," I say to her, then look at him. "We'll meet you in there."

With no choice but to agree, Kaisin nods, saying, "Yeah, okay."

"Subtle," she tsks as soon as he's gone, but I don't care. Subtlety wasn't my goal. Getting his body off hers was.

"Got my wallet for me?"

Without looking at me, she holds it up between her trigger and middle finger. I snatch it and immediately search its contents.

"Did you take anything?"

Out of the corner of my eye, I notice her shrug a bare shoulder.

Everything in my wallet accounted for, I return it where it belongs.

"Like what? The grand I just gifted you?"

She might not have stolen anything but she did go through my wallet because the ten hundred-dollar bills she attached to the Chaste Tree are the only bills I got on hand right now.

Finger-combing my hair, droplets of sweat fly in all different directions, a few onto Lex's back. I eye them, wanting to lick each one off before sucking the porcelain skin clean.

"I thought you would've put that money toward your wedding."

The bartender approaches, so I order a snakebite shot using top shelf whiskey, making sure it goes on Lenox Debrosse's tab.

"You go through my phone, too?" I say instead.

"Without the passcode?" she asks just as evasively, not exactly denying it.

"I'm gonna need that back now."

She finally turns her head, not meeting my gaze but dragging hers along the length of my body, raising my temperature quicker than anything on that stage did.

With her other hand, she slides my phone across the bar top to the spot next to her. I take that seat just as our glasses are set in front of us, hers an old-fashioned full of crystal clear liquid I can't identify.

Lex's gaze never straying from my face, I finish mine in one swallow.

"Do you always treat Kordin's employees to nights out?"

"No, never."

"Then why now?"

"You can't throw a bachelor party after the wedding."

I shake my head and face forward again, tipping my glass at the bartender for another when I catch his eye.

"That's not what I meant. Why go through all this trouble for someone you hate, especially if you've never done anything like this before?"

"I don't hate you. I just don't want you anywhere near me."

I force out a laugh that's anything but humorous. "You hate me. You toss out every gift I buy you."

"You should reevaluate your spending habits."

"You gave me a Monk's Pepper."

"Do you mean the Chaste Tree?"

"I knew you knew what it was." It's called both but they mean the same thing, it's to reduce sexual desire—allegedly. Its history goes all the way back to goddess Hera's birth under one.

"You almost cheated on your fiancée. I thought I was helping."

I love how she turns it around on me like I'm the only one who got off that day in her office.

"You almost cheated on your husband."

"Don't flatter yourself, rookie."

I gesture at her. "You're either insulting me by calling me rookie or sweet."

"Both are accurate assessments of what I've seen so far."

"You don't trust me with fucking anything."

"I trust you to fuck your future wife," she says, bringing us right back to my fake fiancée. "Even if you do lack…creativity."

I scoff. I had three women at once. No other man in this club could even dream of handling three women at the same time.

I don't bother pointing that out because I don't want to waste another second on those women. Lex is actually talking to me, which feels better than the public four-way dry hump that just took place. So I just ask, "What position would you've done?"

"It's hard to explain."

"Try."

Rotating on her stool, Lex faces me and I do the same, both our gazes full of flames—mine raging while hers is dancing mischievously.

"The man lies flat on his back."

I nod, nervous to speak.

She glances around before lowering herself off the stool, shortening some of the distance between us.

"I climb on top and put my hand on him. Here." Flattening her hand on my abs, she gently presses in, then up, like she's burrowing under my ribs. "Then I reach inside."

Inside?

"And I take out his kidneys."

A chuckle-like noise rumbles somewhere deep inside her as she selfishly keeps it to herself.

"Is this that tonic-immobility shit again?"

"Sly fox."

She's getting every man at Kordin's company annihilated tonight. She already got their balls. Now she's going after their kidneys.

"Killer whale."

"You have no idea," she murmurs, taking a step back and looking behind her for her seat.

"I just wanna see if it's her."

My head snaps to the voice and the drunk idiot it belongs to suddenly next to us, some guy and his friend pushing into our space.

Wide eyes latched on Lex's face, he says, "Oh man, it is."

"You're sure?" His friend sips off his beer, his own gaze roaming every visible inch of Lex like she's naked.

The bartender drops off my drink, giving me something to do with my hands while I wait this out, see where it goes. They're fucking aching though.

Lex doesn't say anything either way, just holds her ground by spinning toward both guys, her elbows propped on the bar behind her once again like she's *that* fucking unbothered.

The first guy asks, "Do you remember me?"

Tilting her head to the side, she gives him a quick once-over. "Should I?"

"You took my virginity."

"Doesn't sound like me. Virgins are notoriously bad in bed." She leans forward just a bit and lowers her voice to say, "Clingy, too."

His friend chuckles, making him scowl.

"I remember you...Lexi."

Okay. He had to have been one of her customers at The Playground. That makes a lot more sense than her wanting to outright fuck him.

Eyes still wandering, the friend butts in, asking, "What will a c-note get me?"

Lex pushes herself off the bar and shrugs. "A handful of drinks. I recommend their snakebites. They're delicious." She looks at me for the first time since these assholes arrived. "At least that's how my friend made it look."

Suppressing a smirk, I arch an eyebrow at her. Friend? And I did what…make a cocktail look delicious? All I did was drink it.

If I didn't know any better, I'd think she just gave me a compliment. Maybe even two.

Is she flirting with me?

"I meant with you. We can go in the bath—"

I'm on my feet, standing to my full height, chest fucking swollen around a heart that's already racing as I put myself in front of Lex. "She said you got the wrong person. Get the fuck out of here."

I shove on both of them, but the first guy ducks around me, saying, "I'll prove it." Shooting out his hand, he yanks down the zipper on Lex's dress, too quick for me to stop. My eyes follow the movement behind me a second too late, already finding Lex's tits showing.

Instantly, I grab the tops of her dress with one hand, leaving the middle unzipped and gaping wide open. Her nipples are covered but the small inner swells of her cleavage aren't.

"See? The Polish tattoo on your chest. I knew it'd be there."

I lower my gaze to the black cursive word tattooed at the base of her sternum. *Rozbita.*

Lex keeps her head down as she tries to get the slider up the teeth of the zipper, but with the two pieces of the dress so far apart, it doesn't move.

"Let go," she tells me.

Her eyes still downcast, she doesn't see me shake my head.

"Keep trying." If I let go, her tits will be out all over again, and this time, people are paying attention.

"I looked it up, you know." The fucker keeps talking. "It means broken, as in a broken. Dirty. Slu—"

My free hand collides with his mouth, silencing the rest of that sentence.

His friend rushes me, knocking me sideways, and since I'm still clutching Lex, she comes with.

The people around us scatter out of the way, making me fly further than anticipated. I manage to catch myself just before I lose my footing, never once releasing my grip.

"Asshole," I hear, then another crunch, this one not quite as satisfying as the one I just produced.

When I look back, Lex is shaking her fist out and the friend has blood dripping from his nose. *She hit him?*

She hit him.

With a menacing step in her direction, he says, "Fucking whore."

Tugging Lex toward me, I spin her so her back's against my front and my arm's half-wrapped around her as I hold her dress together, then I punch him myself, right between the eyes, making his nose fucking *gush*.

The bartender yells at us, but without any weapons in his hands, I'm not too worried.

Watching the first guy get up, I pivot us to put my free arm forward.

"Zip it up," I growl close to Lex's ear.

"Let go first."

I tighten my hold on both the dress and her. "No."

She groans, and I can tell without even seeing her face, her eyes are rolling.

Back on his feet, Lex's old customer charges us, and I swing out my hand, palm open, and box his ear so fucking hard he stops to cradle his head. Since he's still within reach, I do it again, but much, much harder. Motherfucker.

"Shit!" he shouts over another bartender's shrieks for security.

"You can't fight one-handed."

I ignore Lex because not only can I, I fucking will.

Making a fist, I clip the same spot on his jaw I hit the first time, his head thrashing to the side before his body goes lax and drops to the floor.

Bent over, his friend takes in the pathetic heap next to him and snarls, blood spewing everywhere.

I start forward, ready to finish him, too, but Lex saying, "Reece, let *go*," has me freezing. Not because I forgot where I go right now, she goes, but because she said my name. My fucking name. Not rookie, not rook, not Mr. Souza. Reece. She called me Reece.

I glance down at her, our noses almost touching. "Say it again."

"Let—"

"My name. Say it again."

"Rook—"

"No. My real name."

Unblinking, she says, "Reece," making my cock harden against her hip.

Lex wets her bottom lip with her tongue before saying, "On your right."

Without looking away from her mouth, I blindly jab my fist out to my right, hitting the friend's...something. Point is, he drops and Lex said my name.

This isn't the greatest night of my life, but it's up there. Now.

Fifteen

Reece

I ROTATE THE ARM WITH LEX INWARD UNTIL I FEEL HER CHEST graze mine, then I release the material to zip both pieces back together again. My right hand is covered in blood and won't stop shaking, but I can't tell if the shaking's from fighting or being this close to Lex.

"Reece." A look of pain flashes on Lex's face before she whispers, "Go home to your fiancée."

"Why?"

I stare into her eyes, full of her own lies and secrets and mysteries, hoping she reveals something more, something I can understand because a lot of the things she says and does, I don't. I don't understand why she worked at The Playground. I don't understand why she married Kordin. I don't understand why she's still married to him. She deserves better than Cyrus, better than Kordin, better than Fox Hollow.

"I got this one," I hear before a security guard hooks Lex's elbow, hauling her out of my grasp and through the circle of onlookers.

I'm on their fucking heels, two more meatheads hot on mine.

Lex's hand lifts to her bun, her fingers hastily tucking hairs back into place. Her hair. She's fucking concerned about her hair right now. The hollow life got to her more than she'd like to admit.

"Hey, where are you taking her?" I shout as soon as we enter a dark hallway with a neon-red exit sign above it. The long stretch of hall doesn't have the same effects as the one from earlier, but with only a single sconce, it's got just enough light to make out Lex being dragged along, her free hand up to her mouth now.

Both her and the man currently treating her like a motherfucking ragdoll ignore me.

"I said where the fuck are you taking her?" And why isn't Lex demanding to know the same thing?

Catching me from behind, one pair of hands mashes the side of my face into the wall as the other jerks my arms behind my back.

"Now, now. Where do you think you're going?"

My eyes never leave Lex. Why isn't she putting up a fight? I know from personal experience she knows how.

"You have two choices. You can walk through that door, or we can drag you through it."

There are only two doors, one off to the side and one at the very end with another exit sign above it.

"The door to the exit?" I breathe against the goddamn wall, making both men at my back chuckle.

"Nice try. The one to the office."

"Then one to a squad car." The other one laughs darkly.

Squad car? Fuck. Of all the shit I've pulled, a fucking bar fight is what's gonna land me behind bars.

But what does that mean for Lex?

"What about her?"

"Her?" one of the assholes behind me echoes. "She gets the exit."

"He's letting her go?"

There's a pause before one mumbles, "Eventually."

At the end of the hall, the guard kicks the exit door open, then yanks Lex over the threshold. Before the door even gets the chance to shut all the way, I lose my fucking shit.

I stomp on one of the four feet behind me, only freeing my head when the motherfucker eases off my face. The fucker with my arms gets a head-butt as I thrash my body off the wall, then a backward kick to the nuts.

The face smasher comes at me again, but this time I've got my arms. I give an uppercut to his chest, making him stumble back, falling right on his ass.

Using the momentary break, I sprint down the hall, bursting out into the cold night air. It does nothing to cool my inflamed body as I take in my surroundings. Barbed wire tops a chain-link fence running the perimeter of an employee-only parking lot. It's dark and deserted, making it a perfect place for the worst sins imaginable.

Beside the door, the guard who took Lex is caging her in, telling her, "This doesn't have to hurt. You just—"

He stops his advance at my intrusion, asking, "What are you doing out here?"

I ignore him to give Lex a quick head-to-toe scan. She's not kicking and screaming like I expected but she doesn't look scared either. There's a strange, checked-out expression on her face as she peers at the son of a bitch who was just predatorily backing her into a brick wall, his intention crystal fucking clear.

Shit. She could be in shock.

He better not have touched her already.

Red closing in on me, I rip the shoulder closest to me, throwing the guard on the ground with a follow-up haymaker to his temple.

With him laid out, I reach for Lex, asking, "Are you okay?"

Her hand fits into mine without further prompting, and she nods, so I pull her forward, both of us freezing when the door opens, the two guards spilling out from the other side of it.

Lex's grip loosens as her body prepares for the same thing as mine—carnage. Technically, with Lex's guard sitting up, it might end up being three against two, but I'm gonna try like hell to keep it to three against one. Lex can fight, when she chooses to, but I won't be able to concentrate if one of these motherfuckers hurts her.

I'm barely restraining myself as it is.

Easing Lex behind me, I say, "Come on," daring the guard sporting a fresh goose egg above his eyebrow to make the first move. He takes a step in my direction, but at the sound of a gun being cocked, I forget all about him and spin, giving my back to all three men to put Lex's against the wall again. Absolutely zero hesitation in my decision, I block her body with mine, my breath caught in my lungs as I wait for the bullet.

Lex's eyes widen—the first real reaction she's given since she was ripped from my arms—and she blurts, "Lexi Andeno." The sound is lispy and nothing like her usual voice.

Lexi Andeno, as in *Cyrus* Andeno?

"Cyrus's daughter?" someone behind me voices my thoughts.

Someone else asks, "What of her?"

Lex blinks long and slow, then spits a wad of saliva mixed with blood into her hand.

Did he fucking hit her? Is that why she wasn't saying anything?

"*I'm* her. I'm Lexi Andeno."

Cyrus's daughter?

Cyrus's.

Daughter.

That's the "family shit" Promise was talking about. They are fucking family.

What the fuck was up with that moment in Lost and Found then? The one where Cyrus jerked off to me describing his…his…

No. No. It can't be. She *can't* be.

"Miss Andeno."

"Fuck!" another guard shouts.

"We didn't know."

Lex spreads her fingers, letting the liquid seep between them until all that's left on her palm is a single-edge razor blade.

She had that in her mouth?

"Now you do." The blade in hand, Lex steps away from me, her chin raised in complete defiance, and I turn in place to follow. The guard on the ground still has his gun out, but it's lowered. "Let us go and I won't tell Cyrus about any of this."

Looking up between us, he says, "You can go…but he stays."

"I feel like I'm talking to a child," she tells him. "Stand up."

Too low for me to hear, the guard mutters something.

Lex does though because as soon as he's semi-upright, she hocks right into his face, a spray of pink-tinged spit coating the man's already strained features. It's the most fox-like thing I've ever seen Lex do and maybe even the sexiest.

The hand with the gun trembles, but Lex doesn't back down whatsoever.

She meets every man's gaze as she shifts her weight to her back foot, the blade at her side no longer hidden from view. It's only an inch and a half long, but the way Lex is wielding it, it might as well be a fucking machete.

"We both leave or none of us do."

Now that's sexy. She won't leave without me, even if it kills her. Goddamn.

If we survive this, I'm wringing her fucking neck, but still, goddamn.

"The cops are already on their way," the guy by the door says regretfully as a police siren wails from a distance.

His partner nods, adding, "They're expecting to take somebody in."

"The two men we left decorating your dance floor…one of them assaulted me. Give him to the cops."

Mid face-wipe, Lex's guard says, "That's not—"

"I wasn't *fucking* asking!" she yells, cutting off all other sound.

I've never heard her talk like this to anyone. She's always confident but in a calculated, sometimes even manufactured way. This is genuine confidence that was built, and tested, over time. Like this, she not only sounds like an apex predator, she could pass as one.

After a few beats of staring at Lex, his face still coated with her spit, he drops his gaze to his feet, defeat wafting off him like a week-old stench.

Lex doesn't waste another second, immediately leading me over to a part of the fence that's been snipped and pulled back.

Her hands disappear behind her head, then reappear again, the blade nowhere to be seen.

That's what she was doing inside—relocating the blade from her bun to her mouth. That explains why she couldn't talk. Not why she didn't fight back though.

"So that's it?"

She shrugs. "Yeah."

"He was gonna rape you."

"He was gonna try."

I catch her elbow. "Lex?"

Her body goes stiff under my touch.

"That's not good enough for me. I can't just leave it like that."

With a hand out to pinch my chin, she says, "You're gonna have to." Then, she lets go and ducks through the break in the fence.

Glancing at the three guards still watching us, I commit the one to memory. I know where he works and where he parks. I'll be back.

Out on the sidewalk, I switch spots with Lex so I'm closest to the street, careful to keep an eye out until we're clear of the lot and in front of another building.

Lex makes a sound in her throat.

"What?"

"Stop trying to save me."

Just like she did when I told her to stop fighting me, I say, "I can't."

Another noise from her throat.

"In this neighborhood…" She intentionally surveys the deserted street. "I'm more likely to get mugged than hit by a car."

I switch our positions again. "Happy?"

She roots her feet but throws her hands up. "No!"

She's mad at *me*? For trying to protect her? The urge to actually wring her fucking neck creeping up again, all I can do is scowl at her. Her and the thousands of goose bumps dotting her skin. The cold is a welcome relief to me now, but Lex, she's not wearing much. And she runs cold…sometimes. Her body temperature seems to fluctuate.

"You're freezing." I take a step toward her, but she counters it with one of her own backward. On God, I might actually choke this bitch.

"You're exhausting. Everything you do, it's…exhausting and un-necessary and…" Her expression hardens. "…not as sweet as you think it is."

"I'm not trying to be sweet. I just don't want you hurt." What's so fucking bad about that?

"You're an even bigger idiot than I thought."

Now my hands are airborne.

"What the fuck? I'm sweet. I'm exhausting. I'm an idiot. I'm sly. I'm Reece. I'm rookie. Make up your fucking mind!"

Instead of saying *anything*, she spins on her heels and resumes walking, her heels whacking the chipped concrete angrily, but I don't let her get more than a couple of steps ahead of me, keeping her within arm's reach, because she's absolutely right about this neighborhood. She almost got raped and we had a gun pulled on us, both out in the open. The residents around here couldn't give less of a fuck.

Lex hugs herself as her shoulders start shaking uncontrollably.

"Where's your car?" I snap, glancing around. This is a pretty far walk to make alone at night for anyone, especially such a tempting hollow look-alike. She's the idiot if she thinks she'd only get mugged. "Didn't you get valet?"

"I don't let strangers touch my shit."

"But you were fine with a club full of strangers seeing your shit."

She rounds on me so fast, she's a fucking blur of black and white and sexy-as-fuck irritation. It's actually refreshing to see emotion on her.

Refreshing but infuriating. Where was all this anger before I came outside? Why does she save it all for me?

"Do you know how many people have seen my tits, rookie?"

And we're back to rookie. Fuck!

"Thousands."

She's on the move again, scurrying away from me as fast as those sky-high heels will take her.

"So what?" I shout, my feet eating up the pavement between us until I do reach for her. Reach for her. Grab her. Hold her. Press my body into hers so my heat becomes hers. My nose buried in that white hair, I say, "Thousands of people have seen your body, touched your body, *fucked* your body." Said body shivers against mine, making me have to swallow a groan to finish. "That doesn't make it any less valuable. That doesn't make *you* any less valuable."

"Valuable?" She scoffs. "Now you sound like Cyrus."

"Funny. A second ago I was thinking the same thing. Your daddy—"

"Don't call him that."

"What should I call him?"

"Boss, like everybody else working for him does."

"Back there—"

"Back there, I was just trying to save myself."

"Bull. Shit." Her head shakes but I press the fuck on. "If you were only worried about saving your own ass, you would've dropped your maiden name long before there was a gun pointed at mine."

"I had a blade under my tongue."

"When were you planning on using it? Huh?" I feel myself get mad all over again. He could've... He was going to...

And she just...

When she doesn't answer, I lower my voice to tell her, "I didn't mean valuable as in money. I meant valuable as in precious. I don't care about the sacrifices you've made to survive. I've had to make my own."

Her voice is a shadow of what it just was when she says, "We're nothing alike."

"I think we are," I whisper back.

"You don't know anything about me."

"I know you're just as protective as I am. Otherwise you would've let me get robbed. Or shot. Or arrested."

"I should've."

"But you didn't." My cock growing to full mast against her ass, I nip at her earlobe. "Lex."

"If you know me so well, stop calling me Lex. It's not my name."

"It is to me. With me, you're not Lenox Debrosse, and you're not Lexi...Andeno. You're Lex."

She spins in my arms, her eyes locked on my chest.

"Lex?"

Despite her not looking at me, I nod. "Lex."

"Go. *Home*," she stresses, still refusing to meet my eyes. "Go home to your fiancée before I…"

My grip on her sides tightens, the material of her dress bunching in my fists. "Before you what?"

She peers up at me. "Before I break up a marriage."

"Your husband already broke it," I rasp, mesmerized by her eyes, her lips, her everything.

"I'm not talking about mine, rook."

My marriage? She's worried about breaking up *my* marriage?

"I'm not getting married," I admit.

She pulls out of my grasp. "Don't be—"

"I lied." An arm around her waist, I drag Lex back to me so her front's flush with mine, my hard cock trapped right between us. "The girl, the engagement, I made it all up—"

Lex's lips crash into mine. Plump, soft, and greedy, they're everything I remember. I deepen the kiss, licking her tongue inside her mouth over and over again until she moans, low and throaty. There's a distinct metallic taste, but oddly, no alcohol.

My hands on her ass, I lift her a couple inches off the ground and carry her over to a dark alcove on the abandoned building.

Her hands go to my pants, undoing the button, but I grab both with one of mine and shake my head. She releases a little growl that makes me smile.

Pulling back, she breathes against my lips, "Don't ruin this by being sweet."

"I'm not." Jesus.

"I don't want sweet. I want you to fuck me right here, right—"

My lips cut her off this time. She's getting fucked right here, but it's not gonna be right now. I need to do something first. Something I've been fucking dying to do since my first day working for her.

After releasing her hands, I unzip the bottom of her dress several inches, then lean back to tell her, "Mine's covered in blood, so you're gonna help me."

My right hand over hers, I push us both down the front of her panties.

Tone scathing, she says, "The lack of creativity… You want me to finger myself while you watch…again."

I guide her fingers to her slick slit, pressing her middle and ring finger between those fat lips I've only glimpsed from across a room. Despite her annoyance, she drops her head back and moans.

"You're the one that chose that song."

Her chest makes the same noise from before. It's kind of like a laugh, but not quite.

"In the song, he licks her up after," she argues.

I already considered getting on my knees and eating Lex out, but I can't. Not here. And I'm not waiting to get a taste.

Pulling her fingers back out, I promise, "I'll lick every fucking drop," then thrust them inside once again, the tips of my fingers brushing her soaked lips. She's shaved smooth and motherfucking *drenched*.

Leaning over her, I hike her leg up my thigh, to my hip, earning another moan as she bucks forward. I kiss the column of her throat, wishing I had a third hand to wrap around it. I don't want to just hear her moans, I want to feel them.

She increases the speed of our pumps, jamming her fingers so deep into her fucking pussy, the tips of my fingers go in, too. Dropping my forehead to her lifted chin, I lose myself in watching our conjoined effort of finger-fucking her hot, wet cunt. Up to my second knuckles, I can feel her walls spasm as she comes.

Before she can recover, I rip both our hands out of her panties because with her milk lubing up my hand, I want to bury my entire fist in her pussy. Unfortunately, that fist is currently fucking filthy with other people's DNA.

Immediately, I bring her hand up to my mouth, sucking her shiny fingers between my lips. Keeping my gaze locked on hers, I swirl my tongue around them, smearing every taste bud until she's all I taste.

Eyes blazing, Lex crooks the fingers in my mouth into my bottom jaw and pulls me forward.

"Don't think you're done, rook."

Wasn't fucking planning on it, Snow.

Keeping me fish-hooked with one hand, she uses her other to

push my pants and boxer briefs low enough for my rock-hard cock to spring free. Finally breaking eye contact, she looks down and bites her bottom lip.

She grips just under my mushroom-head and strokes the top third of my shaft, and I have to chew her fingers to keep from blowing my load.

Pushing under my jaw with her palm, she forces me to bite her fingers harder, the taste of blood filling my mouth as she pants, "Fuck."

I knew there'd be blood.

I yank her panties to the side. Understanding, Lex lines us up, then I thrust inside her pussy, her leg on my hip allowing my cock to go *deep* and those fat lips to swallow me *whole*. When the base of my cock hits her clit, she groans and pulls my jaw down. I stay where I am, not retreating an inch, and grind up into her, brutally mashing her clit.

Each groan I give is met with an equally desperate moan from her, and if anyone were to walk by right now, they'd hear exactly what we're doing. They won't be able to see Lex though, which is all that matters. That and her coming all over my cock because I'm not leaving until she does.

I shake her hand off my mouth to tell her so.

"Reece," she warns.

"Lex," I warn right back.

Her mouth falling open makes my balls throb. *Shit.*

I start pounding into her unchecked.

"Fucking rookie," I hear and freeze. Lex's eyes are raised above our heads, not in bliss but in frustration.

"Why? What'd I do now?"

"You got greedy."

"You said you didn't want sweet."

"Sweet would be letting me fuck you. You're going to help me fuck you."

I can't help but laugh, shaking my head. She just talked shit on me for saying the same thing.

"I need more than penetration to come on your cock."

"Tell me what you need, and I'll do it."

I dip down to tease her mouth but she latches on to my bottom lip, biting it viciously before quickly sucking away the pain. When she releases it, her lips are ruby red with my blood. Or hers. I don't know. We're both fucking bloody right now.

Unable to resist, I pull out of her before *slowly* pushing back in. Instinctively, Lex bows her back, sucking my cock in even further. Fuuuck, that feels good. She feels good. Better than good, fucking phenomenal.

"Tell me how you want me, Lex, or I'm gonna fuck you into the wall."

Listening to her instructions, I lift her other leg off the ground, then hook both my arms under her knees.

"Now…" Her hands gripping my neck, her nails break the skin below my hairline as she pulls her face up to mine, then starts rolling her hips, rubbing her clit just above my shaft. "Don't fucking move."

"I've never wanted to fuck a mouth more," I confess, eyes glued to hers.

Her chest rumbles again and I realize it's her version of laughter.

A laugh? While she's on my cock? Maybe I did get shot and this is the devil's way of teasing my ass by giving me a taste of heaven before dragging me to hell. If this is how I go out, I'm doing it motherfucking basking in glory.

"Make sure you fucking coat me in cum. I want to be soaked."

"Mine or yours?"

I grin. "Yours."

"Eyes on me."

"I'm not blinking," I promise her, staring into eyes as silver as Earl Grey Roses.

Using my neck and arms as leverage, Lex rides me midair. It doesn't take long for the tension in my groin to return, this time doubled in intensity.

"Lex," I'm the one warning now, but Lex doesn't get a chance to reciprocate because she presses her lips to mine just before her body seizes up, her walls spasming for a second time. I kiss her, feeling every part of her shake as she comes. All. Over. My. Cock.

If this is heaven, I'm not fucking leaving. The devil can suck my—
Oh fuck.

My balls tighten, the sensation spreading up my cock until I fucking explode deep inside her pussy.

Our mouths still connected, Lex and I kiss and bite and suck through the aftershocks.

Fuck, I never want her to stop kissing me. Lex doesn't just kiss, she devours, she consumes, she fucking conquers.

This isn't heaven. It's better.

Sixteen

Lex

REALIZATION DAWNS AND I REAR BACK, BREAKING THE KISS. He came. Of course he fucking came, but he came *in me*.

"You didn't pull out."

Did he mean to? Or did he just get caught up in the moment like I did?

"Fuck no," he says unapologetically before trying to steal another kiss, but I whip my head to the side to block it. Against my cheek, he whispers, "You told me not to move. If you wanted something different, you should've said so."

Slowly, I turn to look at him again. Reece's obsidian eyes stare back at me, unblinking, but with that shot of unadulterated endorphins still coursing through his bloodstream, they're completely unreadable.

"And if I get pregnant?"

His eyebrows furrow. "You're not on birth control?"

"No." There's no reason for me to be. Kordin wears a condom *and* pulls out.

Reece shrugs a shoulder. "Good."

"Good?"

I shove on his chest but he doesn't let me down. Or pull out. In fact, he surges into me even more despite his cock softening inside me

"Yeah. Good," he growls. "It'd split you and Kordin up because that motherfucker's not raising my kid."

My heart pounds wildly against my ribs, making it difficult to breathe.

"Rookie, don't be an idiot."

"Use my fucking name when I'm inside you."

"Get the fuck out of me." My palms press into his shoulders, not moving them, or him, an inch.

Practically spearing me into the wall, he growls, "No."

I roll my eyes and snap harsher than necessary, "Reece, don't be an idiot."

"How am I an idiot? Kordin said it himself."

"What? What'd he say?"

"When he offered you up to me. He said I couldn't nut in you because he wasn't going to raise a defect."

"He used the word 'defect'?"

"I think it was 'another defect,' you know ..." His jaw flexes. "... like me."

No, not like Reece. Like *me*. Kordin wasn't referring to Reece's genes. He was referring to mine.

My throat burns.

This time when I push at Reece, he actually puts me down. The moment his body leaves mine, I begin mourning the loss because I know this will never happen again. It was a huge mistake. I was running on adrenaline and hormones. My fucking hormones. They're the bane of my entire existence.

I right my underwear, sliding the material back over my wet, swollen pussy so I can zip my dress.

I just... I wanted to see what it felt like again, to have someone's mouth on mine, to have someone's front on mine.

The way Kordin fucks me now, it's premeditated. When he first started doing it, I hated him, even more than I already did, because despite being fucked in the same way more times than I care to admit while I worked at The Playground, I never felt...worthless. I had a job to do then, and I did it. I went through the motions of sex but never the emotions associated with it. Then I married Kordin and I became less robotic, less mechanical. I let myself *feel*. Not much but enough to get my hopes up. Hopes that were crushed the second I got that diagnosis.

Reece not being disgusted by the prospect of impregnating me doesn't change the fact I can't get pregnant. Not by him, not by anybody.

Not right now. I don't even know what my right now is. Everything's fucked.

"For the record, it'd be my choice if I kept the baby," I say before I forget to. The fucking audacity.

"*Our* baby," he says without looking up from his pants as he tucks himself back into them.

I ignore him and the things those words do to my insides.

"Just like it'd be my choice when, how, and why I leave Kordin."

His hands still and he meets my gaze. "Not would be. Will be. You're fucking leaving him. I told you once I touched you, no other man would. That hollow piece of shit's name is at the top of that list, Lex."

"God. Don't tell me I took your virginity, too."

"I'm not clingy. I'm fucking territorial. What's mine is mine."

I stare at Reece long and hard, a thousand replies running through my mind. I settle on the simplest, saying, "Don't do that."

"Don't do what?"

"Don't turn this into something it doesn't need to be."

He comes over, cups my pussy, and says, "Too late."

I smack his hand off, and when he sends his other one out, I smack that, too.

Reece's nostrils flare a second before he shoots forward, so I jab his chest, making him crouch over with a loud exhale. Not slowing his advance one bit, he plants his shoulder into my side, throwing me off-balance. Fisting the back of his shirt to catch myself, I bring my knee up into his ribs. The sound he makes has my lips twitching.

On a growl, Reece rips one of my legs out from under me, causing me to fall flat on my ass.

Towering over me, he grinds out, "Do you *ever* stop fighting?"

"Never," I pant before flipping a hand toward him. "Aren't you supposed to be sweet?"

"I tried telling you I wasn't, but you didn't listen. Why'd you hit me?"

I cock an eyebrow up at him. "Why'd you grab me?"

"To show you who you—"

"As a thief you're used to stealing what doesn't belong to you, but I'm no man's, therefore I can't be stolen. You want something from me, earn it."

"We just fucking—"

"One test drive does not an owner make, rook," I tsk.

Without any notice whatsoever, Reece yanks me up to standing again, then one hand pressed to the small of my back, he crushes my front to his.

"Mm," I hum at the feel of his new erection. What a nice surprise. Most men go back to being useless after climax.

Sliding his other hand lower, he kneads my ass cheek, causing a delicious friction with each squeeze.

"On God, you're the only woman to get me hard again fresh off a nut."

"You're the only man to soothe the pain he caused me," I confess quietly. He did the same thing with my scalp at The Playground. I hated it then, but this time, I…don't.

"We can keep at each other's throats out here and risk catching some unwanted attention, or we can settle this shit right now."

"What exactly are we settling?" I ask more out of curiosity than anything.

"You fuck with me, you fuck *only* with me." Eyes darker than the night sky overhead drill into mine.

Exhausting, I remind myself. *Absolutely exhausting.*

"Anything else?" I ask.

"Yeah."

He kisses me again, deep and rough, leaving me breathless before he steps back suddenly, taking his warmth with him.

I almost ask for clarification on that last point, just to feel his lips again, but force myself to turn away instead. "Act like a newly married man Monday morning or don't bother showing up," I tell him, then step off the curb to cross the road. I need distance from him.

Predictably—annoyingly—he doesn't give it to me. Reece follows immediately after, his footsteps so heavy it sounds like I'm being stalked by a pissed-off bull.

"You heard what I said. The engagement is fake."

"Kordin doesn't know that. The rest of the firm doesn't know that. And if you insist on doing Cyrus's bidding under the guise of working there, then I'd prefer to keep it that way."

"Lex?"

I stop to look back at him. This approach is soundless and he doesn't stop until we're face to face again, his hands fidgety at his sides like he doesn't know what to do with them.

Before he can say something sweet, I ask the question I can't get out of my head. "What does Cyrus have on you?"

He lied the first time I asked him. And judging by the way the muscle in his jaw pulses, he's about to again.

"Nothing. It's you I owe."

"I know you're lying."

He throws my own words back in my face, telling me, "You don't know anything about me."

A hand on his waistband, I walk him backward until his back hits a boarded-up door.

I stretch up so our lips can touch one final time, whispering against them, "I know your heart was broken by a cheater. I know your last job was blindsided by your sudden departure. I know they'd take you back in a heartbeat, so you ignoring my repeated firings is not because you need the money. I know your reason for working at the firm is Cyrus, not me, because I know Cyrus best of all, which is how I know he would've warned you away from me by now. I know you dislike authority, specifically his because you stay late every night to watch me walk to my car, you constantly buy me gifts, you risked your life to save mine, and…" I step back. "You just fucked me."

His voice low and gravelly, he says, "I didn't do any of that out of rebellion. I did it because I wanted to. And you're the one that fucked me."

My nod is sad because this next truth is the worst kind of tragedy—an avoidable one.

"I also know that when the time comes for Cyrus to get what he wants, you're going to struggle to give it to him. When you do, he will follow through on his threat. I may not know what that threat is, but I can guarantee you I'm not worth it."

Someone shouts, "Lenox!"

My hand still between us, I push Reece further into the shadows before turning to see Phil headed this way. He's still on the other side of the road, so I quickly take stock of my appearance, straightening my neckline and tucking a stray hair behind my ear. Noticing the blood both on my fingers and caked under my nails, I try wiping it all off on the back of my dress. The taste of copper gone from my mouth, I lick over both lips, making sure there aren't any stray drops.

"My cum's running down your leg and you're about to entertain this fucking guy?"

With one hard swipe, I fling most of the thick rivulet off my thigh and onto the cement.

"So much for licking every drop."

Reece scoffs, rumbling, "Not my own spunk."

"*Our* spunk," I whisper through unmoving lips before walking away from him.

"He better not touch you."

Pretending I don't hear Reece, I stride out to the middle of the street to meet Phil on the dividing line.

"Where have you been? What are you doing out here all alone?"

"Can you keep a secret?" I circle him to keep his attention on me, and nowhere near Reece.

Phil looks me up and down before nodding his head. "Anything."

"I thought it'd be good for me to get out, get my mind off things, but I miss Kordin. I miss our home." I make my body sway on my heels.

"Is that where you're headed?" Phil glances around, so I clamp my hands on his forearms, willing his eyes to stay on me.

Fortunately, they do.

Unfortunately, so do Reece's. I don't even have to see him to know he's riveted from his darkened spot.

"I'm so embarrassed to bow out this early. I really thought tonight would be a nice break from everything going on."

"Everybody had a great time. I don't think anyone but me even noticed you were gone." His hand finds my bare back, massaging the skin side to side. "Why don't you come back with me so I can drive you home myself?"

Faking a heave, I cover my mouth like I'm holding back vomit, causing Phil to leap backward, his hand disappearing from my skin as if it caught fire.

"After spending the last thirty minutes in the bathroom, you'd think there wasn't anything left in my stomach to puke up." I do it again, throwing in a loud gagging noise, too.

"Maybe I should call you a cab instead."

I straighten my spine. "I think I'll be okay to drive."

He starts to argue, so I look around with doe eyes.

"Phil? Would you mind walking me to my car? This area isn't what I'm used to and I'd feel safer having you with me."

Jumping on the opportunity to be my knight in shining armor, Phil escorts me all the way to my Range Rover, miraculously forgetting all about me being too wasted to walk, let alone drive. Not once do I feel the COO remove his hand from my elbow, and not once do I feel Reece remove his eyes from the COO.

DIP MY INDEX FINGER INTO THE CUP OF WATER, THEN RUN IT along the outer rim of the dough in my other hand. Using my middle finger to tamp down the potato filling in the middle, I fold the pierogi in half, pressing the edges together tightly. I place it on the counter, fork ready, but the moment I press the tines down, crimping the edges, pain radiates from my hand, past my wrist, and up my entire arm, reminding me of Friday night. The fighting, the fucking, Reece during all of it. Alternating between being defiantly in control and voluntarily giving me the power, he was a perfect storm of dominance and submission. As much as I wanted to look away, I couldn't, and in the end, I was swept up anyway.

"Marzycielka."

My mother's voice brings my attention back to the task at hand as we sit across the peninsula-style counter from each other in her quaint kitchen, making potato pierogis—Polish dumplings—from scratch. It's Halloween, and even though it's a Sunday, her doorbell will be ringing starting as soon as the sun goes down until midnight, when the teens are finally called back inside. Due to the long driveways, my neighborhood doesn't get trick-or-treaters. At least that's what Kordin says. I spend Halloweens here, with my mom, because she gets…nervous. More nervous than usual.

"I'm not a daydreamer," I argue, using the English translation for marzycielka. I'm not any kind of dreamer.

"Where's your head? In the clouds?"

Not in the clouds. In bottomless pits of obsidian.

My leg bouncing hard enough to make the stool under me squeak, I finish sealing my pierogi, then add it to the tray.

"I have a lot going on right now."

"Boy trouble?"

The kitchen goes silent.

"Mum?" I wait for her to look at me before saying, "I'm twenty-six," reminding her I'm not sixteen anymore. She still treats me like I'm sixteen sometimes, not because she's one of those helicopter parents who doesn't respect boundaries, but because that's how old I was when a bullet tore through her head.

Quieter, I add, "And married."

My mom pauses for a moment, organizing her thoughts and memories. Ten years and numerous surgeries later, the time both immediately before and after the accident remain scrambled for her, making her occasionally mistake her life for the way it was before. Before everything—every single part of my life—went to fucking shit. Hers was already on its way there, she just can't remember the explosion, the fallout, or the catalyst for either.

As for the after, most of it was spent in the hospital, in and out of surgeries, so those fourteen months are better off forgotten. She does remember the months of physical therapy followed by the rehabilitation center where she learned how to live on her own again, mostly because of the people she was forced to interact with and their "scrutiny" of her.

"I know that," my mom says finally. "To Kordin."

Exactly, Kordin. That's who deserves my concentration, not the fox I abandoned like the building he was standing next to.

Reece Souza has become a distraction from my main goal. More than that, he's a temptation—the sexiest, sweetest temptation to exist since Eve's infamous apple. Like her, I succumbed to my overwhelming urge to satisfy my own desire once, just fucking once.

While Eve's downfall is notorious, her backstory isn't. It was bliss. That's it? Because she lived in a fucking garden with Adam? What kind of man was her only companion? Does anyone really know how he treated her? Was he as selfless as history would like us to believe? Or was he overindulging all along, leaving Eve positively deprived and reckless by the time that snake appeared offering her the first real flavor after a lifetime of bland leaves and twigs?

If a single bite is responsible for the fall of man, then maybe man was already rife with faults.

Everybody assumes my life is a paradise because of how it's painted. But nobody knows the truth. They don't feel the absolute void beneath the brushstrokes. And although Eve was banished from her alleged utopia, I'm still bound to my veiled hell. Which is why yesterday, I bought a morning-after pill, to ensure Reece's life cannot be eternally entwined with mine. Then tomorrow, I'll fire him. For good this time.

Back to assembling her own pierogi, my mom asks, "How is Kordin?"

"He's..." I let out a pent-up sigh. "Kordin."

Her entire body tenses as she tilts her head ever so slightly to the side, hiding her right cheek from view.

"Sorry," I murmur.

My mother's never met my husband, so she has no idea what he's like. Not only because I don't make a habit of talking about him, but also, she's a complete recluse with a debilitating phobia of anyone seeing her. The only times she even leaves the house are for doctor appointments where she hides most of her face under a babushka. If something needs fixed inside, I have to personally deal with the service workers while she hides in another room until they're gone.

This house was supposed to liberate us, both of us; instead, it's trapped us. Her inside its walls, me in Fox Hollow.

Kordin gifted me the Cape Cod-style house as a refuge the night we met. As far as tips go, it was by far the most substantial I'd ever received, and although I knew it probably wasn't string-free, I didn't particularly care. I figured any strings Kordin held were looser than the ones Cyrus had me on.

Earlier that same night, I'd reached a breaking point with Cyrus. I'd started looking at places to move into so that when my mom graduated from rehab, she'd have somewhere to feel safe. Somewhere to *be* safe. Somewhere away from Cyrus. And because I'd just turned eighteen, legally, there was no one to stop me.

Since breaking laws is as commonplace to Cyrus as flossing is to dentists, he went off the fucking rails trying to control me, trying to keep me—basically holding me hostage—and eventually, I did, too.

With his cane crushed to his trachea in one of the Lost rooms, I very nearly succeeded in killing him until one of his men interrupted. By the time Tommy was finished punishing me, I was barely hanging by a thread, but one is all an evil master needs to control his puppet, so I was forced to perform. I *owed* Cyrus.

Then Kordin Debrosse walked into The Playground, presenting a way out. He was already successful, had just started his own real estate firm, and when I told him I'd been house hunting, he offered me the small Cape on the spot. It was one of his own rental properties in a neighborhood he couldn't coax solid renters into, and as long as I kept up with its maintenance, I could live there for free.

I accepted with the intention of moving my mom in first, then joining her as soon as possible. *If* possible. I really just needed her out of Cyrus's grasp. She couldn't come live with us. I wouldn't let her.

Kordin didn't leave it at that though. He became a regular, visiting me at The Playground every night. Even buying me a phone when I told him I'd lost mine.

I didn't lose it. Cyrus had taken it from me in order to cut me off from the outside world, including my mother.

On the sixth night of knowing him, after I came clean about who'd be living in the Cape, he proposed, promising to give it to me outright if only I'd marry him, and so, I accepted that, too.

At thirteen years my senior, Kordin was still only thirty-one. A young thirty-one with a head full of good hair, and a fit body just teeming with unspent libido. Kordin was handsome, supportive, and understanding, unlike any man I'd ever met.

"*Family's important to me, too,*" he'd said. He'd even recently hired his younger brother, Kaisin, as his chief financial officer, so they could work alongside each other.

It wasn't until Kordin and I were already married that I learned the truth about him and his brother's relationship only existing in accordance with the Debrosse Group's hours of operation.

That was my first mistake—listening to Kordin Debrosse, because while Cyrus will *do* anything to get what he wants, Kordin will *say* anything to get what he wants. He's more strategic with his love bombs than a B-52 dropping atomic bombs during an air strike.

But if what Reece said is true and Kaisin knew me back when I was still working at The Playground, when exactly did he see me? Was it before his brother did? Or after? Once I met Kordin, I was only putting in shifts for a matter of days, less than a week, before I quit and walked away entirely to start a new life with him.

Neither brother has ever breathed a word about Kaisin's previous knowledge of me or my place of employment, but considering I've interacted with my brother-in-law more this past week than the last eight years combined, that's not exactly surprising.

I need that laptop. It holds everything, not just my entire life, but also my mother's because if anything happens to me, she'll die. That's not an exaggeration. Not only does she refuse to leave her house for any reason whatsoever, she's unable to afford her basic day-to-day expenses, much less anything larger. She can't drive, she's partially blind in one eye, and she can't always remember what year we're in. With the exception of the astronomically priced surgeries I couldn't cover by myself for those first couple years, I now pay for everything in her life. Outside of myself and her small team of doctors, there isn't a single person she's willing to meet face to face, not even my husband. And, even if by some miracle she managed to get over her debilitating dread of having people look at her, I don't trust anyone to care for her the way I have, especially not my husband.

I need something that'll force Kordin to get his laptop out of his safe. As much as I've enjoyed my reprieve from him, I think it's time he come home.

My leg resumes its movement, quicker than before.

"Read anything good lately?" my mom asks over the violent squeaking.

Reading is an escape for us both. Books are a way for us to leave our own warped realities behind temporarily. Occasionally, she'll read large-print books, but most of the time she listens to audiobooks; unless I'm over, then she lets me read for her.

"One," I say, picturing the last book Reece got me, the one currently sitting on my nightstand with a bookmark sticking out the top. It's about a single-dad firefighter and his young daughter's nanny. I thought it'd be super taboo but so far there's just been a little steamy oral in the pantry. No penetration…yet. I always read the epilogue first to make sure there's a happily ever after before I invest in a story, and there was a phenomenal sex scene in that, so I know it's coming.

I have no idea what goes through Reece's mind when he shops for me, but I'm glad he finally found a book with some explicit sex in it.

"Boy trouble," my mom repeats.

"What are you talking about?"

She points at my face, so I smooth out my features, giving her my most indifferent expression.

"I'm married," I also repeat.

"So was I," she says, making my breath catch. *Does she remember?*

Brows plummeting, her hands freeze as her hazel eyes get swept up in some kind of memory. Is it a good one? A bad one? A real one?

Or one I fabricated and made her believe was real?

"Have you seen him lately?"

"Who?" I ask carefully.

"Your father."

Slowly, I shake my head.

She clucks her tongue. "You should go see him."

"I told you, I'm really busy."

Dropping the pierogi in her hold to point a finger at me, she says, "I wasn't asking."

"Yes, Mum," I tell her automatically, very much feeling like that sixteen-year-old she confuses me with.

"Promise me."

Tears build in my eyes as I pin them to the counter. I force myself to do it, saying, "I promise."

This is why I'm stuck in Fox Hollow, because my father's here, and since he is, so is my mom. She *loves* him. Still. She won't go see him herself, but just being close is enough for her. Because she doesn't remember correctly.

But I do. I'm reminded every time I look at her face.

Eighteen

Lex

A FRESH, FLORAL FRAGRANCE ENTERS MY OFFICE THE SAME time Reece does.

I keep my hands under my desk, tightly clasped together.

"Morning, Snow," he greets, but I don't respond.

Undeterred, he takes a seat across from me and places his usual offerings on my desk, this time instead of one flower, it's a bunch and it's in a…ring.

I narrow my eyes on it, breathing a sigh of relief that it's a male wedding band.

"Shouldn't you be wearing that?" I nod at the ring, then his naked ring finger.

"It's not mine."

"Whose…" My mind flickers back to Phil, who arrived wearing a cast on his left hand this morning. Apparently, after escorting me to my car Friday night, on his trek back to The Pen, he was attacked and mugged. The thief stole his wallet and wedding band before stomping on his hand and breaking it. "Phil."

Reece smirks, causing me to release another sigh, this one audible.

"The flowers—"

"I don't care."

"—are white Heather, and they mean protection."

The bunch looks like white Lavender but smells like Honeysuckle.

Unlike the other flowers he's given me, these will actually look good in my house.

"No one's touching you anymore."

I meet his black eyes, and without blinking, he adds, "Except me."

Breaking the connection, I eye the book strategically hiding the white Heather.

"Before you ask—"

"I wasn't going to."

"—this one has lots of sex in it. Consensual sex. I can personally guarantee it."

"How?"

Reece taps his lips like he's thinking, before saying, "Missionary, cowgirl, a position called prone bone where the—"

"I meant how can you personally guarantee there's consensual sex in it?"

"Because I read it myself."

"You read it?"

He nods.

"The whole thing?"

Another nod.

"Do you read a lot?"

"Not since it was a requirement in school."

"So, you just…felt like reading this one?"

"Not really." He chuckles. "I wanted to make sure it met your standards."

He read a book, a romance book, cover to cover, just to see if I'd like it. Seeing Reece read one of my books would be sexy. Hearing him read one would be even sexier.

The frown that overtakes my face hurts every muscle. If I don't frown, I will do something stupid…like smile. Why does he have to make everything harder than it needs to be?

"Mr. Souza—"

"Lex, I've memorized exactly how your sopping wet cunt looks, feels, and tastes. We're fucking done with the last-name shit."

Bringing my hands out from under the desk, I grab both the flowers and the book, then deposit them into the trash can.

My thinned eyes on his hardened ones, I repeat, "Mr. Souza. I regret to inform you that your employment here is no long—"

"What happened when you were sixteen?"

"Excuse me?"

"Something happened when you were sixteen and I want to know what it was. That's when you started working at The Playground, isn't it?" He doesn't wait for a reply before asking, "Why?"

I lift a hand flippantly. "I had to survive." He said it himself. We're both survivors forced to do things others haven't. Or wouldn't.

Or couldn't.

"All of a sudden at sixteen? What made Cyrus let—"

"Cyrus is the one that wanted me to work there."

"His own daughter?"

I fight an involuntary grimace to remain apathetic.

"At sixteen years old?"

"Why do you keep repeating my age?"

"I don't understand—"

"I killed someone." I give him a moment to process that before continuing, "When I was sixteen years old, I killed a man. Cyrus helped cover it up. As you're well aware, Cyrus doesn't do anything out of the kindness of his own heart, not even for…me, so I became indebted to him. I dropped out of high school and started working at The Playground, where almost two years later, I met my philandering husband and decided I'd rather be Kordin's whore than Cyrus's. The job was safer, the pay was better, and the living conditions were much, much grander. Do you understand now?"

"Was it Tommy?"

How the hell does he know about Tommy?

It doesn't matter. None of this does. It's all just…pointless.

As indifferent as I can, I inform him, "Tommy was later. When I was eighteen."

"For giving you that scar?"

He points at my forehead, and I hesitate briefly before nodding. Somebody at The Playground's been telling my business.

But not all of it. I didn't kill Tommy for putting his hands on me. I killed him for threatening to use them on my mother.

"Then who'd you off when you were sixteen?"

"Someone that deserved far worse."

"What'd he do to you?"

"To me? Nothing." I shrug. "I *wanted* to kill him."

Reece is quiet for a moment, then quietly, he says, "My heart wasn't broken by a cheater. It was a liar. My father." He tells the story of how his dad was secretly gambling at Cyrus's establishment, and after losing a particularly large bet, he chose to take his own life.

"Cyrus—"

I hold up a hand to stop him.

The next words out of his mouth will most likely be the reason for why he works for Cyrus, and while I was curious before, I can't afford to be now. I can't listen to what he's about to say. It'd make this already difficult situation impossible.

My throat congested, I make myself say, "This isn't group therapy. I don't give a shit about you or your life. Now, you have ten seconds to get the fuck out of my office before I have you physically removed. You're fired, Mr. Souza. I don't *ever* want to see your face again. Not here. Not anywhere."

He glowers at me, his chest the only part on his body moving as air rushes in and out of his nostrils.

Nine.

Eight.

My eyes plead with his. *Just leave.*

Six.

Five.

I reach for my phone.

Three.

Two.

Reece shoves out of the chair and storms from my office without a backward glance.

I did it. I got rid of him. No more seeing his face first thing every morning. No more seeing his face last as I leave the building every evening, pretending not to notice him spying on me. No more straining to hear his voice around the office as different people attempt to engage him in small talk.

No fucking more.

I stare at my laptop, purposely typing a random word every few seconds. It takes me thirty minutes to realize I never even powered it on.

"Lenox Debrosse," I hear someone say, snapping me out of my... fog. I twist to see Reece Souza back and filling my doorway yet again.

"I told you—"

"I got someone I want you to meet."

"I don't want—"

"This is Breckyn Souza." Reece steps to the side and lets a beautiful young woman in.

Breckyn Souza? So he did get married after all.

A pang of something foreign twists my internal organs until I feel like I'm going to puke.

Beads of sweat gather at my hairline as my heart rate picks up.

Shit. Is it my thyroid?

Or something else? Something *worse?*

Grin in place, the woman strides right over to me and sticks her hand out, saying, "Hi. You can call me Breck. I appreciate this, like, above."

Like, above? *How young is she?*

I study both Souzas before me, noting similarities between the two.

Somehow getting to my feet, I shake her hand, my palm clammy and sensitive. "Yes. Reece's..."

"Sister," Reece supplies, inviting himself into my office like he wasn't *just* kicked out of it. "This is my sister."

My body relaxes as I fold my arms over my chest. "Just how many siblings do you have, Mr. Souza?" During our party planning, Kaisin said Reece had a brother.

"Just Breck and Charlie."

"Charlie's your brother?"

Breckyn's smile grows. "No, Charlie's my twin sister…"

So he lied.

"…but she already has someone to shadow."

"Shadow?"

"Breck is here to shadow you for a high school project."

"Ugh. Reece. You told me she agreed," Breckyn whines, revealing even more of her age. I've always struggled to relate to teenagers because while the girls in my grade were getting lattes and talking boys, I was serving shots and screwing their dads.

My eyes fly to Reece. That's what he wanted to understand. It's not my teenage innocence he was worried about, it's his sisters'. Cyrus wants them at The Playground, and having a set of actual twins would be a huge draw.

What Reece fails to realize is, if Cyrus wants something, it's as good as his. Nothing can stop him, not even the police because they're some of his best customers.

Reece opens his mouth, but I rush to say, "That's right, the shadowing. It somehow slipped my mind that we were doing that today. I apologize for being so ill-prepared. My husband was just in an accident and my brain has been…scattered."

Reece's jaw remains slack.

"That's okay. I'm just happy to be here, you know, a fly on the wall, taking it all in." Breckyn surveys my office and its view before looking back at me. "You're the only person to agree to let me shadow them."

"In real estate, it's all about who you know."

Reece's little sister leans toward me, and pretending to whisper, asks, "Is Reece as annoying here as he is at home?"

"I don't know what he's like at home." My gaze switches between the siblings. "Is he annoying?"

"Above annoying."

Her brother tilts his head at her, silently threatening her. All it does is make her laugh. And me want to.

Watching Reece—tall, dark, and menacing Reece—joke around with his sister makes me feel like someone turned the gravity off.

Reece catches my lips pulled to one side before I can fix them, but instead of saying something idiotic, he just grins back.

I tear my gaze away from his mouth to see if I actually am levitating. Surprisingly, my feet are still rooted to the floor. I can't remember ever feeling weightless, not once in twenty-six years.

"I'll be back at the end of the day," Reece says. "Be good," he warns Breckyn in another brotherly threat, but then he looks at me and I think he might've meant it for me, too.

He should know better.

Breckyn gives him a salute that makes him chuckle on his way out my door.

"So…" I turn to her.

"I didn't mean any of that."

"Any of what?" Is this another one of Reece's lies?

"That Reece is annoying. He's not. Charlie and I just like to tease him because he's so serious all the time."

Never having siblings of my own, I'm unsure how to navigate typical family dynamics…especially while trying to remain professional, so settling back into my chair as gingerly as I can, I just say, "Oh."

Breckyn sits across from me, but instantly leans forward, her forearms planted on my desk. "He's actually really great. Overprotective but great. You should've seen him last week when he found out we weren't going to homecoming. He was so pissed."

"Neither of you got asked?"

Breckyn's a very beautiful young woman. Her features are dark like her brother's, and they both have the same golden-beige skin tone, but Breckyn has an unmistakably softer, friendlier face.

When her head wobbles from side to side noncommittally, I tell her, "You should've asked someone."

She smiles. "That's what Reece said."

"So, it was a matter of not wanting to go?"

"We wanted to go, but…" The smile wanes. "Our mom can't afford extras."

My vision blurs and I have to look up at the ceiling to blink several times to clear it. Extras. I went without extras my entire childhood.

"Doesn't Reece help?" I ask once I'm able.

"He tries to, a lot, but my mom doesn't always let him."

"Did she let him this time?"

"He didn't really give her the option to. He just did it. We tried telling him there wasn't enough time to get nice outfits, but he wouldn't listen to us. He even took us to this exclusive boutique and let us get whatever we wanted."

"Do you have any pictures?"

She hands over her phone with instructions of which way to scroll to see more. In the photos, Breckyn's wearing a dapper suit while a girl almost identical to her is in a gold floor-length gown.

The suit and dress he needed on short notice.

"Reece paid for us to have a limo and everything."

"Did you have fun?"

"It was...nothing above."

I glance up from the screen. "Nothing above?"

"Yeah. Like when something's the best. Top tier. Nothing above it."

Her brother said the same thing about apex predators.

Nodding, I return her phone.

"You both looked amazing." More importantly, they looked happy. Their faces were radiating joy in every picture. "Did your brother help with the flowers, too? He seems to have a great appreciation for them." Charlie had a gorgeous corsage that complemented her dress, and Breckyn had a simple boutonniere that fit perfectly with her suit. Although small, a lot of thought went into the arrangements.

Breckyn's laugh is light and fond as she says, "No, our mom made those."

"Your mom could be a florist," I tell her honestly.

"She is. She runs Silvy's."

I rack my brain, trying to place it. "Over on Saint and Fifth?"

"Uh-huh."

More pieces of the puzzle that is Reece Souza start to fall into place. Some, but not all. Silvy's is busy, if not the busiest flower shop in Fox Hollow. Why isn't their mother able to afford extras?

Just how big was that bet Reece's father took on and lost?

"Sorry. Reece probably doesn't want me telling you about our family. He's...private."

On the contrary, I think Reece did want Breckyn to tell me what he can't. What I wouldn't let him.

"If he's as great as you say, then I'm sure he won't mind," I reassure her while also mentally making a note to keep her in my office as much as possible today, so she can't reveal Reece's personal business to anybody else. "Why don't we get started with you telling me what your interest in real estate is?"

"Rehabilitation."

"Like flipping houses?"

Breckyn's eyes sparkle like polished onyx as she shakes her head. "Fox Hollow."

Nineteen

Reece

"**S**HE'S, LIKE, LITERALLY GOR-GEOUS."

"Who?"

Breckyn's knowing scoff echoes throughout my car. "Your boss, Lenox."

"Mm."

"You didn't notice?"

"I noticed she has a husband."

"That's right, the CEO... He seems mean."

"Why? What'd Lenox tell you?"

"Nothing. I just overheard their phone conversation."

"Breck."

"I wasn't trying to eavesdrop, okay? It was hard not to when his voice was booming."

Was he yelling at Lex?

Not for the first time, I find myself wishing I'd inflicted more injuries on Kordin Debrosse—like ripping out his goddamn vocal cords.

"What was he saying?"

"I can't remember all of it. He talked *a lot*. It was actually kinda cringe. He would go on and on saying really nice stuff to her, but then he'd follow it up with an order."

"What kind of orders? For work?"

She thinks to herself for a second. "For everything. When I was listening to him talk, I just kept thinking of this one thing Charlie told me about. She said cult leaders will shower new members with attention and affection as a way to make them easier to manipulate. Technically, it's abuse, but it's… It's disguised as love."

I frown.

"So, anyway, just make sure you never ask for anything after you give her flowers."

I did do that. But not to manipulate Lex. Is that how she took it? Fuck.

I notice out of my periphery Breck turn my way.

Wait. How'd she know about the flowers?

"What are you talking about?" I ask way too fucking late.

"Her office smelled exactly like the white Heather you just so happened to ask Mom for yesterday."

I take my eyes off the road to shoot her a flat look.

All innocence, she says, "She's nice."

Now I'm the one scoffing.

"What? She was nice to me."

"Yeah, well, you're…not a man." Lex hates men. Every one of us. Unfortunately.

Come to think of it, the only person I've seen Lex be nice to, that wasn't an act, was Cat. They had a genuine friendship, or at least an understanding of one another.

My sister chuckles softly. "She reminds me of you."

"How?"

"Have you ever watched a swan swimming?"

"Probably. Why?"

"On the surface, the swan appears calm and confident, but under the surface, it's a constant struggle to stay afloat. Just like you two. You both keep what you're really going through out of view from others."

I tried opening up to Lex and she spit in my fucking face. I knew she wouldn't in Breck's though, that's why I brought my sister in for her shadowing project today.

I don't respond to Breck and she doesn't press me for the rest of the ride.

At the apartment, we eat dinner with Mom and Charlie, and not once does she bring up Lex, but then when I'm about to head out, my mom hands me an Orchid. The petals and sepals are white, while the labellum, column, and anther cap are all purple. It's easy to remember what Orchids symbolize—femininity—because they look like pussies.

"What's this?" I ask her. I hadn't thought of another flower to give Lex yet. I was just going to swing by Silvy's on my way to work tomorrow and snag whichever one caught my eye first.

"For her beauty."

"Breckyn," I drawl, making her and her twin laugh. So she told both Charlie and my mom.

Fucking females. They stick together tighter than sardines in a can.

Closing a cupboard, Breckyn tosses me a bag that I manage to catch one-handed. "Give her these, too."

I eye the assortment of chocolates. "Why?"

"Because the people that get the most looks... What is it again, Charlie?"

Scowl in place, I glance back up at my sisters.

After a yawn, Charlie recites, "The people that get looked at the most are usually the ones that don't have anyone to look out for them," most likely from her research for a career in counseling.

I've tried to look out for Lex, even without understanding why. She's been nothing but a raging fucking bitch ever since we met face to face. From hitting and choking me that first night to constantly berating and firing me now, she's given me every reason to stop looking out for her. Yet, I can't—absolutely motherfucking cannot—make myself.

"But why the chocolates?"

"Oh. She's going to start her period soon."

"How do you know that?"

"She changed from sweating to shivering several times throughout the day."

Snuggling deeper into her two-sizes-too-big sweater, Charlie mumbles, "Dead giveaway."

My mom nods and says, "White witch," in reference to women's cycles mirroring the moon cycle. I can't remember what all of them are but white witches must bleed on the new moon because the new moon's coming up in a couple days.

"She always does that," I say.

Breck shrugs. "Maybe she's pregnant."

"What do you know about being pregnant?" I growl, earning identical eye rolls from both twins before Charlie buries her nose in her phone, her blinks slower than normal. I don't know what all she's got going on lately, but whatever it is, she's exhausted. And it's not just from this past weekend having Halloween and homecoming. The last couple times I've been here, she's either just waking up or dozing off.

It better not be a boy. Motherfucker'll be getting a Chaste Tree down the throat. I got just the fucking one.

"Does that happen during pregnancy, too? Or just from PMS?" Breckyn questions our mom.

With a thoughtful expression, Mom answers, "Everyone's different," before looking at me directly to ask, "Could she be pregnant?"

Could Lex be pregnant? I guess technically she *could*. But it'd be too early to be showing symptoms. I think.

I don't fucking know. Like my mom said, everybody's different. I do know Lex's body temperature's been unstable since before we had sex.

Maybe she was already pregnant.

The thought of knocking up Lex myself didn't faze me at the time—and truthfully, still doesn't—but the idea she could be carrying Kordin's kid…

If she was though, why'd she bring up becoming pregnant right after I nutted in her like the possibility was a genuine concern?

Turning to leave, I give a blanket goodbye to the room, ending the conversation. I'm not talking to them about Lex. I'm not talking to anyone about Lex. Even if I could, I don't know what to fucking say. She's…

And I'm…

Fuck.

My sisters follow me out.

Without breaking stride, I lift the hand with the chocolates by my head, telling Breckyn, "Thanks."

"Thank *you*."

Charlie adds, "For everything."

This finally stops me and I pivot to see both of them standing at the threshold, staring at me with open adoration. I tuck the image away. It'll serve as the fuel for the absolute inferno I'll need to make to keep Cyrus's hands from reaching them.

"Get inside and lock the door."

"Love you, too," they say in unison, then close the door. I wait until I hear the deadbolt click into place to turn back around, a small grin tugging at my lips.

I love them. They know I do. The deepest love isn't spoken, it's shown. Mouths lie, but actions reveal the truth.

Darkness greets me as I close the door to my loft, but I don't bother turning on any lights. I can walk this apartment blindfolded and not run into a single thing. It's furnished to my liking; I just try to practice walking with limited visibility as much as I can, so when I have to navigate other unfamiliar places at night, it's like second nature.

Dropping the shopping bag on the table by the door, I cross to the wall of eight-foot windows on the opposite side. Not one of them is covered, allowing the view to be seen from anywhere inside.

Arms crossed at my chest, I stare out at the dark river below, taking a long full inhale while listening to the powerful rush of water. With twilight just sinking away for the night, the waterfalls are hard to see but thankfully still easy to hear, even with the doors and windows closed.

I hate city life. I hate even being close to city life. If I could, I'd live where there were no people around. Just trees and water and wildlife. I found this nineteenth-century cotton factory turned loft-style apartment complex and knew it was as close as I'd get in Fox Hollow.

Sitting high above a river that runs into the Hudson, the building overlooks a large waterfall.

In addition to the refinished wood floors being original, as well as the high ceilings, they kept a lot of the pipes, vents, and cast-iron support columns exposed to give the updated sleek design an industrial feel.

This isn't my forever home, but it is my home. I don't bring anybody here, not even hookups.

Something unusual catches my eye in the glass, and I realize it's not on the outside but a reflection of what's inside—a person.

Slowly, I lower one arm, about to twist and reach for my gun at the same time, when I hear, "What's with the punching bag?"

I grit my fucking teeth so hard I hear a crack.

I could've shot her. I would've.

Spinning around, I face Lex. She's sitting in my oversized accent chair with her legs crossed and her arms by her sides like it's her throne. The seat's not quite a loveseat but almost. If I were to join her on it, part of my body would be on hers. More than part.

I'm tempted to try it right now to find out exactly how much.

Instead, I walk to the kitchen.

"I like it," I tell her as I get myself a glass of water. "Helps clear my head after a long day at the office." Her office specifically.

"Why in the living room?"

"Why not?" I take in the open space. "There's enough room and it's just me living here."

"Mm," she says to herself, then stands.

My throat working quietly to drain half my glass, I track her every step across the living room over to the window I was just at.

"How'd you know where I live?" I gave the firm a virtual address.

Gazing outside, she says, "I came across it somewhere."

"Where, Lex?"

"Your driver's license."

My wallet. She fucking ransacked that thing for the short time she had it in her possession.

She puts her back to the window, telling me, "It's quicker and more cost effective than following someone after work."

Shit. She caught me.

"Aren't you going to ask me how I got in here?"

I shake my head. "I know who you are."

"Do you?"

"Daughter of Cyrus Andeno. Wife of Kordin Debrosse. One way or another, doors open for you." Either using skill or money, Lex can probably get in anywhere she wants.

After a slow nod, she abandons her spot at the window for the other side of the room.

My arms tingle, wanting to reach out and… I don't know. Tell her not to go. Not yet.

But she says, "Let's go."

"Where?"

She doesn't answer, only opens the door. The light darts inside in an angry slash, illuminating Lex's slender form. No surprise, she's head to toe in black, except instead of her usual dressy attire, she's wearing skintight pants tucked into heavy boots and a long-sleeve shirt that has a cowl-neck hood bunched around her throat. Hair the color of a Magnolia Brittany doesn't offset the dangerous-looking outfit one bit, only enhances it, making her look nothing like the hollow I work for and everything like a deadly assassin.

"Grab what you need."

"For?"

Before disappearing into the hall, she says quietly, "A job."

What the fuck? A job? *With* Lex?

Kit in hand, I jog out after her. Outside, we part ways as I head for my car.

"We're taking this," she says, pointing at a maroon Mustang crossover.

"Is it yours?" I've only seen her Range Rover.

On God, she gives me a lip snarl as she says, "It's red."

We have that in common. I like my cars and clothes black, too.

"Where are the plates?" I ask as we approach, the taillights flashing from the doors being unlocked.

"Inside."

"If a cop sees it without plates—"

Lex taps the back window on her way to the driver's side. Taped on the inside is a paper that looks like what dealerships send new owners home with until the real license plates arrive. *Smart.*

Getting in, I immediately notice a booster seat in the backseat and freeze.

"You stole some soccer mom's car, with the fucking child seat still in it?"

"That's presumptuous," she mutters while starting it up.

"This car isn't stolen?"

"It is, but how do you know the kid plays soccer?"

Without waiting for a response, she proceeds to back out.

"Lex."

Eyes on the road, she ignores me.

"Lex?"

Her voice is barely above a whisper when she says, "I'm not the sweet one here."

I bark out a harsh laugh. No shit.

The ride is smooth and quiet until eventually Lex pulls off into a field. Fifteen minutes of off-roading later, a huge warehouse comes into view. Lex parks a good distance away, leaving only the top of the roof visible.

The Mustang goes dark and we sit in silence for a full minute.

Lex is the first to break it, saying, "Case it."

I put on my gloves and grasp the handle.

"Are you gonna wait?"

"I've waited this long."

"How long were you at my place?"

"Long enough to almost fall asleep."

My cock thickens at the idea of finding Lex sleeping in my apartment, Lex *staying* in my apartment.

"If you ignore the punching bag in the middle of the living room, it's actually cozy in there. It shouldn't be as comfortable as it is."

I smirk. "I know."

"Fifteen-foot ceilings?"

"Seventeen."

"You bought it?"

"Renting."

Her whole body shudders. "You're just throwing money away."

"I don't want to live there long term."

"Where do you want to live long term?"

I shake my head. "You get mad when I share things about myself."

"No, I don't."

"Bullsh—"

"I get mad that I *want* you to share things about yourself."

My eyes on hers, another heavy moment passes before I tell her, "In the woods. Away from everybody."

She lets out a long sigh, but doesn't reply.

"I should've made you wait longer." I drag my gaze down her body. "Could've had some fun waking you up."

"I thought you said you wouldn't touch me while I'm asleep."

Pulling my balaclava down over my head, I say through the material, "That was before I knew what you felt like." Then, I get out to go scout the grounds.

At first glance, it's just an abandoned warehouse with a dozen storage containers sitting forgotten in its barren yard, but in reality, the building itself has a sophisticated security system, and the containers are all locked up tight.

"What the fuck's in there?" I ask Lex as soon as I make it back to the small SUV.

She's leaning against the driver's door, pulling her hood up over her hair and lower half of her face, taking special care to hide all the stark-white strands. She's also wearing her own gloves now and some kind of bag around her waist that she didn't have before.

Pushing away from the Mustang, she says, "Let's go find out."

A pit in the bottom of my stomach forming, I turn to follow her.

She's not telling me something. Technically, she hasn't told me any-thing. Even Cyrus gives me more information to go off of than this when he sends me on a job.

Lex leads me to the side of the warehouse closest to us, directly over to a ventilation shaft. She takes a screwdriver out of her waist bag and uses it to remove every screw, tucking each one safely into her bag, then together, we ease the vent away from its notch in the wall. Thankfully, no alarm sounds.

"After you," she says, motioning to the black tunnel.

My head's already shaking. "After *you*."

"I have to take care of this," she says, still holding the vent. "We can't leave it lying on the ground."

"You go in first or I'm not going in at all."

"You think I'm going to lock you in there?"

I don't answer her. I shouldn't really have to.

She shoves the vent into my chest, then ducks inside, bending down onto her hands and knees.

I take a moment to admire the view before following her in, sit-ting right at the opening with my legs half scrunched up the curved wall while I get the panel back in place.

Lex reaches over me to help, her sweet, frozen Jasmine scent clos-ing in on me more than the tight space.

We get it situated just enough that it doesn't move, then Lex low-ers her face to mine. Her covered mouth against my covered ear, she whispers, "Stay close and don't talk," making my dick instantly hard.

We crawl through the tunnel agonizingly slow. I prefer to take my time during jobs, so the speed itself isn't what's bothering me, it's Lex's ass in front of my face the entire time, because as tempting as it is to press my face to her pussy at this angle, I can't. Each time my masked jaw brushes her pants, I have to stifle a groan. By the time we reach the end, my mouth is watering and that pit in my stomach has become an insatiable hunger. Judging by the distinct smell of Lex's desire, I'm not the only one suffering.

Lex jimmies another vent out of our way, allowing us to climb out between two industrial-sized washing machines and into a large space that must've been a laundry room once upon a time.

Taking my hand, she pulls me through a couple more rooms, neither of us making any unnecessary movements or sounds.

If she knew this place so well, why'd she have me case it?

My gaze touches on everything around us. While some of the interior hasn't been changed from whenever this building was a functioning factory, most of it's been renovated—sloppily—into semi-livable accommodations. Meaning someone fucking lives here. I don't know who the fuck would want to. If it weren't for the pricey security system, I'd think squatters. It's dingy, dark, and freezing. Basically it's the exact opposite of my loft. There is zero comfort here.

Old warehouses are refurbished all the time around Fox Hollow, but usually for apartments—like mine and my mom's. From all I'm seeing, this warehouse isn't housing several units, just one, and probably not even legally.

In some kind of office, we come to a stop in front of a tall gun safe, and Lex nods, silently telling me to open it.

One look at it and I pocket my kit. It's a combination lock, one of the worst fucking locks ever made. With my ear against the cool metal, I turn the dial until I hear the first click. As I'm listening for the second, I notice a *tick, tick, tick* noise and stop, angling my head away from the safe. *What the fuck is that?*

Next to me, Lex's leg is jiggling.

Gripping her ankle, I press a kiss to her inner thigh. All movement halts, so I pull back to look up at her. I give the other thigh a kiss, then return to the safe. Lex remains quiet as I work, but I do feel her hand on my back, her finger tracing my shoulder blade. I don't know if it's absentmindedly or if she's doing it to keep herself calm, but I like it and hope she never stops.

A motherfucking shoulder blade. Jesus Christ, I'm fucked.

Once I get all the numbers in, I crank the handle, making the safe pop open. Lex and I both stand back to survey its contents. It's cash. Stacks and stacks of cash. More cash than I've ever seen at once.

But...whose cash is it?

I look at Lex, her finger already up to her mouth.

Stepping forward, she runs a gloved hand over the fronts of the stacks, hesitating by a folder tucked against the side of the safe before sliding it out. Her body sways to one side, blocking my view, and I think she's going to sway right back, but she doesn't. When I try to look over her shoulder, the folder's closed.

Somewhere in the warehouse a motor kicks on. It's hard to tell if the steady whirring is a heater or something else, but Lex springs into action, quickly returning the folder and shutting the safe door.

We're not taking anything?

Lifting the handle, she spins the dial until the arrow is pointing at the same number it was before I touched it.

We retrace our steps, moving much faster through the shaft, but at the end of it, Lex grabs me, making me freeze. Through the slats, I see a Brabus 900 XLP pickup truck waiting at one of the dock's opening doors.

This time when my eyes fly to Lex, she ignores me completely. Is she fucking for real right now?

As soon as the half-mill supercar disappears inside the warehouse, we get out, replace the vent, then break into full-on sprints back to the Mustang.

The second we're seated, my mask's ripped off, and I'm snarling, "What the fuck was that?"

Lex, removing her face covering at a normal, unhurried pace, doesn't answer.

She doesn't fucking answer.

"What's Cyrus doing here?" There's no possible way that Brabus could be anyone else's. There's a *very* limited supply of the luxury pickup circulating the planet and only one in Fox Hollow.

She shrugs her narrow shoulders, and says, "We didn't trip anything, so I don't know why he's home early."

"Home? Are you fucking crazy?"

Her face nearly exposed again, she shoots me a sideways glare.

"That's not Cyrus's home. I've seen where he lives. I've been in it. It's a house."

"Do you really think Cyrus would let just anybody know where he sleeps? The house you're talking about is where he fucks, where he parties, where he lets others fuck and party. It's where he makes everybody else *think* he lives, but it is not where he actually sleeps." She points at the warehouse. "*That* is where he sleeps. That is where he keeps anything of real value to him."

I want to rage at her but settle on running a hand through my sweaty hair instead as I grind out, "Why'd we just break into it?"

"I thought it was obvious. To rob him."

Now I do yell. "What?"

"To *rob*—"

"I fucking heard what you said, Lex. I'm trying to figure out why the fuck you said it. Rob him? That's a suicide mission."

"It's only suicide if you get caught, so next time when you—"

"I'm not robbing Cyrus motherfucking Andeno."

"Yes, you are. You're going to come back another time, alone, and you're going to do *exactly* what we just did, then you're going to take enough cash out of that safe to get you and your sisters and your mom out of here."

"What are you talking about?"

"I'm talking about Silvy's. Your mom's floral shop that should be bringing in good money but isn't. After Breckyn left, I looked up who owns the building."

Then she knows it's Cyrus.

"That was the bet your dad lost, huh?"

My elbow on the door, I prop my head in my hand, then jerk out a nod. What the fuck did I get myself into?

"And he keeps you at his beck and call by threatening to put your sisters to work at The Playground?"

Lex pauses, waiting for me to give her some sort of response but I'm still reeling. I just broke into Cyrus Andeno's "house," with his daughter's help. She used to live with him? Here? No wonder she thinks my place is comfortable, she grew up in a literal fucking warehouse.

"Reece, you wanted me to figure it out—"

"Whose fault is that? Huh, Lex? Maybe if you weren't so fucking cold, you would've let me finish telling you myself, instead of firing my ass and kicking me out of your fucking life!" Spit flies out of my mouth at the last part because that's what hurt the most. That's what hurts the most. Even if… No, even *when* I stop working at the Debrosse Group, I still want to be able to see Lex, but she tried taking that away from me.

Just like she's trying right now.

"I'm…"

We stare at each other. Is she going to apologize?

Lex blinks first before tearing her gaze away.

Of course not. I'm such a fucking dumbass for thinking she might.

"That folder?"

"The one you hid from me?"

"It's full of deeds. Cyrus probably owns half of Fox Hollow."

I make a sound in my throat. "At least."

"Don't you fucking get it, Reece? The same way he's never going to give that business up, he's never going to stop holding your sisters over your head. The only way to get out from under his thumb is to get out of Fox Hollow."

"Cyrus doesn't own you anymore and you're still here."

"He had to let me go. He's a businessman first and foremost, and I paid my debt. I was only one person. You're not. He wants your entire family and all the profit he's currently making, and stands to make, off them. You guys need to leave. All of you. Soon. Now."

I swallow hard, the sound deafening to my own ears.

"Would you come with?"

Her head whips my way. "What?"

"If I'm leaving, you should, too."

"Don't be an idi—"

"I'm dead fucking serious. We can leave Fox Hollow, and everyone in it, behind."

She doesn't answer right away as she studies something outside. There's a dense gray fog weighing down the sky, an indication snow is on its way. If not tonight, soon. Very soon. We're close enough to New York City and the Atlantic that we don't get hit with as much snow as the rest of the state, but we do get some.

"Your sister thinks Fox Hollow can be saved. Flipped. Turned into something good."

"My sister's naïve."

"Thanks to you. You've done a good job keeping her that way. Naiveté is a luxury I didn't have growing up."

"Let me take you away from it. All of it, even Kordin."

"Isn't it enough to get your mom and sisters out?"

My answer leaves my lips before I finish thinking it. "No."

A few weeks ago it would've been enough. It would've been everything.

But now it's not.

Lex breaks our connection to start the car, then we leave the same way we came in—silent.

Twenty

Lex

"CAN YOU AT LEAST COME UP?" REECE ASKS WHEN WE reach his apartment building like this was some sort of date gone wrong and he's hoping to talk things out, smooth everything over. *Rookie.*

I pull alongside his black Alfa Romeo. "I need you to follow me."

"For what?"

"To dump this," I say impatiently.

Without another word, Reece gets out.

Watching him stalk over to his car, I release my grip on the steering wheel, my hands shaking uncontrollably. I can't fucking stand to be in this Mustang another minute, but I have to get rid of it completely so it can't be traced back to me in any way. Kordin has to be the one to get the call it's missing, not the cops, so that he can concentrate on purchasing a replacement. For that, he'll need his laptop.

At least that's the hope.

His scent is in here. His and his knockoff girlfriend's and their...

I glance in the rearview mirror at the booster seat.

I was under the impression Kordin's affairs started two years ago, but this kid is school age. I never saw the child, only the mom, so while I don't know that Kordin's the father, I don't know that he's not either.

My chest feels like it's being held in a giant's fist, the viselike grip crushing my rib cage until I'm wheezing.

There's so much I don't know about the man I'm married to. There's too much I don't know about him.

Reece follows me forty minutes north of town, the temperature outside dropping the further we go. It hasn't snowed in Fox Hollow yet but several surrounding areas have already gotten a couple inches, so it's only a matter of time.

Despite the landscape having a thin white dusting, the roads are clear, making the drive easy.

By the time I park at the top of a powder-coated ravine, my hands are still jittery but my breathing's once again under control.

I gather everything I need before emptying a bottle of sap all over the interior. Just as I'm climbing out, I shift it into neutral.

"Did you get the VIN number?"

I lift it to show Reece, careful to keep the numbers facing me in case he has a photographic memory and wants to look it up later.

"Sometimes there's another—"

"I thought you said you knew me, rook?" I hold up the other one. "Do you have a lighter?"

He scowls. "No."

"What kind of criminal doesn't carry a lighter?"

"One that doesn't smoke."

I roll my eyes at him but pull a box of matches from my hip pack.

Scoffing, he says, "You don't smoke either."

"I could," I counter before striking a single match and throwing it in through the open driver's door. I shut it, then meet Reece by the Mustang's rear end, the growing orange light from inside already spreading up his sharp jawline.

Wordlessly, Reece and I push the Mustang over the edge, where it rolls down the frozen-over hillside, picking up speed in its descent. We watch as it crashes into the bottom, the entire interior consumed by flames.

"You don't smoke," Reece says quietly. "Lighters are to destroy yourself, matches are to destroy everybody else."

The Mustang explodes into a thunderous blaze of screeching metal and sizzling leather. Everything around it brightens from the fire, its glowing reflection gyrating on the surrounding vegetation, making it look like a sea of restless energy.

Pulling myself away from the hypnotic scene, I turn my gaze on Reece. "I've never used matches to kill somebody."

"Just a bike chain?" Amongst the flames mirrored in his dark eyes, there's also humor.

He's not scared of me. Or repulsed by me.

Because he doesn't actually know me.

If he did, he would've never asked me to leave Fox Hollow with him.

"We got one more stop," I say before I can change my mind.

Once we're through the cemetery's wrought-iron gate, I tell him where to park. Out in the open air, I weave us between headstones ranging from small to large and simple to ornate. My steps slow a few away from the one I'm here for. It's both simple and small, yet not simple or small enough. I wish it was a nondescript pebble I could throw into the ocean, so I could be free of him once and for all.

There aren't any lights this far in, and the sky is nothing but rolling white clouds like a fleet of pirate ships, sails fully billowed on the horizon, yet the waning crescent moon—a mere sliver above us—still manages to battle its way through the opaque coverage just enough to cast a hazy spotlight on his name and his name alone.

I stop directly on top of his grave and ask Reece, "Can you give me some privacy?"

He throws me a strange look, but faces the other way.

I lower my leggings and underwear to my thighs, then squat with my feet as far apart as they'll go. As soon as my stream hits the frigid, unforgiving earth, Reece spins right back around, staring down at me.

"Privacy, please."

"Snow…" Thrusting a hand out in my direction, his eyes lift to the churning sky. "What are you doing?"

I raise my eyes skyward, too. "Relieving myself."

"Why didn't you tell me you had to go? I would've pulled off somewhere."

"I'd rather piss on him." I finish and stand, quickly covering myself before my ass gets frostbite. Thankfully Reece had an extra coat in his car that he insisted I wear, otherwise I'd be half frozen by now.

Reece drops his gaze to me again. "Him?"

"You wanted to know about the man I killed when I was sixteen." I wave at the headstone.

"Aleksander Obuchowski," Reece reads aloud. "Who was he?"

"My father."

"You killed your… But I thought you said…"

"I never said Cyrus was my father. I said my name was Lexi Andeno, and it was. For a time."

"He was your stepfather?"

"Temporary legal guardian. When I went to live with him at sixteen, he had my last name changed so everybody would know I was off-limits." I cock my head. "Outside of The Playground anyway."

Reece studies my father's engraved name, a crease forming between his black eyebrows. "Tell me what he did to you or I'll dig him up and get it out of him myself."

I'm tempted to stay quiet just to watch him try. But then I'd have to see my dad—whatever's left of him.

"I'm supposed to believe you keep a shovel with you when you don't even carry a lighter?"

"You know what… Why don't you give me a list of everything we might need before we leave the house next time? That way I'll be better prepared for whatever you chose to do."

He says it like we're the married couple and this is a regular occurrence, like it could be—us leaving the same house together—and for a brief second, I let myself imagine what that'd look like. With Reece's apartment still fresh in my memory, it's easy to imagine our house. Sitting among his things, surrounded by his zesty, spicy scent, it was the closest I've ever felt to being home.

While my house is cold and insipid and untouched, his place is warm and cozy and lived in. I miss it already and I was barely in it.

We're the hard part to wrap my head around because Reece and I... A marriage between us wouldn't be anything like mine and Kordin's. It'd be full. Of noise. Of passion. And I don't know if I could turn a cheek to him cheating on me.

Would he cheat on me?

"Have you ever cheated on anyone?"

"What does cheating have to do with this?"

"Everything." This starts with a cheater. And ends with a cheater.

I am my mother's daughter.

Nodding, he tilts his head up. Tiny snowflakes flutter down around us, sparkling on their lazy descent, some of them sticking to Reece's raven hair and eyelashes before melting completely.

I tug his coat tighter to my body.

"I haven't been with anybody seriously since I got mixed up with Cyrus. This life, it's..." He blows out a breath and drops his obsidian eyes to mine. "No, I've never cheated on anyone."

I tear my gaze away. The life he resents so thoroughly, it's mine. It's the only life I've ever known and will ever know. Reece can get out. Him and his family, they can go live in the woods, away from everybody, away from Cyrus, away from me.

And hopefully, after hearing what I'm about to tell him, he will.

This is why I brought him here. Not to bond or bring him further into my life, but to shove him out of it. To show him exactly what Fox Hollow does to families. Exactly what it did to mine.

I lean against my father's headstone, the chill of the marble instantly slicing through my thin leggings like a finely sharpened sword.

"The story goes like this... One day, while stopping by to talk to my father about getting a new tattoo, Cyrus walked in on him having a psychotic break. He was trying to kill my mom when Cyrus intervened. My father shot at Cyrus, hitting him in his foot, then turned the gun on himself and committed suicide."

That crease between Reece's eyebrows deepens. "The story?"

"That's what the cops were told. That's what my mom was told. That's what everybody was told."

"Cyrus saved your mom?"

"I…" My throat clogs and I have to look away from him, scanning the copse of evergreens just outside the fence line. The only two people who know what actually happened are me and Cyrus. This will be my first time saying it to someone else. I've lived with the guilt, the fucking shame, for a decade, keeping it all locked up tight inside me so nobody would know the truth. Now that I'm about to tell Reece, the words are stuck. They're literally fucking stuck in my throat.

"Lex."

Bringing my attention back to Reece, I watch him take a step toward me, his arms out like he wants to wrap me up in them.

But I can't let him. If I do, I don't know if I'll be able to pull myself back out of them.

So, I put a hand up, stopping him in his tracks. "Don't. Just… Just wait."

He shoves his hands in his pockets, the perfect impression of patience even though we both know he has none.

"My father was a tattoo artist. He did tattoos for everyone, even Cyrus and his employees. He got fired from every shop that was gullible enough to hire him because he would accept anything as payment—rims, shoes, favors, tickets to basketball games, you name it, my dad would give a tattoo for it. He *rarely* had enough money to cover even the bare necessities." I shake my head, remembering the truly asinine things he'd accept, like the used kayak he left sitting outside because it was too big to store in our house. Of course, it was stolen soon after, probably from the same guy who gave it to him. "Eventually he started working right out of our house, days, nights, holidays, it didn't matter, we always had people over, so my mom and I were familiar with his clients. Some of them were like family. One of them more than the rest."

"Cyrus?"

"My mom…" My voice catches again, making me frown at myself. At my fucking weakness. She's the only person that makes me weak because she's the only person I let myself love.

"My mom had to pick up the slack. A lot. I don't know what came first or when exactly either started, but she wound up working at The Playground *and* having an affair with Cyrus, all behind my dad's back."

"In Lost and Found only?"

I take in the man in front of me, wondering how he knows so little about a world he hates so much. Lost and Found wasn't always what it is today. Cyrus made it up after I started working there as a way to "train me" for it himself. He wanted a reason to fuck me, so he invented one. The fact that it ultimately earned him more money was just a bonus.

But that's my business and not part of this story. His compassion is useless, it's his apprehension I'm after.

"Cheating is cheating, rookie. It doesn't matter where it happens."

"Fuck, I know, it's just… She willingly fucked Cyrus? Off the clock?"

"He was generous to us. Both of us. She fell for him, while also loving my dad."

Back then it was her heart that ruled her, not her fear.

"Did your dad find out?"

"That's why he's six feet under." I point at the ground below my feet, and Reece follows my finger.

With his focus off me, I force the words out before my throat stops working a third time.

"The truth is this… One day my dad was tattooing a Playground girl and she let it slip that his wife was not only working for Cyrus, but also sleeping with him."

"Shit," Reece mutters, his attention snapping up to me again.

"After beating my mom and raping her, he held her down and tattooed dziwka, whore in Polish, on her cheek." I tap under my right eye with a numb fingertip. "Just off the school bus, I walked in on him still pinning her to the living room floor where she was naked, bleeding, and had a face sporting almost every fucking color including black from the fresh ink as he was just finishing up."

"You saved her. You shot him."

I nod, then clench my eyes closed, visualizing the scene in vivid clarity. I was aiming for my dad's head, but I'd never shot anyone before. It was a clusterfuck, a daunting fucking clusterfuck. I was scrambling, they were scrambling. I was screaming, my dad was cursing. I was crying, my mom was…howling. She was *howling* in pain, in misery, in utter fucking humiliation and devastation. I tried to save her. I tried my fucking best.

"Goddamn. You were only sixteen."

I open my eyes, somehow finding Reece's locked on mine through a veil of tears as he resumes his approach, this time much slower, like I'm a wild animal he's afraid of.

As he should be.

"You did what you had to. You saved your mom. I would've done the same thing."

He's misreading my silence, my emotion.

I shake my head, but he keeps going, drawing nearer.

"I would've done the same thing for *less*. My dad never laid a hand on my mom, but if he ever even fucking flinched at her or my sisters, I wouldn't have hesitated to put a bullet in his head."

A foot away from me now, I grab his chin. "Reece, the only thing I regret about shooting my father is not having better aim." I release him just as quickly. "I fired off more than one shot. I hit my mom, too."

"She's…"

"She's alive. The bullet that clipped her skull split, thankfully missing the most vital parts."

Her memory's missing her darkest deeds as well as my father's, so she has no recollection of anything regarding The Playground, Cyrus, or her husband abusing the literal piss out of her when he discovered her involvement with both.

She knows our life before wasn't easy or glamorous, but she doesn't know the full extent of how bad everything got. How bad she got, my dad got, or how bad I got.

And I protect the small bit of peace she does have these days by sparing her the truth. She still loves my dad, even thinking he tried to kill her during his breakdown, and she'll never let us leave this town. She refuses to visit his grave, but makes me because I carry his blood.

If I could bleed myself dry of him without killing myself, I would.

When I was younger and didn't see a way out for either of us, I tried anyway. I tried *because* I thought it'd kill me. Hoped it would.

It never did and it never severed the last tie to my father either. All it did was leave me scarred and give Cyrus a reason to keep a closer eye on me.

"So what about Cyrus? Where does he come in?"

"The bullet I caught my dad with was fatal, killed him instantly, but… My mom had a pulse. She was unresponsive but alive. I knew Cyrus had money and connections, so I begged him to help." If I'd confessed to shooting my parents, I would've been locked up with no way to pay for the life-saving surgeries my mom suddenly required—the life-saving surgeries I caused her to suddenly require. We had nothing to help cover the cost, no health insurance, no life insurance, no savings, no friends or family to pitch in, no caring community to start a fundraiser. We had fucking nothing. It was all on me to find a way to keep her alive. So I did. "He made me promise to go live with him and do anything he asked, then he shot himself in the foot to make the story he came up with more believable before the police showed up."

"I don't understand. You called Cyrus?"

"I didn't have to. He was already there."

"There? Cyrus was fucking there?"

"Him randomly stopping by to talk tattoos was the only part of the story that was true. According to him."

"You don't think he was?"

"At the time, I didn't know any better, couldn't have even fathomed anything other than what I was told. Now though… One of his employees spilled Playground business as well as Cyrus's personal business to someone that wasn't on his official payroll. The reason my dad had an unregistered gun in the house was because a few weeks prior, Cyrus paid him with it in exchange for a tattoo. You saw his safe. He didn't need to make trades back then any more than he does now. He was nearby when everything came to a head, close enough to walk through our front door while the gunshots were still echoing off the walls.

"When he was discharged from the hospital for his foot injury, he took me straight to his warehouse where I lived with him until I was eighteen. I got to know Cyrus better than anyone. He put the whole thing into motion, orchestrated every fucking part of it, then sat back and waited for it to unfold." I pause for a moment to consider his particular predicament. "You said your dad used a gun to commit suicide. Did you ever find out whose gun it was? Or even how he came to have it in his possession?"

His jaw flexes and he shakes his head.

"Cyrus doesn't buy loyalty because loyalty bought is loyalty that can be resold. So he creates scenarios that earn true loyalty, priceless loyalty—the kind only given freely, usually between family members. When he finds a family housing someone he's deemed useful to his business in some way, he picks them apart until they're unrecognizable, until they're either on the brink of ruin or just past it. Then, and only then, does he swoop in." I've seen him do it numerous times.

"So…what? You think Cyrus wanted your mom to himself? How? By just hoping your dad would commit suicide? He could've just as easily killed your mom, too. Cyrus was better off taking your dad out—" His face turns murderous. "He wanted you."

I nod once. Whether Cyrus wanted me by myself or me and my mom together, I'll probably never know for certain, but yes, his sights were set my way.

"Jesus Christ, Lex. Then why the *fuck* did you go to him for help?"

"I didn't know him as Cyrus Andeno, Fox Hollow's tyrant. I only knew how he treated me and my mom." I never could've guessed what my life would become being indebted to Cyrus. Every time he'd come over, he'd pull out two candy bars from his pocket, one for me and one for my mom. He'd tell us the cost was a smile, then wait patiently until we each gave him one before handing them over.

And now I can't stomach either.

"I'm not talking about then. I'm talking about now. A PI could've trailed Kordin and gotten you proof of his affairs. You should've never gone back to Cyrus for anything."

He turns to pace while I eye him carefully. This isn't going the way I expected. He's not reacting the way he's supposed to.

"Both times I went to Cyrus for help were for the same reason…"

Reece stops, his hair glistening with delicate dots of snow on the verge of disappearing.

"Her."

"Your mom?"

"The prenup I signed gives Kordin everything he started out with before we were married, my mom's house included," I say before telling Reece about Kordin gifting me the house, as well as my mom's reluctance to ever leave it and why.

"Kordin gave you a fucking house *and* a duffel bag full of cash the first week he knew you?"

Dozens of tiny pinpricks break out on the back of my skull as "Yes" leaves my lips. Whoever told Reece about Tommy didn't leave anything out of the story. *The* story, because that's not *my* story. Nobody knows my story but me. That bag was full of *my* money, earned by *my* hands before I ever even met Kordin. During my two years working at The Playground, I managed to save enough to get a place for me and my mom.

Unfortunately, Cyrus didn't just put me on lockdown on my eighteenth birthday, he also handed me a detailed list of every single expense he'd covered for my mom's care. If I wanted out, I'd have to reimburse him for the full amount. I didn't have enough for both, which he knew.

My mom didn't even know who Cyrus was anymore, but he wanted her to come live with us, at the warehouse, and become some kind of fucked-up family. I wasn't going to let him into her life, her bed, or her heart again, so I snapped and tried to kill him myself.

Then when Kordin appeared and presented me with an offer I couldn't refuse—a way for us both to get out—I didn't fucking blink to take it. I moved my mom into the Cape, handed Cyrus every dollar to my name, and married the hollow.

Eight years later, I'm no closer to being free but at least my mom is. And she'll continue to be as long as I'm able to make it so.

"If Kordin's got that kind of cash, why didn't you just get him to buy your mom another house? It's his mother-in-law."

I bristle at the insinuation that I can't afford to buy one by myself, but answer him anyway, explaining, "They don't have a relationship. They've never even met. My mom is chained to that house. It's her refuge as much as her prison. She won't leave it for anything other than mandatory medical appointments."

"Not even in the middle of the night? We could—"

"Don't insert yourself in this. If she won't let her own son-in-law see her, she definitely wouldn't let you."

He's quiet for a minute, his face made of stone. I'm not taking it back. It's true. Kordin is my husband and Reece is…not.

"The eye she's partially blind in…is it her right eye? The same eye with the tattoo under it?"

"Yes."

"She could wear an eye patch. There's gotta be ones that'd be able to cover her tattoo."

I shake my head, a pressure building behind my eyeballs. "Stop, stop, stop."

"No, you fucking stop."

"Stop what?"

"Stop acting like you've been brainwashed into thinking you're just as stuck as your mom. You're not stuck, Lex."

"Yes, I am. My mom's here because *he's* here." Pushing off the headstone, I jab a hand toward the ground. "Which means I'm here, too."

"Then understand that I am, too. Because my mom is."

"Why?"

"Same as yours, loyalty."

"To who? Your dad?" I hold back a laugh, a real fucking laugh because neither of our dads deserve an ounce of loyalty, not from us and certainly not from our mothers.

He gestures around us. "This place. Fox Hollow. The customers that've been going to her for years."

My momentary humor evaporates.

"It's misplaced loyalty."

"To me and you, yeah, but it's what keeps them going."

"Everybody needs a purpose," I sigh.

"We're more alike than you think. We both sacrifice our own lives for those we love most."

"Love is a parasite. All it does is take while giving nothing in return."

"You really believe that?"

"With every cell in my body."

"Did you ever love Kordin?"

I just stare at Reece, losing myself in his intense black pools focused solely on me. I like his full attention on me. I shouldn't but I do.

"Lex?" he finally prompts.

"No. Never."

"Are you going after his company?"

I shrug, my shoulders hidden deep within Reece's large coat. "I helped him grow it into the success it is today. I deserve at least half."

I don't want Kordin's company. I want the Senior Leadership Team on my side. If Kordin has another income he's hiding, it's because he's obtaining it illegally and can't report it. Until I have proof saying otherwise, I have no choice but to assume it's coming from Debrosse Investment Properties Group. And by using my name to spend that money, he's made me an accomplice, if not a conspirator. Whenever Kordin's transgressions come to light, I need the SLT to dismiss the notion that I could've been involved.

"How much time do you spend at the office?" Reece asks out of nowhere.

"You seem to know my schedule inside and out, why don't you tell me?"

"I meant during your workday. Do you ever get out? To check up on properties?"

"Hardly ever."

Reece's gaze plummets to my feet.

"Why?"

"You acted like it was a surprise Cyrus owns half of Fox Hollow. I thought you would've already known that."

I'll admit I was a bit taken aback to find that folder and see just how much real estate Cyrus has usurped. He's been very busy these past eight years.

"It's not like you can tell who owns a building by looking at it."

His eyes float up to mine again.

"You can tell a lot about a building by looking at it."

It feels like he's provoking me, but why?

"Like what?" I ask to push this along, see where he's taking it.

"Like what kind of state it's in. Whether it's had upgrades or not."

I nod despite my eyebrows knitting together. I'm not sure why Reece is wasting time pointing out something so incredibly well-known. Of course you can tell what state a building is in by looking at it—superficially speaking. Just because an exterior looks good doesn't mean the interior isn't downright rotten.

Or in my case, broken.

"You're going to need a lot of money to fight Kordin in court."

"I'm aware," I state dryly, wondering—again—why he's stating the obvious.

"Do you have it?"

I avoid answering with my own question. "Why?"

Reece and I remain locked in a stare-off, so much distrust swirling between us.

"Cyrus's—"

"I'm not stealing from Cyrus. I almost killed my mother, Reece. I won't risk doing it again by abandoning her." Whether voluntarily or not, I won't do it. I can't leave her alone, which means I *have* to get to the bottom of what Kordin's up to. If I end up in jail…

"Who said anything about abandoning your mom?"

I throw up my hands, the sleeves longer than my arms disrupting the light snowfall by making flakes scatter away from me.

"Oh my fucking God, have you been listening at all? If I stole from Cyrus, I wouldn't settle for a few stacks of cash, rook. I'd take *everything* from him and that'd start a war. A war I have no interest in waging singlehandedly, so I'd be forced to leave Fox Hollow…without my mom."

"So much for being an apex predator."

"Apex predators don't go around fighting unprovoked. It's how they remain at the top. They choose their battles."

"It wouldn't have to be singlehandedly."

I press my fingertips into my eyelids until there's more white spots behind them than were just in front of them, and say quietly, "You're not going up against Cyrus."

"You got a soft spot for him or something?" Reece says it mockingly but jealousy tinges his voice, giving him away.

"I don't have soft spots."

He chuffs out a laugh, causing me to drop my hands.

"That's not true."

"Only the one for my mother."

More sarcastic laughter. "That's not true. You wouldn't have brought me out here if it was."

"I brought you out here to show you what kind of person I am. The person *you* asked to leave Fox Hollow with. The person *you* wanted as the mother of your child."

"*Our* child," he practically growls on a step in my direction.

I take one, too, putting us only a few feet apart. Directly atop my father's resting place that I pray to God is anything but restful, I say the words I've thought thousands of times but have never actually spoken aloud. "I'm a murderer. I've murdered two people and almost killed another."

Reece's chest rumbles with a noise deeper than his eyes. "I don't care."

Time freezes as we hold each other's gazes, the silver flurries falling around us seeming to slow as well until it feels like we're in a snow globe, just the two of us in our own cocooned world of suspended sparkly serenity. If there was one moment in my life I could pinpoint as wanting to stay in, it'd be this—standing so peacefully over the man who caused me nothing but angst.

"You have terrible taste," I whisper to Reece, reluctant to completely break the silence just yet.

"You like my apartment," he whispers back with a playful scowl.

"I meant in women."

Those lips of his spread, showcasing his top row of straight white teeth. A solitary snowflake lands on his plump bottom lip, melting almost instantly, and I lick mine wishing it was his.

My eyes latch on to his, the lust I feel building in me mirrored there. Reece grabs two large handfuls of his jacket and pulls me to him. He keeps our fronts close without actually touching.

But I don't want him to hold back. I'm so tired of always holding back.

"Would you kiss me right now if I asked you to?"

"Kiss you? Lex, I'd fuck you right here, right now, out in the open, on top of your dad's grave."

That's not what I want. Fucking is…fucking. It's a basic need that doesn't require much effort or thought to accomplish. Men can fuck an empty flashlight. A couple short pumps later, they're fulfilled. Normally it's over as quick as it started.

Kissing is intimate. It's personal. It takes finesse and restraint, and usually, emotion. If done right, it can last all night.

Fucking is fast food, but kissing is fine dining, and my diet's been strictly fast food for so long. Maybe always, because nobody's ever kissed me like Reece.

"If I asked you to *only* kiss me, would you?"

"I'd do anything you asked me to, Snow."

"Except leave."

I don't pose it as a question yet he validates it anyway by nodding, and saying, "Except leave."

This isn't what was supposed to happen tonight. Not at all. Reece was supposed to be fleeing, now if possible, from Fox Hollow, from this life, from me. Instead, he's digging his heels in, refusing to escape what we both know is a dead end.

And I'm…dying to kiss him.

"You're exhausting," I remind him for at least the fiftieth time since our paths have crossed.

"Only to you."

"Your sisters might say otherwise."

At the mention of his sisters, the most magnetizing little half-grin transforms Reece's face.

I deny myself so much, so fucking much, and all it's gotten me is miserable and devoid. I want to be full for once.

Again. I want to be full again. The only time in my life I've felt full was outside The Pen, when I let myself indulge.

"Kiss me," leaves my lips so quiet, I'm not even sure Reece hears it.

But then he says, "Ask me," just as softly, confirming he did.

Why does he insist on making everything *so* difficult?

I twist away but his grip on my arms tightens, hauling me right back, then his lips clash with mine, wedging between the two as his tongue slips in. He licks and licks and licks, the motion like waves lapping at the shoreline until I bite his tongue, keeping him in place so I can suck on it. His lips close over mine, then we're kissing again, each of us lapping up the other.

Ten shards of ice nip at my cheeks and jaw as Reece gingerly grazes my face with his fingertips, tilting my head back for a better angle. I thread my wrists inside his, my own freezing digits clasping the sides of his throat. The vibrations from his moan tickle their tips, and I clutch harder until I'm digging my nails into his skin. His pulse races under my touch, fulfilling me in a way actual food never has.

Our kiss lasts for several days, erasing everything about our regular lives save for each other. Except when Reece pulls back, it's only been minutes and we're still very much ourselves. Disoriented at the realization, I sway on my feet, but he's quick to steady me.

"Tell me something honest," I beg. This moment is too raw to only have deceit between us.

"The first time I saw you, I thought you were soft, just like the Snow—"

"You mean cold like the snow?"

He rubs his kiss-swollen lips together.

"That night you were running hot."

My gaze flutters to his chin. Night sweats. I've been getting them more and more recently.

He dips his head to catch my eye again.

"Sheets all tangled around you, one milky thigh sticking out, begging to be kissed."

"Yet it wasn't."

"It wasn't." He pauses, his features darkening for a split second.

It's not hard to guess what he's thinking. Kordin could've kissed my thigh.

He didn't, sits restless on the tip of my tongue. Instead of unleashing the words of comfort and confusing him further, I lift my jaw, swallowing them down. I only wanted a kiss. I can't be what he said—only his. I can't promise not to let another man touch me… I'm married. Kordin can and will touch me whenever it suits him.

"But I did kiss something on you."

Sly fox. "What?"

"Your eye mask."

My eyes yearn to break from Reece's again, to hide. Despite being in remission, the prospect of developing Graves' ophthalmopathy weighs heavily on me. It all weighs heavily on me.

"Even with part of your face hidden, I could tell you were…"

"Beautiful?" That's what he said was the reason for the nickname originally, that I'm beautiful and cold. If anything, tonight should've given him a better understanding as to why I'm deliberately both.

"Beautiful… No, Snow, you were fucking breathtaking. I thought you should be cherished."

I shouldn't though. I've lied, stolen, killed, and now, cheated, and I've never felt bad about any of it, not once. Reece does, I can tell, not just by the soccer-mom comment earlier, but in general. He's a good person, better than I've ever been or could hope to be. He commits crimes, but ruefully.

Some people have a motto or an affirmation they repeat to themselves to get them through a hard time. My life is my hard time and the only thing I repeat to myself is po trupach do celu, a Polish term for when you'll do anything, regardless how awful, to achieve something. Reece's moral compass has been temporarily skewed for the sake of his family. I permanently smashed mine for my mom. There is *nothing* I won't do for her and I make zero apologies for it.

"Now you," Reece demands, and I have to think for a minute.

"When I first saw you at The Playground, I thought you were hard."

"That's because I was," he says, referencing an entirely different meaning for the word.

Clearly remembering our meeting in Lost and Found better than him, I shake my head, and throw back at him, "That night you were running soft."

"Fuck." He thrusts his bottom half against mine, his noticeable erection between us. "The feel of your pussy fixed that."

"Liar." He was grinding into me for an entire song only half-cocked and we both know it.

"You're right. It was your fight. I fucking loved it. Still do. The more you fight, the harder I get. I'd take your worst over anyone else's best."

I give Reece an obligatory eye roll, making him groan as his already stiff cock expands against my thigh.

Terrible, terrible taste in women.

Sticking to the same testimony he gave, I say slowly, "I thought you would be…a good hate fuck."

Laughter bursts out of him, making me bite my lips together to keep in my own.

"I thought you didn't joke."

"I don't," I tell him at the same time my phone's alarm goes off, pulsing through the pouch on my stomach. Four hours felt like four minutes.

Four hours *with him* felt like four minutes.

"Well?" he questions, more serious now. "Was I?"

"You were okay."

"Just okay?" He rears back, visibly wounded. "Where the fuck did you get just okay from? You came twice."

An internalized sigh ripples through my chest, inflating it to capacity. The male ego is more fragile than a bubble, I swear to God.

"Two orgasms is not the ceiling, rook. It's the bare minimum." It *should* be the bare minimum but Reece is the only man I've met willing to accept guidance, so I'm taking a few liberties with his tutelage—for his benefit and any woman he sleeps with from here on out.

My chest deflates, leaving it feeling achy.

"I need to get home," I say suddenly, accurately. I do need to go. It's been four hours since I left, and the officer patrolling my house could wake up any time now.

Every night after work, I've been taking Officer Manning a paczki—Polish doughnut—I get from a local bakery before sprinkling the top with a mixture of sleeping powder and powdered sugar, just enough to make him sleepy without actually causing him to fall asleep. Tonight, I handed him one with enough to knock him out while making an off-handed comment about him looking tired. When he wakes up from his impromptu nap, he'll worry at first before eventually recalling my earlier assessment. *Maybe he really was tired.* Then tomorrow, when I give him another one, but without any sleeping powder, I'll tell him he looks better, well-rested, and he'll forgive himself for sleeping on the job, concluding it must be true, he did need that nap.

Since some of the reviews I read on the product said the deep sleep only lasted four hours, I need to return before he gets the chance to come out of it and notice me driving back up my driveway.

"Now?"

"Yes, now."

I don't wait for Reece as I shrug out of his hold to return to his black sedan.

"What's the ceiling?" he calls out, following close behind me.

Hidden from his view, I release a smile, feeling it spread to the rest of my body—a phenomenon I didn't know was possible—and say, "There isn't one."

There's a reason women can climax more than men. We deserve it.

Twenty-One

Reece

NEXT TO LEX'S RANGE ROVER, I KEEP MY FINGER ON THE lock button, pressing it every time she hits the unlock button, stretching my time with her by only seconds. They're seconds I need though. The first time I tried this, we had a stolen car to get rid of. Now, we don't.

"There's a skylight in my apartment," I say.

Lex gives me a thoughtful look that launches my hopes into outer fucking space. She's considering.

I tell her, "We can see the moon through it," even though I have no idea if that's true. It's barely visible right now. The snow already stopped, but it's still pretty overcast.

"Why would that interest me?"

"Because you're a lunatic."

"Excuse me?"

"Your moon tattoo. Originally, lunatic just meant moonstruck, but since so much crazy shit happens during full moons, the term took on worse and worse implications over time until eventually it had nothing to do with the moon at all. At its core though, lunatic still means someone affected by the moon. Because bodies are made up of over fifty percent water, technically we're all lunatics, most females even more so if their cycle syncs up with the moon's."

If I could remember who bleeds when, I'd explain the kind of witches there are—white, red, pink, and purple—and see if she'd tell me which one she is. I highly doubt she would though.

Glancing down at the finger tat, she says softly, "I've never heard that before, only that the moon was feminine. I'm a fan of feminine energy."

"Me, too." Lex's specifically.

She leans across my center console, and I switch between staring at her lips and eyes as silver as the moon.

"You want to be a lunatic with me, rookie?"

"If that's…" I choke down all the saliva building in my mouth like an actual fucking rookie. "Yeah."

"From your bed?"

My eyebrows skydive. How'd she know—

Her lips touch mine, gently at first, then rougher.

She climbs to her knees, causing me to tilt my head back to accommodate her higher position, then there's some sort of thump sound I can't pinpoint. Ignoring it, I reach out both hands, ready to drag her over the console and let her ride me here and now, but before I can grab hold of her, she's backing up…out of the car.

She set me up. Distracted me just long enough to unlock the doors and make her escape.

I growl, about to fucking follow her, but her grin stops me cold. Her. Grin. Lex is fucking grinning.

She's still distracting me.

"You were in my bedroom?" That's where my skylight is, right above my bed.

She nods, and says, "I was everywhere," then slams the door shut, leaving me in motherfucking shock.

Everywhere? What does that mean? She went through my shit?

Lex pulls away in her Range Rover with an innocent little wave and a double honk that has me shaking my head.

She went through my shit. My question now is, how much?

I head home to find out, the entire drive something telling me to search my dresser first.

As soon as I do, I see why. She took them—her black panties. Technically, she took them back because I stole them first.

They were hidden in the bottom of my t-shirt drawer, which means Lex wasn't lying, she was *everywhere*. Every fucking bit of it. The first person to set foot in my apartment and she searches it top to bottom. What a bitch.

Honestly, I'm not even that mad. I just wish I was here to watch as she wandered around, rooting through my things, touching them, maybe even asking about them. I would've told her, too. I would've done anything to keep her here, with me.

I know what earlier was about. Lex took me to the cemetery to warn me away from her true self, but all it did was make me like her more because that's *my* true self. I like her dark side. I'm drawn to hers because it matches mine. Her drive, her fucking ruthlessness— it stems from pain inflicted by those closest to you.

I like the other side of her, too. The one she swears she doesn't have but was plain as day the moment she started talking about her mom. She cares for her mom the same way I care for mine—without limits. And that only comes from deep-rooted love.

Lex cares about me, too. Or at the very fucking least, my safety. Her actions proved that, especially tonight's.

Tonight. What a night.

After everything that went down, we just…went our separate ways. Her to her sterile mansion, me to my peaceful loft.

I should've never taken her back to her car. I should've brought her here and shown her my feelings through my actions.

I feel restless. The same way I get sometimes before a big job.

Lex told me anything I wanted from her I had to earn, but that's *from* her. Right now I just want her. Luckily, I know exactly where to find her.

Pulling a drive-by through Lex's neighborhood, I find some motherfucker parked at the bottom of her driveway. The man in the Dodge

Durango is too busy rubbing at his eyes when I pass to get a good look at me, but I see all I need to. He's definitely an undercover.

A fucking cop outside her house? Is he here about the Mustang?

Parking at the back of the hill Lex's house is perched on, I get out and start jogging up through the frost-encrusted woods. While the snow isn't actively falling at the moment, its bite is still thick in the air, gnawing on every exposed surface it can.

My mask already on, I break from the icy fog clinging to the tree line to approach the Colonial from the rear and do my usual sweep. Using the same door I did the first time, I pick the lock and let myself in. I don't go as slow as before, but I take my time making my way through the kitchen, keeping an ear out for any activity.

A shiver runs through me when I reach the spot I first locked eyes with the whimpering hollow. She had me fucking fooled. She's good at fooling people. Had to be. Has to be.

Not with me though. Now that she's shared her past with me, she doesn't have to pretend to be anything with me. She can pull me to her darkest depths and I'll go freely. Eagerly. I've had a lot of practice holding my breath.

At the fish tank, a light streams through from the other side—a light different from the tank's blue glow.

Someone's up.

Kordin's still at the hospital, so it can't be him. The only cars in the garage were his and Lex's, and the part of the driveway I could make out was clear. It's gotta be Lex but she left me almost an hour ago. I thought she'd be asleep by now. I kinda hoped she would be.

Through the spotless tank full of colorful anemones, coral, and fish, I spy Lex coming out of the primary bathroom, scrunching her white hair with a towel. She's wearing another black sleep set that looks just as expensive as the first one I saw her in. Just as tempting, too.

I don't know how the fuck I was able to stop myself from touching her then.

I'm not even gonna try now.

I position myself in front of the tank, shamelessly watching her flit around the room, brushing her hair out with one hand while skimming a book in the other. During her pacing, I catch sight of the cover and almost fucking snort. It's the book I gave her this morning, the one she threw away right in front of my ass.

Lex doesn't make eye contact with me, hell, her eyes don't come anywhere near where I am, but I can tell the moment she becomes aware of my presence because her body language changes from relaxed to hyperaware in a blink.

I drift past the tank, to the room's threshold, lazily propping a shoulder against the jamb.

Still not letting on that she's noticed me, Lex lets out a curse as her book falls from her hands by the foot of the bed. She drops to her knees immediately after, but doesn't retrieve the book, just waits… on me? She's waiting on me.

Eyes on her bowed head, I take a tentative step into the room, my limbs prickly from the electricity zipping through my veins.

Lex's jaw swivels in my direction ever so slightly before I hear the faintest inhale.

"I almost shot you, rook."

Damn. I forgot about the cologne I put on this morning.

She looks up at me and meets my gaze. I don't see a gun in her hand but that doesn't mean one isn't in reach. She wouldn't have put herself in such a compromising position if there wasn't.

"Then we're even."

"You would've pulled a gun on me?"

I nod.

"What else would you've done?"

"To you?"

Now she nods.

"Stand up."

"Lose the mask."

A few strides, then I'm gripping both shoulders, lifting her up off the floor, and setting her on her feet—all with my mask still on.

"You're not in charge anymore, Snow." I let her call the shots the first time we fucked, but this one's all me.

"Show me what you got," she says mockingly.

Leaning in close to her ear, I tell her, "Don't talk."

"Why?"

Goddamn it.

"Because you've got a cop watching your house."

"Officer Manning's too far away to hear anything."

She knows he's there? And his name?

I pull back, trying to read her eyes. Other than the color—Globe Thistle at dusk—I can't make out anything.

"Why's Officer Manning outside your house?" I bite out.

Those grayish-blue eyes go lax just like they did when she was talking to Phil outside The Pen, right before I jumped him from behind and broke the hand he was touching Lex with. He didn't know it was me. Without my mask, I had to use my shirt to cover my face, but he was so dopey-eyed after his interaction with Lex, he never even saw me coming.

Before she can get too far into her victim-act, I say, "Cut the bullshit, Lex."

Blowing out a breath, she pushes some wet strands over her shoulder. "It's in case the burglars return." She adds an eyebrow arch that I don't take personal.

Yeah, I returned, but I'm as alone now as I was before. And I'm not here to steal anything that isn't already mine.

"The driveway's not the only way up here." Me standing here is proof of that.

"If Officer Manning was good at his job, he wouldn't be on babysitting duty, now would he?"

"Did Kordin hire him?"

She shakes her head, but glances away. "No, it's standard protocol after a home invasion."

"Hollows," I sneer.

Still focused on the floor, she shrugs and says, "We like our possessions," like she's actually one of them.

Using my fist, I lift her chin, bringing her attention back to me. I pull her top over her head, letting it fall from my hands to the floor as I take in every inch of her naked torso. Shoulders back, Lex's thin frame stands tall, not shrinking from my gaze whatsoever. Her small, perky tits come to enticing stiff peaks I could hold on to while hammering into her from behind.

I guide her shorts off her hips, down her thighs until they pool at her feet, then help her step out of them one foot at a time before standing back up. The only other color in this room besides the clothes on my body are her two delicate tattoos and the V of material covering her pussy.

"I like mine, too," I tell her, eyes still roaming all the porcelain skin before me.

"I'm not your possession."

I stop my perusal to lean in until my forehead almost touches hers. One hand at the base of her skull, I grasp the roots and angle her head so she's looking up at me.

"I wasn't talking about you."

On a moan, Lex's hands come up to cup my cheeks, then both her thumbs stab between my lips, making a tear in the mask's fabric. I let my jaw go slack, so she can split the hole wider, just enough to expose my mouth.

Our mouths race to meet each other's, a collision of lips and tongue and frenzied need. Each time she tries to take control, I reposition her head and go a little deeper so it's me kissing her. At the cemetery, she wanted me to kiss her and I did, I kissed her and kissed her and kissed her, not once asking for more, but now, I'm fucking her mouth with mine and I'm not asking for anything. I'm motherfucking taking.

With her preoccupied, I grab a handful of her thong and rip it right off her body.

Breaking the kiss, she says, "Those cost two hundred dollars."

"I don't care." I jam the pricey panties in my front pocket. "You stole the other ones."

"Stole them? They were mine."

"*Were* yours. They became mine when you forgot them in your office." I thought I earned that pair, but I guess I didn't. Tonight's not a matter of guessing. I'm walking away knowing what I earned.

"You're—"

I push her backward, cutting her off as she falls onto the mattress.

"We can go round and round about it all night, but I'm not leaving without a pair of your underwear. If you want them back, you know where they'll be." *Just like I know where she'll be.*

I rake my gaze across her completely naked body. This is the first time I'm seeing all of Lex at once and goddamn is she a fucking vision.

"Think you can take me on, rookie?" Bending her knees just a bit, she spreads her feet apart, giving me a glimpse of her clit. The white comforter is slightly bunched between her thighs, keeping most of her pussy out of sight. It's not enough. I need an unobstructed view from every angle possible. I want to see her lips split as she takes me in—my tongue, my fingers, my cock.

Leaning over her with a knee on the bed, I grip one side of her hips before locking eyes with her. "Yeah, Snow. I do."

"Remember the ceiling."

"What ceiling?"

The sound of her chest-imprisoned chuckle washes over me.

I fucking love her laugh. It's secretive, just like her.

With a smirk, I flip her over.

All humor evaporates and "What the fuuuck?" comes out hoarse as I tear my mask off my head.

Both her ass cheeks are marred by bruises. Black and blue splotches with yellowing edges, they're new but not brand new. When the fuck…

How the fuck…

Who the—

Lex sighs. She fucking sighs.

I drop down, draping my body alongside hers, eyeing her entire backside while ghosting a hand over the wounded skin.

"Lex? Who the fuck did this to you?"

"You."

My gaze snaps to hers.

"Remember? You tripped me on the sidewalk."

Shiiiit. I didn't mean to hurt her. I was just trying to get her to stop hitting me.

"Fuck. I'm sorry." I press my forehead to her temple, filling my nose with her wintry scent. "I'm so fucking sorry." I kiss her cheek, then her jaw before moving to the side of her throat, murmuring, "I'm gonna take good care of you." I could add "tonight," but I don't mean just tonight, so I keep it open-ended.

I leave kisses all the way down her back, lingering at her tailbone to glance up at her. She's got her arms folded out in front of her, with her head turned sideways, resting on the top one. She looks relaxed, which is good, but possibly approaching boredom, which is not.

My lips stretch against her skin before I move lower, kissing one ass cheek from top to bottom and side to side, then the other exactly the same way.

Lex's hips buck, so I slide an arm under her from below, making her lower abdomen rest on my hand while her clit kisses my wrist. Lifting her even higher, her cheeks spread apart enough to give me a better glimpse of both her holes. It takes everything in me not to dive right in and devour her now.

Reaching out to my side, I grab the pillow closest to me, then think better of it, snatching the one further away instead, and stick it through Lex's legs, trapping my arm between her and the pillow.

With her bottom half propped up, I drag my tongue over the same path I just kissed, soothing the skin I bruised before dipping down into Lex's crack and licking up that, too. When my tongue passes over her tight asshole, Lex moans out a curse and arches her back to give me better access. The move makes her clit rub against my wrist, so I retract my arm until I'm palming her pussy.

Something's not right though. I've only had a small taste of Lex and this wasn't it.

I stop all movement and pull back, causing Lex to groan like she's in pain.

"Why the hell are you stopping?"

"You taste too clean, like soap."

Pushing up to her hands, Lex looks at me over her shoulder and says, "I should. I just got out of the shower."

I shake my head as I step up behind her, gripping one of her shoulders with my free hand, my thumb at the base of her neck. "Fuck the pillow."

"What?"

"The first time I eat you out, I want to know I'm tasting you. Fuck the pillow until you're dripping sweat."

With a little guidance, I get her to start moving her hips, front to back, riding both my palm and the pillow.

"You broke into my house just to watch me fuck a pillow?"

My lips at her ear, I rasp, "Not just any pillow. Kordin's pillow."

Her speed increases.

"That's right. Fuck your husband's pillow so the next time he lays his head on it, he'll smell what I stole from him."

Drawing my hand back a couple inches, I line two fingers up with her pussy, then push right in, making us both curse. My palm mashing her split ass crack, I keep pace with Lex, thrusting in and out of her warm, slick pussy as she fucks Kordin's pillow.

I fit my other hand to the front of her throat and squeeze, turning her head over her shoulder.

Automatically, her hands come up to the back of my neck.

"Right out from under his fucking nose," I tell her before sealing my lips to hers.

I kiss and finger-fuck her until she comes, her walls pulsing around my fingers as her movements grow chaotic and her body becomes dotted with sweat.

Breaking my mouth from hers, I let Lex slump forward, sending her ass into the air, then I bend down and eat. Still slowly pumping inside her, I explore every inch of her ass, licking and sucking until she's shaking and screaming, her pussy walls choking my fingers again as they throb furiously.

I ease out of her despite her protests and wipe her cum off my fingers on Kordin's pillow, telling her, "Sit up."

Lex obeys without argument. If this is how she always behaves after multiple orgasms, I might have to make this my new daily habit. Jesus, this woman.

"Don't think you're done, Snow," I say, using her own words.

She gives another one of her chuckles, this one actually strong enough to pass through her lips. That or she's too tired to hold it in.

I press my lips to the back of her head, briefly closing my eyes to savor the moment.

"There's my sweet boy."

She can insult me any way she fucking pleases as long as she puts "my" in front of it, because goddamn, does it sound better than any compliment I've ever received.

A few of her white strands stick to my face as I pull away, then I rip the pillow out from under her and drop to my back, fitting my head between her knees.

My rigid cock leaks in my pants, needing a taste of Lex as much as, maybe even more than, my mouth, but he's gonna have to wait. I'm getting my fill first.

Hands full of ass and my gaze on hers just above her glistening pussy, I say, "Fuck my face."

Staring down at me, she quirks an eyebrow, then gathers her hair into a hand-held ponytail. "And if you drown?"

My lips spread so wide my cheeks ache. She is fucking soaked and I haven't even got a third out of her yet.

Holding her eyes, I flick my tongue out, teasing her slit. My first lick doesn't hold any hint of soap whatsoever, so I go for another. Then another. Then another. Fuck, is she delicious.

Her arms fall to her sides, a waterfall of hair cascading around her face as she gazes down at me. "Reece—"

"Drown me, Lex." I pull on her ass, causing her pussy to land directly on my mouth, then I'm eating again.

Lex forgets all about what she was gonna say and starts riding my face just like she did the pillow, except easier, faster, and louder thanks to all the natural lube. She gasps in rhythm with her swollen clit slamming against my nose on each drive forward, the sounds going right to my cock.

Releasing an ass cheek, I push one of her thighs up above my head and out to the side, making Lex have to prop herself up with her hands. The new angle, fuck, it lets me go even deeper, licking into her pussy like I'm cleaning every last drop off a fucking spoon.

"Reece," she warns in a trembling tone I could get addicted to.

Fuck that, I'm already addicted—to her saying my name, to her saying it like *that*. I'm addicted to Lex straight, no chaser; I'll take her in her rawest fucking form.

Lex makes a sound that's more scream than word before her arms give out completely, all of her weight falling on top of me. Without breaking pace, I spin us so she's flat on her back and I'm on top, one of her legs over my shoulder, the other pushed out to the side by my elbow, and I continue lapping at her pussy while nosing her clit with every upward thrust.

A soundless cry rips from her throat as she claws at my head, both her legs fighting to clamp shut, but like I told her, she's not in charge anymore. She's fucking coming again, and she's coming on my goddamn tongue.

I'm licking into her so quick and pulling her back to me so hard, the bedframe creaks in time with my thrusts. I don't always open my eyes when I'm going down on a woman, but I want to see Lex fall apart. I need to. And for whatever reason, she always needs it, too. So I keep my eyes open and on her, watching her stomach rise and fall, her tits strain in the air, and her mouth release the many incoherent noises she's making.

Lex's top half catapults off the bed like she's possessed, and she latches on to my hair, pulling, but I don't stop. I don't ease up. I don't slow. I keep going, tongue-fucking her until finally, she comes again, coating my tongue, and teeth, and lips, and nose, and fuck if I couldn't go for some motherfucking mouth to mouth right now. Not for breath. Just for her.

I. Want. More.

Lex's grip in my hair loosens right as she rolls backward onto the mattress, her entire body limp. I crawl up her, kissing her without wiping my face first so she can taste what I coaxed out of her. At first she kisses me back eagerly, roughly, then her motions slow to soft and lazy before eventually stopping altogether.

She's fucking wrecked.

But she's not finished. We're *far* from done.

I climb off the bed to undress.

"Lex?"

No answer. No eye crack. Nothing.

"Lex?" I repeat as I get back on, concern quickly replacing every other emotion.

"Hold on. Just…wait," is all she says, but then I notice tears streaming from the corner of her closed eyelids down her temples into her hairline. "It's been a while."

I almost ask what she means—it's been a while since what?—but I don't actually want to hear the answer, so I stay quiet. I have a feeling it has to do with Kordin and that motherfucker's the last thing I want on either of our minds right now. I'm gifting him a cum-covered pillow courtesy of his wife's mouthwatering cunt, that's all the consideration I'm willing to give him tonight. Or any night.

"Bend your knees and spread your legs for me."

Lex's eyes fly open and lock on mine, two silver cyclones zeroed in on me. How are they silver right now without any hint of blue? We're in the same lighting.

When she doesn't move a muscle, I plant my elbows on both sides of her, my face hovering above hers as I thumb her temples dry.

"Where's the ceiling?"

Her lips part, but I beat her to it, saying, "That's right, there isn't one. I'm gonna fuck you now and you're gonna come at least one more time, then I'll let you rest for a little bit before we do it all over again." I press a gentle kiss to her pliant lips, asking against them, "Okay, Snow White?"

If she notices my slipup with the nickname, she doesn't say anything, just exhales as her knees come up to frame my sides.

"There's my good girl," I tease while sitting back on my heels, earning myself an eye roll. I butt my knees up against the backs of her thighs, then lift her lower half off the mattress using both hands.

Fuck. She's drying up already. This is one of those times where patience doesn't actually pay off.

Gathering as much moisture in my mouth as I can, I spit directly on her clit before bending down and using my tongue to spread it around her lips.

"Reece," she pants, her hips twitching in my hold. "I'm gonna…"

I stay where I am, mopping her clit with my flattened tongue. It only takes seconds for her body to start convulsing as she comes again, her stomach and thighs visibly quivering.

Quickly rising up off my heels, I meet Lex's hips with mine and line my cock up with her now sopping wet pussy to notch myself at her entrance.

She's staring up at me with pure exhaustion and what I swear to fuck could be admiration, making me feel like a god.

"You're so fucking perfect right now. I could blow just looking at you."

A small smile flirts with her lips, teasing them apart. "You have."

"My hand doesn't compare to being inside you." I thrust forward until I'm bottomed out inside her, then swivel my hips, grinding into her. "Nothing does."

One long moan purrs in Lex's throat as she massages her tits, trapping her pink nipples between her knuckles. She doesn't break eye contact though and neither do I.

"No blinking," I vow. Shit, I like her eyes on me, too.

I like all of her on me better.

With my hands clutching her sides, I lower my hips, then lift them again, pumping in and out of her slowly, deeply, so each inch of my cock strokes every bit of her pussy, leaving a mark—my mark. It's mine. *She's* mine.

I dare anyone to tell me otherwise, and that includes Lex.

I've been aching for this all night, all day, all weekend, ever since Lex walked away from me with another man at her side. I want to be the man at her side. I want to be the only man at her side, ever.

The realization hits me hard, all of my muscles tensing from the sudden sensation buildup.

"Touch your clit," I practically grind out, barely able to speak.

Somehow finding the energy, Lex wraps her legs around my back, and says, "You want another orgasm from me, you do it."

A feral growl rips out of me, and I move one hand to her stomach, circling her clit with a thumb. Still driving into Lex, I press my palm down, feeling my cock move deep inside her.

"Oh, God!" she screams, her pussy contracting around my cock so tight, her walls try to push me out, strangling my shaft.

Like striking a match, a fire ignites from my balls to my cock, making cum gush out, my body shuddering against Lex's as I flood her pussy, even forcing more out when I feel the geyser tapering off. I want to stain this woman from the inside out.

"Next time, call my name," I tell Lex before collapsing half on top of her, only held up by two shaky elbows. "Not God's."

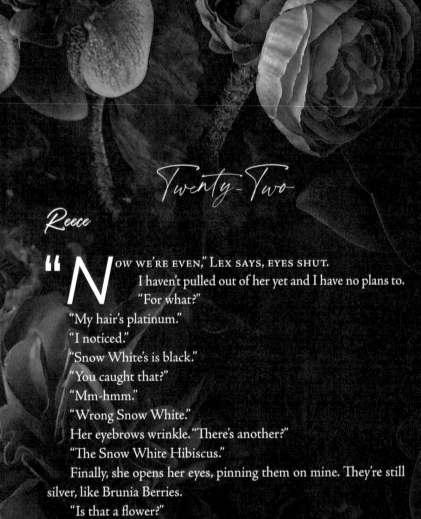

Twenty-Two

Reece

"**N**OW WE'RE EVEN," LEX SAYS, EYES SHUT.

I haven't pulled out of her yet and I have no plans to.

"For what?"

"My hair's platinum."

"I noticed."

"Snow White's is black."

"You caught that?"

"Mm-hmm."

"Wrong Snow White."

Her eyebrows wrinkle. "There's another?"

"The Snow White Hibiscus."

Finally, she opens her eyes, pinning them on mine. They're still silver, like Brunia Berries.

"Is that a flower?"

"Mm-hmm," I mimic her answer. "It's a perennial. Pure white. Root-hardy. Intelligent. Patient."

I brush some hair off her forehead, running my fingers through the damp strands until I hit a snag that Lex frowns at but doesn't scold me for like she usually would. Multiple orgasms—that's the key.

My schedule just got busier.

And hotter.

"What makes it intelligent and patient?" she asks.

"They're slow to surface in the spring. So slow most gardeners either forget about them or assume they're dead. But they're smart enough, and patient enough, to wait for the perfect time to rise above the soil. It's a surprise to everybody when they finally do."

Lex stares at me intently, her eyes shifting between mine.

"And root-hardy? What's that?"

"Over time they develop larger and larger roots, allowing for more and more flowers to bloom. Even though it may not look like it, the Snow White Hibiscus is a strong, resilient, survivor of a plant. Most of its strength is under the surface, out of sight."

"Thanks," she mutters.

I laugh, still careful to keep most of my weight off her.

"Speaking of flowers." I nod over at the bunch of white Heather sitting on Lex's nightstand, still held together by Phil's wedding ring.

She avoids their general direction, telling me, "One of my co-workers gave those to me."

A growl claws up my tongue, out between my lips before I can stop it. I know it's dumb as fuck but just the thought of another man showing Lex affection pisses me off. Luckily not many do at the office. It's weird. Everyone will walk by her office and stare at her through the glass, but no one ever goes inside to talk to her.

"You're jealous of yourself."

"I'm jealous of the air in your lungs," I admit without an ounce of shame.

"Why?"

I kiss her collarbone, whispering against the thin skin, "Because you let it in."

"That explains why you refuse to pull out."

I hadn't really thought about it like that before, but yeah, I do like knowing a part of me is still inside Lex even when I'm not. I like it a lot. I'll pump her full of my cum every chance I fucking get from now on…if she keeps letting me, because that's what's really happening—Lex *lets* me come in her. Even when she's not in charge, she is in charge. She knows that as well as I do. Both times we fucked, if she would've told me to pull out, I would've. It would've damn near killed me, but I would've listened to her.

"Shit." Lex sighs, her rib cage under me deflating. "I still need to take the morning-after pill."

"You don't *need* to," I say, pushing myself up again.

"Yes, I do."

"No, you don't. I already told you—"

"That you want me to get knocked up so I'll leave my husband? Yes, you did tell me. Except I didn't agree to that."

"You didn't protest either."

Lex blinks twice, very slowly. "I don't want kids."

"With me or with anyone?"

"With anyone."

"Why?"

"Because I don't—"

"Deserve them?" I guess, grazing her lips with mine to tell her, "You're not broken, Lex."

"I am. I broke myself the second I pulled that trigger. I don't deserve to bring life into this world. Not when I've taken away so much."

I make sure I'm looking into her eyes when I say, "You don't know what would've happened if you didn't pull that trigger. Nobody knows, not even Cyrus. Your dad could've killed your mom. Hell, he could've killed you. Your mom could've shot your dad and ended up in prison. There are more than a hundred different outcomes of what could've happened that day...maybe this was the best."

"The best would be my mom alive, happy, with her memories intact."

"Who's to say she would've been happy? You lived with Cyrus; were you happy? You have all your memories from your childhood and from The Playground; are you happy?"

Her silence is deafening.

"Your mom's face was already tatted when you got there. You think Cyrus would've let her stop working just because of a face tat? I know every girl at The Playground and not one of them is happy. You rid this earth of two lowlifes, you got your mom out of a tough situation, and you figured out a way to get yourself out, too. Your hands are covered in blood but it's blood nobody but you is crying over."

"I'm not crying."

"You're punishing yourself."

She sighs again and glances at the flowers. "I deprive myself of anything that makes me happy."

"I noticed," I repeat quietly.

That's the real reason she throws my presents away—she acts like it's to hurt me, but really, it's to hurt herself. She wants them. She likes them. But she thinks she doesn't deserve them.

She does the same thing with me. She insults me at every turn as a way to talk herself out of wanting me.

"I can make you happy, Lex."

Her expression darkens and she drags her gaze back to mine.

"In another life, I'm sure you could. In this one, you'll never get the chance. Even if you did impregnate me, Kordin wouldn't let me go that easily. An abortion is cheaper and much quicker to obtain than a divorce."

He wouldn't? Why? He's already fucking around. Why hang on to a broken marriage?

Probably for appearances. Shallow fuck.

"It's your body. It's—"

Lex's scoff throws me off. "Is it?"

"Why wouldn't it be?"

Acting like she doesn't hear me, she shakes her head and continues, "There is no future with us, Reece, because while Kordin has mine in his hands, Cyrus has yours, and neither of them are letting go anytime soon. This is all we'll ever be, this moment, this secret, this mistake."

"All the mistakes I've made in my life, none of them ever felt this right."

"Say that to me when your cock isn't in my—"

I pull out of her, making both of us wince.

"I've never made a mistake that felt this right."

With a shove to my shoulders, she tries to sit up, saying, "You're still young. There will be plenty more."

"You're young, too." I bear down on her, preventing her from going anywhere. She's only one year older than me. She just presents older because she's always had to.

"I can't offer you what you're looking for."

"I haven't even told you what I'm looking for."

"You didn't have to." Her touch turns thoughtful as she trails her fingers up my arms, to my back. "It's obvious."

How is it obvious to her when it's not to me? I don't give myself the freedom to envision my future. Like Lex pointed out, it's useless.

We remain staring at each other, our breaths drowned out by the fish tank's steady thrum and sporadic burst of bubbles. Soon the goose bumps she's creating on my body will start to spread to hers but not for the same reason. She's been hot since I got here and she never stays hot for long.

"If this is all we have, then I'm stretching this moment to make it last." Fisting as much of the comforter as I can reach, I fold it over my back, wrapping us in a blanket cocoon. I don't particularly like fucking under any covers, but for Lex, I'll do anything.

"We have until sunrise," she says, gazing at me.

I grin as I settle myself on top of her again. "Before dawn's when I do all my best work."

I leave Lex's house when the sky is just waking up, the horizon a seamless blend of pink to orange to blue. Without any more snow falling overnight I don't need to worry about making a trail of footprints as I jog over to the woods and hike back down to my car. I haven't gotten a wink of sleep and Lex barely any herself. I worked that pussy over until she was on the verge of hysteria. I knew women could come multiple times but I didn't know there wasn't a firm limit for how many times. It's basically when the body can't take anymore.

Lex's reached that point about an hour ago. I finally let her pass out, but stayed awake myself, watching her instead. When I was sure she wasn't going to wake up, I took a look around the house. The safe Kordin locked his laptop inside of isn't as big as Cyrus's, but it's better as far as being theft-proof. It's one of the best on the market for home safes. To open it, you need an electronic password and a thumbprint. Unfortunately, it's too thick for me to drill through, and with anti-pry hinges and solid door bolts, I can't break my way into it either.

I still think Kaisin is the key to figuring out what the fuck is really going on at Debrosse Group, so that's where I'll focus. The more I get to know Lex, the more convinced I am she has no idea her husband's firm is a fraud. She's already confessed her darkest sins to me and none of them stemmed from greed. I can't picture her fucking over innocent, hard-working people just trying to survive in Fox Hollow.

If Kordin is involved somehow and I can find a way to prove it, I might be able to blackmail him into giving Lex a divorce and her mom's house. Then, only after she's off the hook, would I hand the info over to Cyrus. He's planning on using whatever intel I give him to trick Lex somehow, but I'm not gonna let that happen.

Both men had their time with Lex but they didn't appreciate it. That's because they didn't earn any of it.

Now I'm going to do everything I can to earn my time with her, because once it starts, I'm making it last forever.

Twenty-Three

Reece

I'M SITTING AT MY CUBICLE, STARING AT THE SAME FORM FOR the last hour and a half, wondering where the fuck Lex is. When I left her in bed this morning, I woke her up with a long kiss goodbye and a promise to see her later at work. She didn't say anything to make me think she wouldn't be in today, but here I am, at the firm, and she's nowhere to be found. I've already checked her office a half dozen times, hoping I missed her come in this morning, but find it empty every pass by. I don't know where she is, nobody else seems to know where she is, and the longer I sit here, the more I have to talk myself out of going in search of her.

Hearing Kaisin's raised voice bark at one of the interns to get a double cappuccino, I shuffle the papers in front of me around, blankly studying whichever one lands at the top of the pile.

What if that undercover went up to Lex's house after I left? Something about him being there rubs me the wrong way. I've ripped off a lot of people, and none of them, not even the hollows, ever got their own night patrol afterward.

Maybe Kordin hired him to keep an eye on his wife, make sure she's not fucking around on him while he's in the hospital.

The thought makes me grin.

Until Kaisin's order comes back to me, then I scowl. He drinks green tea only. He told me all about it, as well as his reasoning, during one of our countless run-ins around this place. Kaisin's always out of his office, wandering the halls aimlessly, talking to anyone that'll listen. The guy bullshits more than works.

My mind goes to the person it's been on all morning—Lex—but she likes her coffee as black as her outfits. So who's the cappuccino for? As long as I've been here, Kaisin hasn't met with any clients, or even a single prospect. I don't know what the CFO actually does on a day-to-day basis, which is probably the point. Every evil mastermind needs a fall guy and Kaisin is the perfect scapegoat for Kordin. He's in a prominent position with very little, if any, supervision; he's in love with his brother's wife; he resents him for marrying her; and most importantly, he's stupid without being too stupid—just competent enough to not raise suspicions outright while still being believably incompetent in case shit goes sideways. Which means if something is passing through the cracks, it'll be cracks Kaisin oversees.

I spin in my chair, eyeing Lex's brother-in-law rushing around.

She's been going after the wrong laptop all along. It's Kaisin's we need. He won't have the same safeguards in place that Kordin would, because he may not even realize he needs them.

"What's going on?" I ask him as I stand, tucking my hand in a pocket.

"It's my brother."

"Did he die?"

The warmest feeling fills my chest until it's swollen with hot air, practically lifting me off the floor. On God, I will break into laughter if Kordin's dead.

Kaisin pauses to frown at me. "Die? No. He's back. He's on his way up right now." He's on the move again, tidying random things in his path like a fucking fake potted plant in the corner.

Another feeling kicks all the happiness out of my body, turning my insides to cold hard cement, bonding my feet in place. That's where Lex has been…with him. And now I have to face him. And her. Him *with* her.

What if he touches her?

I won't be able to stop myself from removing Kordin's throat from the rest of his body if he does.

But what if she touches him?

I know where I stand. I felt it when we first fucked, maybe even before, but last night and this morning confirmed it. Lex is mine. I accept all of her—every dark, twisted part, along with every light, honest part—but does she feel the same? Am I hers? She's made no claim either way.

"I deprive myself of anything that makes me happy."

That's why she hasn't made a claim, because I do make her happy. And she won't until I convince her she deserves it, that she deserves me. I can't do that if I'm in prison for Kordin Debrosse's murder.

This is a waiting game, and for someone as impatient as Lex alleges I am, the ultimate test of determination.

The elevator's ding rings in my ears, making my head pound and my blood boil, then the doors slide open and it all comes to a halt as Kordin, in a wheelchair, rolls out followed by Lex pushing him.

The entire office converges for the reunion with the boss.

While Lex's gaze never reaches me, Kordin's does a couple times.

Once the crowd thins and people return to their work, Kordin beckons me forward.

Prying one lead foot off the floor, then the other, I approach with a tight expression.

Kaisin clears his throat. "Kordin, this is Reece Souza, our new regional marketing and research coordinator."

Kordin cocks his head to the side as he regards me, but luckily, no recognition registers. His right arm's in a cast as well as his right leg. I force myself to remain stoic while fondly remembering how they got that way. What I wouldn't give to beat his ass all over again.

"Souza, where have I heard that name?"

"From me, when I told you about him," Lex says, still avoiding my vicinity. A half-inch layer of my cum is coating her pussy walls right now, millions of my sperm fucking fighting for their lives in there, and she's talking to her husband about me like I'm not even here.

"The one that couldn't get the stain out for you?" he asks her, also ignoring my presence.

She told him that?

"Mm-hmm."

"Souza." Kordin sticks his left hand out, and I shake it awkwardly with mine, squeezing harder than necessary even though it's my left, too. He still doesn't meet my eyes. "Welcome to the team."

"Thank you, sir. Happy to be here."

I hate myself right now, so much I want to sock my own jaw to prevent me from having to say another word.

"I hope you'll forgive my wife's first-day hazing. It was her first, and last, attempt at it."

"Already forgiven." That and everything else she's done to rile me up.

"Is he the one that just got married?" Kordin directs the question over his shoulder to Lex.

"One and the same," she says lazily like she's so fucking bored she might fall asleep. I know she's gotta be tired enough to.

"How's the newlywed life treating you so far?" Kordin asks me.

"Still getting used to it."

"I can see that. Did you forget your ring at home?" His grasp on my hand tightens as his eyes drop to my empty ring finger.

I flash a tight smile, telling him, "I lost it," then pull my hand from his. I shouldn't have let the handshake go on that long. I shouldn't have touched him, period.

Without looking away from…somewhere on my face, he says, "Lenox, remember the time I lost my wedding band?"

Licking her lips, Lex shakes her head, her gaze on the ceiling like she's embarrassed. Oh, she's awake now.

Kordin reaches his hand over his shoulder, covering Lex's on the handle, and looks up at her.

The only thing on me that moves are my nostrils as they flare.

They have history. There's a familiarity between them I expected but wasn't ready to have shoved down my throat. He's touching her. He's gazing at her. He's openly flirting with her. He's…loving her.

And he's doing it all with no effort, no resistance, no consequences whatsoever.

I want that. All of it. With Lex.

Next to me, Kaisin shifts on his feet. He wants it, too.

He's not getting it. Not with her.

Tearing his attention from his wife, Kordin starts to explain with a chuckle, "We thought we were going to have to take Lenox to the hospital—"

"This is hardly appropriate conversation for the workplace," Lex rushes to say.

"—luckily, I was able to retrieve it on my own."

Jesus fucking Christ. His wedding band came off in Lex's pussy, I'm gonna assume while he was fingering her.

I wonder if he'd still be laughing if I told him what I left behind in there just hours ago. My saliva and cum won't land Lex in the hospital, but Kordin's begging for me to send his ass back there with stories like this. First time meeting a brand-new employee and he's talking about finger-fucking his wife. He's either trying to rub it in my face or Kaisin's.

Or both since he's an entitled hollow prick that like.

I should stroke his ego so he doesn't see me as a threat, but I can't pass up the opportunity to rock his confidence at least a little.

"Thankfully, I'm a righty." I lift said hand, crooking both my middle and ring finger to show these fucking stiffs how a woman is supposed to be fingered. "So right hand only for my wife."

Lex finally looks at me, her green eyes piercing, but I'm not sure if it's because I said "my wife" or because I insinuated Kordin doesn't know how to please his.

"I'm right-handed, too," Kordin says.

I already figured he was, and the weak, clumsy handshake with his left confirmed it, so what the fuck was he doing using his left hand to finger Lex?

"Mm," I hum with a thoughtful head-nod, tucking my hand away again.

"That was a long time ago," Lex adds in. "I've trained him well since then." She pats Kordin's shoulder, never breaking eye contact with me.

Is she standing up for him? Or getting me back?

Both feel like a knife through the gut.

"Excuse me, Lenox, the men are talking," Kordin snaps, all traces of tenderness gone.

The hand in my pocket clenches into a fist, my short nails biting my palm. This is more like the Kordin I first met, when he offered his wife's sweet cunt to me in exchange for absolutely fuck all. I've been through his house, there's not a single thing in it I'd let another man stick his dick in Lex for.

"If you don't want me joining a conversation about me, then have it when I'm not around," Lex says before strutting away, leaving the three of us to watch as she sashays toward her office.

The younger Debrosse attempts to mask a snicker with a cough, saying, "Where's the fun in that?"

"Where indeed," Kordin murmurs, focus solely on Lex's ass in a tight black pencil skirt like he's in a trance before asking, "Why'd you let her stay?"

Kaisin sobers. "She said she was fine. She insisted."

Kordin turns his attention on his brother. "I told you she would."

"I tried." He waves where Lex just was. "But she…"

"You should've tried harder." Kordin notices me still here, listening, and releases another chuckle. "My wife, she's far too ambitious. Sometimes to her own detriment."

That's an odd thing to say. Then again, so is admitting he lost his ring inside his wife's pussy.

"Actually, Lenox hasn't been sec—"

"For fuck's sake," Kordin interrupts, his voice sharp. "What do I have to do to get some coffee around here?"

Kaisin snaps his fingers, and like magic, an intern appears holding a mug of light-brown liquid.

"How's it taste?"

The intern's eyes widen as he stammers, "I…I don't know. I didn't try it."

"Better not have. You heard what I did the last time someone touched what belongs to me?"

Between Kordin puffing up his chest, acting like he actually did something to me—the someone he's referring to—and the intern's head almost snapping off his neck from nodding too hard, I almost crack up laughing. Hollows are so fucking pathetic.

"Kaisin, take me to my office. I've got a pressing matter to attend to."

Kaisin positions himself behind his brother's wheelchair, brows furrowed as he tries to figure out how to operate it. The short side of a laptop sticks out from the back pouch like a lighthouse on a jagged shore, illuminating the preferred path.

It's not the only one though.

"Follow," Kordin orders the intern without sparing him another glance.

I wait until they're gone from sight before returning to my cubicle for the bag I brought in this morning, then I start in the direction of Lex's office.

"Did you know he was getting released today?" I ask once her door's closed.

"I had an inkling," Lex answers without taking her eyes off her laptop.

An inkling? What does that mean?

"I don't want you to fuck him."

"Your jealousy's going to be the death of you."

Unconcerned, I shrug, telling her, "Doubt it." Jealousy's new for me. I've never felt it like I do over Lex.

"Anyway, Kordin's my—"

"I know who he is. I don't care. I don't want you fucking him anymore."

She stops typing to meet my stare. I drop the bag on her desk as I sit, and she points at it. "Another book and flower?"

Rubbing my jaw, I nod absentmindedly, recalling Kordin and Kaisin's conversation. Is that the trouble Kaisin was referring to at The Pen?

I never understood why Kaisin wanted Lex to go home so bad, but now I'm wondering why Kordin didn't want her working in his absence either. Lex made it sound like the brothers don't talk outside of work, but that's not how they seem to me.

A loud thud snaps me out of it.

Lex threw away the bag, this time without even seeing the Orchid or rock-star romance inside.

"You're just going to fish them out later and take them home with you, so why'd you even bother?"

"As you just saw, my husband is back."

"So what? He's sleeping with someone else, too."

"I'm not *sleeping* with anybody."

I smirk, and ask her, "Are you tired?"

She pops a shoulder. "No. I'm used to going without sleep."

My smirk slips. There are so many ways I could take that. What keeps her up? Not Kordin...right?

"However..." She sighs in a way that could be considered as being pleased. "I am sore."

Now I'm wearing a full-blown smile. It's not Kordin. Her pussy, her body, wouldn't be worn out if she were getting dick regularly.

"I don't like how he talked to you. Does he always snap at you like that?" I nod toward the hallway.

"Always? No, I wouldn't say that. Usually, my husband's quite kind. Doting, in fact."

Doting. He didn't come across as doting in either of the times I've been around him.

Then I remember Breck's assessment of Kordin. He's doting...intentionally. He dotes on Lex as a way to get her to do what he wants.

It's when she doesn't, that he snaps.

"Although..." Lex says. "Today in particular, he has a lot on his mind."

"Because he just got out of the hospital?"

Lex returns her attention to whatever she was working on before I came in here, but says, "That's the story."

"What really happened?"

"His mistress's car was stolen last night."

That's a hell of a coincidence.

I study Lex.

Or is it?

"Ford Mustang? Red? With a car seat in the back?"

Nothing on Lex moves other than her fingers flying across the keyboard.

"Lex?"

The room goes silent as she looks at me.

I smile, then she does, a cruel slash across her face. It's there one moment, gone the next. She stole Kordin's fuck buddy's car and set it on fire.

My cock grows in my pants. I could bend her over her desk right here and now. Give all her spectators a real show.

"Can I see you tonight?"

"No."

She resumes typing.

"When can I see you again?"

"What's wrong with right now?"

"Our clothes are still on and some part of me isn't buried deep inside some part of you."

Lex raises her eyebrows before dropping them back into place.

"As long as you're employed by Debrosse Investment Properties Group, you can see me every weekday, between the hours of eight AM and five PM."

"What about after office hours? Or before?" I can wake up an extra hour or two early.

Her head shakes side to side.

Fuck. This can't be over already. We just fucking started.

I rap my knuckles on her desk, making her stop to acknowledge me again.

"Why not?"

"My husband's back," she repeats slower.

"What's that supposed to mean?"

"Aside from the extra care he now requires, it means my schedule is back to that of a dutiful wife's."

I purse my lips as I nod, then I shake it all away, telling her, "You're not fucking him. You do whatever wife-shit you need to, except that. Your pussy is off-limits to him."

"Just to him?"

On fucking God, as soon as her bruises are healed, her ass is getting smacked for that.

"To everybody. But me," I add so there's no confusion whatsoever.

"In what capacity?"

"Every capacity. No touching, no licking, no sucking, no fucking. I don't want anyone getting close enough to even catch a whiff. That shit you pulled in the conference room…" I shake my head, remembering the effect her arousal had on not just me but everybody. "That won't happen again."

"Where'd all that 'it's your body' talk go?"

"It is your body and you can do whatever the fuck you want to it—"

"How gracious of you."

"—as long as you don't put it in jeopardy."

"Put it in jeopardy?" She frowns. "I'm the one that's kept myself alive all this time. Me."

"Alive, but not unharmed."

"Reece—"

"Lex, Kordin tried to give me your body for practically nothing in return."

"It's been said before that my husband's a generous man." Her voice is straight deadpan, no emotion at all, but it *has* to bother her knowing Kordin did that. It bothers me. A lot.

"Cyrus handed your body out to anybody willing to pay."

All she does is take a deep inhale because we both know there's not a generous bone in Cyrus's body.

"Your tits were exposed to an entire nightclub and you didn't flinch."

She rolls her eyes, so quick I almost miss it.

"You were about to be raped and you didn't so much as put up a fight."

"All I had on me was a tiny blade. I had to be smart. I had to be patient. I had to wait until the right moment, when he was at his most vulnerable, or else it would've been for nothing. And as for my breasts, we already went over that. I don't—"

"Care? Yeah, that's my fucking point. You don't care what happens to your body."

"More like I've been through enough to understand public humiliation is only temporary. Physical pain is temporary. Having a man inside me that I don't want inside me is temporary. Real torture is watching someone I care about suffer and not being able to do a damn thing about it."

"Exactly."

The air around us turns frigid.

"Don't do that."

Oh, it's too fucking late now, Snow.

"I care," I admit.

"Do not fucking do that."

"I care…" How deep should I go here? How deep can I go without scaring her off? I settle on saying, "About your body. As long as we're together, nobody gets to mistreat it, not even you."

Suddenly she's standing, both palms planted on her desk as she leans over it, invading my personal space in a way that only makes my cock harder.

"We are not together."

Head tilted to the side, I peer up at her and lick my bottom lip before telling her, "We're together."

Her scoff echoes off the glass walls. "You said you wouldn't, but here you are, trying to make me your whore…just like they did."

"I'm nothing like them, Lex. I don't want you as my whore. I just want you as mine." There. I said it. Last night should've clued her in, but since it didn't, I'll do it my-goddamn-self.

Her voice is as icy as her nickname as she grits, "I'm no man's."

She's right—kind of. She hasn't been a man's up until now because Kordin and Cyrus aren't real men. If they were, they wouldn't have allowed any harm to come to her.

I get to my feet, refusing to back down on this. Looking between those Bells of Ireland eyes, I tell her, "No, you were no man's. Now, you are. You're mine." Then I leave her office before she can argue.

Twenty-Four

Lex

THE WHITE ANEMONE REECE GAVE ME THIS MORNING stares up at me accusingly from the bottom drawer of my desk. It's the newest addition to my hidden floral shrine. With snowy-white petals and a black center, it's simple yet sophisticated. Too sophisticated to be kept in a drawer, but I can't take it home. Not anymore. Not with Kordin around. That hasn't stopped Reece from bringing me his daily offerings the last few days. I wish he would stop as much as I wish he wouldn't. The books I can still get use out of. As long as I wrap them in butcher paper, Kordin can't tell the difference. He's never paid any attention to my books, only that they're covered discreetly and aesthetically once they enter our home.

The flowers though, I have nowhere to put them that won't raise questions, and the thought of throwing them completely away makes my stomach cramp, so the bottom drawer it is. With no way to keep them watered, most of them are wilting already, but I prefer half-dead things. They're far more relatable.

As usual, I researched today's flower after Reece left my office, and the white Anemone has several meanings—both positive and negative. While I don't know which manner Reece gave it to me in, I know which one I should want. I *should* want the negative, the one that stands for fading hope. It'd mean Reece is finally coming to terms with the fact that we aren't together, that we can't be together.

Unfortunately, as I gaze down at the delicate bloom, I find myself wanting the positive—the one that represents anticipation. Every morning Reece enters my office, I feel an impatience to be alone with him again, but not in this room where anyone walking by can see us. I want to spend hours alone with him, somewhere no one could ever find us.

Since Tuesday, I've been cold to Reece, colder than normal, but it hasn't lessened the heat in my belly when I remember our night together. My entire body is ablaze with longing, and not just for the physical part either, but for all of it. Reece listened, he watched, he pushed, he waited, he paid attention. He was selfless, intuitive, careful. He was everything I didn't know could exist in one man. He was…perfect.

And for a split second, I felt like I was, too. My past, my future, everything outside of the present melted away, leaving only the two of us in our own stolen hiccup in time.

It's that feeling alone I blame for my momentary lapse in judgement when I bought him something I had no business buying anyone, least of all Cyrus's fox.

Tonight I have to face Reece in that same place and act like I have nothing for him. Not a gift and certainly not anything else. Anything *more*. Like feelings.

I've invited several Debrosse Group employees, including the Senior Leadership Team, for a dinner party to celebrate Kordin's return. Kordin hasn't let his laptop out of his sight since his release which makes tonight that much more important. Whether or not I can get my hands on it, as well as everything it contains, I have to leave a lasting impression on the SLT, so that by the time the night's over, they believe I wholeheartedly love and trust my husband. Although we see these people on a daily basis, we've typically kept public displays of affection out of the workplace. They all know we're married, there's no need to rub their noses in it…until now.

I close the drawer, then lock it before getting up and slipping on my coat. Down the hall, past Kordin's office, I give a single knock on the open door to Kaisin's.

He looks up instantly, his murky blue eyes bulging. "Lenox? Uh… Everything okay?"

"I think so," I say while strategically placing a breadcrumb by letting my tone imply *but how could I really know?*

I enter the room that's somehow cooler than the rest of this floor, instinctively hugging my coat tighter against my body before rethinking it and letting it gape open.

Kaisin gives my form-fitting dress a once-over.

"That doesn't sound very reassuring. Is something wrong?"

A couple exaggerated glimpses behind me, then I say vaguely, "It's Kordin."

Kaisin pushes to his feet, confusion in his features but silence on his tongue.

Even if Reece is right about Kaisin having feelings for me, he'd still have to know what Kordin's up to in order to be useful. Sadly, it seems my brother-in-law, like most men, is purely ornamental.

"Can you give him a ride home for me? I need to leave early to let the caterers in."

It's going to be a four-course meal with a full bar. Since our formal dining room isn't big enough, dinner will be held in our garage. Luckily, Kordin not only insists on keeping the inside spotless, but heated as well.

"Sure. Anything."

Anything. That's two members of the board who've promised they'd do anything for me.

"Thank you, Kaisin. Anything I can do to return the favor, let me know," I say before pivoting away.

"Before you go…"

I look back.

"Is there, uh… This is kind of delicate, I guess, but is there somebody you've been seeing? You know, lately."

"Excuse me?" I ask with the most incredulous tone I can muster, prepared to deny anything and everything to the absolute death.

"Like a therapist."

A therapist?

"You said you were fine, but um… Maybe you weren't?"

Is he referring to The Pen when I left early?

I decide to stick to the story I gave Phil in case he is.

"It's honestly quite embarrassing to admit but I think I under-estimated how challenging this whole ordeal would be. It's such a relief to have Kordin back home and on the mend."

"Yeah. Of course." He waves a hand at me. "You seem much more yourself this week. That's why I thought maybe you were get-ting some help."

Much more myself? How did he come to that conclusion? Excluding Kordin's arrival on Tuesday, we haven't spoken a word to each other since The Pen.

"Oh. No, no therapist." I take a step forward. "As for this week—"

Something bangs into the threshold behind me, but I don't have to look to know what it is. Kordin's wheelchair has already de-stroyed almost every doorjamb in our house. It fits through them just fine. It's Kordin that's the problem. He's been irritable all week, and our home's trim has paid the price.

"Lenox, my love," Kordin coos. "I thought I saw you come in here."

I spin to face my husband. When he doesn't expand any fur-ther, I give him an expectant expression.

He gives one right back though, asking, "So, what are you doing?"

Shaking my head, I say, "I was just asking Kaisin if he'd be able to take you home, that way I can go ahead now and get everything ready."

"Am I not capable of asking him myself?" His tone is teetering on that line between civil and hostile.

"I know you are, but you looked very busy when I walked by, so I thought I'd save you the trouble."

Kordin looks from me to Kaisin, then back. "Since I have

you both here, we should discuss tonight. Everything needs to go smoothly."

I couldn't agree more.

"It will," I promise.

"Kaisin." He rotates his head toward his brother, his eyes following a moment after. "No hard alcohol tonight. Stick to beer, two max. And for fuck's sake, lay off the powder, would you?"

Kaisin's entire face reddens, including his ears, but he nods. I noticed at The Pen he was coked out as well. If his habit is bad enough for his brother to take notice, it must be a problem.

"As for you, my beautiful wife…" Kordin returns his focus on me. "Maybe, for once, you could try to not dress like a gold-digger at her late husband's funeral, hmm?"

"Kordin," Kaisin says with an awkward chuckle.

"She knows I'm kidding. Lenox, tell him I'm kidding."

He's not kidding.

"He's kidding," I tell Kaisin in an unconvincing tone.

"I would like it if you could see about pulling that stick out of your ass for the night though."

"I thought you preferred me with something up my ass."

Kaisin makes a sound in his throat.

"Darling," Kordin reprimands through clenched teeth. It's okay for him to tell two men, one his brother and the other a subordinate he'd only met seconds prior, about the time his wedding band came loose in my vagina, but this…this is crossing a line. I wasn't even talking about anal anyway. I was referencing what he said to me in the hospital.

"I'll find something fit for the occasion," I assure him despite having absolutely zero intention of actually fulfilling his wishes. My attire is a constant point of contention for us. Kordin often instructs me on what to wear, but eight years in, I have yet to listen. I'm usually able to smooth things over with him in one way or another. Tonight will be no different.

At The Playground, when I wasn't naked, I was forced to don ridiculously colorful outfits. People go to strip clubs to forget their misery, and black's too morose to let them. White was impractical because it stains too easily, so the rule was always the gaudier the better.

I abhor bright colors now. Luckily, Kordin does too, except where I prefer black, he favors white. Everything in his life is kept white—pure, he calls it.

But I'm not pure. I'll never be pure. Black suits me as much as it soothes me.

Seeing the color on Reece—his eyes, his hair, his clothes, his car—it's like he was designed to my exact specifications. If I hadn't seen his apartment for myself, I would've thought he was. He doesn't keep his home monochromatic. He's decorated it using a multitude of colors, all of them dark and masculine and cozy. I wasn't really at risk of falling asleep there because he took too long. I was just relaxed enough to.

"I better get going," I say with a glance at my watch. Without another word, I spin on my heel and leave.

All the way out to my car, I feel eyes on me, and all the way home, I imagine them being black.

Studying my reflection in the mirror, I tug each sleeve of my dress down over my wrists, making sure the scars beneath are hidden.

Kordin comes into the bathroom, eyes my dress, and shakes his head. It's an off-the-shoulder long-sleeve minidress with ruching at the waist and hips. It's also black.

"What about the Versace I just bought you? I spent thirty five hundred dollars on that dress."

Slowly, I turn around, the ruched material brushing against the counter's edge. "Precisely. It's far too extravagant for such an intimate gathering. I thought understated would be best."

"You can't be understated in white?"

"With my pale complexion, no. White would wash me out."

"The last time I saw you with a tan was in St. Maarten five years ago."

"You and everyone else on that island."

Kordin chuckles. "If I recall correctly, it was your idea to go to that nude beach."

"I don't remember hearing any complaints from you."

It hasn't all been bad with Kordin. It was just better when I could get drunk and he didn't find me repulsive.

"My wife was the sexiest woman on the island. I didn't mind showing you off."

And yet now he can't even stomach to look at me himself.

The nostalgia dies off as quickly as it formed.

But the subject change might be useful.

"We could use another vacation. In Jamaica maybe?" I twist my hands at my sides, fingers rubbing against each other painfully as I search his expression. "Or the Caymans." The Cayman Islands are a well-known location for criminals to keep secret *illegal* offshore accounts.

Kordin's slow to respond, his face completely devoid of emotion, then he says, "We don't need to go anywhere to reenact St. Maarten." One-handed, he undoes his pants, freeing his semi-erect cock. "Do we, dear?"

Thankfully, sex hasn't come up since Kordin's been home. Love for my husband's never been in the picture, but physical attraction has. At least until recently. Something about the last few weeks has changed my entire view of Kordin, and as I stand here, regarding his soon-to-be upright cock, it's more apparent than ever. I feel nothing. Not even the slightest stirring of arousal. I half-wonder if I can even get wet with him at all anymore.

Keeping his gaze, I approach the wheelchair, and run my hand up his shoulder to his jaw. It's not as sharp as Reece's and his eyes aren't as dark either. There's nothing outwardly dangerous about Kordin. He keeps his menace tucked away.

Just like I do mine.

"Let's get you over to the bed. I'll ride you just like I did at the beach."

Kordin visibly blanches, breaking the connection. "We're not alone and our bedroom might as well have a window right into it."

"We weren't alone that day either."

The rental cabanas on the beach had beds. It was broad daylight, there was a steady breeze coming off the water, and the walls were sheets. People saw. A lot of people saw. And heard. Discretion wasn't on our drunken minds in the slightest. That was back when I still drank alcohol.

Not that I'm opposed to public displays now that I'm sober. I just haven't been presented with many opportunities for it…until Reece came along.

"I'm not feeling quite as gratuitous." He shakes his head. "Turn around."

The ever-present scream inside me churns, swirling faster and faster like a tornado of silent protest, tearing at the walls of my throat. *Why do I have to turn around?*

What's wrong with me?

Quicker than I thought possible, Kordin shoots out his good arm, and with a handful of my dress, yanks me down on his lap so my back's against his front, his now solid erection trying to emerge between my clamped-together thighs.

"Ah, my love. We fit so well together. Lift up your dress for me."

I was prepared to do this, do anything to appease Kordin. During our eight-year marriage, I've never hesitated to fulfill his sexual urges. Whenever, wherever, however, I submitted to him, giving him what he needed, what he wanted.

And despite Reece's outlandish instruction to stop, as well as his even more ludicrous belief I would, I had no real intention to. As long as he's my husband, I would still fuck Kordin. I've always done what needed to be done, and usually, without complaint.

But sitting here, being forced yet again to face away from him, for *his* aversion, for *his* comfort, for *his* fucking pleasure, I…can't. Physically, emotionally—I cannot make myself do it.

While lying in bed together, hot, sticky, and staring up at a ceiling I now wish had a skylight, Reece told me memories are like flowers. While their existence is inevitable, their cultivation is not. Depending on how much effort you put in, you can choose which ones die, survive, or thrive. He then told me that by propagating our sex together, reproducing the act as many times as he could in one night, he was raising the memory's survival rate in his mind, and even though he didn't say it, I'm assuming he meant mine as well.

I took the opposite approach, attempting to treat our night together like a weed, using eradication to rid myself of it. I've tried all week to forget about Reece's midnight eyes, and how he refused to let them stray from mine the entire time his body worshipped mine.

Like a true weed, the memory is still here and it spread all on its own. Now it's a whole meadow, obscuring all other memories.

We had sex so many times, and Reece kept eye contact with me through every one. That wasn't because of his aversion, or comfort, or pleasure. It wasn't about him at all. It was about me. He *made* it about me and he did a damn good job ensuring I'd never forget it.

Kordin grabs me by my hair and twists my head to the side, so I'm half looking at him.

Normally having my hair pulled turns me on, but this isn't for my benefit. It's for his. Again.

"Kordin, I just did my hair." I try to shake free to no avail.

It's just shy of painful but only because I'm letting him move me. If I fight him at all, it will hurt.

"I give you everything you want, right?"

"Mm-hmm."

"I provide for you, treat you well, let you do whatever it is that pleases you."

"Yes. Always."

"Is it so unreasonable to get a little of that in return every now and then?"

I hate what I see in his eyes. It's nothing like what Reece looks at me with.

"No. It's not."

"Then please, lift up your dress," he repeats.

"What about a condom?" I ask, grasping at straws. I don't want to fuck him, but…

I will.

"We don't need one for what I have in mind."

For a split second I feel a quiver in my belly, until he says, "It's your fault for putting that visual in my head earlier," reminding me he wouldn't need a condom for anal.

I try to right my head again, but his hold at the crown tightens, keeping me bent at the unnatural angle and moving into painful territory. My cry drowns in my throat. *It's only temporary.*

"We'll need lube."

"Allow me."

Releasing my hair, he sticks his hand up my dress and jabs at my entrance, four fingers all at once. I've watched SWAT teams break into crack houses with more tact.

Unsurprisingly, my pussy remains as dry as the Atacama Desert, so even if he made it past the two barriers of undergarments currently playing my own personal gatekeepers, he wouldn't get very far. And he definitely wouldn't produce enough to lubricate an asshole.

"What is that?" Kordin continues poking around, huffing.

"Pantyhose."

With a sigh, he pushes on my back, saying, "Give me a towel."

I stand, then hand him one from the heated drying rack. Seeing the mess my hair is now, I try in vain to fix it by tousling the strands, then throw the top over to one side, giving it a deep side-part instead of the middle-part I styled it for.

"You're better off putting it up so it doesn't get in your mouth," I hear, and freeze.

My mouth?

Kordin drops his gaze to the spot in front of him.

"You want me to blow you?"

"You're not leaving me with any other options."

I eye the towel. "Is that for my knees?"

Shifting in his wheelchair, he dabs at his forehead and says, "I better hang on to it. The withdrawal from the painkillers has been making me perspire more than usual."

He's lying. The towel's to cover my head.

I don't think there's a word to describe what this feels like, to know your very presence disgusts someone. Agony, degradation, anguish—none of them do this feeling inside me justice.

The doorbell chimes out in the foyer.

"Rain check?" I offer half-heartedly.

After a long stare-off that neither of us blinks during, Kordin gives a solitary nod, excusing me.

As soon as I'm out of the bathroom, I hear him mutter, "Not with you." Instead of that internal scream boiling in the pit of my stomach, I feel a laugh bubbling up.

Now that getting even is a possibility, I'm done getting angry.

Twenty-Five

Reece

LEX OPENS THE DOOR, AND FOR A SECOND, I FORGET HOW TO breathe. Hair the color of Daisy petals falls in loose waves with a deep part from one side, like she flipped it over her head roughly while riding some dick.

She did that exact move while riding mine without even breaking pace and it was fucking hot.

The tight black dress molded to her body leaves absolutely nothing to my overactive imagination. The things I could do to her in it…

The things I could do to her *out* of it.

"Mr. Souza, glad you could make it. Any trouble finding the house?"

I hold in a chuckle. "None."

She looks like she's fighting a smile of her own as she says, "Good," before inviting me in and closing the door.

"You look…" I drag my hand across her stomach when we revolve around each other. "Incredible," I whisper, then give her the pot containing three bulbs of newly bloomed yellow Hyacinth. "These are for you."

Taking it, she examines the flowers with furrowed brows. I don't always tell her what the flowers mean, but these ones I need her to know.

"They're a sign of jealousy."

Her eyes lift to mine. Despite the brightness of the room, it's hard to make out their color. I've witnessed them in three distinct shades now—green, blue, and silver, as well as different combinations of the three—and still don't understand what amount of lighting determines which color.

"You were right," I say before dropping my voice to a whisper again to admit, "it's fucking killing me." Turns out jealousy will be the death of me, and soon if something doesn't change. Last night I broke in here again just to see Lex. She was asleep and I wore a brand-new outfit without any identifiable scents on it, so she wouldn't sense me, but I was here with her...and Kordin. It took everything in me not to smother him and let Lex think sleep apnea widowed her. Unfortunately, I didn't. Couldn't. Not yet. I need to see this thing through first.

Kordin hasn't taken any steps to protect his wife after my break-in, but he has secured his laptop. He must be storing it in his safe now because I wasn't able to find that thing anywhere. His priorities and mine couldn't be more different.

"So it was anticipation?" Lex questions softly.

Anticipation?

"The Anemone?" I ask, and she nods.

Now I'm the one wearing a confused look. She wasn't sure? Any one flower can have several different meanings, sometimes on opposite ends of the emotional spectrum, so it's all in the intention they're given with. White Anemones can also have a hopeless connotation. Is that how she thought I meant this morning's?

"It was anticipation," I tell her. She can say the other night was all she's willing to give but I never agreed that's all I'm planning to take.

"Keep that out of view." She bows her head at my left hand.

"This?" I flip my palm over, showing her it's completely empty.

"Uh-huh. Will you find me later?"

Later when?

Lex's nostrils suddenly flare, then she makes a show of inhaling the Hyacinth before saying loudly, "They smell like spring."

A second later, the distinct sound of wheels rolling over flooring hits my ears, so I whisper, "I'll find you." Nothing could stop me.

Anything she asks for, I'll give her.

Holding the pot out to the side, she turns around.

I stick my left hand in my pocket as I follow after her.

Pretending to just notice her husband stationed at the entrance to the hallway, she pulls up short, saying, "Oh, Kordin, look what Mr. Souza brought us."

She goes over to stand next to him, showing him the yellow flowers.

"Hydrangeas. Same as the ones we have out front." Kordin grins up at his wife fondly, his hand settling on the swell of her ass.

Chaos erupts inside me, and I actually take a step forward before I know what I'm doing.

Lex moves away from Kordin, only a couple inches, but enough to make his hand fall away. The second he's no longer touching her, my internal temperature plunges back to somewhere closer to normal.

I still don't like him being near her.

She angles her body to address him. "The big bushes with purple flowers?"

"Yes. Gorgeous in the summer, aren't they?"

Lex eyes the Hyacinth. "They are…but I don't remember them looking like these."

"They're the same flower, just a different color."

"They're not the same at all," I interrupt to correct. "They're two different flowers from two different families."

Kordin redirects his narrowed eyes from his wife to me.

"The plants you have outside are Hydrangeas, shrubs from the Hydrangea family." There's another name, too, but it's hard to pronounce and Kordin wouldn't understand anyway, so I save my time, only telling him, "Those are Hyacinth," while pointing at the pot. "An herb belonging to the Hyacinth family." *Two completely different families, dumbfuck.*

Kordin looks like he just got punched in the stomach, and since

I actually did punch him in the stomach before, I know. He's pissed. Kordin Debrosse doesn't like *anyone* getting *anything* over on him.

"Where's Mrs. Souza this evening? I was looking forward to meeting her."

Now's his shot at offense, putting me in the hot seat.

"She's not feeling well. Some kind of stomach bug."

"Any chance she could be pregnant?"

I look right at Lex when I say, "Several actually."

Lex clears her throat, then points me in the direction of the garage with a suggestion to help myself to a drink.

Inside the decked-out garage, I find Kaisin double-fisting a couple of beers at the bar. Neither are open; he's just staring at them.

"Thirsty?" I ask to announce my presence.

He raises his eyebrows at me in greeting. "Uh, no. Just debating."

After putting in my order with the bartender, I ask him, "What are you debating?"

"If two beers is enough."

Kordin must've put a limit on how much his CFO can consume tonight. Unfortunately, two beers won't work for what I have planned. I'm not sure what Kaisin's got in mind but I'm guessing stopping at two beers wasn't it.

"Enough for what?"

When he doesn't answer right away, I glance over to see his attention glued to the doorway I just came through. Lex is there, a gift-wrapped bottle of wine in one hand and a new candle in the other as she ushers in more guests.

"Who answered the door for you?" Kaisin questions instead.

"Lenox."

"What was she like?"

Frowning, I cock my head at him. "What do you mean?"

He drags his gaze down his sister-in-law's body like he's the one with the fucking right to. These goddamn Debrosse brothers…

"Earlier, Kordin told her not to wear black. When we got here, he went off to find her, then they were in their bathroom for a while…"

In *their* bathroom? That means their attached bath which can be seen from the hallway through the fish tank. What the fuck was he doing snooping on Lex and Kordin? And what all did he see?

"...now, she's wearing black."

Lex scans the decorated space, lingering on me for a split second longer than everyone else before she gives some kind of excuse for needing to disappear briefly. Her mascara or something.

"You think there's trouble in paradise? Maybe they were arguing?"

Kaisin shakes his head. "Kordin *always* gets what he wants."

"Apparently not."

"Have you ever seen Lenox wear anything other than black?"

Making it look like I have to think about it first, I take my time to shake my head.

He unscrews the cap to one of the beers and tips its neck at me, saying, "That's not what big bro wanted," before taking a long drink.

He wanted...

What'd he want?

In his wife's absence, Kordin singlehandedly wheels himself into the garage ahead of another group of Debrosse Group associates, bragging about the custom epoxy-coated flooring he had put in. "So clean you could eat off it," he tells them, earning a round of impressed laughs.

He rolls right by us, and from this higher vantage point, I can see his pants' zipper is only half-zipped. That, plus Lex's hair when she opened the door...

Mother. Fucker.

He wanted Lex to either ask for permission or beg for forgiveness to wear black, knowing damn well she'd be wearing it regardless.

Did she though? Did Lex do what he wanted?

I ask Kaisin where the bathroom is, pushing away from the bar before he's even done explaining. Every face I pass, every corner I scour, all I see is red, until I spot the blue glow in the hall and remember Lex went to fix her makeup.

She's just coming out of her closet when she looks up, locking eyes with me standing next to the fish tank. The bedroom door on my other side is already closed and locked, keeping me out of view from anyone who might walk past, so it's just us. Finally.

Head to toe and back, I check out Lex, finding nothing different from when she first greeted me. Both hands are empty, her make-up's still flawless, the dress is in place, and not a single strand of that sexy-as-fuck bedhead has been touched. But...

If there's one thing I've learned from Lex, it's that looks can be deceiving. Especially hers.

"Need something?"

"Yeah, you," I answer automatically.

Her brow arches. "I've found men often confuse their wants and needs."

"Not me."

"No?"

"No, see, I want to kiss your pussy, but I *need* to kiss your lips. No confusion whatsoever."

"Mm, well, I'm wearing lipstick."

"Then I'll take what I want instead."

"I'm wearing pantyhose."

This fucking woman always trying me. I swear I had patience... until I met Lex.

"Lipstick or tights, pick which one you don't mind replacing because I'm kissing one pair of lips before I leave this room and I don't give a fuck what I have to ruin to do it."

She rolls her eyes, saying, "I don't have time for this," then moves for the door.

With a hand on each bare shoulder, I intercept her and spin us so her back's against the wall now.

"Did you fuck him?"

"Who?"

Who? Who the fuck does she think?

"Kordin. Did you fuck him before I got here?"

Shaking her head, her white locks dance over her exposed collarbone. Unable to control myself, I dip down and press a kiss to each side, making her shiver under my lips.

"Did he try?" I ask against her skin. I lied. I don't just want to kiss her pussy. I want to kiss every inch of her.

"No, just a blow job."

I rear back to look between her eyes.

She plays coy, asking, "What?"

"Lex," I grit.

"What would you do to me?"

"To you? Nothing. It's him I'd punish." I'm already counting down the seconds until I get to put my hands on that motherfucker again.

Avoiding my stare, she says, "You never said anything about my mouth being off-limits."

My face hardens to granite. "Did you suck his—"

"No. God, you're exhausting."

"Why didn't you just say that? You got me over here getting all worked up over nothing."

Probably because she likes it.

"You like it," I accuse, only half-sure it's true.

"I don't…" She straightens her neck and lifts her chin in that way hollows do when they're trying to act all superior. "…dislike it."

It's the closest she's come to admitting she likes anything about me. Other than my apartment.

I flatten myself against her, burying my nose in the crook of her neck and dragging the tip along the sensitive skin.

"You look like a Before the Storm Iris and smell like icicles."

"Reece," comes out all breathy, making my cock that much harder as he seeks out the heat of her pussy.

I feel her tongue on the shell of my ear and pull back, zeroing in on that open mouth of hers.

"Choose. Now."

Before I can lose all control and seal mine over hers anyway, she twists her head to the side, telling me, "Pantyhose. I choose pantyhose."

I drop to my knees fucking instantly and hike up her dress.

"Why the fuck are you wearing these?" I say with a curled lip at the tan-colored tights covering the only thing I came here hungry for.

It's like being served a filet mignon wrapped in cling wrap. What's the fucking point?

"Warmth," she says, reminding of the conversation my family and I had about that exact topic.

Using both hands at her crotch, I rip a hole in the thin material, revealing black panties underneath.

"When's your period?"

"When my uterine wall sheds."

A chuckle slips past my lips. Bitch.

I tug her panties to one side, only to stop when I feel…something. Not blood. *Fuck, like that'd stop me.* It's the material. It's not as thin as other panties, almost like it's weighted.

A bell maybe?

A lock?

Why the fuck would she have a lock on her underwear?

"What—"

"Every pair of women's underwear has an extra piece of fabric at the crotch. It's called a gusset."

"A gusset?" I echo, glancing up at her.

"It makes a little pocket, not exactly big enough to hold anything…normally."

A pocket. Okay. So she's got something stored in there. It doesn't sound like a bell.

It better not be a lock. She knows I'd just pick that shit anyway.

I dip a finger in and scoop out whatever's in Lex's secret pocket before dropping it in my other hand. A ring sits in the middle of my palm. A matte-black ring. It's not dainty enough to be a woman's ring. It's thick and looks like a—

"It's a wedding band, rookie." Lex fingers a piece of my hair. "Your wedding band."

The outside is plain, smooth and black, nothing fancy whatsoever. But the inside has some sort of engraving. Twisting it at all different angles, I finally make out flowers—simple with only five slim petals each—but I can't tell what type they are.

"What kind?"

Her voice takes on a softness I've never heard her use. "Lemon Blossoms."

Lemon Blossoms are a promise to be faithful.

This is the first gift I've ever received from someone outside of my family and it's not just that the piece of jewelry is something I'd pick out for myself, it's the deep significance tied to it. It's a fucking vow of loyalty. It hasn't escaped my notice that every time I tell Lex not to fuck her husband, or anyone else, that she doesn't comply verbally. Or if she does, it's more performance than genuine cooperation.

This though, this fucking says more than words ever could. There's a quote on the wall at Silvy's. It's from one of Tennessee Williams's plays, and eventually, it became his epitaph. "The violets in the mountains have broken the rocks." I've seen it for years but never really understood its depth until this moment. Sometimes the smallest flower, the smallest gesture, can have the biggest impact.

My throat gets clogged when I try to thank her, making me have to clear it a couple times first.

"Don't make this into something," Lex cuts me off. "It's just to shut Kordin up. That's it."

She had the *inside* of my fake wedding ring custom-engraved for…appearances.

Right. It doesn't mean anything.

Just like the flowers and books I handpick specifically for her every day. No meaning at all.

"How'd you know I'd find it?" She could've been walking around all night with this ring tucked against her pussy. That's best-case scenario because it could've easily fallen out at some point. That useless pouch wasn't very deep or tight.

"Because I asked you to."

She asked me to find her, not her pussy.

But she knew I'd come looking for both.

I smirk. She's finally starting to understand me.

I try putting it on, but the skin around my knuckle bunches up, preventing it from moving any further.

Lex takes it from me. "Do you remember the story about Kordin's wedding band?"

Remember it? I haven't been able to get it out of my fucking head.

"Yeah," I say, wishing she hadn't just used that asshole's name.

Lex sticks the hand with my ring up her dress before pulling it back out, no ring in sight.

"Replace the memory." Her gentle caress at my hairline turns rough as she grabs hold.

Fuck, that hurts.

My cock digging into my jeans hurts worse though. I'm *that* hard right now.

"Replace it? How about I fucking obliterate it?" I say, easing two fingers up her pussy until I feel the ring with my fingertips.

I'm not fingering her with my left hand…much.

With the band secure between my fingers, I do play with her a little before bringing the ring out, slick with clear fluid. With the addition of her pussy's milk, it glides right over my knuckle, all the way up my finger to its rightful place.

Damn, it looks good.

"Lick your plate clean, rook," I hear as I lean forward, and almost laugh. Like there's even a chance I won't. Not even Kordin showing up, banging down the door to his own bedroom could stop me from finishing off his wife properly. Shit, motherfucker can park it and watch, maybe learn a thing or two.

Fisting Lex's panties with my right hand, I kiss her pussy lips as if I'm kissing her mouth. I pour all my emotions from getting her gift, her promise, into the kiss, making out with her lips—kissing them, sucking them, fucking inhaling them—and licking my tongue in between her slick walls exactly like I would her other lips. The tang of Lex's arousal awakens every one of my taste buds, flooding my mouth with a thirst for more. She tastes so fucking good. Different than the first time I went down on her because she's not fresh out of the shower, but still good. Better actually because she's more *her*.

"Oh, God," Lex pants above me, her other hand grabbing at my hair, too.

That's not gonna fly. I told her whose name to call. Mine.

With a glimpse up at her flushed face, I spear my tongue into her pussy, penetrating her until I'm nose-deep, then I press my left thumb to her clit and rub tight circles while continuing to fuck her with my tongue.

"Reece," she half-squeals, half-whispers, both of her hands slamming me into her harder and harder until finally, she locks up, her head thrown back as her knees shake on either side of me.

Her body starts to sag, but I grip both thighs from underneath and stand, pushing her up the fucking wall, my tongue still buried in her sopping wet cunt.

If her feet don't touch the floor, she can't get away.

Lex's hands scramble to my ears, shoulders, then back of my neck as she tries to hold on. "What are you doing?"

In response, I growl. That's it—one single growl. This is mine. Lex is mine and she's been kept from me for the past few days. It was a few days too many, and now, I'm feral, absolutely fucking feral for her.

Supporting Lex's lower half, I'm able to bring her to me, drawing her pussy toward my mouth on a more consistent pace. The angle opens her up to me, too, allowing for deeper, harder penetration.

Lex finds a motion that stimulates her clit with each hip rotation and drops her head back, her soft moans echoing off the ceiling as she fucks my face.

On God, she's perfect.

The points of her high heels stab into my shoulder blades, piercing the skin under my black dress shirt. The sharp pain makes my balls ache, the tip of my cock leak, and my stomach contract. I'm fucking dying to come, but don't even consider letting myself. This is about Lex. Only Lex. I'll come later, in my bed, gazing up at the fiery flowers in the sky, while stroking my cock with the panties I ripped off Lex's body last time I was here while she was awake. I'll imagine this exact moment when I felt full enough to fucking explode and I will, I'll *explode*. I'll douse her panties with cum, that way if she ever does steal them back, she'll get a piece of me, too.

I push Lex's thighs apart, spreading her wide open to expose her clit out from under its hood, then latch on and suck the swollen nub. Unable to thrust anymore, Lex diverts all her energy into keeping her screams quiet as she comes again, her clit throbbing violently against my lips.

I press a kiss to her clit, and lips, before I mop her cum up with my tongue until only my saliva remains. I lower Lex back to the floor, watching her dazed eyes as I fix her panties, then dress.

"That's how you show appreciation for a gift," I tell her.

Without opening her mouth, Lex laughs, her chest bouncing from it, and I smile, shaking my head. How am I prouder earning one laugh from her than back-to-back orgasms?

Lex removes her high heels before rolling her pantyhose down her thighs and throwing them into her closet.

"Aren't you gonna put new ones on?" I ask when she starts replacing her shoes.

"No."

"Why didn't you take them off to begin with?"

"I wanted to see if it'd stop you."

She does like it. She likes me to prove myself because nobody else has.

I make my own promise, telling her, "It'd take a hell of a lot more than nylon to keep me from you, Snow."

If we had work tomorrow, I'd bring her Kalmia. They're a symbol for perseverance.

Maybe I will on Monday.

Once we're sure the coast is clear, we take turns returning to the garage.

Twenty-Six

Reece

Kordin's still chirping about his garage, and Kaisin's already on his second beer, so I join him at the bar, ordering us a pair of shots.

Looking him over, I tell him, "Hey, you got some dandruff flaking."

"Really? Where?"

Kaisin wipes at his forehead.

"Almost got it. Just... Here." With the roller bottle tucked in my palm and hidden along my trigger finger, I reach up and roll the tip on his left temple, then the right one. "Oh shit." Wiping roughly, I dab more on, making sure I get a good amount on there. "Fuck, man, it's going everywhere." I swipe the Nightshade oil on his neck as I pat his shoulders.

Nightshade—sometimes called Belladonna—is one of the most toxic plants to humans. The entire plant is lethal. It's been used throughout history for assassinations by spies, even kings back in the day when they didn't want to get their hands dirty. Since it affects the nervous system, small doses in ointments and oils applied directly to the skin can be used for pain relief, anxiety, all kinds of shit…including insomnia. With the right dose, it's a sedative. Luckily, I was able to steal a bottle from my mom. She uses Nightshade oil for period cramps and migraines, but not only does she know how much to use, she's built up a tolerance to it over the years. Kaisin hasn't

Right as our shots arrive, I pocket the bottle, lifting the glasses between us to mask any scent of the Nightshade. While Kaisin's draining his, I spit mine into the beer bottle I've been nursing.

Every move I make, that black ring standing out against my usually naked hand catches my eye and makes me fight a grin. I love it. I love how it looks, how it feels, what it means. Lex can say it means nothing all she wants but it means something to me. It means a lot.

I get two more shots in Kaisin before everyone starts making their way over to the three rows of long tables end to end. I stay close to him, watching him closely. I've seen my mom use the oil an hour or two before bed, so that's the timeframe I'm banking on.

He goes straight for the same table as Lex, which unfortunately, Kordin's already at the head of. Lex sits to her husband's left and Kaisin posts himself on her other side.

Standing behind Kaisin, I tell Lex, "Your house looks brand new. How long have you lived in it?"

The second she opens her mouth to respond, I pat Kaisin on the back a couple times, slathering more oil at the base of his neck. His shoulders jump, but he's so absorbed in his sister-in-law speaking, he doesn't even blink away from her.

All the other chairs get filled, so I quickly take the spot directly across from Lex, putting me on Kordin's right. His right arm and his right leg are in casts, and the fact that they're closest to the person responsible for breaking both makes me want to laugh.

The first thing that motherfucker does is notice my wedding band, asking, "Is that the original or did you have to buy a replacement?" which I do laugh at because Lex called it. She knew he'd be checking tonight. I've run into Kordin plenty of times around the firm the last few days and he's brought up my wife or marriage during every one of them. I think he's trying to embarrass me, like I'm some sort of chump of a husband, but it wasn't my wife who just came on another man's face while I was in the other room showing off a fucking floor. It was his.

Before answering, I flick my tongue out to taste if Lex's cum is still clinging to my top lip.

It is.

"Replacement," I tell him with a smug smile.

"Wife's happy?"

"Very."

Multiple orgasms have that effect on her, I think before catching myself. She's not my wife.

"Then that's all that matters. Nothing beats the original, but any ring's better than no ring."

I can't help my even smugger tone as I say, "This replacement beats the original."

"Oh yeah? You think you found the exception?"

Elbows on the table, Lex steeples her hands, props her chin on her intertwined fingers, and cocks her head at me.

Lex didn't have to tell me I'm better than Kordin. Her body did it for her.

"I know I did," I say, ending the conversation. I didn't find the exception. I *am* the exception.

I spend the evening watching Lex cut up Kordin's food, cater to his every whim, gaze into his eyes, whisper kind words, all while touching him practically nonstop. Her hand is everywhere—his cheek, his shoulder, his hand, his knee under the table where only I can see it because as much as I want to stop looking, I fucking can't.

Then there's Kaisin. He's barely removed his arm from the back of Lex's seat since he sat down next to her. I've lost count of how many times he's "accidentally" brushed her hair, or worse, bare skin.

By the time dessert is served, I'm clutching my fork so hard my knuckles are about to pierce through my flesh.

I'm glad Phil's wife made him sit at the other end. If I had to deal with him groping Lex too right now, I'd stab a motherfucker. Any motherfucker.

Maybe I will anyway. This is bullshit. Lex didn't give me any kind of heads-up that she'd be affectionate to this pompous prick while her chickenshit brother-in-law gets to rub on her.

Either the Nightshade isn't working or I didn't use enough because

Kaisin has yet to show any signs of drowsiness and it's been almost two hours since the first application.

After clinking her glass, Lex asks everyone to raise theirs in a toast to Kordin while her dessert remains uneaten. She didn't eat much of her dinner either. She was too busy using her hands to stroke Kordin.

Why the fuck is there so goddamn much touching going on? Fuck!

"Before we get to that..." Kordin says, cutting off his wife. "I'd like to give a couple of my own. Lenox, my dear, will you please stand up?"

Lex hesitates before eventually indulging her husband.

Gazing up at her, he says, "Give us a smile, love," like she's his marionette.

Her chest rises and falls twice, but then she cracks the smallest, fakest grin I've ever seen. It's nothing like the ones I've gotten from her. The ones I earned.

Hand to his heart, Kordin croons, "And that, ladies and gentlemen, is how I was taken off the market. One smile from Lenox and I was forever changed."

"Oohs" and "aahs" surround me like an obnoxious laugh track as spots fill my vision.

The CEO lifts his wineglass. "To my wife. Lenox has taken on so much recently. More than any one person should. I'm grateful to have such an intelligent, capable wife."

Capable. A capable wife. It sounds like a compliment but I'm having a hard time believing it is.

Dabbing under her eyes, Lex half bends to kiss Kordin. Before she can make contact, he picks up his wineglass, and says, "Cheers," putting it to his lips.

While everybody takes sips off their drinks, Lex doesn't. She waits for Kordin to finish with his. Keeping eye contact with her, he drains more than half the glass of red wine despite lecturing someone not ten minutes ago for doing the same thing. Apparently the good stuff's supposed to be "savored."

My mom drinks wine from a motherfucking box, and the best way to drink that shit is to chug it. No glass required. You can straight pour it right from the spout into your mouth.

Kordin finally takes a break, lowering his glass.

Like she can't wait another second, Lex immediately leans in and presses her lips to his.

With his eyes squeezed shut and a noise in his throat, Kordin savors his wife like an eighteen-thousand-dollar bottle of vintage French wine.

I know this is all an act and there's no way she was actually crying over being called a capable wife, but a kiss? A fucking kiss. In front of me?

Next chance I get I'm erasing Kordin from Lex's mouth, too. Soon, there'll be no trace of Kordin Debrosse left.

Inches from his lips, Lex tells him, "I love you," then she settles back into her seat, flipping her hair over a shoulder.

My eyes fall to my ring, picturing the carved Lemon Blossoms just beneath. She doesn't mean it. She told me herself she doesn't love him.

"And now, my brother."

There's a brief pause, and then a throat being cleared.

"Kaisin, your glass."

I glance up to find Kordin glaring at his brother who's waving a hand above his wineglass.

"Kaisin, raise your glass," Kordin bites out.

Kaisin hunches over until his chin's resting on the tablecloth, and eyes wide, says, "It is raised."

Another thing about Nightshade is that it can produce hallucinations. That's how the myth about witches being able to fly got started—hallucinations after using Nightshade in their potions.

Kaisin's finally having some kind of reaction. Thank fucking God.

"Is everything okay?" Lex says close to her brother-in-law's ear, making him jump up out of his chair, lifting the table a few inches in the process before its legs slam back to the floor, causing a clatter of dishware.

Everybody startles, worried looks flying around the room faster than any witch ever could.

"What are you?" he asks her, voice husky.

Head back, Lex side-eyes me. Me. Not Kordin.

But is it because she knows I'll protect her or that I'm the reason she might need protecting?

Just like she didn't inform me of her plans for tonight, I didn't bother telling her mine.

"Kaisin!" Kordin shouts. "What's gotten into you?"

Lowering himself so he's eye level with Lex, Kaisin repeats, "What. Are."

I'm out of my seat, around both the table and Kordin's wheelchair before he can even finish. I grab him by the scruff of his neck and shove him away from Lex, making him stumble around, dazed, so I don't have to kick his ass for getting in Lex's face. Delirious or not, don't fuck with my girl.

"All those shots before dinner must've caught up with him," I say with a twist of my lips.

Focused on his baby brother, Kordin's face turns the same color as a red Dahlia. "Get him out of here."

Just the words I was looking for.

After thanking the hosts for the best meal I ever had—the food was decent; Lex was incomparable—and tossing out a handful of random goodbyes, I grasp on to Kaisin's elbow and drag him through the house. Outside, more than a dozen flashy luxury cars greet us as I stop off at Kaisin's Aston Martin to retrieve his garage door opener before pulling him down the steep driveway, my estimate of total value well over five million dollars by the time we reach the bottom.

Unlocking my Alfa Romero, I push Kaisin into the backseat. Almost instantly, a shrieking noise erupts from his throat.

"I need my ticket. Help me find my ticket," he begs, still very much awake and alert, even if he is tripping absolute fucking balls.

I pinch the bridge of my nose. Why isn't he drowsy yet? He was supposed to be sleepy now, then hopefully passed out by the time we made it to his place. What the fuck do I do with this shit? I don't want to babysit him, especially not after he was touching Lex.

He was touching Lex.

Leaning in, I pat Kaisin's pockets, checking that his phone is on him as well as which pocket it's in—front right.

"Got your ticket," I tell him, quickly hiding my empty hand behind my back. "Just sit back and enjoy the ride. All right, man?" I shut the door on a string of incoherent rambling.

Since I already know his address from following him home several times, I drive around for a while, giving him enough time to wear himself out. Once I notice him spread out on the backseat, his eyelids struggling to stay open, I head to a busy shopping center, where I wait until he's fully under to park. After a quick trip inside, I go to his place.

Parking in his garage, I wait until the door is closed behind my car to pull my laptop out, then open it up on the passenger seat. Once it's fired up and the program I need is ready, I slide Kaisin's phone out of his pocket and plug it in, immediately starting the process of retrieving every single piece of data from it and imaging it all.

Relaxing in my seat, I angle my rearview mirror on the backseat so I can watch Kaisin's body for any movement. Other than the occasional rise and fall of his chest, he doesn't stir.

Two hours and seven minutes later, it's done. I put everything back, then half-carry, half-drag Kaisin inside his house, laying him on the floor next to his bed. His shoes and socks are off next, dropped carelessly along the path to his room like he did it himself in his drunken stupor.

Thankfully, he's got an opened jar of peanut butter in one of his cupboards, so I grab that along with a spoon before going back out to the garage to get the small box from my trunk. Claws scamper around inside and tiny whiskers poke through a few of the holes in the cardboard when I lift it.

Returning to Kaisin, I dab some peanut butter around his mouth, nothing too crazy, just enough to be noticeable when he looks in the mirror later, then using his right hand—the hand he had all over Lex—I scoop out a good two-fingers worth before positioning his arm out to his side.

Our house used to get mice in the winter, usually in the attic, sometimes in the walls, but no matter where we heard that telltale scratching, my dad would set the traps the same way, with a tiny smear of peanut butter in the middle. And he'd catch them every fucking time, too.

The spoon plunged in the peanut butter, I set the jar on the nightstand, then go over to the threshold to release the rat I bought earlier. He doesn't go straight for Kaisin, instead scurrying to the nearest wall, but he'll get there. Mice and rats have that in common—they can't resist peanut butter.

I close the door and walk away.

At home, I settle in on my couch and start sorting through Kaisin's phone content, searching his call logs and messages first for anything with Lex's name. There's nothing. Well, next to nothing. There is one text from Lex, asking Kaisin if he has a wine opener. That was Thanksgiving six years ago. Other than that, there aren't any messages or calls between the two before or after, which is strange considering they're family.

I check the emails, too, just in case. Only eleven emails appear. That's it. In all the time Lex has worked at Debrosse Group, she's only emailed back and forth with the CFO less than a dozen times. Excluding the two coming together to plan my bachelor party, they haven't had any sit-downs in the time I've been there either. I've made it my business to make sure.

Judging by how little communication Kaisin and Lex have with each other, it's safe to say nothing's ever happened between them, but they do work together, so why don't they interact at all?

Next, I scour all correspondence with Kordin. An hour into it with no obvious red flags, I move on, checking every folder in Kaisin's email, starting at the top and *slowly* making my way down because this motherfucker puts everything in its own folder. He has a few labelled RENO followed by two more letters, and after combing the first one, I realize they're initials of whoever submitted the bills for renovations. RENO-LD is obviously Lex's, but when I open it, the contents are completely different from the other one. They're emails sent from Kaisin to himself and the bodies are empty. The only thing keeping them from being completely blank is the single attachment each one has. The attachments are just like the other invoices in that they're for work on different properties the Debrosse Group manages. They range from simple repairs to elaborate upgrades, all invoiced to Lenox Debrosse. But one look at them and I can spot the major difference—they're fake. Even if I hadn't been to some of these properties myself and seen the state they're in, I'd know these invoices were forged. For one, they're all printed. They weren't emailed to Lex, then forwarded on from her to the CFO for review. They were printed, then Kaisin scanned them himself—by the looks of the backgrounds and sloppy cropping, he just used his phone to take the pictures—before emailing each one to his own account. I'm sure some companies are still doing paper invoices, but every one of them? That'd be a huge fucking coincidence. It's not like I could check either because there's not a single company name to be found. Invoices almost always have a logo somewhere on them, just not always in the same spot, but the ones Lex submitted to Kaisin have a blacked-out square at the top left corner—*only* ever in the top left corner—indicating there was a logo there before someone took a marker to it.

What are the odds every company Lex hired does their invoices the exact same way? Slim to fucking none.

It's Lex scamming Debrosse Investment Properties Group, not Kordin. Of course it's Lex. Once a fox, always a motherfucking fox.

What's the real reason she wanted Kordin's laptop then? So she could frame him? Or did he discover what she's been doing, making her scramble to cover her own tracks?

Does she even want a divorce? It wouldn't make sense for her to. She'd lose her opportunity to keep embezzling funds from her husband's company.

Some of these invoices go back eight years, around the time she married Kordin, so she's been playing him all along, just like she plays everyone, including me.

And Kaisin…he approves everything she submits to him because he's in love with her, which she knows.

She knows…

Except she acted like she didn't know the day I told her.

She's a con artist. Her entire life is an act.

All of it though? Even the story about her mom? That, at least, I thought was true. I felt it. The way Lex talked about her, the raw fucking pain in her voice. How could she fake that?

But according to these records, Lex has conned millions of dollars out of the Debrosse Group, giving her more than enough money to buy a new house for her mom. She could afford anything—brand-new identities for both of them to start over, a new grave for her dad.

Was that grave her dad's? I never even looked him up. I just… trusted her.

Goddamn it.

Just like every other encounter with Lex, I'm left with too many questions and not enough answers. Even if I bring this to her, would she answer me? Honestly? Because lies roll off her tongue as effortlessly as they roll off mine. But my lies are to protect the people I care about from Cyrus…

Shit. Cyrus. If he gets ahold of this information, who knows what he'll do with it. With the ability to send her to prison, he could make Lex do anything, literally fucking anything for the rest of her goddamn life.

I thumb the black band on my finger, twisting it around and around.

What if it's not all bullshit?

Opening up a new tab, I type "Aleksander Obuchowski" in the search bar. Luckily, not many results pop up, only a handful of newspaper articles from the same year that gravestone listed as his death. The story Lex told me Cyrus came up with is all laid out, detail by detail, along with a picture of the house Aleksander lived, and ultimately died, in. Each article lists Cyrus Andeno and his wife—Yetta Obuchowski—as the victims he shot and almost killed before turning the gun on himself. Only one article even mentions Aleksander and Yetta having a daughter, but doesn't use her name, I'm assuming because she was a minor at the time.

I search both parents' names plus "Lenox Obuchowski," but nothing comes up, so then I do their names and "baby girl," and get a birth announcement from twenty-six years ago. Aleksandra Obuchowski, born April first. No wonder she doesn't joke; she was born on April Fools and probably got teased for it in the same way that kids get teased for every little thing.

So she changed her identity. She shapeshifted. Because she chose to? Or because someone made the choice for her?

Kaisin visited The Playground before Kordin did. If Cyrus crossed paths with baby Debrosse, all it would've taken was the smallest amount of prompting to get him blabbing about his brother and his real estate firm.

Shit. Kordin was targeted from the beginning, manipulated by Lex via her orders from Cyrus.

And now he wants Lex to return. Whether because the arrangement was only supposed to be temporary or Lex got greedy and has been skimming off the top, keeping some of the money for herself. Whatever the reason, Cyrus is calling his fox back.

But she's not listening.

She's too smart for that. She's…using me. She's been using me. Even when I didn't, she knew exactly why I was forced to take a job with her husband's company, and she's been jerking me around, telling me sob stories to make me care, make me *fall* for her.

Did I fall for her?

Rubbing the back of my neck, I press the base of my skull down onto the heel of my palm until both sting.

I don't want her to end up in prison.

I don't want her back under Cyrus's thumb either.

I just want…

I think back to earlier, when I saw Lex coming out of her closet and she asked me if I needed anything. It was her.

And if I'm being just as honest with myself, it still is.

I don't know how to protect Lex without wanting her, needing her…loving her.

Fuck. I did. I fell for her.

Twenty-Seven

Lex

"NEED ANYTHING BEFORE I LEAVE?"

"No," Kordin says automatically before looking up from his cell and doing a double take. He lowers the phone, face side down. "Where are you going?"

"The Wellness Den." All weekend I've been cleaning up the aftermath from Friday night's dinner party. The caterers may have taken away the leftovers and dishes, but they left the mess. Without Kordin helping, it took me all day yesterday and most of this morning. Because it's Sunday, I'm lucky I was able to grab the last massage before they close early.

"You have to be a member to get in."

"I know. I gave them your name."

"And it worked?" he asks, surprise written across his face.

"Well, you are my husband."

"I thought I canceled my membership there."

How could that be true if Reagan Hull sees him there?

"Hmm, no." I cock my head. "It was still valid during my last visit."

The skin around his eyes crinkles.

"You've already been there?"

"I went for a massage while you were in the hospital." I wait for a moment before adding, "That reminds me. I ran into one of your friends. Reagan Hull. She introduced herself to me."

Kordin doesn't say a word.

"Apparently her husband's on the police force."

My husband's lips pull to one side as he half-laughs, the sound twisting my stomach. "Matthew Hull isn't *on* the police force, darling. He *is* the police force. In fact, he's the chief of police."

"Oh," I say like this is news to me.

"I'm surprised you don't remember. I introduced you to the Hulls years ago."

No, he didn't.

"Must've been during one of your bouts of brain fog."

"Must've."

Brain fog was one of the hardest symptoms to open up about. All my thoughts felt like they were in a wind tunnel, constantly flying out of reach. Even trying to describe the experience alone was a challenge. And now, Kordin's using it against me.

"You should invite them over for dinner sometime."

"And subject them to your cooking?" This chuckle is just as nauseating.

I can cook, just not the kind of food Kordin's accustomed to. I wasn't raised on crab legs and ribeye, so I have no idea how to prepare them. I don't even like them enough to try. Crab legs are too much work for too little meat and ribeyes are mostly fat. Just because rich-people food costs more money doesn't necessarily mean it tastes better.

"We can go out."

His humor dissolves. "I don't think that's appropriate."

"Why not? I could get to know your friends bet—"

"You're going to make me spell it out?"

I wave a hand. "By all means."

"Chief Hull can't be seen out in public with a prostitute."

That's why I would've remembered meeting the Hulls. Even if I wanted to forget, my past would never allow me to. Nor would my husband. He still calls me a prostitute—not former—despite me retiring eight years ago. No matter what I wear, how much I make, who I marry, my past is always here with me because to people like

Kordin Debrosse and the Hulls, it is me—then, now, forever. Half the police force were regulars at The Playground, both up front and back in Lost and Found, but I'm the only one branded for the rest of my life. Not them. Not the ones who repeatedly and unabashedly cheated on their spouses. Not the ones who got too rough because they knew they could. There are no consequences for men in power; only the women who could easily take it all away. Sex workers hold all the cards because if we ever chose to show them, it'd be a clean sweep in every single tax bracket.

But we're told we don't have any power. We're told we're nothing. We're *treated* like nothing. And after a while, we believe it. It's easier to fall down a waterfall than swim up one. The constant deluge at the bottom becomes…familiar. It's anything else—No, everything else, that you become wary of. Kindness is just a tactic you learn to spot instantly. Gifts are physical tokens of manipulation. And love… Love is the most lethal weapon in existence because it's more addicting than crack, it's priceless, and it's invisible. You cannot see it until it's too late, and by then, you're already hooked. Once you experience love, you'll do anything to feel it, to keep it, to protect it. I've seen people loan out their bodies trying to buy drugs, but I've seen people lose themselves entirely trying to find love.

Love is the world's biggest serial killer, yet it'll never make headlines.

"I, however, have no reservations. I'd love to go out with you," Kordin says, as if that lessens the sting of the blow he just delivered.

Fake love is a gateway emotion; it opens the door to real love.

Unless you keep it closed and locked.

I lift my eyebrows. "How about tomorrow after work?"

"I was thinking right now. I'm sick of ordering in."

"My massage—"

"That? After everything you've been through, you deserve more than one massage. I'll book you a whole wellness package somewhere else." Bringing his phone back up, Kordin starts typing with his thumb. "Somewhere nicer."

Nicer. He means farther away.

"Tonight?" Reece's face flashes in my mind. I wouldn't get to say goodbye.

Do I need to say goodbye? We're not anything...serious. Technically we're not anything at all.

Are we? I gave him a ring, which could've really muddled things if I hadn't made it clear that it meant nothing.

"No, I need you at the office right now. Next weekend." Kordin holds up his phone to show me the hotel confirmation. "All booked. Luxury wellness resort in the Catskills. You'll go up Friday evening and return home to me Sunday afternoon."

He didn't even pretend to search for a place to ship me off to. He already had one lined up, awaiting his credit card number.

"Go ahead and cancel tonight's appointment, then we can leave."

"I already had dinner."

"Lenox. Not everyone enjoys drinking their meals. I'm craving a juicy porterhouse." His stare sharpens as he uses his left foot to propel his wheelchair forward several inches in my direction. "So, call. I'll wait."

After a deep breath, I pull my phone out and make the call.

"Good," Kordin says when I'm finished. "Tomorrow I'll let them know to cancel my membership."

Two birds just met their demise and there's nothing I can do about it. Despite only having his left hand, Kordin still pitched his one stone with perfect precision. I'm once again cut off from his secret connections and he gets a weekend with whichever girlfriend he chooses.

"Thank you, Kordin. You think of everything."

"Anything for my wife," comes out in an equally placating, borderline patronizing, tone as mine.

Twenty-Eight

Lex

REECE ENTERS MY OFFICE, STANDS ACROSS FROM ME, AND sets the flower and dark-looking romance down without bothering to sit. It's the same energy he's been using all week, like he's on autopilot. He's doing what he's done every day he's worked here, and yet now he's doing it *wrong*.

"Have anything new to tell me?" I ask him despite already knowing his answer.

"No," he says for the fifth day in a row before twisting away so he's no longer facing me.

I leave for the mountains in a matter of hours and I still haven't told Reece, mainly because he doesn't stick around long enough for me to be able to, but also because of this…indifference. He barely meets my eyes, he speaks in a clipped tone, and he doesn't bring us up at all—not what happened between us, not what he wishes would happen between us, nothing. He just gives me a rundown of his work-day—his actual workday—before walking right back out.

The ring I gave him is still on his finger though. I can't help seeking it out each and every time I look at him. Even when I see him watching me out in the parking lot, his fist tightened on the top of his steering wheel, I search for the custom band.

It means nothing, I remind myself.

Unlike today's flower, a black Dahlia, which I know has a meaning.

Probably an ominous one. Yesterday's was a Begonia. I looked it up and none of its meanings were good. Lots about caution and warnings, but also deep thinking.

If he has a warning for me, I need to know now. I'm still just as out of the loop as I've always been. In spite of requiring Reece's eyes and ears, all I've managed to utilize so far is his cock.

It is a fabulous cock though. The man attached to it isn't that bad either, not that I could ever tell him that.

With a sigh, I relocate both gifts to my bottom drawer, careful not to smash any of the other flowers.

"I've gotta check out a building over on Birch and—"

"What does it mean?" I ask him point-blank, a little mad at myself for caring so much. Not a little. A lot. I shouldn't care at all. I wish he'd stop giving me flowers altogether.

Reece releases his own heavy exhale. "Some countries think birch is a symbol of good luck."

"What does the Dahlia mean?" I snap, because the truth is I hope he never stops giving me flowers.

And that's the problem. I don't like him being distant and I should. I should be ecstatic he's finally heeding my own warning. I should be, but I'm not.

Reece stares into my eyes for the first time in a week. I hold the black volcanic glass pools, desperately wanting to understand what's below their surface.

"Dishonesty. Betrayal," he bites out, the disapproval rattling my ears like a clap of thunder, the finality ringing long after. It hurts my ears, but more than that, it hurts something deeper inside me.

Nobody was supposed to ever reach that.

"You're sure you weren't able to get anything out of Kaisin?"

I know he got Kaisin drunk on purpose. He took him home, too, which gave him the perfect opportunity to get some answers— assuming Kaisin had any to give—but every time I ask, Reece acts oblivious. Something changed over the weekend to make him behave like this. Why won't he tell me what it was?

His shrug is too easy, too relaxed. "He didn't say a word."

298 | A. MARIE

Either Reece is a terrible spy, he's lying, or both.

"And you're sure you're not responsible for his hand being injured?"

Monday morning Kaisin had a thick padding of gauze wrapped around his right hand. On my way into my office, I heard somebody ask him what happened, causing his face to turn a very perplexing shade of red as he muttered through a completely implausible story.

"I didn't hurt his hand."

"Uh-huh." I didn't miss Reece's scowl trained on Kaisin's hand every time it brushed my back during Friday night's dinner. "Since you came into my life, every man that's touched me, coincidentally all have hand injuries. At least in this office." It is no coincidence. It is only Reece.

My panties grow wet, my pussy lips twitching at the realization.

"Why'd you add 'in this office'? Did somebody else touch you?" he asks, finally dropping the monotone he's used all week.

"The guard at The Pen." I let that hang in the air, waiting to see if he'll confess to anything. When he doesn't, I add, "But that was before we fucked, so technically, your rule wasn't in effect yet."

A deep frown is his only response.

Kordin rolls by my office, glancing in at us, and my pussy recoils in absolute fucking horror. Reece hasn't broken our morning routine once, so this is nothing out of the ordinary, however Reece staring the CEO down is.

Bringing my hand up to my mouth, I pretend to chew on a nail, saying around it, "Sit or he might come in here, thinking this is just a social call, and try to join."

As I speak, Kordin's wheelchair slows to a stop.

Reece lowers himself into the chair opposite me, and after a moment, Kordin begins moving again.

Turning his glare on me, Reece asks, "You wanna tell me why you're still with him?"

I study him long and hard before answering, "I already did."

"How can I trust anything that comes out of your mouth? You're a liar."

"You've known that since our first encounter, rook," I say evenly. "Why get distraught about it now?"

"I'm not distraught. I'm pissed."

"Why? What happened? Did I do something to offend you?"

"Other than that make-out session you pulled right in front of my fucking face?"

"You found that offensive? Do kisses not fall under 'wife-duties,' the ones you so *generously* gave me permission to fulfill?"

"Not that kind of kiss."

A noise of sadness cloaked in incredulity rushes out of me. That kind of kiss. The kind I used in retaliation against Kordin for making me smile in front of others. The kind that caused my husband to nearly vomit the second my lips touched his. Us having an audience might've been the only reason he allowed me to kiss him, but it's also how he managed to keep his dinner down, otherwise I'm positive he would've thrown up.

Didn't Reece hear the gag? See the warning Kordin shot me using his eyes before *and* after the kiss? Like he pointed out, it was right in front of his face.

I triggered physical illness with that kiss. Not just Kordin's, and not just my own. But apparently, Reece's as well.

I fold my trembling arms over my chest, adding another layer of protection since evidently my ribs aren't doing a suitable job.

I need to put an end to whatever it is Reece and I are doing once and for all. After vowing not to, I stupidly gave him an inch—the same inch I've given hundreds of others—but like the thief he is, he thought he'd take a fucking mile. A foot in and now I'm the one wanting more. I don't like him being hurt. I don't even like the idea of it.

Yet that's exactly what I have to do to get this to stop. I have to hurt him. Right now. Before everything comes to a head. And it will. I'm no closer to getting the dirt I need on Kordin than when I first went to Cyrus for help.

This conversation proves I can't trust Reece any more than he can trust me. I practically told him not to at The Pen. If it comes down to

me or his family, he *should* drop me, because if it were between him or mine, I know my choice and I make no qualms about it.

I don't…but I might start to.

So I'm dropping him before that can happen.

"You're right," I tell him, altering my version of what took place to his. "There was more to that kiss than met the eye."

His brows knit together. "What are you talking about?"

"I'm talking about what that kiss ultimately led to after our guests left."

"Fucking?"

"Mm."

"You're lying."

I raise both shoulders as if to say *you'll never know.*

"You let Kordin fuck you?"

As eyes colder than the dark side of the moon bore into mine, all I can muster is a nod.

"Are you telling me this because you can smell Cia on me?"

My shoulders droop like gravity just kicked back on. "What?"

"Cia? Last time she and I…"

"Fucked?" I hear myself ask without feeling my lips move.

"Yeah. Last time we fucked."

My lungs seize up, the oxygen flowing between my lips catching, loud enough for Reece to notice and smirk triumphantly.

"You smelled her on me afterward, and since we were just together last night, I thought—"

"That I was a hothead with unreasonable expectations like you?" I shake both my head and my discomfort. "Who you fuck is not my concern."

Reece drops the smile. "Just who I marry?"

"You're not married." As hard as I try not to, I glance down at his ring finger. I also take a surreptitious inhale through my nose, seeking any hint of Cia's atrocious perfume.

God, this is pathetic. I'm pathetic.

"But when you thought I was, you got mad when I brought my sister in because you assumed she was my wife."

"I wasn't mad. I was preoccupied with formulating a plan to dismember you because she was clearly a minor."

"You were mad. And you were so relieved when I told you the truth, that I made the engagement up, that you even fucked my mouth with yours."

"Don't delude yourself. I kissed you because I was drunk and you were easy."

"You were jealous."

"You're projecting, Mr. Souza. And reaching."

"Fuck you, *Lenox*," he spits, pinching my nerve in the same way I just pinched his. "I'm open with my possession. You try to hide yours. Like you're doing now."

I fake a partial laugh, feeling my own anger rise up.

"How could I possibly be possessive if my husband cheats on me constantly?"

"Because your husband doesn't make you happy."

The truth squeezes my heart in my chest. Again. *Damn it.*

I fight through the pain to tell him, "I found what I need."

It takes a moment for Reece to respond before he questions, "Did you?"

"Yes. And now that I've obtained enough evidence to prove Kordin's infidelity—"

"You're leaving him?"

"I was going to say your involvement with this company is—"

"Are you leaving him? Yes or no?"

Relocating my concentration to a pen, I say, "Eventually."

Pitching to his feet suddenly, he tells me, "Meet me on the stairs in ten minutes." Then, he stalks out of the room.

I wait twenty seven and a half minutes before approaching the stairwell.

The second the door closes behind me, Reece asks, "How'd he fuck you?"

Remembering the saying *ask stupid questions, get stupid answers,* I tell him, "Like a sex addict on ecstasy," because his question is by far the stupidest.

"So he took you from the back." That triumphant smirk reappears. "Once."

"Like I said in my office, Mr. Souza, I no longer require your assistance."

"My assistance. You admit you've been using me?"

"I…tried," I say truthfully. "Why else would I allow you to work here? Out of charity? No. I thought keeping Cyrus's mole close could be useful, but unfortunately, you only proved incompetent, again, leaving me no choice but to fir—"

He gets in my face. "Fire me again. See what happens."

Looking between his eyes, I see the threat there. No, not threat. Promise.

He's really not going to make this easy on me, is he?

"I don't need to. I'll have HR do it."

I turn to leave, but when I try to open the door, Reece props his big hand on the wood above my head, keeping it closed. Taking another step closer to me, I can feel his front pressing in on my back and close my eyes tight.

"I know you've been using me," he whispers near my ear. "And I don't care."

"You're an idiot," I whisper back.

"Only for you."

"Your attachment issues are disturbing. You should seek help. Immediately."

"What about your attachment issues?"

"I don't—"

"You're pushing me away because you're scared I'll make you happy. You're even more scared I already do."

Scared is too weak a word, I think, but say, "You don't have that kind of effect on me."

His other hand finds my heart. "I have some kind of effect on you. Your heart's about to beat out of your chest."

Heart palpitations. *Are they heart palpitations?*

"A result from having a dangerous thug block my escape," I bite

back, trying to convince myself as much as Reece. It can't be heart palpitations.

It can't be what he's implying either though.

It.

Can't.

Because other than the one to my mother, I don't have attachments.

"I'm not dangerous to you," he says, making a scoff tear from my throat before I can stop it. If that were true, I wouldn't be in this predicament.

"I didn't fuck Cia."

The tension in my body thaws a fraction, the air in my lungs pumping easier. I open my eyes, keeping them focused on the wall in front of me.

"You could've."

"No, Snow, I couldn't. She doesn't have—"

"A mean bone in her body and you like being treated like shit?"

His chest shakes against my back.

"Your eyes. She doesn't have your eyes. Or your hair. Or your scent." He buries his nose in my hair, inhaling, then pushing my cheek, he turns my head to the side. "Or your mouth."

He kisses me and my lips respond out of pure reflex. I missed this. *I missed him.*

That last thought has me ripping my mouth away.

"She's not you," he says fiercely despite his quiet tone. "Whether you admit to claiming me or not, I'm yours, and I don't fuck with anybody else. Not anymore. Not ever again."

Thoughts swirl like they're in a wind tunnel all over again, making it difficult to pluck the right one out.

Pain. Focus on pain. For me, for Reece.

"That doesn't change the fact that I did fuck Kordin."

"I don't believe you. I don't believe you even let him lay a finger on you."

"He didn't use his fingers, rookie."

"Prove it. Bend over and let me see what that hollow did to *my* pussy."

I struggle to get out of the cage his body has me in but just end up rubbing my ass against his stiffening cock. "I'm ending this. We're over. And—"

Removing his hand from the door, he yanks my hips away from the wall a few feet.

"And you're so turned on I could fucking smell you from over your desk."

"Kordin's a very attractive man."

"You were dripping before you saw him."

"You don't know—"

He grinds his stiff cock into my backside, causing me to end my sentence in a moan.

"Hands on the door. There aren't any cameras in here, but there's no lock either, so hold the door closed for me."

His large hands over mine, he flattens my palms to the door, my body bent with my ass rooting side to side against him as I seek out that friction my pussy likes so much.

"Is this how he fucked you?" Reece asks, his nails trailing up my wrists, arms, then shoulders.

Gripping my neck for leverage, he thrusts against me, and I lift my head on a hiss, arching my back.

"Is it?" Another thrust.

"Yes."

The heat of his body disappears before cold hits my ass from my skirt being lifted.

"Tights again?" he mumbles.

A second later there's multiple ripping sounds. Nudging my panties to the side, Reece shoves two fingers right in my tight hole, his palm wedged in my ass crack, right up against my even tighter hole.

"God," I groan, clenching around his digits as hard as I can before widening my stance to rock against his hand, my pussy's cream already making for a slick glide.

"Why'd you lie about fucking Kordin?"

"I didn't."

"You did." He crooks his fingers and I shudder over his wrist. "Was it because you wanted me to fight for you?"

"I wanted you to leave."

His movements falter. "You wanted me to break up with you?"

"We're not together."

Reece tears his hand away, so I go to straighten, but he grips a handful of my hair, his fist on my spine keeping me bowed. I hear his pants being unzipped and the material shifting, then feel his cock's tip at my entrance.

"We're not together?"

I roll my eyes. He thinks I'll fold for dick. *Rookie.* I'm the MVP of this game. I used to make a killing teasing sex, and I *never* gave in until after I won.

I ease backward, crowning his cock. "We're not together. We just fucked a couple times behind my husband's back."

Keeping just his head inside my entrance, Reece slowly bobs himself in and out until we're both breathing heavy.

Right as I push against the door, trying to back up into him, he withdraws entirely, leaving my pussy aching and tightening painfully around nothing.

"You'll get more when you say we're together. You'll get it all, every fucking inch, Snow White. Just tell me the truth."

My lips remain sealed.

He tugs on my hair, sending my chin toward the ceiling. The lack of pain gives me hope. Neck sensitivity was another one of my symptoms, but now I feel none.

"Admit it."

How do I get him inside me without letting him win?

Challenges always work.

"Why would I work for something that I can go down the hall and get for free?"

In one hard plunge, Reece fills me completely before instantly pulling back out and repeating the move. My mouth falls open on a silent scream, tears leaking from the corners of my eyes as he drives into me again.

"Fucking. Liar. This pussy hasn't been stretched recently."

That's a myth men made up to make women feel guilty for having different partners. A woman can have sex with fifty different men and her pussy will be in the same shape it'd be from having sex with the same man fifty times. Pussies aren't beaches. They don't erode. They're muscular canals that can be tightened back up with a few simple exercises.

I do one of them now, squeezing my vaginal muscles during Reece's deep plunge, and he croaks out a strained, "Fuuuck."

"You can't tell when I last had sex."

"I can. Aside from your tight cunt choking my cock like a goddamn virgin, your body's stiff as a board."

That we actually can thank Kordin for. I wouldn't be if I'd gotten that massage.

"Probably because it feels like Kordin is fucking me. He neglects my clit, too."

Reece growls, but releases my hair. A second later he's rubbing tight circles over my swollen clit.

My legs quaking beneath me, I gasp, "Jesus."

"Wrong man again."

"Reece."

"There we go. You like me fucking you?"

"Mm," I hum noncommittally since it's pretty obvious I do... when he's doing it right.

Switching hands at my clit, Reece holds his wet fingers up to my mouth, and I lick my own juices off each one before sucking them into my mouth.

"Show me how much you like me fucking you. Soak me, Snow. Soak my cock."

Still massaging my clit, he pounds into me from behind, and I have to bite his fingers to keep from screaming.

"Fuck, you're gonna bite my fingers off."

I bite even harder, the metallic tang of blood filling my mouth, and his speed increases. The sound of our bodies slamming together echoes in the stairwell, then suddenly Reece thrusts into me one final time, grumbling my name as his cum surges out of him.

Instead of withdrawing, Reece circles his hips, forcing a deeper penetration to massage my cervix with his cock's tip. What feels like a ball of tension in my gut spins faster and faster, growing bigger and bigger.

My jaw drops, releasing his fingers, but he's quick to cover my mouth before any noise can escape.

Voices on the other side of the door have me tensing up and taking a step forward, but Reece snarls, "Mine," dragging me right back to continue teasing my cervix. He even bites my shoulder like a fucking animal, keeping me in place. It is single-handedly the most erotic thing I've ever experienced, and just when I think I can't take anymore, the knot deep within unfurls like one of Reece's flowers, sending petals of bliss outward to the rest of my body. Wave after wave, pleasure crashes over me and through me until I feel like I'm glowing inside and out.

"That's why we're together," he pants. "Because we get off on each other's darkest parts. I like you rough and you like me possessive."

"Maybe I just like that your cock's bigger than my husband's," I say, equally breathless, my body still buzzing what feels like audibly. My God, I've never felt anything like that in my life.

"You didn't let him fuck you. Your body tells me truths your mouth refuses to."

As soon as he pulls out, I spin around, slumping against the door to fix my clothes.

"Even if you did, it'd take more than that to get me to walk away."

"What would it take?"

Tucking his shirt into his pants, Reece scoffs. "A blade through my heart?" he guesses, like he's not even sure that would do the trick.

"I'm going straight to HR after this. It's over."

He looks up at me. "How many times did you come?"

"Once."

"Shit," he murmurs, closing the distance between us.

I try sliding right, but he mirrors the move, one hand cupping my cheek while the other disappears beneath my skirt.

I knee him in the balls, and he drops to his knees at my feet. It's a beautiful sight until he glares up at me, his eyes full of unshed tears as he sputters, "What the *fuck?*"

"HR's gonna be looking for you, so when you're able to, use the stairs and go down to a lower level, then take the elevator back up—"

"I don't care if I work here or not…" Shaking his head, he pulls himself up to his feet using the handrail. "We're not fucking done."

"Yes, we are. We're done." I have to fight to keep my voice low. "We have to be," I grit one of the few truths I've said all day.

"Lex—"

"Reece, don't walk away. *Run.* Do what we talked about. What I showed you." I give him a pointed look. "Then run as fast and as far as you can."

His posture seems to double as he straightens his spine. "Why the fuck did you bother getting me on your side if you were just going to push me away?"

I never wanted him on my side. I wanted him as far from me as possible. I thought by showing him my side, he'd realize that. But he didn't because he's a fucking masochist who mistakes my every warning to leave as an invitation to come closer.

"You've been mistaken from the start. I'm the black Dahlia, not the Snow White Hibiscus. Dishonesty and betrayal, rookie. That's all I'm capable of."

"No, it's not. I've seen—"

"You've seen what I wanted you to!" I whisper-shout.

"What about the loyalty you promised me? What were you showing me with that?"

"A reminder apparently. That promises are like shells on a beach. They look pretty on the surface, but underneath they're almost always broken." *Like me.*

I frown.

"Not my promises. Not my fucking promises, Snow. I don't break my promises."

I make myself turn my back on him, saying softly, "You will if you stay." Reece has made promises to his family as I have to mine. It doesn't matter how good the sex is between us, those promises aren't worth breaking.

"Coward."

He has no idea how much courage this is taking. How much pain it's causing.

Pain is still safer. I can live through pain. I *do* live through pain and I will continue to…with a lot less orgasms.

Twenty-Nine

Reece

WE'RE NOT FUCKING THROUGH. I DON'T GIVE A FUCK what Lex says.

The elevator doors open to floor forty-two with Kordin's wheelchair blocking my way out. The motherfucker blinks up at me, frowning.

"Souza, didn't I just see you in Lenox's office?"

"Yeah, she, uh…" He doesn't know yet? I'm not gonna be the one to tell him and give him another reason to look down on me. "She asked me to check out a property."

"Did she now? She's such a go-getter."

"I got all the way to the lobby before I realized I forgot my keys in my desk."

He studies me. "Are you one of those guys that'd forget his head if it wasn't attached?"

Trying my hand at looking guilty, I shrug. I spend so much of my time feigning innocence, it's actually pretty fucking difficult. I think of his wife's cum still coating my cock and balls and have to press my lips together.

I must pull it off because rolling himself forward, Kordin parks on the track and jerks his head to the side. "Get your keys, we'll ride down together. I've been meaning to talk to you anyway."

After a brief hesitation, I slip by him, then head in the direction of my cubicle. The only thing I've bothered keeping here is my lap-top case, so I grab that, leaving behind the company-issued laptop I barely touched.

Back in the elevator, I hit the button for the ground level, notic-ing the one for the sixth floor already lit up.

"So what was it you wanted to talk to me about?"

"Your meetings with my wife..."

Curling my fingers, I slowly form my free hand into a tight fist. "Who approved those?"

Approved them? Why would a meeting with Lex need approval?

I look over at him, but he's focused on the doors, his chin lifted like a king on his throne.

"Uh..." I shake my head. "Lenox, I believe."

He makes a noise in his chest, but doesn't say anything else on the subject, just asks, "Any plans for the weekend?"

As I face forward too, I try to think of the most mundane married-thing possible.

"The wife wants to go furniture shopping."

"Where are you thinking?"

"We'll probably go down to the city. Make a whole getaway out of it."

Out of the corner of my eye, I see Kordin turn his head my way before he murmurs, "Must be in the air."

"Furniture shopping?"

"Travel. My wife...she's an angel." He chuffs out a laugh, and I glance at him again, but he immediately rights his face. "Even while playing nurse to me at the hospital, she didn't miss a beat here."

My hold on my bag's strap tightens. Lex wasn't his nurse. If any-thing, his wife was tending to *my* needs.

"It really is a mystery how she does it all. I had to coerce her into taking a break for a weekend away."

A silence surrounds us as I replay every word Lex said to me today. She didn't even hint at going out of town with Kordin. If there was anything she could rub in my face, it'd be that. A fuck with Kordin, especially the way he does it—all impersonal and shit—I could write that off. But her taking a trip with him? Willingly? That's harder to swallow because I didn't just claim Lex's pussy. I claimed all of her.

What if he wants to reconcile?

"In the city?"

"No, no. The Catskills."

That's a very extensive, very rural area. What if he confronts her about the money she's stealing and she kills him?

What if he kills her?

Watching the falling numbers, I ask as casually as I can, "You two getting a cabin up there?"

"Lenox in a cabin?" Another laugh, this one unmistakably phony. "It's nothing but extravagance for that woman. She has... Well, let's just say, my wife's acquired quite the taste for luxury over the years."

I fight to keep a neutral expression. She wouldn't have been exposed to her current hollow lifestyle, and probably never would've been, if it weren't for Kordin. So if Lex is a monster, she's the monster he created.

"She wouldn't even consider anything less than five-star accommodations, so I set her up in a lavish resort."

I side-eye him. "You're not going?"

He shakes his head. "Lenox will be too busy getting pampered to even remember I exist. That's the dream anyway," he adds with an even faker laugh.

I force one, too. "Right."

Too busy to remember her husband...and the woman he's planning on fucking while she's not around.

I knew Lex was lying. She didn't fuck Kordin. If she did, he wouldn't need to schedule a fuckfest with somebody else.

"Since she'll be leaving early for the day, go ahead and come to me with your findings."

The elevator stops at the sixth floor.

An arm on the door, I say, "I'll have everything typed up and emailed to you by the end of the day," knowing damn well I won't.

The CEO doesn't move, just remains where he is, not even

looking at me as he says, "We can go over everything together during our morning meetup on Monday."

"Morning meetup?"

"Yeah. Going forward, I think it'd be more beneficial for you to meet with me instead of Lenox."

More beneficial for who?

Kordin wheels himself out but does a clunky two-point pivot to address me again, his eyes rising to only my chest. "Let's keep this between us. Lenox has enough on her plate."

"Consider it forgotten," I tell him with a tap to my head, referencing his earlier remark.

"I knew I could count on you."

His words hold a weight to them that sounds almost like, but I'm not sure why, triumph.

A pretty blonde with her hands behind her back and her perky tits piercing the sky, approaches, greeting, "Mr. Debrosse. Back so soon? It's only been a few days."

The large sign behind her reads, "Summit Enhancements" with a smaller motto underneath that says, "Elevate your vision."

There are several other medical practices in the building, including a doctor who strictly does dental veneers. It's like a one-stop shop for Fox Hollow's elite.

"It's the customer service I can't get enough of," he says before going ahead of her, making her keep pace with him.

I fix my gaze on the backs of their heads, wondering what the fuck just happened. Kordin speaks in endless backhanded compliments. His tone is smooth and concise, while his words are jagged and hard to navigate. In no way do I believe he considers Lex an angel or that he's sending her away to help *her*. I'm the one he offered to let rape her. Where was his great concern for Lex's wellbeing then?

Up until this moment, I thought Lex was the most calculated person I'd ever met, but Kordin Debrosse is the real actor. But *why* is he acting? If he's not the one ripping off his company, what's he hiding? It can't just be the affairs. Most guys try to make their wives sound worse than they actually are as a way to justify their cheating.

Not Kordin. He's over here hyping his wife up. Lenox Debrosse, the extravagance-demanding angel.

Neither of which has been my experience with Lex.

With him busy getting his eyesight checked and Lex talking with HR, that leaves their house empty and free to explore for clues.

Peeling out of the parking lot, I race toward it without a backward glance.

The massive Colonial is still, stiller than it is at night when its occupants are fast asleep. Starting in the kitchen, I scour it top to bottom. Everything's fucking spotless, to the point it reminds me of a model home. There is a pill box holding various pills for each day of the week though, proving it's not. The pantry is pretty bare, mostly stocked with dust-covered half-empty bottles of alcohol, bags of nuts, vitamins—D, B, and Ashwagandha—and some kind of tea that makes me gag when I open the container. Other than fresh fruits and vegetables filling every shelf and drawer in the fridge, there's not a lot of food. No dairy whatsoever. The freezer has tubs of ice cubes in all different shapes and sizes, along with a few eye masks. The eye masks belong to Lex, I know that, but the rest… Is Kordin a health freak?

Someone living here cares a lot about what goes in their body.

Or lack thereof. Who the fuck can live off berries, nuts, and ice? Who'd want to?

It can't be Kordin. No way his rich-blood would tolerate a diet of fucking raspberries. It's gotta be Lex. I've only ever seen her consume black coffee.

I head to their suite next, combing the entire room as well as the bathroom and both attached closets. Other than the drawer of vibrators in Lex's nightstand, the bedroom doesn't have anything of interest. The bathroom doesn't give me much either, not even glasses, lens cleaner, or contact solution for Kordin, only a bottle of eye drops in Lex's side of the drawers. For someone who visits the eye doctor so frequently—twice in one week—I would've thought there'd be some sort of sign.

Kordin's closet is loaded with designer suits, diamond-encrusted watches, matching cuff links and tie bars, while Lex's looks like it's having an identity crisis. Half of her closet mirrors Kordin's— high-price clothing, shiny jewelry, and enough pristine-condition purses to open a handbag store. One look at it and I can tell it's the half that doesn't get worn, not only because of the colorful hues but because all the price tags are still attached. The other half is made up of black items from nice but definitely less-expensive brands, and have Lex's scent all over them.

Who buys the stuff on the untouched side? And why? It doesn't make any sense why Lex would. She literally won't wear any of it. Ever.

But it doesn't make any sense why Kordin would either. In ex-change to get Lex to agree to sex? He's the one who only fucks her from the back. That's not a burning desire you'll do anything for; that's a power move.

Like the one I just got done pulling on Lex.

In a stairwell.

During the workday.

Fuck!

No wonder she doesn't believe we're together. I don't fucking treat her like we are. I fell for a liar, got pissed at her for lying, then punished her for more lies. After ignoring her all week, I fucked her from behind…just like her piece-of-shit husband does.

What the fuck is wrong with me?

If I want her to fall for me, I have to earn it. I have to earn every-thing, including her trust.

After checking the rest of the house, I return to their bedroom, taking it all in again. Like everything else in this place, the primary could pass as a display in a furniture store. Nothing is out of place ex-cept for the rolling suitcase at the end of the bed. The top of Kordin's nightstand has an alarm clock while Lex's is empty. Ever since Kordin's been back, it's been free of anything personal, anything that might bring her joy.

What's she planning on doing with her stolen millions if she barely even spends the legitimate money she's making now? It can't all be for her mom.

Wait.

She barely spends the legitimate money she's making now.

Lex didn't buy that over-the-top neglected wardrobe. She wouldn't have. She doesn't even buy herself nice things she likes, let alone nice things she doesn't. Kordin showers her with expensive shit to back up his claims of her being materialistic.

If Kordin viewed Lex as an angel, her robbing his company would blindside him. But at the same time, if she's as high maintenance as he makes her out to be, her greed wouldn't surprise anybody. And with her past…

Son of a bitch. Kordin Debrosse is framing Lex, a former fox stripper, for embezzlement.

It wasn't Cyrus who set it up. It was Kordin. After hearing Kaisin talk about her, he went to The Playground and plucked her right off the stage to be his scapegoat. He knew that if Kaisin—his CFO—felt that strongly for their portfolio manager, his brother would authorize anything she submitted to him. Any invoices for any amount of money, of course he'd approve it, no questions asked.

Lex has to know about the embezzlement. She has to. She was desperate to get Kordin's laptop. Desperate enough to invite Cyrus back into her life.

Does she know she's being set up though?

I just went through every inch of this house and there's nothing in it to even hint at Kordin's setup. He's too smart to leave evidence around the person he's framing. He's too smart to leave evidence around, period. That's why he keeps everyone at the firm away from Lex. He's isolated her so no one could figure it out, figure *her* out.

His only mistake was trusting a CFO so dumb he's actually smart. Kaisin unknowingly created proof the moment he took pictures of those invoices and emailed them to himself.

Lex would only know that if she hacked her brother-in-law, which she didn't. If she knew how, she would've hacked Kordin to begin with.

Which means she was lying her ass off earlier. Not only did she not let Kordin fuck her, but she didn't find anything incriminating either.

If I want to earn her trust, I've gotta come clean and tell her everything.

Cracking my knuckles, I eye the suitcase.

I'm guessing she didn't demand a luxury resort either. Kordin probably did as a way to keep tabs on her. He's shipping Lex off to the mountains for the weekend, all alone, with spotty cell service. He needed to know exactly when she'll arrive and when she'll leave, and some privately owned cabin wouldn't provide the same information a fully staffed resort could.

She'll be alone.

With a valid excuse for being inaccessible.

All she needs to be physically present for is check-in and checkout.

I jog back out to my car and grab one of the tracking devices I keep on hand. Back inside, I link it to my phone before ripping a small section of the suitcase's interior stitching and tucking it in between the layers of material. Before I can close the lid, a hint of blue among all the black catches my eye, and lifting the flap higher, I find a vibrator sitting on top of her clothing. *She won't be needing that anymore.*

I return the silicone curved wand to her pleasure chest of a drawer.

After zipping the suitcase closed again, I stand it up, exactly where it was, then head back to the kitchen before leaving.

I gotta prepare for the biggest job of my life.

With a couple smaller ones beforehand.

Thirty

Lex

"**M**rs. Debrosse?"

I stop to regard the hotel receptionist, pulling my robe's belt a little tighter around my torso.

"Yes?"

Coming around from behind the front desk, she glances around nervously all the way up until she's within a couple feet of me. I prepare myself for whatever news she's about to break to me.

"I'm sorry to disturb you, but the vehicle you noted at check-in…" She holds up the paperwork I filled out when I first got here. "The black Range Rover with New York license plate—"

"Yes, that's mine."

The woman looks thoroughly chastised, making me instantly regret my snippy tone. I'm in a robe, with hardly anything on underneath, while standing in the middle of the lobby. I just want to go for a swim.

"Sorry. I'm…cold." Cold as snow. Ask Reece.

My chest aches at the thought of him.

The receptionist's head dips. "My apologies, ma'am."

"No need to apologize. Just, um, my car…is something wrong with it?"

"We've had multiple noise complaints regarding it."

"What kind of noise complaints?" I didn't have my music up when I arrived and it's been parked for hours.

She points at the front revolving door where I can make out a faint repetitive siren now that I'm listening for it.

"The alarm. It keeps going off."

I release a sigh and look back at the door leading to the stairwell I just came out of. The only thing I brought down with me is my keycard.

"I'm so sorry."

"It's okay," I say, facing her again with a shake of my head. "I'll handle it."

I forgo the three flights of stairs and take the elevator back up to my room to grab my keys. I don't know what would be setting off the alarm.

The entire way out to the parking lot, I push every button on the key fob, none of them stop—

A bag goes over my head before getting cinched at my neck, obscuring the outside world, then somebody lifts me clear off my feet.

Oh, shit. Not again.

I never should've been distracted while walking in the dark.

Any sound that escapes my mouth before a hand covers it is masked by my car's siren blaring next to me. To us.

How many am I dealing with?

My fist squeezes around my key fob, my house key jutting out between my fingers as I try to punch over my shoulder with it, but one hard retaliatory smack to my hand and the keyring goes sailing out of my hold.

My arms and legs automatically start moving. Elbows fly, feet kick this way and that. I hear a couple grunts from my blows to the person at my back, but no words being exchanged. I don't know if it's because these assholes aren't talking or because the alarm is that loud. My ears continue to ring as I'm tossed into the backseat of a car. I scramble backward, all the way to the other side before getting dragged right back. Judging by the width, it's larger than a sedan. Possibly a truck or an SUV.

I throw my hands over the back of the seat but don't feel a window.

SUV.

An SUV doesn't tell me much.

Someone binds my feet together before moving on to my wrists. Whoever does it isn't nearly as callous as my first captors were. The ties are tight, but not circulation-severing.

Because I don't believe in true altruism, I still kick at them, both feet connecting with a solid stomach.

A grunt as the only reaction turns my blood cold. Colder than if they'd retaliated or threatened me. They're professionals. My first time being kidnapped was when I was seventeen and the men were complete amateurs, acting on all bravado and no brains. Well-acquainted with warehouses, especially sneaking in and out of them unnoticed, I managed to escape the one they were holding me prisoner in. And like a true Stockholm syndrome victim, I ran straight back to Cyrus, the entire reason I was taken to begin with. If it wasn't for the monstrosities he commits, people wouldn't have it out for him and anyone close to him.

Assuming I make it out of this alive, I won't be running to anybody because Cyrus was not my savior then any more than he'd be now. And Kordin... Kordin's just as big of a captor as Cyrus was.

With all the motion, my robe practically drapes off me, so it's incredibly noticeable when two warm hands slowly glide down my bare thighs. I wait until they get to my knees before clenching them together, effectively trapping both hands.

"I don't need my hands to crush every bone in yours," I tell them. "Don't touch me again."

I squeeze my knees as tightly as I can, earning myself a shove to the breastbone, presumably from the person's head, sending me backward and causing my legs to fall open again. I inhale through my nose before the wind gets knocked out of me, but don't smell any identifiable scents other than gasoline. Even without my breath, I bring my knees up, catching a chin before I'm shoved roughly to the side so the door can close, the childproof locks already engaged as I try the handle above my head.

A second later my car's alarm goes silent, allowing me to train my ears on every movement inside this vehicle.

The driver's door opens and closes, then we're on the move, the tires squealing against the asphalt as the driver takes off.

Using the passenger headrest to pull myself up, I stretch my fingers out, but don't feel anyone's head.

One person? That's all they sent?

That's…insulting actually.

I'll just have to use it. If there's only one person, then my best chance of escaping is while they're busy driving.

I pay close attention to each movement the vehicle makes. One left out of the parking lot, one right on the same road I came in on, then two pregnant pauses at what must be stop signs. The resort was forty minutes off the nearest highway, so after ten minutes of straight, quiet driving, I know we're still on a backroad with speed limits ranging between thirty-five and forty-five miles an hour. Fast enough to hurt; slow enough to *probably* survive.

I just need to get off the road and into the woods as quickly as possible. Having memorized the path so far, I *should* be able to make it back to the resort as long as I keep to the side of the road.

Probably.

Should.

They're still better odds than anything I'll face if I stay put.

Throwing myself sideways and on to my back again, I hug my knees to my chest, then kick at the window, the glass making a loud *thud*, but no cracking or breaking. Shit.

I repeat the motion, kicking harder.

"What the *fuck*?" I hear from the front, but ignore it to continue my efforts.

I lost my slippers somewhere between being grabbed from behind and thrown into the car, so each time my bare feet strike the glass, pain not only shoots up my ankles but also burns my soles.

It *hurts*. Pain is only temporary, while death…is not.

322 | A. MARIE

The car swerves before coming to a complete stop. *No.* This was my best shot. Possibly my only shot.

My legs continue pumping as sweat rolls from my hairline into my eyes.

"Stop!"

Every muscle in my body locks up, not because of what was said, but because of who said it. It can't be.

The bag over my head is loosened, then pulled off. After a couple blinks, Reece's angry face comes into view, his mask flipped up over his eyebrows. He's turned around in the driver's seat, on his knees, leaning over the center console to hover above me.

"Shit, Lex. You're gonna hurt yourself."

All ten fingers intertwined, I punch him square in the nose, double-handed, double-irritated.

"Fuck," he groans as he sits back on his heels, a hand over his face as he uses the other to remove his mask.

"Who are you working for?" I ask while repositioning myself so my feet are aimed at him instead. They couldn't break tempered glass but they'll shatter a jaw.

"What do you mean? You know who I work for."

"Cyrus paid you to kidnap me?" I hadn't even considered he'd be behind this.

I should've.

This is what happens when you forget, when you become complacent, comfortable.

This is what happens when you let your guard down.

"No. Jesus Christ." His voice comes out nasally from his nose being pinched. "Cyrus didn't fucking hire me to kidnap you. I meant that's who I usually work for."

"Kordin then? Did Kordin hire you to do it?"

"Are you fucking kidding me? You actually think I'd ever do *any-thing* for that motherfucker?"

The window closest to him starts to fog from his heavy breathing.

"Why'd you kidnap me?"

Reece drops his hand to stare at me. "Because you wouldn't have said yes."

"Said yes to what?"

"To spending the weekend with me."

The intensity in his gaze causes a panic in my chest, and throat, and limbs—worse than when I thought I was going to be tortured and eventually murdered.

Back to Plan A.

I pivot and kick the glass again.

Reece launches himself between the seats, landing with one knee on my gut and the other on the floor. With only one hand, he holds both my legs together, preventing any movement.

"Get off of me," I grit.

Lowering himself into my face, he grits right back, "Stop fucking fighting."

He knows my response—he's heard it, seen it, and felt it—so instead I try a different tactic by holding up my hands being held together with a zip tie. "I will if you cut these off."

"I'll cut them off when I'm sure you won't run."

"They're hurting me," I lie with a slight whine.

"Dishonesty and betrayal," he tsks with a shake of his head, but a smirk on his lips.

"I think you like it."

"I don't…"

Turning his head away, his tongue licks the corner of his mouth as a way to cover the smirk. *Too late, rook. I saw it.*

"…dislike it."

He used my admission as his own. We really are a match made in hell.

"I'm not going with you," I tell him point-blank.

He returns his gaze to mine. "Yes, you are."

Neither of us blink or speak, just stare at one another. He's not backing down on this.

But I don't want to either.

I need to lower *his* guard first, then escape.

"Why is gasoline the only scent in here?" I sniff him. "You don't even smell like you."

Reece gets up, suddenly avoiding eye contact. "What do you take me for?"

"A rookie."

He chuckles as he returns to the front.

I let my body sag onto the leather seat. The more distance I can get between us the better.

Even if his full attention felt like being kissed by the warmest ray of sunshine on a dreary winter day.

"I've been in and out of your house, in and out of your bedroom, almost every night for two weeks now. So maybe…you're just losing your touch."

"Not while I was home. I would've known."

I sit up, my feet screaming, my ankles weak, and my skin covered in goose bumps I don't know one hundred percent are from my current state of undress. My bikini is the only real covering I have at this point. The robe is off my shoulders, the train gathered under my ass, the belt missing completely. Reece is sorely mistaken if he thinks this look won't attract the wrong kind of attention—the kind that results in the cops getting called—anywhere we go.

Looking at me through the rearview mirror, he asks, "How'd I find you?"

"You followed me again?"

The only thing that moves is his head as he rotates it side to side.

I sift through my day, paying special attention to the afternoon and evening portions for anything that was out of the ordinary.

My suitcase. The vibrator I know I packed this morning was missing when I checked in. He must've put some kind of tracker in there when he took it out.

That doesn't explain why he was in my house when I wasn't.

"Why have you been breaking in?"

"To be close to you."

God, that sounds as pathetic as I've felt all day. Why do I like it so much?

"Then why were you there today? To get back at me for…letting you go."

"Letting me go." He scoffs. "No, it wasn't like that. Kordin and I took the elevator down together and—"

"Down where? You mean he went somewhere?" Aside from the two times I've left the office early and needed Kaisin to help out—the night of our dinner party and tonight—I've been Kordin's only means of transportation. When I left earlier, Kordin was still in his office working.

"I don't know if he stuck around or not after his eye appointment."

Why didn't Kordin tell me he had an appointment today? Maybe because I didn't have to drive him?

Or because he's fucking one of the staff members.

"There's an optometrist in the building?"

Reece gives me a weird look before saying, "Apparently. Summit Enhancements. Before he got off on the sixth floor, he told me you were going out of town. I saw my shot, so I took it."

My mind is being pulled in too many different directions right now, but did Reece really just say "I saw my shot" for *abducting* me? Like it was a forgone conclusion?

"Your shot for what?"

"To spend time with you. You, Lex, not Lenox Debrosse, or Lexi Andeno, or whoever you think you should be or need to be. I want to spend a weekend with you, but you were never going to let yourself give me one. So I'm doing what I do best. I'm fucking stealing it."

I open my mouth to say something, but nothing comes out the first try. The second attempt my voice is croaky and mortifying. "I can't give you what you want."

His hand on the shifter freezes, and looking over his shoulder at me, he says, "You know what I want from you? For you to breathe. That's all I need you to do this weekend. That's all I need you to do ever. Just fucking exist, Lex."

It takes me even longer to form words this time. Finally, I whisper, "Dishonesty and betrayal."

But the sly fox hears and grins.

"I've already proved that's not all I'm capable of, but in case you need more proof..." He shifts into Drive and pulls back on to the dark, deserted road. "...in one of the bags behind your seat, there's clothes that'll fit you."

Peeking in the back, I spot several duffle bags and a couple totes.

"Other men have tried to dress me up like a doll, too."

"No, other men tried to dress you up like *their* doll, which didn't work out...because you're mine."

I ignore what that statement does to my pussy.

"And how exactly am I supposed to get dressed if I'm tied up?"

"In another one of the bags, there's a pair of wire cutters."

I'm already scaling the backseat, the robe's train slithering after me like a snake's obedient tail. Once I have a weapon, escaping will be much easier.

Riffling through bag after bag, every article of clothing I come across is black, so it's a little hard to tell what gender or size each one is in the dark, but what's not hard to tell is none of them are small and triangle-shaped.

Still searching, I say, "You forgot underwear." I can't even make out any pairs for Reece.

"I didn't forget."

The energy in the car changes and I stop to glance at the front. With Reece focused on the road ahead, I study the side of his face. He's classically handsome, the way old movie stars were, yet has tattoos and muscles like modern-day gangsters do.

Before I can look away, his eyes lock on to mine in the rearview mirror.

"You're exhausting," I tell him because I honestly don't know what else to say. I do not want to trust him but he makes me believe that maybe someday I could.

"You don't know exhaustion yet, Snow."

I make myself return to the task at hand, saying, "I thought all I'd have to do is breathe."

"Panting is breathing. Moaning is breathing. Screaming is breathing."

I dip my head so he can't see my lips parting, then immediately scowl at myself. What am I doing?

I'm getting out of here. I have to.

What he's saying isn't possible. It's not. I can't just go be with Reece for a weekend.

I can't just go *be*.

Locating the wire cutters, I cradle them between my hands, mindlessly stroking the rubber handles.

I can never just *be*. Like Reece said, I'm always someone—someone else. Never me—this me that I desperately wish I could be.

I want to trust Reece. I want to spend time with Reece. I want to be the person he believes I am.

But he's right. I don't allow myself to.

Awkwardly fitting the wire cutters to the zip tie at my wrists, I crush the handles together until there's a loud *snip*.

The sound makes me flinch. Or maybe it's not the sound, maybe it's the feeling it represents: freedom, in its simplest form.

I cut the one at my ankles next, the same visceral reaction washing over me.

What's so pressing at the resort that I have to rush right back to? Nothing. No one.

So, what if I did? What if I allowed myself to just *be*? If ever there was a time I could give it a try, it's now.

Shedding the robe altogether, I shove a baggy outfit over my bikini, then make my way up to Reece.

The wire cutters up to his throat, I tell him, "If you fuck me over in any way, I'll sever your carotid artery."

Unconcerned, he shakes his head, one of the sharp tips digging a white line into his skin. "Using wire cutters?"

Falling into the passenger seat, I shrug. "It'll get bloody."

My new weapon goes into the pocket of my hoodie.

"It usually is with you."

He wipes his nose and shows me his blood-coated fingertips.

"You abducted me."

"You broke up with me!" he says just as defensively as if the two are remotely comparable.

I take a huge breath, then another. We've been over this. We weren't together.

My eyes wander to his left hand wrapped around the steering wheel, to the ring specifically.

We were something though. Something that definitely pulled us...*not* together, but closer.

We were closer.

The closest I've ever felt to anyone.

"So where are we going?" I ask to change the subject.

"You're coming?"

"I thought I didn't have a choice."

"You know you always have a choice with me."

He's the only one that's ever given me one. That's why I'm currently up here and not cutting random wires at the back hatch.

"Where are we going?" I repeat.

Reece tries to hide another smirk. "Somewhere not quite fox but a lot less hollow."

"To another one of your secret addresses?"

"No, I rented a cabin."

Nodding, I watch through the windshield as the trees break ahead just enough to show a stream. The light from the waxing gibbous bounces off the water's surface, highlighting the rushing current.

"What do you think about that?"

Lost, I shake my head. "About what?"

"Staying in a cabin."

"I think...it'll be more secluded than the place I just left." When he doesn't respond, I add, "Depending on how close the neighbors are, nobody should be able to hear your screams if I need to bleed you out."

Reece laughs. "This weekend should be fun."

I concentrate on that streak of rousing moonlight again, my eyebrows scrunching as my thoughts turn inward.

"I don't think I know how to have fun. I don't joke. I don't smile, especially not on command. I don't show gratitude properly. I don't make claims on anybody. I lie, cheat, steal, and kill. I'm bitchy, I'm broken, and no, actually, I don't…I don't have the first fucking clue how to have fun because I don't know what fun is."

I blink rapidly like I'm coming out of a trance. What was that? Some sort of nature witchcraft? I gazed at a shimmering stream once and now I know what's wrong with me? Without the constant buzz of other people, you're forced to focus on yourself, but I don't even… like…myself… Do I?

I don't.

"I'll teach you."

Reece's voice startles me.

"We know what we learn, so I'll teach you how to have fun, then you will know. The rest of it…" He continues, "That's what makes you *you*. Haven't you noticed I prefer the taste of you when you're *not* freshly cleaned?" He glances at me, but thankfully doesn't wait for my response. "That's because I don't want the watered-down version of you, Lex. I want every fucking part of you, the best, the worst, all of it. I want *you*."

"You're—"

"You don't have to hurt either of us right now. You can let me make you feel good and you can let yourself feel good."

"That's…" I sigh. He's right. My initial reaction was, just like it usually is with him, to act out and say something nasty. In order to give this a real try, I have to actually *try*. That's easily the nicest thing anyone's ever said to me, but the idea of telling Reece that makes me feel like a little girl again. Not in a nostalgic way, or a giddy way, but in a vulnerable way that churns my stomach.

I take in his position. "Remember how you showed gratitude?"

Reece's smile couldn't be any bigger as he says, "Yeah."

"Pull out your cock."

"Now? I'm fucking driving."

This is far more private than some of the other places I've had him pull his cock out.

"Right now." I climb to my knees and angle my top half across the center console.

He doesn't so much as unzip his pants, so I do it for him, freeing his gorgeous cock. Even limp it looks good. I scoop out his balls, too, because those are a package deal.

"Lex, we'll be there in five minutes. Just wait 'til we get to the cabin." Despite his serious tone, his cock swells in my hand.

"It'll take me less than two."

I lick my lips to moisten them, and Reece stretches his right arm out, gripping the passenger headrest.

"Hey," he says when I start to lower my head over his lap. "No teeth this time. I'm not trying to crash out here."

It was one time and it was out of desperation. I had to do something to give my pussy a break the night he stayed at my house. It was like he was the sex addict on ecstasy. The teeth worked because after he came, he was too paralyzed to touch me for a solid twenty or thirty minutes.

As much as I *know* he liked that particular trick, I agree. Now's not the time to pull out anything too crazy. I'm still going to give him a BJ to remember.

Careful to keep my lips tucked over my teeth, I loosen my jaw and suck his length into my mouth until his spongy head pokes the back of my throat, then swallow, the muscles constricting his tip briefly.

"Jesus, Lex."

I cup his balls, applying just enough pressure for him to make a string of incoherent sounds. The faster I bob up and down on Reece's cock, the louder the engine revs. Several deep plunges later, his hot, salty cum fills my mouth. Keeping it pooled on my tongue, I carefully release Reece's shaft, and with my head still horizontal so he can see over it, I kiss him, spitting at least half of the fluid between his lips.

"My c—" he sputters before gulping it down.

He could've spit it out, but he swallowed like a good boy.

I don't know what the big deal is. He's constantly making me taste my own cum.

"What kind of thank-you was that?"

"The blow job was for you being sweet. The kiss was for tracking me down and kidnapping me," I tell him as I sit back and check the time first—less than two, as promised—then the speedometer. Eighty and dropping. "How fast did you get up to?"

Wiping his mouth with the back of his hand, Reece shakes his head. "I lost track after ninety-five."

I scan a darkened building as we zoom past it.

"Imagine if I had used teeth."

Reece turns off into a tiny gravel parking lot with a half-lit sign above a log building, and parks.

"You know, for someone that doesn't joke, you have a wicked sense of humor."

"Speaking of, where did that Chaste Tree go? I didn't see it in your apartment."

"You mean the *one* night you broke into it?"

"Yes." Was he expecting it to be a regular occurrence? And now, he's upset it's not?

"It's in the corner of my sisters' room," Reece says in answer to my question before getting out and going around to the back. Since I'm not wearing shoes, I crawl through the interior.

"They share a room?"

He digs through a bag, pulling out a wallet I've never seen before, another outfit for himself, and a pair of shoes for me.

"Yeah. My mom had to get an apartment for them after my dad…"

"Is it safe?" I ask as I put on the tennis shoes that fit surprisingly well.

Frowning, Reece changes his shirt, his movements jerky. "Not as safe as I'd like."

"I could find them something safer. All of you. I have contacts all over."

"With you?"

We've been over this, too.

I don't respond and neither does Reece. He just finishes switching from jeans into a black pair of sweatpants. When he's finished, he holds his hand out for me and helps me down. Keeping my hand, we lock up the black Ford Explorer and head toward the entrance, passing a row of beach-style bicycles chained up together and three tables with mismatched chairs.

"Gray cars are more common than black cars," I say to lighten the mood.

Glancing back at the SUV, he says, "Yeah, but you like black."

"You like black, too."

He looks at me again. "But I like you more, so I got you what you like."

When he opens the door for me, I pass through, shaking my head. He considered my preferences when stealing a car.

"Good evening," a woman says, coming through a doorway filled with a curtain of beads. "How can I help you?"

Two cats lounging in the middle of the floor barely even acknowledge our presence, making us go around them to meet her at a cluttered counter.

"Checking in," Reece tells the receptionist. "For James Jones."

"Yes, I remember. You said you'd be late." She goes over to the computer and types in something. "Coming up from Fox Hollow, right? Did you hear about the explosion down there?"

A single shake of his head, Reece pouts his already plump bottom lip out.

"It's been all over the news."

"We were on a self-guided tour, checking out some outdoor art exhibits."

"Oh, I've heard about those, but have never done one. How was it?"

"Good. Very easy. You just download the audio from an app and follow the directions, listening while it tells you all about the area's history."

I fight not to side-eye him as I scan for security cameras, thankfully finding none. The Catskills are an art collector's haven with every form of art you can imagine, with some of the galleries outside even, but how did Reece come up with that idea so quickly?

"What kind of explosion?" I ask because it seems like the proper

333 ABOVE | 333

thing to do. Curiosity is human nature. But also, I didn't hear anything about an explosion and I was in Fox Hollow most of the day.

"A car explosion outside a bar called... I can't remember now. It was a prison reference. What was it again? The Slammer maybe?"

"The Pen?"

"That's it."

"Was anybody hurt?"

"Sadly, there was one casualty. A man. An employee of the bar. He went out to get something from his car, nobody knows for sure, and while he was in there, *poof*." She snaps her fingers. "The whole thing went up in flames."

Something inside the Explorer smelled like gasoline, but I didn't come across anything in the back that'd be the source.

Maybe because Reece was the source.

I finally give in and look over at him again. He did change before we came in here, although I assumed that was because he'd just kidnapped a person and didn't want to take any chances in case he was spotted.

This is why I use sap to start fires. It's odorless and you only need a small, concealable amount.

"Crazy," I say.

Nodding, Reece pushes out that bottom lip of his again.

"All right, if I can just get a form of ID and a valid credit card from ya."

Reece passes her a New York driver's license from his wallet before frowning.

"I, uh..." He pulls out another card but keeps it. "I just noticed my credit card's expired. Do you accept cash?"

The receptionist checks the ID for this James Jones before handing it right back.

"Cash works."

Already removing bills, Reece starts stacking them on the counter.

"Much appreciated. Next, I'll have you fill out this form."

After scanning straight to the bottom, Reece says, "I can never remember my license plate number."

"Um…"

My hands rubbing up and down my arms, I offer through chattering teeth, "Do you want me to go back out there and get it?"

"No, no. Stay in here where it's warm. You two are the only ones staying here this weekend anyway, so make and model's fine."

While Reece fills out the paper, I look around the small, warm lobby. It smells like cedar and freshly baked cookies. There's stuff everywhere—paintings, local festival posters, signs with nature sayings, rainbows. In addition to a mini fridge in the corner with drinks and yogurts, there's a shelf of DVDs and an entire bookcase of board games renters can check out.

"What's this one for?" Reece asks, his finger on one of the many bullet points listed.

"Oh, so we're not only a female-owned business but queer-owned as well, and my wife and I just want to make sure we're being respectful to all our guests by using folks' pronouns correctly. It's completely optional though. Please don't feel pressured at all."

My eyes find the numerous rainbows decorating the walls just as another woman pushes through the bead curtain.

"Are you two the owners?" I ask her.

"Guilty as charged," she says with a smile at me, then her wife, before placing a plate of chocolate-chip cookies down in front of us.

They're their own bosses, doing things their own way.

I've always been fascinated by orcas for many reasons, the main one being that although their pods have males in them, they're female-led.

I do something I never do—

I do *two* things I never do. I grab a cookie, and I smile back, both actions making me feel…good.

"I identify as he and hers," Reece says, drawing everybody's attention back to him. "He," he repeats before pointing at me, saying, "And hers."

My lips relax again, and I roll my eyes.

"Oh, my heavens," the woman behind the counter croons. "That is so—"

"Sweet?" I finish for her.

"Only for you," Reece mouths to me.

With a shake of my head, I say, "And my pronouns are she and her—"

"Mine." Catching me by my hips, Reece closes the gap to kiss me like a man possessed, leaving no room for argument.

When we separate, both women have misty eyes as they gaze between us.

"Remember our newlywed-phase, Diane?"

"Fondly."

As the couple continue to reminisce, my mind screams we're not newlyweds, but both me and Reece wearing wedding rings suggests we just might be.

What a rookie move. After, and while, committing a crime, you never want to be remembered. Thanks to Reece's syrupy behavior, these women will never forget us.

He just can't help himself. He really is that sweet.

Behind my hand, I mimic a yawn that turns into a real one.

"Oh, here, we won't keep you two any longer. All that driving around probably wore you out."

Diane gives us a quick rundown of the rules and a map of the grounds with directions where to find our cabin.

"If you two need anything at all, give us a holler. Otherwise feel free to leave the key under the mat when you leave."

"Thank you," I tell her, surprising myself when I mean it.

Thirty-One

Reece

LEX IS ON ME THE SECOND WE'RE ALONE IN THE EXPLORER, saying, "You killed that guard." She also hands me the cookie she grabbed inside. No explanation, just passes it over to me. There's only one small bite missing, so I shove the rest of it in my mouth and start up the stolen SUV.

They thought we were newlyweds. They thought we were married. To each other. And it felt like we were. Or at least we could be.

"Reece?"

Ignoring Lex, I focus on backing out and taking the road that leads up the mountain, passing all the turnoffs to the other cabins in search of the post with the number eight on it.

"Reece."

"You heard Diane, there was an explosion," I say when my mouth is empty.

"An explosion you caused."

I did cause the explosion, but that motherfucker's actions are what really killed him.

Once I spot the eight, I swing in and pull up in front of the cabin.

"He touched me *before*—"

"I don't care. I don't fucking care when he touched you. Before or after we fucked, it doesn't matter. It wasn't just you he tried to rape, you know that as well as I do. Lex. What we don't know is how many women he already succeeded with or how many he would've. He was a fucking parasite on this planet and now he's ashes. I don't feel guilty about it and you're wasting your time trying to make me."

"I'm not trying to guilt you. But... You said you'd sell your soul trying to afford me."

"I'd do more than that," I admit.

Her focus shifts to her hands as she pulls the sleeves over her wrists.

"Have you ever heard po trupach do celu? It's Polish."

"No."

"It means to achieve something no matter what it takes, even climb over dead bodies. It's what I tell myself as a way to justify the unforgivable things I've done. The unforgivable things I *do*. What are you trying to achieve?"

"Achieve? Like a goal? It wasn't... I didn't..."

"Was this your first time taking a life?"

I jerk out a nod before realizing she can't see me. "Yeah." I've roughed up plenty of guys but never enough to end any of their lives.

Head bowed, she says quietly, "Leave the killing to me, rook. Only one of us still has a soul, and in order to keep being you, you need to keep it."

"Are you saying you don't want me to change?"

"I'm saying the same thing I've been saying all along...I'm not worth the trade."

She climbs out, so I follow after.

As soon as we step foot in the quaint cabin, I hang back to watch her. I could've afforded a bigger one but I wanted to see how she'd react to a cabin that could fit in her mansion a hundred times and still have room to spare. Passing through the living room, she takes in the kitchen before moving down the hall to the bathroom and bedroom. When she returns a second later, she doesn't even bring up the copper claw-foot tub in the bathroom, which is the other reason why I chose this place.

She only gestures to the woodstove fireplace, the blaze inside bright red, orange, and yellow like a Marigold Flame. "That's the only source of heat?"

I nod.

"We're going to need more firewood."

The bundle of kindling the owners left us is small, hopefully enough to last the night.

"I'll chop some in the morning." Outside, we passed an ax stuck into a stump with a pile of whole logs next to it.

Lex cocks an eyebrow. "James Jones knows how to chop wood?"

"My childhood home had a woodstove fireplace in the basement we had to keep fed through the winter to heat the rest of the house," I tell her, dropping one of the duffle bags onto the couch. "I mean, James Jones's childhood home."

"How'd you come up with James Jones? Did you just look up the most basic names in America?"

That's exactly what I did.

"Basically. How'd you come up with Lenox Debrosse?"

She angles her body away from me to examine the window above the kitchen sink. It's pitch black outside, and with the lights on inside, it's causing a mirror effect. From where I'm standing, I can't see her reflection, but she probably can.

"That's my married name."

I study her profile. "What's your real name?"

"You mean my maiden name?"

"I mean your real name."

Her attention relocates to the knife block by the stove. There are a few missing, but enough for her to cause some damage if she wanted.

Don't do it. Don't go for them.

She's not ready to go deep yet. She opened up a little in the car, but not completely. I have to time this just right. Her fight-or-flight mode is always activated, and in order for this to work, for me to be able to tell her everything I've discovered, I need her to not only be emotionally ready, but physically, too.

Finally, she tears her gaze away, looking over the rest of the kitchen. "Depends who you talk to."

"Lexi, Lenox…Aleksandra."

She spins around to face me. "Lift up your shirt."

"You think I'm wearing a fucking wire? I just changed right in front of you."

Her eyebrows rise as she waits.

I yank my shirt up and spin in a slow circle, telling her, "You watch too many movies."

"I don't watch any movies."

"Ever?"

"No."

She *never* watches movies?

"What about shows?"

"You've seen what my hobbies consist of."

"Hobbies? I've seen one. Reading smut."

"Unless you read smut, you shouldn't call it smut."

"Not counting the first few, I've read every book I gave you."

"That's impossible. I can't even read that fast."

"Every book I buy you, I get on audio, too, and listen to it myself before giving it to you." Picked up that hack from my mom. I tried reading the physical books, but she's right, I can't read that fast. With audios, I can crank the speed up and knock it out in no time.

"Why?"

She knows this, but I tell her anyway.

"At first it was to make sure there was sex, then that the sex was consensual. After that it was to make sure you'd like it. And…"

"And?"

She doesn't know this.

"Because I want to be able to talk to you about the stories…if you want." Books are the one fucking thing she lets herself have. I don't want her to have to enjoy them alone—if that's what she chooses. If not, then at least I'm broadening my horizons into freaky territory because romances are the best kept-secret into women's fantasies, and I've already picked up a few new tricks.

Lex folds her arms over her chest.

I almost forget I'm still holding my shirt until the fabric falls from my hand.

"Happy? I'm not a cop. I'm not a rat. I just know how to use the internet."

"Why were you using it to look me up?"

"You tell me, black Dahlia."

The sigh she releases could trigger earthquakes, and I start to worry I pushed too hard too soon, but then she says, "My name at birth was Aleksandra Obuchowski. My dad, Aleksander, went by Alex, so almost everybody called me Lexi. Cyrus took the nickname and made it my stage name. You already know he changed my last name to Andeno when he adopted me, so legally I became Aleksandra Andeno, but I was still known as Lexi."

That all checks out with what she previously told me and what I found on my own. We're finally getting somewhere.

"When'd you become Lenox?"

"When I married Kordin. Instead of just changing my last name, I changed both."

"Why Lenox?"

"You'd have to ask Kordin that. It was his idea."

"The name?"

"The whole thing—changing my name, which name to change it to, how and where to change it. It's a much easier process to change your first and last names at the same time than it is separately."

And doesn't raise as many suspicions.

"Did you want a different first name?"

"I didn't want to be the daughter of Aleksander Obuchowski anymore. Or Cyrus Andeno. They each gave me names that they themselves ended up tainting. In order to be Kordin Debrosse's wife, I thought I had to get another new name."

"Kordin made you believe you had to get a new name," I say.

"He made me believe a lot of things."

"How many have been true?"

"I'm not sure I'll ever know the answer to that."

"Has he ever hit you?"

"Never. He uses words." She considers something, then says, "He uses his voice, his tone. It's not what he says, but how."

That's exactly how Breckyn described it.

"It's other things, too."

"Like what?"

In the blink of an eye, Lex's entire demeanor changes. "Is this your idea of fun? An interrogation?"

"What do you have to lose telling me about your life?"

Without missing a beat, she throws right back, "What do you have to gain?"

"Your trust."

Her eyes fly to each of the escape routes. Shit. I'm gonna lose her. If she was willing to hike in the woods barefoot in nothing but a bikini and robe, she won't bat an eye at leaving here fully clothed.

"Look, they say trust is a two-way street. Okay? So—"

"They also say to make lemonade when life hands you lemons, but that's the worst advice ever."

"Why?"

"Because lemonade's disgusting."

"So what do you do with the lemons life gives you?"

She shrugs like it's obvious. "Stockpile them to use as weapons."

I laugh, and she quickly glances away from me. *She's trying not to smile.*

Lex is back. Little by little, she's thawing, but if I move too fast, she's even quicker to freeze back up.

"All right, Snow White, you win. Let's have some fun." I turn for the door, but Lex calling my name has me stopping.

"If it involves board games, tell me now." She removes the wire cutters from the hoodie's pocket.

"Are you gonna use those on me if it does?"

With a shake of her head, she says, "Myself."

I let out another laugh and hold up my hands, palms facing her. "I promise, no board games. I'm just getting the rest of the stuff from the car. Go start a bath. I'll meet you in there when I'm done."

Out on the front porch, I hesitate until Lex disappears into the bathroom, then start unloading everything from the back of the Explorer, taking it all inside two handfuls at a time. The last trip, I'm just closing the rear hatch when my phone rings. The service has been so shitty ever since I got up here, I almost lost Lex earlier. Thankfully she didn't leave the resort once she checked in or I probably would've.

I reposition the tote in my hold to grab it, almost dropping the cell when I see Cyrus's name on the screen.

Fuck.

"Where are you?" are his first words, causing the SUV to blur in front of my eyes.

Sultry music filters through the speaker as Cyrus's voice fades like he's speaking to somebody else. Suddenly, he's back on, full volume again as he asks, "Why the fuck aren't you at The Playground right now giving me an update?"

Everything coming back into focus, I exhale away from the phone.

"I'm out of town, following a lead."

"You didn't think to tell me?"

"I tried. I called you before I left but your voicemail was full."

"Huh. I thought I just cleared that thing."

Shit. Hopefully not. His voicemail is always full, that's why I said it.

"What kind of lead we talking? I thought it was cut and dry. The Debrosse brothers knocking off the Debrosse empire."

"There might be another partner, a silent one. If they're splitting their profit with him, it might not be as big a pot as I originally thought."

"Not as big a pot as you originally thought, huh?"

I don't like the way he keeps saying huh.

"That's why I'm checking it out myself."

"Where's this silent partner live?"

I don't want him thinking I'm too far away that he can try anything while I'm gone, but I don't want him knowing anywhere close to my actual location either, so I tell him a town about the same distance from Fox Hollow as I am right now, just in the opposite direction.

"Bedford."

"Bedford, huh?"

There's that word again. Poppies, the omen for evil, pop up in my mind.

"I know a guy from Bedford. What's his name?"

I say, "Damon Poppy," then add, "the fourth," to make it sound more hollowish.

"The fourth? Elitist snobs," he mutters more to himself. To me, he asks, "When will you have an update for me?"

"Next week."

"You planning on staying in Bedford that long?"

"Maybe."

"I need you back Sunday."

Sunday isn't enough time. I haven't even talked to Lex about all this yet. I'm biding my time, waiting for the perfect opportunity. She's not going to be happy finding out I've been lying to her, but if she trusts me, really fucking trusts me, then it'll be easier to explain why I lied. I'm hoping she'll at least hear me out. If I try telling her now, she wouldn't stick around to hear anything. She'd fight, leave, or most likely fight, then leave.

And because I'm dealing with Lex here, those are best-case scenarios. I'm well aware she might actually use those wire cutters to cut the vein in my neck.

"Sunday? I don't think—"

"I don't pay you to think. I pay you to do. Remember, hollows seek, foxes find. Be here Sunday."

The line goes dead, submerging me in silence louder than the music was. No people, no traffic, no bugs, no noise whatsoever. It's pure silence. Usually I find it peaceful. Day in and day out, I crave this kind of stillness, yearn for it in every part of my body. But right now, I feel like it's just me with the world sitting on my shoulders. Everything rides on me.

I squeeze my phone in my hand. Fuck!

Thirty-Two

Reece

THE BATHROOM'S STEAMY WHEN I REACH IT, THE FLOOR-TO-ceiling window next to the tub fogged up along the edges. Past the glass is nothing but motionless conifers, only identifiable by their moonlight-tipped crowns.

I stand at the threshold, watching Lex scoop up handfuls of water before letting it all trickle down between her fingers. She looks as harmless as the moment I first saw her.

Her hand disappears beneath the water, then her eyes flutter closed as a moan passes her lips. Arching her back, her hard nipples pierce the water's surface.

My cock goes hard at the sight, the sound, the fucking beauty of Lex fingering herself. Goddamn. The only thing better would be feeling her pussy for myself.

Not a moment later, Lex's body relaxes and she returns to her previous task.

What the fuck? She finished that fucking fast?

"You can come closer." Lex turns her head to look at me, so I take a step forward. "I don't bite."

I freeze in my tracks. "Then why would I come closer?"

The room fills with that sound Lex makes when she laughs, her shaking torso causing ripples throughout the water.

Walking over to the claw foot, I set the small bucket on the table beside it, then push my sleeves up to my elbows, one at a time, never breaking eye contact with Lex. When I'm done, I rub my thumb over her lips a couple times, each pass firmer and firmer. Finally, she parts them, granting me access. As soon as my thumb grazes her teeth, she bites down on the tip.

The *only* thing harmless about this woman is her looks.

Thank fucking God.

"What are you doing?" I nod at her lower half where her fingertips keep making lazy swipes over her clit.

After sucking away the pain, she pops off my thumb to tell me, "Edging myself while I wait for you to finish me off."

"Show me."

"Again?"

"Again."

"You're not going to get undressed?"

I shake my head and pick up the bucket again.

"How is that fun?"

"Fucking is fun…"

"Mm, sometimes," she argues, and I dip my head, giving her that. I've always found fucking fun, but I can understand why others might not, especially Lex.

"But it's not the most fun."

"Ooh, what's the most fun?" she questions with a hint of sarcasm, one of her feet leaving the water to massage my erection.

"Everything leading up to fucking."

"Like the BJ that almost got us killed."

I was in control of the car the whole time.

Just not my foot on the gas pedal.

"That was fun." Until she snowballed me. I didn't hate it, but I didn't…

I didn't hate it.

"But now I'm gonna warm you up." I nudge her foot away from my cock before I make the inside of my pants as wet as the outside. One new kink a day.

Tucking her leg back into the water, she says, "I'm warmed up."

"You're not warmed up. Play with your pussy."

"Are you gonna watch?"

"Won't blink."

Lex goes through the same motions as before, her entire body responding to her hand between her thighs. While her eyes are closed, I sprinkle Rose petals all over her, the burgundy petals sticking to the different parts that are exposed—her knees, her shoulders, her collarbone, one of her nipples.

She opens her eyes to see what the new sensation is, but that's no fun at all.

"Close your eyes," I tell her, then press a gentle kiss to her lips. Her moan almost unravels me and my plan to stretch this out. With her head back and her throat up to the ceiling, I fit my hand over the top of it, my fingers squeezing gently on one side as the thumb she just bit rubs a petal into her skin on the other.

"It's coming."

"Stop," I whisper next to her ear before nipping the shell with my teeth.

She listens, so I reward her with another kiss, this one much longer and with tongue. Tongue so deep I have to pull back before I suffocate either of us.

"Again," I gasp against her lips, wanting to bury myself in her right now.

"You do it this time."

I pull back an inch to look in her eyes. "Ask me."

"Do it."

"Ask."

Her swallow knocks against my palm, then, "Now," passes through her kiss-swollen lips.

Close enough.

I release her throat and submerge my hand, wrist, then entire forearm, the fabric around my elbow getting soaked as I fit my hand over Lex's, my fingertips brushing her bare pussy lips.

She hasn't even been finger-fucking herself, just massaging her clit.

I'll fix that.

Plunging two fingers in, I keep them buried in her hot cunt while grinding my palm against her fingers still at her clit.

When Lex pleads, "More," I add a third finger.

When she says, "Harder," I start pumping in and out of her.

When she repeats it, I give up holding back entirely.

Gripping the rim by her head with my free hand, I tell her, "Grab the sides."

Only one of her hands comes up to clench the tub's lip.

"Both," I growl, not slowing one bit.

"God."

Lex removes her hand from her clit to brace herself, so I let loose, driving my fingers into her pussy, my palm clapping against her needy clit, water sloshing out onto my sweatpants, the floor, my feet, everywhere.

"Ah, ah, ah!" Lex screams in time with each thrust, her chin and tits rising higher and higher until her spine looks like a fucking fish hook.

Taking one of her tits in my mouth, I suck the peak, my tongue circling her nipple.

A random combination of vowels and maybe one consonant blasts from Lex's open mouth, then her entire body begins straightening out, her back sinking down to the bottom of the tub again.

"That was…"

"Too hard?" I look down, half-expecting the water to be tinged pink. Fuck. That's not how I was planning to kick this weekend off. She just… I can't get enough of her.

Lex shakes her head, her tongue running along her top lip. "It wasn't too hard, rookie. You can't break what's already broken."

I press a kiss to her forehead, then stand to my full height. "You're not broken. You're perfect." *Perfect for me*, I stop myself from saying.

"Ah, so lying is the most fun."

Pulling one of her legs from the water, I prop her heel on my stomach and massage the arch of her foot with my knuckles. I know they gotta hurt the way she was kicking that window.

348 | A. MARIE

"Ask me anything, I'll answer honestly."

She gives me a long stare and I prepare myself for the worst. No matter what, I will give her the truth.

"What happened to Kaisin's hand?"

I tell her about the rat and the peanut butter, fully expecting a follow-up about everything leading up to Kaisin being unconscious on his floor, but all she does is ask, "Why'd you do that?"

I shrug. "He touched my girl."

Without acknowledging that statement, she changes topics completely, asking, "How often do you see your mom and sisters?"

"A couple times a week usually. How often do you see your mom?"

"I can't go more than three days without visiting her."

"Because you miss her?"

"Because I take care of her."

I switch my attention to her other leg, doing the same thing with that foot.

"Did you see her today?"

"Mm-hmm. Stocked her fridge for the weekend and made sure she had all the necessities while I was away."

I wasn't following Lex's location all day because I was busy, but if she had her suitcase with her already when she went to her mom's house, the address should be in the tracker's history.

"What kind of necessities?"

"Books."

"She's a reader, too?"

Her voice drops several decibels to repeat, "Mm-hmm."

"My mom, too."

Lex snaps out of whatever reverie she just fell into, asking, "Yeah? What kind of books?"

"According to my sisters, smutty ones."

Laughter echoes in Lex's chest, making her slim shoulders bounce.

"Have you two exchanged recommendations yet?"

"No," I snap, making her laugh harder.

"What about your mom? What does she read?" I ask with a smirk.

"Dystopian, sci-fi, fantasy, anything that has a female protagonist who saves the world."

"Why?"

"It gives her hope. I guess it's the same reason I read romance with happy endings. Just because it's not our reality, doesn't mean it couldn't be for someone else. To see the fantasy play out for ourselves, we have to travel to fictional worlds."

My hands stop. "Happy endings exist in this world."

"I'm well aware. I used to provide them for an additional fee."

I do my best impression of her eye roll, and switch legs again.

"That's not what I meant."

Using one of the Roses with all its petals still intact, I drag the head along the inside of Lex's thigh, over her knee and up her calf.

Lex stifles a moan like she's holding her breath.

"Breathe, Snow," I soothe. "Let me make you feel good. Let yourself feel good."

All at once her breath whooshes out of her. "They do exist, just not for people like us."

"People *like* us? Or us?"

"Both."

"So we don't get happy endings?"

"No."

"And we don't get happy beginnings?"

"I didn't."

"Do we get happy middles?"

She thinks about it for a second before asking, "What is happiness?"

Another thing Lex wasn't taught.

"Happiness, like fun, is whatever you make it. It's hard sometimes, but knowing how to first makes it easier." If I didn't have happy times with my family, I wouldn't know how to find that happiness with them now.

"Teach me."

"What? Happiness?"

She nods.

I run through everything I know about Lex, all my encounters with her, the things she's said, the things she's done. There's only one time where she seemed close to happy. It was in the cemetery when she asked me to kiss her—*just* kiss her—and we made out like a couple of teenagers. She was a different person afterward. Playful. Open to affection. She didn't even pull her gun on me when I showed up at her house later.

"Hook your legs over the sides." I position the leg in my hold for her, then wait as she slowly does the other. Even below shifting water, I can see her pussy on full display, nothing stopping me from admiring every pink bit of it.

This is why I'm a thief and not a teacher. I already forgot the fucking lesson.

Fun.

Happiness.

Fuck, I want to feel that pussy again.

Fun. Happiness.

The second I step into the water—still in my sweats and Henley—Lex squeals and tries to scramble up to sitting, but I'm already coming down on top of her, settling between her thighs, water spilling over the edge like a waterfall to accommodate the extra weight and movement. A mesmerizing smile, the kind I'll never forget, stretches Lex's lips, then a laugh, an actual laugh, slowly tumbles from them. It's the most beautiful sound from the most beautiful woman. *My* beautiful laugh and *my* beautiful woman because I earned them both.

Cupping Lex's cheek, I kiss her, deep and deliberate.

Always so responsive, she wraps her legs and arms around me, hugging me just as intentionally.

I think I finally figured it out. Lex doesn't laugh with her vocal cords. She laughs with her heart. That's why she fights so hard to keep them trapped inside. If nothing gets out, nothing can get in.

But I got her to let one out.

Now I'm gonna find a way in.

After I do, she won't have to protect everything so fiercely. I'll do it for her.

Thirty-Three

Reece

"**T**HAT WAS HAPPINESS?"

"That's up to you," I say softly, my lips tickling Lex's ear as she relaxes back against me.

We kissed for so long the water grew cold, so we drained, then refilled the copper bathtub. This time I stripped before getting in though, so now there's nothing between us. *Physically.*

My arm wrapped under her tits shakes her a little. "Are you happy?"

"There's a term your sister used…"

My sister?

"Is it 'cringe'?" I ask with my own. Cringe and literally are the twins' favorite words. Literally doesn't fit the occasion, and I'm really fucking hoping cringe doesn't either.

Turning her head, she looks up at me. "It's not cringe." She pauses, then whispers, "I'm better than happy."

Damn. What else can I teach her? I want a list, a never-ending list, that I go down, teaching Lex different parts of life she's never experienced. That's how you make a life with someone. You literally fucking make it.

We sit with our thoughts for a while, our hands in constant motion over each other's bodies, until my fingers graze the valley between her tits.

"What makes you think you're broken?" I ask, tracing the tattoo there.

"I know I am. My body…it doesn't work right. Well, it didn't, and then it did, but now…I'm not sure what's going on."

"What was wrong?"

"It was just…unbalanced."

"Was it your hormones?" Lex stops drawing circles on my knee. I can't see her face to know what she's thinking, but I can guess. "There've been some things I noticed, but only because—"

"You're a stalker."

"—I grew up in a house full of females."

She releases another one of her earth-shattering sighs. "It was my thyroid."

I figured it was her hormones affecting her; I just didn't know in what way. Now I can officially rule out pregnancy.

"So, what happened?"

"The symptoms started when I was sixteen. My weight began to yo-yo. At first I gained a lot at once, then I couldn't stop losing it, no matter how often I ate. I'd go from sleeping too much to not enough. My anxiety was practically uncontrollable. I just… I didn't know everything was connected, at least not by something treatable. It's not like I could go to a doctor and ask, so I blamed it all on my new lifestyle. It made sense. The stress from…everything with my parents, moving into a warehouse with a stranger, then working at The Playground. Even though I suddenly had access to more food, I still wasn't eating correctly. My schedule was the opposite of what I was used to. My body was under *constant* physical and emotional demand. After a while, I decided to shut one off to make the other more bearable."

"Cyrus wouldn't take you to the doctor?"

Her headshake confirms my suspicions.

"What'd it end up being?"

"Graves' disease."

Disease. "That sounds fucking scary." And fatal. "What is it?"

"It's an autoimmune disease that causes your thyroid to overproduce. It affected all aspects of my life."

"But you got a diagnosis as soon as you married Kordin, right?"

"Not right away, no. After I got married and my lifestyle changed again, some of the symptoms went away while different ones appeared."

"So, when'd you find out?"

"Only a couple years ago."

"Why so long? You had health insurance and money. You could afford any doctor you wanted probably." Unless Kordin also prevented her from seeking medical attention.

"Without an idea what the cause could be, I didn't know where to start. I saw a regular doctor and a gynecologist, but because everybody's symptoms are different, Graves' disease can be hard to diagnose sometimes, impossible if your doctor doesn't listen to you and treat you individually instead of just as another faceless patient they stand to make a profit off of by prescribing you prescription after prescription after prescription. I went years just trying out different birth control methods before I was referred to an endocrinologist."

"Okay, so you found a specialist. Then what? Did they listen to you?"

"Then…I found out I was literally broken, not just metaphorically. My husband started fucking other women who weren't either. I was told I had to start radioactive iodine treatment or get my thyroid removed, so I decided to look into less invasive routes which took me all over while also giving Kordin more time to spend with his mistresses. I discovered a holistic doctor who prescribed me the most disgusting tea to ever exist that I drank three times a day, every day, for a year."

Is that the tea in her pantry? I gagged just smelling it. I can't imagine drinking it once, let alone for that long.

"Did it help?"

"Eventually, yeah. That, along with a compete diet overhaul and other lifestyle changes, I was able to go into remission."

"You're not anymore though?"

"I don't know. I haven't gone and gotten tested again. It's just little things… Like you pointed out, there've been some signs that make me think it might be malfunctioning again."

"Can it just happen randomly, at any time?" That's gotta be hard to live with knowing. Every fucking hiccup from the norm would make a person worried.

"I'll always have Graves' disease, but there are definitely factors that can cause a flare-up."

"Like what?"

"Mm, stress is a big one."

I want to ask her what stress, but not at the risk of causing her more stress, so instead, I say, "I'm sorry I didn't take Kordin's laptop when I had the chance." I've never apologized for it, and even though I'm still not sorry for what I did to Kordin, I feel like shit now that I know why Lex really wanted it.

"Yeah…" Gazing out the window, I think maybe she's going to tell me about her stress, but she just says, "You have a habit of fucking me."

She's not ready. I have a day and a half left to gain her full trust.

Grabbing her chin, I make her look at me. "I'm sorry for my actions that night but I don't regret anything. The moment I laid eyes on you, Lex—"

A look of pure torture crosses her face and she tries to shake her head. "Don't."

"The moment I laid eyes on you, something shifted."

"Don't do that."

"Don't do what?"

"Don't… Don't…"

She can't even say it. But she doesn't have to. I will, because it's fucking done. I already fell in love with Lex. Maybe from the beginning, during that first time seeing her, when she gave me something to work for—no matter what it takes, even over dead bodies. I didn't know my true purpose then, but I do now. It's not to save what's good in this world; it's to save Lex so I can show her what is good in it.

"I lo—"

"Reece, please." She twists around on top of me, her knees resting on my armpits as she sits on my lower abdomen. "I never ask for anything, but I am begging you not to use that word. I got my tattoo over my chest because *I'm* broken, not just my body. Me. I know because I did it myself. I'm incapable of…*that*, and you deserve…*that*."

I try to come up with another way to say what captures how I feel about Lex without scaring her off.

"I'm obsessed with you," I tell her.

"Obsessed?" She rears back. "Obsession is its own disease."

Exactly. I'm fucking *sick* for Lex.

"If you're broken, I'm broken." I'll break myself before I'd ever try fixing her. "Lex…I'm obsessed with you."

Her silver eyes fall to my lips and her breathing speeds up, her collarbone heaving quicker and quicker. "You're sure?" comes out a whisper that turns my cock rock hard.

I glide her hips backward, raising her up until she's straddling my tip.

"I'm sure."

Hands in the hair by my ears, she pulls me to sitting, our faces coming together like magnets.

"I'm so fucking sure," I say against her lips before guiding her down on my rigid shaft and stuffing her pussy to the brim.

Thirty-Four

Lex

I WAKE UP TO THE SOUND OF WOOD BEING SPLIT NEARBY, AND immediately open my eyes to find the spot beside me empty. Past Reece's pillow is the nightstand where soft morning light is reaching through the blinds onto a book that's been propped up, the cover facing me. Judging by the wolf silhouette behind the woman with the wild hair on the front, it's a shifter romance. I reach over and grab it. The description is full of wilderness references, and the chapter headers inside feature a picture of a wolf standing in a forest, howling at a full moon.

If Reece was telling the truth last night, then he's already read this one.

As usual, I flip to the end and read the epilogue.

Setting the book down when I'm done, I don't get up right away. Instead, I close my eyes again to imagine the happily ever after in my head.

Amazing.

But unrealistic.

Gathering the sheet around me, I pad out to the kitchen, the smell of freshly brewed coffee drawing me over to the no-cup-insert, regular old coffee pot. Coffee isn't good for my anxiety, but neither is my husband. If I'm stuck with one, I *need* the other. After pouring myself a mug sans sweetener and dairy to avoid adding more strain on my thyroid, I head outside, passing a bouquet of tall Sunflowers on the countertop. Following last night's bath, we moved things to the bedroom, so this is my first time seeing any of the other stuff Reece brought in aside from the closet full of black clothes for each of us.

Outside, I'm greeted by an intoxicating blend of cedar, juniper, and smoke.

Settling on the top step of the porch, I watch Reece chop wood. Another pair of sweatpants slung low on his hips and no shirt whatsoever, I can see every single muscle on his torso flex and twist as he brings the ax down, cracking the wood into thirds. With no underwear to be found in the matching nightstand-and-dresser combo, I'm all too aware Reece is currently going commando and will be for the rest of our time here. His hair is mostly slicked back but has a few rebellious pieces in the front sticking up that I find adorable.

All around him dainty snowflakes fall from the frothy white sky, their motions as carefree and lively as I feel in this moment.

This is happiness, I remind myself again so I don't take it for granted. Not even for a second.

"Aren't you cold?" I ask once Reece stops to put another piece of wood on the stump.

He wipes his forehead with the back of his forearm, then gestures to the sheet wrapped around my naked body. "Aren't you?"

"Not anymore," I say before taking a sip.

"You keep looking at me like that, Snow…"

"Like I want you to split me in half, too?"

"There's that wicked sense of humor."

"I'm not joking," I tell him seriously.

Reece points the ax at me with a heated look, and I smile behind my mug…still gazing at him exactly the same way.

This is fun.

I never saw my parents tease or flirt or laugh. Now that I know what it looks like and feels like, I wonder what my mom ever saw in my dad. Or Cyrus.

You know what you learn. Sadly, nobody ever taught her what true happiness was either.

Maybe I could teach her someday.

Someday soon, or it might not even happen.

That realization sits heavy on me, and I have to physically roll my shoulders. I've fought so hard for a life I haven't even lived yet. Everybody else only lives one life, meanwhile I'm just trying to live one weekend. One weekend. I'm giving Reece this one weekend—I'm giving *myself* this one weekend—and then I'll return to my reality, but not a moment sooner.

"Did you see your book?"

I nod. "Thank you." Each time I say it with meaning, it gets a little easier. "Did you read it?"

"Listened, yeah."

"What'd you think?"

He shrugs one bare, toned shoulder. "Story was okay. The setting made it better. But the male narrator wasn't my favorite."

I try not to smile. "You have favorites?"

"A couple." He tells me about his favorite narrators, both female and male, and the reasons why he likes each one. I've never cared for audiobooks, but maybe I was choosing the ones with bad narration.

"Will you read it to me?"

"What? The book?"

I give him another nod.

"If you want me to," he says with a grin.

"I want you to."

"Okay. Then I will."

"Are you going to tell me about the flowers?"

"Which ones?" he asks during a powerful downswing.

"What other ones did you bring?"

"The Roses."

From the bath.

"Not the Roses," I say quickly, hoping he'll skip that explanation.

Hand on the exposed top of his Adonis belt, Reece pauses, reading my thoughts.

"Different color Roses have different meanings."

"I know that. I also know what the red ones mean." Everybody knows what those mean.

"They were burgundy. The Roses last night."

"Burgundy is a shade of red, rookie."

"*Burgundy* Roses…" He resumes chopping. "…mean dark beauty, affection…" The last swing, Reece brings the ax down faster and harder, causing the log to shatter into multiple shards. "And passion," he finishes while staring directly at me.

I didn't know that, but like everything else Reece has taught me, I'm glad I do now.

"And the Sunflowers?"

Reece wedges the ax into the stump's surface, and begins collecting wood chunks off the ground, ignoring my question.

"I'll just look them up and jump to my own conclusions."

"You'd need your phone to do that…" Reece purses his lips and squints his eyes in a way that makes him look guiltier than if he'd said it with a straight face.

I almost forgot about that, how I was kidnapped last night with nothing but the measly clothing on my body. Usually, it feels like my phone is another limb, but right now, I feel whole without it. I feel whole without any of that world.

I will have to find a way to call and check up on my mom though. That is a part of me, a permanent part.

Standing with an armful, Reece says, "So I guess I have to tell you," making me roll my eyes.

He dumps the wood into a basket by my feet, then dusts off his hands.

"Do you know how Sunflowers got their name?"

"Because they look like the sun," I say confidently, but he shakes his head.

"Because they follow the sun. At sunrise, they face east." He points east. "Then they follow the sun as it makes its way across the sky." He makes a large arc over his head before pointing west, where the sun sets.

"That doesn't make any sense. Wouldn't they still be facing west when the sun comes up again?"

Gradually reversing the path his arm just took, he says, "Overnight, they slowly turn back toward the east." By the time he finishes, his finger's once again pointing east.

That can't be true. Flowers are that intuitive?

"The sun is completely gone, missing from the sky, but they still know it'll be there again? Even though it was in a different place the last time they saw it? How?"

"Loyalty. Even when they lose sight of the sun, Sunflowers are loyal to it."

"Enough to go an entire night, through total darkness, waiting for something that might not be there anymore?"

"Yeah." He shrugs. "They trust, and they wait, and eventually, they find it again."

So why did he choose that particular flower for this weekend?

No notice whatsoever, Reece scoops me up, sheet and all, and carries me back inside.

"Careful," I say, trying my hardest to keep all the coffee in the mug. "This is scalding."

"If you can take it, so can I."

"Not likely," I mumble. "I have a much longer history of enduring pain."

"What do you want for breakfast?" he asks once he sets me down on the counter, next to the vase of loyal Sunflowers. I wait until Reece goes to the fridge to spin them to face the other way.

I'm nobody's sun.

"I don't eat breakfast," I say when Reece holds up a cartoon of eggs and a package of bacon. "I drink it."

He frowns. "Coffee?"

"No." *Well...* "Not *just* coffee. I drink fruit and vegetable juice. It's part of my treatment plan."

"Didn't that stop a year ago? When you went into remission?"

I study the mug in my hands and shrug a shoulder. "I didn't feel like stopping."

The sound of Reece dropping his arms by his sides echoes in the toasty kitchen.

"You've been scared to."

My head shakes all on its own. "I'm not scared. It's not a fear thing. It's a…"

I clung to every component of the treatment plan like it was my life raft, because at the time each one felt like it was, and since remission, it's been hard to even relax my grip, let alone give it up completely. My body was failing me for *years*. That's difficult to forget. It's even more difficult to forgive.

Not just difficult, I've found, but impossible.

"I'm not a Sunflower, Reece. I don't trust anything blindly, especially something that's already failed me once." And may possibly be failing me again.

"Did Kordin always fuck you from behind?" he asks randomly.

"No, that's something he picked up recently."

"Two-years-ago recently?"

Oh. He's connecting the dots.

"It's hard to say exactly. In a long string of bad sex, it all kind of blends together."

"Right," Reece says before putting the eggs and bacon back in the fridge. "We're going out for breakfast."

"Ree—"

"You can have your fruit, even your vegetables, but not in juice form. This area has more crystal shops, spiritual centers, health-food stores, and specialty restaurants than any other part of the state. We'll find you something to eat. Then I'm going to bring you back here and fuck you while staring at the face I go to sleep every night picturing."

He presses a quick kiss to my lips.

"I don't need you to pity me."

"I don't pity you, Lex. I…"

I suck in a breath.

"…am obsessed with you." He nods at the cupboard by the sink. "Your vitamins are in there. I don't know how many you take, so hopefully there's enough. If not, we'll get more in town."

"What vitamins?"

"The ones in your pantry. I didn't know what you needed them for, just that you might. And I figured you probably wouldn't have your luggage on you when I grabbed you last night, so I took several of each before I left your house."

A normal person would be appalled at this entire situation, at every crime that's been committed to get us here, but me, I let the sheet slide off my body as I put the mug down beside me because my pussy is soaked and aching.

"Lex," Reece warns, his gaze on my thighs as I slowly pull them apart. "You haven't eaten yet."

"Neither have you."

Legs wide open, I grip the edge and roll my hips forward, then back, my pussy kissing the countertop noisily, greedily. I moan his name so he knows it's him I picture, too.

Brows creased, Reece takes a step toward me, nudges me backward a couple inches, leans down, and proceeds to run his tongue over the part of the countertop my pussy just grazed. Glancing up at me, he rasps, "Mine," his voice unrecognizable, his intention unmistakable.

He's jealous of the counter.

I have never been more turned on in my twenty-six years.

He drops to his knees before I can say a word. His hands under my thighs, he drags me to the edge, right to his mouth, and begins sucking my pussy. Fingers, lips, tongue, and spit, Reece devours my pussy how I imagine a lumberjack eats a pork chop. So much slurping, so much sensation until finally I come on his tongue, his face glistening when he stands and shoves his sweatpants down one-handed, freeing his upright cock that's already swollen and leaking.

"Enjoy your meal?" I ask before I dab the precum on his tip and suck it off my finger, moaning at the memory of having him in my mouth.

"That was just the appetizer."

An appetite of a lumberjack, too. The mountains might be growing on me after all.

Stepping between my thighs, Reece aligns his cock with my entrance.

Just as hungry for him, I use my heels against his ass to pull him into me, his shaft gliding into my pussy as far as our bodies will allow. Both of us cling to the other, not wanting air to come between us.

"Don't pull out," I pant over his wet lips, flicking out my tongue for a taste of that, too.

"Teach me." He licks my tongue.

It's not just me who's been getting lessons from Reece; we've both been learning from each other all along.

"Stay deep, but go on your toes."

As soon as Reece does, the topside of his cock stimulates the underside of my clit, causing my mouth to fall open on a silent scream and my nails to dig into his shoulder blades.

"There's no one around to catch us this time. This weekend you're all fucking mine and I'm all fucking yours. So." He flattens his feet against the floor again before rising up to his toes. "Give me." He repeats the move. "Every." Down. "Fucking." Up. "Sound." Down. "You got." Up.

I throw my head back on a guttural groan, arching my back so my clit presses down on the base of his cock fully.

"Nuh-uh, Snow. Eyes on mine. I want to see your face, every beautiful inch of it, when we come together."

Somehow I roll my head forward, my forehead landing on his, and we stare into each other's eyes as we slowly, methodically fuck. The deep penetration combined with the constant stimulation on my clit has me screaming and clawing and cursing and praising, and between it all Reece and I kiss, our mouths just as intentional as our bottom halves.

"I... I... I..." I pant against his lips, my voice growing more and more urgent, more and more high-pitched.

Understanding, Reece breathes, "Me, too. Ready?"

All I can manage is a frantic half-nod, our foreheads still conjoined, then one more drive upward from Reece and everything goes numb from my toes to my hairline.

Shaking, Reece wheezes, "Holy fuck."

"Reece," rumbles from my chest, up my throat, and through my lips.

While Reece peppers me with kisses, my body starts to sag, a complete relaxation taking over my every muscle.

Before I can recline, Reece catches me, saying, "Just...wait." Lowering to his knees again, he looks up, and says, "Eyes on mine, Lex," then gathers the cum—his cum—leaking from my pussy with his tongue before spearing it between my folds, licking inside with exaggerated swirls that make me dizzy. With our eyes on each other's, neither of us blinking, I moan his name again. It's almost too much. Too much sensation, too much emotion, too much everything.

He latches on to my very engorged, very sensitive clit, crossing that line I was just teetering, and on an open-mouth scream, I clench his hair with both hands, trying to push him away, but he doesn't let up, only sucks harder. Almost instantly another orgasm starts to build, and I switch from pushing Reece to pulling him closer, not wanting him to stop or slow down or—

The knot in my abdomen explodes into a searing release of mind-bending, life-altering ecstasy.

"Oh my fucking God!" I scream at the top of my lungs, oblivious to Reece climbing to his feet until he snatches my face with both hands.

Between sloppy, sodden kisses that taste like cum and sweat, he whispers, "I'm obsessed with you. I'm fucking *obsessed* with you."

"I'm...starving."

His laugh tickles my lips, and he pulls back. "Works every time."

Thirty-Five

Lex

AFTER A BREAKFAST CONSISTING OF SOLID FOOD, WE HANG around the picturesque downtown, walking from one unconventional store to another. The businesses are all locally owned and operated and just as eclectic as Reece promised. Inside an independent bookstore, Reece tells me to get whatever I want, then follows me around to carry all the books I choose. Each one I hand him, he inspects before looking up the title on his phone. And any that don't fit whatever criteria he's using but refuses to share, he reshelves. When I ask him if he's texting his mom to get her opinion, I get a look of horror so amusing I almost laugh out loud. *Almost.*

"If you want to know what my mom reads, you can ask her yourself."

"How would I do that?" I question while skimming the local author selection. Unfortunately, there's not a single romance to be found.

Next to the shelf is a poster with different crystals, their meanings listed below each picture. My eyes automatically seek out obsidian. *Stone of protection.*

I smile to myself.

"When you meet her," Reece says casually.

Meanwhile every part of my body comes to a standstill, possibly even my heart. "Did you invite her here?"

"No."

My body resumes its normal functions. "Thank God."

"What?"

"I'm married."

"I'm aware."

"To another man."

Reece scoffs. "I wouldn't call him a man."

"I'm still married to him."

"She already knows."

I spin around to face him. "Knows what?"

"That you're married."

"And that you're..." I gesture at him, feeling my body wanting to lock up again.

"Obsessed with you?" He casually leans on a bookshelf. "Yeah. She and my sisters probably figured it out before I did."

"Reece," I hiss before realizing my mistake and pulling the hood on my head tighter. I've been careful to keep my hair covered since we left the cabin. That's all I need is someone to recognize me.

"What's the big deal? You already met Breckyn. It's only a matter of time before you meet the rest of my family."

I nod at the stack in his arms. "Do you have enough cash for all those?"

"Yes?" he says like a question.

"I'll be outside while you check out." I sidestep him and leave without another word.

Sooner than I was hoping, Reece finds me across the street, standing in the flurries, staring at a mural between two buildings.

I point at the larger-than-life white flower floating atop sparkling water with stars soaring from the petals up to billowing clouds. "Is that a Water Lily?"

Bag in hand, Reece keeps his distance from me, but glances at the painting, immediately answering, "It's a Lotus."

It's ethereal-looking.

"What does it stand for?"

"Beauty. Purity. Hope. Rebirth. Perseverance. The Lotus grows in shallow waters, mostly ponds. It's born in the mud at the bottom of

the water, where the seed takes root. Without knowing what's waiting for it overhead, the bud pushes up through the filth and darkness
to bloom above the surface, perfectly clean. It's one of the most beautiful flowers in the world, but the fact that it overcomes its hopeless
beginnings, makes it one of the most revered, too."

I side-eye Reece.

"What flower are you?"

He shifts on his feet. "Not a Lotus."

Me neither. But here, I feel like I could be.

Unfortunately, here is not reality. Here is a fictional story Reece
and I are writing in real time, except when we reach the end, that's it,
it'll just end. There is no clean, untouched happily ever after for us.

I close my eyes and imagine what it would look like if there was—
our families blended, a pod of females with Reece right at home in the
middle. He'd be comfortable because that's what he already knows.
I'm the one who didn't learn that life. I only know how to survive like
an apex predator, not thrive like one.

"Can you call her?"

"Who? My mom? You want to talk to her?"

I shake my head but open my eyes. "You talk. I'll listen."

We find a café open for afternoon tea service and use their com-
plimentary Wi-Fi at a back booth, away from the other patrons. I
remove my coat but keep my sweatshirt's hood up.

Putting his phone on speaker, Reece calls his mom.

"What's her name?" I ask while it rings.

"Gwen. Gwendolyn, but no one calls her that."

Gwen Souza answers, a smile in her voice.

"Hey, Ma."

"What's today's order?"

Reece smiles, too. "No order. I picked up enough flowers yesterday to last through the weekend."

He did? I've only seen the Roses and the Sunflowers. Did he
bring up more?

Of course he did. He's Reece.

"I hope she likes all these flowers you keep giving her."

Reece eyes me, and I bow my head.

"She does."

"That's something," Reece's mom murmurs like she's preoccupied. "Everything okay?"

"Oh, Mrs. Edwards, you remember her? Well, her cat attacked her last night after picking up her weekly order."

"Did she ask for Eucalyptus in it?"

"Yes. I feel terrible, but she never mentioned having a cat. All this time she's been coming and she never said anything."

"Eucalyptus smells like cat piss," Reece explains to me quietly.

"Anyway, tell me what's going on with you. Anything new?"

"No, nothing new."

"There never is. I don't know why I even ask."

I divert my attention to a passing server holding a tray of steaming teas and sugar-dusted crepes.

Reece keeps the ugly parts of his life from his family. He's their protector just like I am for mine.

Whatever it takes.

"Ask Reece about the chocolate," someone in the background says.

"Here. You do it," Gwen says before there's a shuffling sound.

"Did the chocolate work?"

"Breck," Reece mouths to me, then to his sister, "It wasn't that."

"Chocolate?" I mouth as well.

Leaning back, Reece reaches into his front pocket and pulls out a square piece of chocolate wrapped in shiny packaging. "They gave me chocolate for you."

"For me?"

"For your PMS. During her shadowing with you, Breck picked up on some of the same things I did."

His family was concerned about me, about my health? They had a conversation about it? And Reece has been carrying chocolate around on him ever since? Chocolate they gave him. For me.

"Why didn't you try it?"

"Because I found a better way to combat your mood swings."

What way?

His words before we left the cabin come back to me. *"Works every time."* Sex is the better way?

If it's between chocolate and sex, of course I'm going to choose the latter.

"Is Lenox there? Oh my God, Reece, you could've told us. Hi, Lenox."

I silently beg Reece to say something, but all he does is angle the phone toward me.

After several blinks, I say, "Hello, Breckyn. How've you been?"

Breckyn launches into telling me everything new in her life, clearly not as private as her brother, then pauses to ask, "So…am I going to be an aunt?" causing me to almost choke on my own saliva. Where did that come from?

"Breck," Reece barks while giving me an apologetic look. "It's not that either. It's just…"

"Her thyroid?" she guesses, her voice small but curious.

"What makes you say that?"

"Because Charlie's been having some trouble lately, and after looking up her symptoms, we think it might be that."

Reece looks like he got slapped across the face. "What trouble?"

"I don't know, just, like, feeling like crap all the time. Ask Charlie yourself."

Another voice gets on, this one deeper than Breckyn's.

"Why didn't you tell me something was wrong?" Reece demands instantly.

"Because I didn't know it was?"

I ease the phone out of Reece's hold. Considering I was barely one myself, I'm no expert on teenagers, but that—a man making this about himself—is *not* what Charlie needs right now.

First, I take the phone off speaker, then I draw a deep breath and greet Reece's other sister.

"Hi." She laughs awkwardly.

"I had an overactive thyroid when I was around your age, so I might know a little about what you're going through. Do you want to talk about it?"

Emotion replaces humor, and her voice takes on a croaky tone as she tells me all the symptoms she's been experiencing lately, including hair loss.

"I lost a lot of my hair, too," I tell her, feeling the heat of Reece's stare on the side of my face. "I dyed it as light as I could to make the bald spots less noticeable." This is my first time telling someone the real reason for my hair color.

"Really? I've been so tired, too. I'll wake up and get ready, then boom, I just want to curl up and pass out again. I assumed it was from school and...you know..."

"Yeah. I do." Life for women, in general, is draining. Our bodies turning on us makes it that much harder. Charlie sounds exactly how I felt facing so many signs with no real idea what any of them were indicating. Without anyone to talk to about it, I went to great lengths to cover up my suffering. I don't want that for Charlie. It definitely sounds like something could be going on with her thyroid, but whether it's underactive or overactive I don't know. The internet can help cast a net, but she needs professional assistance to narrow it down to an actual diagnosis.

"Have you seen any doctors yet?"

"Only our pediatrician."

"Did they order any tests? Or refer you out?"

"No, she just prescribed me the pill."

Charlie could go the next ten years down the same path I was on, one wrong prescription after another, one wrong diagnosis after another. That alone is enough stress to cause hormonal imbalances.

"I'm going to give your brother my functional medicine doctor's information and he'll send it to your mom so she can set up an appointment for you. He's amazing and will figure out exactly what's going on and what the next steps are to get you feeling like yourself again."

Gwen mumbles something I can't make out.

"My mom doesn't think our insurance will cover that kind of doctor."

Most insurances don't. That's why so few people seek out functional medicine.

I glance at Reece before quickly looking away. "They don't accept insurance but they do accept sponsorships. So when you call, make sure you tell them my name and they'll—"

"Lex." Using his arm around my shoulders, Reece rotates me his way. "I take care of my family."

I push mute.

"It's just like with the boutique, rook. My name will get her through the door, then the rest is up to you," I lie. Kordin's never audited my medical expenses before and I don't see why he'd start, so as long as Charlie uses the same doctor I do, any bills I receive will be paid in full. I just have to speak to the billing department before her brother does.

The moment Reece nods, I unmute the phone, asking, "How does that sound, Charlie?"

"Okay. Yeah. We can try. Thank you. You're literally a lifesaver."

Water coats my vision as I whisper, "It's nothing."

Most things I do for my mom she doesn't even realize. But this, doing something for someone else, someone I don't owe anything to, it feels…good. Nice. I *like* it.

I may not be a Lotus, but maybe my core isn't as polluted as I've always believed.

Gwen calls her son's name, so I hit the speaker button again and blindly give the phone back to him.

"Can I expect you two for dinner tonight?" she asks.

"No. We're going to the movies."

We are? He didn't tell me that.

When he ends the call a few minutes later, his eyebrows are puckered.

"My sister's broken."

"She's not broken," I argue, feeling irrationally protective over Charlie. "Her body's out of balance right now. Lots of women go through hormone imbalances. Once the root of the problem is determined, she can get proper treatment."

"So you'll give a stranger more compassion than you'll give yourself?"

"It's not…" I stop to thoroughly consider my response—the one I gave about Charlie—then Reece's. He was baiting me, trying to prove a point. While I understand where he's trying to come from, he'll never fully grasp where I actually do come from.

"I told you my tattoo isn't just about my thyroid." I got it before I even knew about my Graves' disease.

"And if I said she shot someone to save my mom…would you let me call her broken?"

"She…" My chest rising and falling rapidly, I shake my head. *No, I wouldn't.*

Gripping my chin and looking between my eyes, Reece says, "Charlie's not broken and neither are you. You're fucking perfect." He seals his lips to mine before pulling back an inch, whispering over them, "For me."

But Charlie didn't shoot her mom in the fucking head. Charlie didn't rob her mom of a normal life. That's what Reece is missing. That's what Reece will never wholly comprehend.

"I don't know how," I confess quietly.

"How to what?"

"How to…" Love myself. Forgive myself. Give myself an ounce of fucking grace.

"I'll teach you," Reece says.

"You don't even know what I was going to say."

"I don't need to. Whatever you don't know, I'll teach you."

"And if you don't know it?"

"I'll learn it first."

I have to be open to learning too though.

Taking his phone, I dial my mom.

"Who are you calling?"

I don't answer Reece, only say, "Hi, Mum," when my mom picks up.

"Where are you calling me from? The caller ID says—"

"My phone died and I don't have a charger with me, so I borrowed someone else's to check in on you. How are you feeling today?"

Reece's smile is as gentle as his touch when he presses a hand to my knee to stop its incessant movement.

"You didn't have to do that. I'm fine. I've got that bottle of wine you dropped off, a new book to dive into, and the whole day to enjoy both. What else could I possibly want?"

Reece narrows his dark eyes.

Doesn't he see? She could want a lot more. She could have a lot more. *If it weren't for me.*

I abandon his stare for the table.

Would I think that about Charlie?

No.

I change my perspective to an outsider looking in, examining the entire situation. It didn't *really* start with me, did it? I put a hole in my mom's head, but before that happened, both Cyrus and my dad had already torn a hole in her fate.

"Sounds like a perfect night to me," I tell her.

"Are you going to be home at a reasonable hour tonight or am I going to have to ground you again for missing curfew?"

"Mum, I don't live with you anymore because I'm an adult now. I told you yesterday I'm out of town this weekend, remember?"

"Oh." This pause is quicker than some as she puts everything in the right order. "Where'd you get away to this time?"

"The mountains."

"Are they lovely?"

I take a grounding inhale through my nose, picking up Reece's zesty cologne next to me, the comforting cocoon of sweet, delicate crepe batter surrounding us, the earthy call of the firs outside drifting through the front door every time someone opens it.

"Better than fiction."

"Better than fiction? I didn't think such a thing existed."

"I didn't either," I admit to her. *Until him*, I admit to myself. Reece is better than any fictional man.

My mom and I talk for a while longer, then hang up.

"She thinks you're still a kid?" Reece asks as he waves over a server.

"She occasionally thinks I'm sixteen, yes."

We put in an order for lunch, then while we wait, I explain to Reece how my mom's injury affected her memory and what those first couple years following the accident were like. He listens intently and asks questions throughout, never once making me feel judged or pitied. Judgement I deserve. Pity I don't. But Reece gives me neither, only an open mind as I tell him more about my life than I've ever told anyone.

When we're finished eating, and my voice is hoarse from talking so much, Reece covers the check with more than enough bills, then stands, looks down at me seriously, and says, "Thank you."

"For what? You paid." Without my wallet, he's had to pay for everything.

I fit my hand in his warm palm, his fingers closing snugly around mine.

Shaking his head, he pulls me up, hugging my front against his, and close to my cheek, he whispers, "For letting me in."

A break from the snow finally comes after the sun goes down, giving the moon a chance to light our walk to the movie theater.

After buying tickets, we stop at a long counter selling popcorn, drinks, candy, sub sandwiches, and ice cream. Reece tells me to get whatever I want, so I order a water and a separate cup of ice.

"Why don't you put the water with the ice?"

Keeping my voice low, I tell him, "Eating ice helps me cool down. In case I get overheated."

"You've been fine all day, haven't you?"

"I..." I have been fine all day. Last night, too. I was overheated yesterday practically the entire drive to the resort, but since I've been with Reece, I haven't tipped one way or the other. My body temp's been normal. Apart from my brief bout of unease at the café earlier, I haven't had anxiety either.

I run through my mental checklist of other symptoms, not finding any applicable in the last twenty-four hours.

Maybe my thyroid isn't malfunctioning again. Maybe it's something else.

I stare at Reece, his lips pulling into a secretive smile.

Maybe it's some*one* else. Kordin has always caused me stress, but lately it's been worse. The daily onslaught of extra cortisol from constantly being in survival mode is affecting my system, and my body's been letting me know.

"Will you get popcorn?" I ask Reece.

"Do you want me to get popcorn?"

"Yes."

"Then I will."

"Are all movie theaters like this?" I ask once we're inside the dimly lit theater. The back two-thirds is made up of tightly packed rows of plush red chairs, while the front section has six booth-style tables, the seats only on one side, facing the screen.

Carefully holding his drink and popcorn in one arm, Reece settles his free hand on the small of my back, guiding me forward. "None I've ever been to."

We sit at one of the middle tables, perfectly centered to the screen. I wait until the theater goes dark to lower my hood.

During the previews, I reach over and grab Reece's hand, placing it on the inside of my thigh, right up against my crotch. He gives it a squeeze before withdrawing his hand altogether. I do it again and get the same results.

Leaning over, he whispers, "That's not why we're here."

Someone shushes him, making me scowl.

Reece grins.

"Why are we here? We could've watched a movie at the cabin."

"You want your first movie to be on a twenty-four-inch screen with a thirteen-year-old DVD that most likely skips?"

Maybe? I can honestly say I've never put any thought into what my first movie experience would be like.

"Why is this so important?"

"Because I don't want you ending up like your mom thinking a bottle of wine and a book are the best life has to offer."

My scoff triggers more shushes.

This time Reece sends out threatening glares.

376 | A. MARIE

"At least she gets wine. That's an upgrade from my Saturday nights."

"You don't drink wine?"

I shake my head. "I don't drink at all."

"But I saw you... At The Pen..."

"Did you see what was actually poured into the glasses I drank from?"

His eyes harden.

"Dishonesty and betrayal, rookie."

He leans forward until his lips brush mine, my heartbeat spiking significantly.

"You're capable of more than that." Just when I think he's going to kiss me, he sticks a piece of popcorn between my lips, and says, "Now watch the movie."

A laugh builds behind my ribs until the buttery, salty popcorn touches my tongue, then it becomes an internalized moan. Grabbing a handful for myself, I focus on the gigantic screen before us, where my eyes stay for the next hour and forty-nine minutes until the credits roll.

"What'd you think? Did you like it?" Reece asks next to me, my legs on his lap, one of his hands rubbing my calves, the other on the back of my head, palming my skull.

I nod and grin. "I liked it. I liked this." I point to the empty popcorn bucket, then over our heads, all around us. "I liked all of it, everything. Thank you."

"For what?" he asks, wearing his own smile.

"For teaching me what else fun can be." We could've made this sexual, but I'm grateful Reece insisted we didn't.

I lean forward to show him just how grateful, and his eyes trail down to my lips.

Suddenly, the lights come on, making me scramble to replace my hood. *I almost forgot.*

"Let's get out of here." Reece springs into action, setting my feet back down on the floor before standing up.

"Okay..."

His previous rejections were explicable—I didn't understand that at the time, only after the fact—but this one hits a little too close to home. Why won't he kiss me?

Outside, the snowstorm's returned with renewed vigor.

Coming to an intersection, Reece grabs my hand and pulls me along behind him on to the crosswalk before stopping in the middle of it and spinning around to face me.

Multiple cars honk, but Reece doesn't budge an inch, just flicks my hood backward, off my head.

Instead of worrying about my hair, my eyes lift on their own accord, admiring the clusters of snow crystals cascading around us and on us. I fill my lungs with a long inhale, my nose picking up a hint of forest, but mostly a fresh, clean scent from nature's raw reset.

"Lex."

Out of the corner of my eye, I see the stoplight parallel to us switch to green, but I can't pull my attention away from the show overhead.

"Yes?" I say without looking at him, a smirk flirting with my lips as I try to hold it back. We're going to get hit.

"I don't want to hide you."

First I lower my gaze, then head, Reece's sincere expression evident the entire time, despite the flakes clinging to my lashes.

"Not in there. Not anywhere. In private or public, in the dark or light, I want to treat you the same." He pauses to pull my body to his, our fronts mashed together as tightly as our padded coats allow. "Like you're mine." Driving his point home, he seizes my lips in a searing kiss that ignites my whole body. From the top of my head to the tips of my toes, I'm engulfed by Reece.

Before my eyes drift closed, I catch his shoulder rotating as he waves for traffic to go around us, and a sense of security washes over me. In the middle of a snowstorm, in an intersection during a green light, where we are vulnerable and exposed and in danger's direct path, I feel…safe. Because of him.

Bringing my arms up around Reece's neck, I tilt my head and deepen the kiss, never wanting this fantasy to end.

Our lips slow to lazy, sensual caresses, our mouths making love, until eventually they stop moving entirely. Still, we don't separate.

"I'm obsessed with you," Reece whispers, his words traveling down my throat, burrowing into my chest and encasing my heart in something I thought I banned myself from ever feeling again. Not only do I feel it from Reece, I feel it *for* him, too.

"Let's go home," he says.

Home.

For one more moment I remain in the fantasy that we are together and we do live under the same roof, and I nod.

"Do any flowers stand for happiness?" I ask as we turn toward the sidewalk, my skin tingling beneath my layers.

"I can think of a couple."

We wait for a car to pass, the driver giving us the finger that we return instantly, simultaneously.

After Reece puts himself closest to the road, he tucks me under his arm, keeping the flame kindled by the kiss alive between us as we walk side by side.

"Honeysuckle symbolizes pure happiness."

Honeysuckle. That's it. That's what this weekend feels like— pure happiness.

"Lily of the Valley has a lot of meanings, including happiness. Except…"

I gaze up at him. "Except?"

"It's also poisonous."

Lethal bliss. Sounds a lot like blind trust to me.

"You didn't bring any Lily of the Valley along, did you?"

The way he stares down at me, I feel something simmering, and expect him to tell me he did, but then he shakes his head and looks forward, saying, "No. Only Peruvian Lilies. Alstroemerias."

"What do those signify?"

"Devotion, since their leaves grow upside down."

"I'm not seeing the connection."

"As the leaves grow out from the stems," he explains, using a hand to demonstrate, "they twist so the bottoms are facing up, mimicking the twists and turns of a relationship."

Reality rains down on me like an abrupt onslaught of sleet, extinguishing any previous warmth. A relationship? This is a fantasy, and not even a full-length novel, but a weekend-long novella. The kind the author wouldn't be able to sell, so they throw it up on their website for free. We're an unmarketable passion-project, not a relationship.

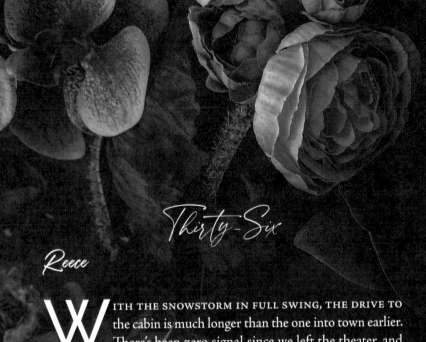

Thirty-Six

Reece

WITH THE SNOWSTORM IN FULL SWING, THE DRIVE TO the cabin is much longer than the one into town earlier. There's been zero signal since we left the theater, and we haven't passed a single car on the deserted backroad, so I'm taking my time, going well under the speed limit to avoid a crash.

Every time I catch a glimpse of Lex she's riveted by the big, fat flakes showering the windshield as we round a mountain, her expression equal parts fear and fascination. I can tell because that's exactly how I feel looking at her.

Our time together up here has been perfect, and I'm scared of ruining it. While I *think* I've earned her trust, I don't know for sure.

The only way to find out is to come clean and see how she reacts.

But I'm not doing that right now. Once we're safe inside the cabin, I will.

"What do you think? Would you ever live out here?" I ask, breaking the silence.

Focused out the glass, she says, "A house away from everybody?"

"Yeah."

"With a brook on the property, a vase of flowers on the counter, and a punching bag in the living room?"

Despite her teasing tone, or maybe because of it, I smile. "Don't forget the smut on the shelves and a skylight over the bed."

She finally tears her attention away from the scenery to glance my way, her eyebrows pinched. The skylight is my thing, but it should be hers, too.

I nod ahead of us, explaining, "For the moon and the snow. You like both." And now so do I. "I told you we were alike. You want to live out here just as much as I do."

Her knee begins jumping, so I place my right hand on her thigh, my fingers curling around the curve until the nervous tic stops.

"Do you know what your ring's made of?"

"Only what you told me…broken promises." Not that I believe her.

"Black diamond."

"A fucking diamond?" I study my hand on top of the steering wheel, the band almost sinister-looking against my skin.

"It's formed by immense pressure and heat over a long period of time. The only thing that can ever scratch it is another diamond. Like may attract like, but like also destroys like."

She fixes her gaze on the windshield, the wipers working at max speed to clear the glass.

"Snow?" I say after a while.

"Hmm?"

"If your scratches destroy me, draw my death out. Make it as long and brutally painful as you can." I'll go into the ground smashed, slashed, and having lived out a fantasy worth dying for. What better ending is there?

"You're a masochist."

"Only for you."

Her lips form a small smirk, then she shakes her head, muttering, "Exhausting."

I'll show her exhausting. *Then* we'll talk, because that's the best way to get through to Lex. And because…she does hold the power to destroy me. Not because we're alike, but because with every breath she takes, I feel myself falling deeper and deeper in love with her. I told her all she had to do was breathe but I left out the most important part. I need her to breathe *near me*. If she runs, she won't be anymore. So I'm hoping, I'm fucking praying, that after several orgasms, she won't have the energy to even try.

All four tires powering through the foot and a half of undisturbed snow, we make it up the steep incline to the cabin without incident.

"Are you ready to read me my bedtime story?" Lex asks once we're inside, shoes off at the door and placed in the provided boot tray.

"I'll read to you, but you're not going to bed anytime soon."

I don't miss her eye roll as she turns away. Catching her with an arm around her middle, I heave her off the floor and carry her to the bedroom, tossing her onto the bed so she's staring up at me, another smile teasing her lips.

"Strip," is all I say.

"You can't afford me."

"I'm not trying to buy you, Lex."

I'm trying to keep her. Forever.

I can't tell her that though. At least not yet.

Gripping the fabric at her ankles, I say, "I'm trying to eat you." Then, I yank both pant legs down at the same time, half-dragging Lex across the mattress, too.

"Reece!" she yells while breaking into barely suppressed laughter.

I continue pulling on her pants until her bare pussy comes into view.

Not packing any underwear for this weekend was pure fucking genius.

Dropping down on my stomach, I take one long lick up her slit.

"No," Lex says, trying to twist away. "You said you'd read to me."

Holding her in place, I say against her plump, pink pussy lips, "I can read while I eat," before giving them a sloppy tongue kiss.

A scoff has me stopping to glance up at Lex's face, that arched eyebrow of hers taunting me.

It's not a total lie. I *listen* to books while I eat.

I brace myself on my elbows and tell her, "Give me the book."

Opening the fated-mates romance, I set it on Lex's lower abdomen, the pages spread right above her clit, making her the sexiest book stand to ever fucking exist. Goddamn.

I get another lick in, then start reading.

By the time I reach chapter two, I've managed to get Lex's pants the rest of the way off—one-handed, without skipping a single word. Chapter three, we're both shirtless. Chapter four, I'm completely naked, too, my cock like granite. I steal tastes of Lex every time I turn a page, keeping her nice and wet for me. In chapter five we get the couple's dramatic first kiss and I reenact it on Lex's pussy until she comes on my tongue. Chapter six never comes, but Lex does two more times—once around my fingers and once when I bite the inside of her thigh like her own personal werewolf alpha. After that I add vampire romances to the top of the tbr list I keep in my phone's notes because I have every intention of capitalizing on that kink. If Lex can come from a single bite, she's about to be permanently imprinted with my teeth marks because I plan on biting her every chance I get.

Settling between her quivering thighs, I drag my shaft along her pussy, coating myself in her milk. Her arms fold over top of me, her nails scraping my lats before crisscrossing over my back to trail down to my ass, squeezing my cheeks and pulling me into her. My cock parts her slick, warm walls, the fit once I'm buried like a motherfucking glove.

Lex's grip on my ass loosens before falling away completely.

"Are you tired already?" That was only three.

"I'm always tired, rook."

"From what? Your thyroid?"

She shakes her head, the motion slow and…sad?

"It's exhausting pretending to be okay."

I search her eyes. Despite being in the dark now, they're still silver, like the leaves of Woolly Lavender.

"So stop."

"I can't. It's all I know."

Just like fighting, pretending's all she's ever known.

"Nobody's okay all the time."

"Not even you?"

I remember my dad's death and how I handled it. How I'm still handling it. I took on a role I wasn't prepared for and I've been playing catch-up ever since, never quite getting ahead, somehow always falling behind. What I can't seem to remember is what okay felt like, because I don't know when the last time I actually was.

"Not even me," I admit.

Her eyes explore mine this time, and I reach up to brush an invisible hair off her forehead, causing her to break the connection with a blink.

"You don't have to be okay for me. I'll still be obsessed with you if you're not. *When* you're not. I just…" I stop and lower my head to hers. After swallowing thickly, I start again, whispering, "I just need you to breathe."

Her damp eyes locked on my even damper ones, Lex says, "Be sweet."

"You never want me to be sweet."

"Tonight I do."

Sealing my lips to hers, I rock my hips back and forth instead of thrusting up and down because just the thought of leaving her in any way right now, even an inch, a half-inch, a quarter, is unbearable.

Lex returns her hands to my body, one on my shoulder blade, the other under my ass, her nails burrowing under the skin in both spots as she clutches me to her. Crossing her legs and hooking her ankles behind me brings us closer, so fucking close we're one.

Eyebrows crushed together painfully, air pours through my nose, my exhales growing as heavy as my balls.

Fuck, I love her. I love her when she's hurting me. I love her when she's hurting, because she is, always. We all are. We just bury our pain like we bury our dead—in the same soil we resent but do nothing to change.

I want to change. I want to change it all. For her. *With* her. And

I'm going to. Tomorrow. Tonight is about confronting our pasts to understand our present. Tomorrow we'll figure out a way to have a future—together because the only life I want is with her in it.

I tell her everything I'm feeling, physically, emotionally, all of it.

Lex comes first, with me following right after, then I tuck her against my side and press a kiss to her white hair, telling her, "Sleep, Snow White."

We stay wrapped up in each other's arms until Lex passes out. Just before I drift off, I realize I don't care if I ever feel okay again. As long as I have this, have *her*, I'm better than okay.

Thirty-Seven

Reece

A CRUNCHING NOISE PRICKS MY EARS, SENDING AWARENESS throughout the rest of my body like an electric current. With around two feet of snow outside, if not more by now, crunching means something's out there, walking on it. Something...

Or somebody.

I stretch the arm under Lex's pillow to reach for my Glock without waking her.

My hand feels around the smooth surface of the nightstand, finding fucking nothing. Shit!

I open my eyes to see Lex's already on mine.

Before I can say a word, she brings my gun up to her lips, silently shushing me with its barrel.

Holding the sheet over her tits with her other hand, she sits up, saying loudly, "Some things never change."

Oh fuck. Did she find—

A man using a cane steps out from behind the wall, filling the bedroom's doorway, and I snap to sitting, too, my heartbeat pounding in my ears.

Cyrus stares back at me before shifting his gaze to Lex...and the thin sheet covering her naked body.

Goddamn it.

What is he doing here? How did he find us? Was it that kiss in town? Did someone recognize Lex? Us?

"Smile, Lexi. You don't seem happy to see me."

"I'm not," she says emotionlessly.

"Don't fucking smile," I murmur to her, loud enough for Cyrus to hear.

A beat of tense silence passes before he waves a hand at Lex. "Some things do change. I see you're not wearing head-to-toe sweats to bed anymore. Did the hollow get you to kick the habit? Or was it my employee's doing?" He jabs a finger in my direction.

"Mmm." Lex doesn't waste time acting surprised at Cyrus's bombshell about my identity, just answers him with, "I did it myself. It was fairly easy once I was out of your house and no longer sleeping in a room with a pedophile standing in the corner, tugging on his cock."

Now I'm looking at Lex, too. Cyrus did that when she lived with him?

With my head turned her way, I search out my piece. She's still got it in her hand, the hand furthest from me, keeping it out of Cyrus's sight under the sheet by her thigh. It's a reach. It's a fucking reach to try to grab it *and* cover Lex, but I'll do it.

If there's someone else stalking around outside, guaranteed they're strapped, too, making us outgunned as well. Possibly even outnumbered, depending on how many men he's got out there.

Cyrus sighs. "Everything in this world is a transaction. I let you live with me, covered all your expenses as well as your mother's, and you expected me to get nothing in return?"

"All I did was give to you, including the idea for Lost and Found."

Cyrus licks his lips, biting the bottom one before releasing it noisily. "I'll admit you provided the incentive for Lost and Found, however you were not its creator."

Incentive? Motherfucker.

Lex gives the same sigh as Cyrus, making her sound like his real daughter. "What do you want?"

Leaning against the doorframe, he nods toward me. "You mean

388 | A. MARIE

you didn't get it out of Reece here? You used to make hollows sing like canaries. Now you can't even get one fox to talk?"

Beside me, Lex's body stiffens, but she keeps her attention on Cyrus. "Considering he was sent to me by you, I assumed anything out of his mouth would be regurgitated bullshit straight from yours."

"It's not like that," I swear to her.

"So why, may I ask, did you still fuck him?"

"I said his mouth was of no use to me, not that his cock wasn't."

Cyrus shifts on his feet.

"Why do you seem so surprised? You orchestrated the affair yourself, did you not?"

I try again, telling her, "He didn't—"

"As much as I'd love to take credit for this little tryst, my sights have been set a bit higher, on your husband and his side endeavors."

"Kordin's affairs?"

"Of all the roles you've taken on, naïve never did suit you. Everybody in this room is aware that hollow's need for numerous cum receptacles is not the real reason you sought out my assistance."

Here it is. She has to say it.

Will she?

Lex cocks her head toward me, staring at my exposed chest. She knows I know.

She's quiet for a minute, then scoffs, glancing back at Cyrus.

"You're here about Kordin's greed?"

Cyrus chuckles menacingly.

She chose her words carefully, but at least she acknowledged what Kordin's really up to. For once.

I wish it wasn't like this. I wish she'd confided in me hours ago when it was just us. I could've confessed my part in this, because it's nothing like what she's implying. I never gave Cyrus any intel on her. He didn't even want me near her.

"What does that have to do with me?" Lex asks.

My boss tuts.

"No." She shakes her head. "I'm out. I've been out. I paid my way out."

"That hollow cunt paid."

"Regardless, you got your money and I got my freedom. You said it yourself, everything's a transaction. That one's complete. It's been complete. You're wasting your time—"

After retrieving something from his back pocket, Cyrus holds out a black-and-orange USB.

"What is that?"

I'm the one who answers her, saying, "My flash drive."

For the first time since Cyrus appeared, Lex meets my eyes, dishonesty and betrayal not in hers this time, but in mine.

I'm fucking sorry, I try telling her with them. On God, I was going to show her everything on it as soon as we woke up. And ate. And… Fuck! I was going to show her!

"I wonder which one Kordin will be more willing to give up: you or the funds he's been illegally pocketing from his own company."

Lex remains tight-lipped, her mind working louder than any words she could possibly say.

Cyrus tells her with a serious tone, "I need you, Lexi. There's nothing in this world more valuable to me."

"You've been getting by just fine without me."

"Imagine how much better I'll be with you."

"On your stage?"

"By my side. You and me, we'll rule all of Fox Hollow."

"Fox Hollow doesn't need rulers. It needs an overhaul."

"With your real estate expertise, we can do that."

That's it. Cyrus wants to own all of Fox Hollow, not just the worst half. Anyone can get their real estate license, but not everyone can be Lenox Debrosse, a fox who can pass as a hollow. Cyrus doesn't value Lex, he values the profit he can make off her, off her reputation, and he's been waiting as she built it.

Cyrus did play a part in putting Lex in the Debrosse brothers' path, not for scamming them like I originally thought, but for the name, the experience, the knowledge, the contacts only they could provide her. It's like what Lex told Breckyn, that business is all about who you know, and Lex knows a lot of people now thanks to Kordin

Debrosse. People she would've never worked with if she were involved with Cyrus.

"You're not getting her," erupts out of me in a snarled growl I feel from the pit of my soul.

"You fucking…"

The second Cyrus points his gun at me, Lex whips mine out, her finger positioned on the trigger as she aims at the window above the nightstand.

"Shoot him and I shoot your fox on the other side of this glass."

Cyrus chuckles. "Be my guest. I don't give a fuck about hi—"

Lex turns the gun on herself, the muzzle to her temple.

Another dose of adrenaline shoots through my body, my limbs vibrating with it.

"What the fuck, Lex?"

Ignoring me, she asks Cyrus, "How valuable am I to you dead?"

"This was always your last-ditch threat. The amount of times I caught you with a razorblade at your wrists, and yet here you sit, still alive."

The scars. Stripper poles didn't cause them; Lex did.

"That's because you wouldn't let me die," she grits between clenched teeth.

She wasn't just threatening to kill herself. She tried to, but Cyrus stopped her…for his own reasons. For his own gain.

Lex has been through a lot of shit in her life, more than she's shared with me and probably ever will share with anyone, but most of the best flowers start in the dirt. Some just need more tending than others.

"But I've upgraded from razorblades and I'm promising you if you pull that trigger, I pull mine."

"Lex, don't," I plead through a tight throat.

My eyes trained on Lex with Cyrus in my periphery, I can see him sizing me up. He's weighing his options, calculating his chances.

Across the mattress's surface, I slowly reach out to touch Lex's hip, rubbing her smooth skin with the back of my fingers, silently begging her not to do it. I don't care if he kills me, she can't shoot herself. She fucking can't.

After a few more seconds that feel like hours, Cyrus finally lowers his gun. Lex waits until it's holstered to drop mine by her side again.

"You're fucking dead," Cyrus spits at me. "Your sisters will—"

"What's the number?"

"Number?" he asks Lex.

"The one you're planning on going to Kordin with."

"I don't want his money. I want his wife."

"You plan for every scenario, including Kordin refusing to give me up, so what was the number you were willing to settle for in case he did?"

Cyrus swings his gaze back and forth between the two of us.

"Five million."

Lex closes her eyes, breathing through her nose, and for a moment I think she's going to risk the counterattack waiting for us outside and just kill Cyrus now.

If she does, at least one of us is getting shot.

I prepare my body to tackle hers, so it's me. It can *only* be me.

Her eyes open again. "I'll get you your five million dollars."

"You have until midnight tonight otherwise the deal's off and you're mine."

"I need more time. Banks are closed on Sundays."

"I might be persuaded to extending my patience and generosity another day."

"How much?"

"Double."

Ten million dollars. Ten million motherfucking dollars. There's no way she can—

"Done," Lex says.

What? How the fuck does she have access to ten million dollars?

"But if you so much as go near Reece or anyone in his family between now and Monday night, I'll blow my brains out, leaving you with nothing."

"Nothing?" A humorless laugh leaves Cyrus's lips. "I'd be front row at your funeral, squeezing Kordin Debrosse for every penny he's worth before the first scoop of dirt hits your casket."

"Now who's naïve? How could Kordin possibly attend my funeral if he's in prison for my murder? It'd be his gun after all, and I know *exactly* how to make it look believable." At Cyrus's stunned silence, she adds, "Thanks to your tutelage."

Cyrus's expression hardens as he looks from her to me. "If you let anything happen to her before Monday—"

"I won't," I promise, not for his sake or mine, but for hers. Only fucking hers. Goddamn it, how did we get to this? Everything was perfect—fucking *perfect*—when Lex and I went to sleep. Now it's all shit.

Cyrus points his cane at me. "Any harm she inflicts on herself will be replicated on your mother." His aim shifts to Lex. "Then yours. Don't think that mediocre security system you have on that white-and-blue Cape with the window boxes will keep me away from Yetta."

Lex doesn't react in any way whatsoever.

With a sinister smile, he says, "Tomorrow night. Midnight. The Playground. See you then."

We hold our positions until we hear the footsteps outside recede, then fade completely, an engine in the distance starting up before fading away as well.

Lex springs from the bed to pace beside it, naked, with my gun still in her hold.

"You fucked me *again*."

Fucked *her*? Is she serious? We're both fucked.

"How'd you know he was here?" I ask, making her stop and acknowledge me directly.

"You know how, fox."

I try not to balk at the insult. It's true, but not entirely.

So she smelled Cyrus. That doesn't explain…anything else. Why was that my first fucking question?

I'm losing my mind. I'm losing…everything.

I can't lose everything.

I can't lose anything.

First thing's first. I gotta make sure we're alone.

"I need to do a sweep outside."

"How'd he know we were here?"

I've been asking myself that this whole time and still have zero theories. It couldn't have been the kiss, could it?

"I don't know." I shake my head and get up from the bed.

Lex raises the gun, tracking my every move.

"Don't do that," I warn while slowly sliding my legs into my sweatpants. She's not gonna shoot me, otherwise she would've let Cyrus.

"Don't do what?"

"Lock me out."

Lowering the gun, she passes it off to me handle first, and says, "Too late."

Thirty-Eight

Reece

NOD, MY TONGUE RUNNING BETWEEN MY TEETH AND MY BOTTOM lip.

I wish she would've shot me. I'd be in a hell of a lot less pain.

Glock in hand, I storm from the room, shove on my boots, then burst out the front door.

The icy flakes hitting my skin dissolve on contact, the chill not even registering as I check the cabin's perimeter and surrounding area.

Judging from the tracks in the snow, it was Cyrus and two others—not just the one outside the window—who got out on foot. They left in either an SUV or truck they had waiting on the road coming up here. They're gone though. They're gone, leaving us alone again.

Again? Were we ever alone? Was Cyrus following me the whole time? Lex? Was he following her?

I don't fucking know!

I take a swing at a tree trunk, the bark tearing the skin on my knuckles open, but I don't feel it.

Jogging back to the cabin, I lean against the cold metal of the Explorer, drop my head in my numb, bleeding hands, and breathe.

Air in, air out.

Air in, air out.

No matter how hard I try getting oxygen to my lungs, I don't feel any make it past the lump in my throat.

After everything that happened this weekend, it's all gone. Done. Right back to square fucking one. I should've told her when we first got here. I should've told her last weekend when I found the invoices. I should've fucking told her.

Then we wouldn't have been fucking blindsided. And we would've been able to come up with a plan. A better one than...

What is the plan? Pay Cyrus hush money...then what? What about Lex? What about me and my family? None of us will be safe just because Cyrus gets another ten million dollars added to his stash. He's already got more than that at his warehouse.

And now he's got my flash drive, which without knowing what he's looking for...

He doesn't know what to look for. He doesn't know what's on it. Nobody does. Not even...Lex?

I yank the passenger door open, and with my bare hands, pry off the cover for the blind spot mirror mounting nuts. I used a screwdriver to do it earlier but I don't need to worry about damaging it anymore. Cyrus would've had the whole car searched and cleared first thing.

Due to the current freezing conditions, the flash drive is half hanging from the plastic I taped it to on Friday.

Stomping up the porch steps, I go back inside, my eyes sweeping Lex—dressed and sitting on the counter, facing the front door like she's waiting for me—then the rest of the cabin. Just like the Explorer, Cyrus checked the whole cabin without leaving a single hint he was even here. My laptop is still in the same place it was before. Nothing else is moved, broken, or new, but something in here is different. Something's missing.

Past Lex is the knife block. There were seven in it when we got here; now there's six.

She took one. She's getting ready to run. Why hasn't she yet? There are a number of windows in this cabin she could've fit through while I was outside.

Maybe because she knows as well as I do, it's time.

"We need to talk," I tell her, my tongue and skin itchy. I want to tear it all off until all that's left is my core, so she can see—can *feel*—I'm not the enemy. At least not hers.

She doesn't react, just continues staring at me quietly.

"First, you were not my assignment. You were *never* my assignment."

The only response she gives is a clipped, "I know."

That's one thing cleared up.

"Why didn't you tell me you knew what Kordin was doing?" I ask next.

"Why didn't you tell me *you* knew?"

"I thought I was protecting you."

"Protecting me? From what?"

"Cyrus. I knew he'd do this."

"That's precisely why you should've told me."

"If you'd been honest from the start—"

"I couldn't!" she shouts.

"Why?" I'm not accepting that answer. Not anymore.

"Because *I* was protecting *you*!"

"Why?" I yell even louder, ready for some goddamn honesty.

She hops off the counter and comes right up to me, the knife to my throat before I even see it get pulled. "Because you're weak. You can't choose between me and your family. But I can choose between you and mine." Gritting, she repeats, "I. Can."

"I can't choose because you *are* my family. You are my fucking family, Lex!"

Tears well in her eyes, spilling over long, unblinking lashes to stream down her cheeks, but she doesn't reciprocate the sentiment.

Fine. I'm not hers. I knew I probably wasn't, but...

Fuck, it still hurts.

"Then let me make it easy on you." I crowd her, the knife's edge digging into the skin under my jaw. "I'll choose for you."

We hold each other's eyes, every moment from the last couple days passing between us.

"Make it hurt," comes out of my mouth quiet but steady.

Stepping back, Lex throws the knife at the wall, burying the tip into one of the logs the cabin's made of.

"I already chose. Cyrus knows, Reece. He *knows*." She clamps a hand over her mouth like she's about to puke.

"Knows what? What does he know?"

Through her fingers, she whispers, "He knows everything. He knows where my mom lives, he knows we're…" She gestures between us with her free hand. "He probably even knows I can't pay ten million dollars."

"Why the fuck did you agree to?"

Lex doesn't answer, just shakes her head.

"Lex! Fucking talk to me!"

Her hand falls away from her mouth, her face red and wet and so fucking broken it kills me. "I chose my family."

"What does that mean?"

"It means in order to keep my mom out of it, he'll get…"

Don't say it. Don't fucking say it.

"…me."

"No."

"I have to. I *have* to."

"No. You don't. We'll find another way."

"There's no other way."

"If you knew you couldn't pay, why'd you even fucking offer?"

"To buy time."

"For what?"

"For you and your family to get out of town."

"Lex," I growl out of pure exhaustion from repeating this. "I'm. Not. Leaving—"

"Tuesday morning, no matter if he has ten million dollars in his pocket, me at his side, or nothing but his dick in his hand, Cyrus will go after you, your mom, and your sisters. You did the unthinkable, Reece. You betrayed him. He won't just punish you. He'll make an example out of you. If you don't disappear, you and everyone you love will die."

"But not including you?"

"Don't."

"Oh, we're way past that, Snow. After everything that's happened, there's no fucking denying I love you with every jagged piece of my fucked-up, shattered heart."

"Reece." She takes another step back.

I grab her face, not letting her go anywhere. "I. Love. You."

"Why did you do that?" she cries.

"Fall for you?"

Her eyebrows caving in, she nods.

How do I explain it? What is there to explain? It wasn't even me. It was all her.

"I didn't have a choice, Lex. You knocked me on my ass."

Despite the pain on her face and in her posture, her chest manages to create one of those laughs I fucking crave more than water, and I brush my lips over hers, coaxing them open so I can quench my thirst. She responds, giving me exactly what I need while also taking what she wants. Even if she won't admit she loves me back, this feels close enough.

"I thought I was the one that got knocked on my ass," she whispers into my mouth.

I stop to pull back and look at her. "Did you?" I physically knocked her on her ass, but did I emotionally, too?

She shakes her head, conflict etched in her features.

I have to remind myself, seeds don't bloom overnight. Everything worthwhile takes time.

"Please go."

"Only if you come with me."

Immediately, she starts to argue, so I tell her, "You can't stay here either. You're not safe, not with Cyrus or Kordin."

Extracting herself from my grasp, she returns to the kitchen counter, her arms wrapped tightly around her front.

We're not done here.

"Do you know what's on the flash drive Cyrus took?"

Her head shakes. "But I think I have a pretty good idea."

I'm not sure she does.

"I can show you."

She spins around to face me. I've already got the backup flash drive out for her to see.

"This is just a copy," I tell her before she can get her hopes up. Luckily, I made a copy of everything from Kaisin's phone and stored it on a separate flash drive. Hiding it in the Explorer's door panel felt like paranoia at the time but now I'm grateful I did it.

Moving my laptop over to the coffee table, I take a seat on the couch, then plug in the flash drive.

Cyrus was in the cabin for a while and neither of us knew. He could've done anything, even killed us. Not Lex, because he has a use for her, but me, he could've killed easily.

Opening my laptop and hitting the Power button, I study Lex while it fires up. What would she have done if Cyrus had killed me? She put a gun to her own head just to prevent him from trying.

She chose all right. Without even knowing the full extent of the danger she's in, she made the decision to face it alone. She chose everybody else's safety—her family's and mine—over her own.

That's love. And there's nothing weak about it.

After pulling up the folder I need, I spin my laptop around so Lex can see the screen.

Glancing at it, she asks, "What is that?"

"Kaisin's email."

Her eyes jump to mine. "You said—"

"Kaisin didn't tell me anything…but his phone did."

"You stole it?"

"Didn't have to." I tell her all about the Nightshade oil at her house, then how I imaged her brother-in-law's phone afterward at his.

"What made you think to hack Kaisin's phone?"

"It took me working there two days to notice something was off. The Debrosse Group prides itself on dealing exclusively with high-tech buildings."

"Because we do." She slips into her Lenox Debrosse role like a sundress, saying, "As one of our portfolio managers—"

"Lex," I say, cutting her off before she can get too comfortable. "They don't."

"Maybe at first some of them may not be, but part of our strategy is to modernize any property that requires it."

"And the ones that do, who do those expenses go through?"

"You mean the work orders? The CFO."

"Kaisin?"

"Correct. But why—"

"Kaisin has the power to approve any work order that passes his desk?"

"If this were the eighties, maybe. But since it's not and everything's submitted electronically now, yes, one of Kaisin's responsibilities is to review each work order he receives, then approve or deny them."

Old school is exactly the way Kordin's been submitting them, and with decoy cameras at all three of their offices, nobody can prove who approaches Kaisin's desk to do it.

"Does he deny any of yours?"

"Kordin has me handle our higher-end clients who've already made tremendous upgrades, so I rarely submit work orders."

I gesture to the laptop. "Then what are those?"

She goes right for it, asking once she's gotten a good look, "These were emailed to Kaisin?"

"Kind of."

Freezing, she pins me with a confused look.

"He emailed them to himself."

"Kaisin did this?"

"I don't think so."

Her expression remains skeptical.

"Look for yourself."

I hear a couple clicks as Lex dives into her own investigation.

"I didn't..."

Her eyes ping-pong around the screen, her eyebrows getting closer and closer.

"These aren't even..."

Fully engrossed, she lowers her knees to the floor.

"But where are the…"

After several more minutes and at least a hundred more clicks, she says, "According to these, I'm the one committing fraud."

I assume she's still talking to herself until she looks over the screen at me.

I nod once. "According to them, you are."

"You don't believe I am?"

"No."

"The evidence showing I am is very compelling."

"Very. Enough to fool me for a minute."

"What convinced you otherwise?"

"Not what. Who."

"Who?"

"The person whose hard drive you were after. The person who heard his brother going on and on about the stripper he thought he might be in love with; the person who got to that stripper first, married her, gave her a new identity and new job working under that same brother so he would approve anything that had her name on it; the person who brags about his wife to anyone that'll listen, making her seem like a money-hungry saint, but treats her like shit, fucks her even worse, and offers her pussy up to a cat burglar."

"Shit. *Shit.* Kordin's been playing the long game our entire marriage." She checks the laptop again and nods. "These work orders go back to the first month I was working there."

"It makes sense why he didn't want you at the office while he wasn't around."

"What are you talking about? It was Kaisin that didn't want me there."

"It was Kordin. Kaisin was just following his brother's orders. They talked about it right in front of me." Because people like them don't view people like me as equals.

"Kaisin kept saying something about my numbers fluctuating and seeming more like myself after Kordin's return."

She ducks her head, clicking through the invoices, probably to the more recent ones.

"That's why. Kordin couldn't submit anything while he was in the hospital, but he started right back up as soon as he was released."

Which backs up my theory as to how he's been delivering the invoices to Kaisin.

"That's proof right there it wasn't you."

Straightening, she scoffs. "Hardly. That's a drop in the ocean compared to the evidence stacked against me."

"What else is there?"

Lex tells me about the speeding ticket she got in the mail for the Mustang in her name.

"Not only is he framing you for stealing the money but he's framing you for spending it, too."

"Yeah."

"Fuck, Lex. You should've told me."

"I didn't know."

I sit forward, my elbows on my knees. "You knew something."

"I knew he was using my name for big purchases that weren't coming out of our joint account. I *assumed* the money was coming from the Debrosse Group in some means other than his regular salary. And given the fact that those purchases were in my name, I *suspected* it was at my expense, but I had no idea how he was going about it. Or for how long."

"Where's Kordin keeping the money?"

"That's what I was trying to get off his hard drive—his passwords. I was hoping if I could access the account the money was going into, I could track where it was coming in from."

I could've imaged Kordin's hard drive just like I did his brother's phone. Lex would've had all the information she needed weeks ago.

"Damn. Why didn't you just fucking—"

"Tell Cyrus?" She scoffs again.

"I know. Fuck. I know." He would've kept the hard drive for himself or had me make a copy of it. "That's why I didn't tell him anything about the invoices."

Getting to her feet, she points at the laptop. "He doesn't know how Kordin's been stealing?"

"No. I fucking told you, my loyalty is to you. It has been from the start."

"Look where that got us."

"I'm sorry," I tell her. "Look, right now Cyrus has no idea what's on that flash drive, and unless he goes to every property for every invoice in Kaisin's email, I don't think he will. At least not before Monday night."

"What are you saying?"

"I'm saying…" Fuck. What am I saying? How the fuck can we get out of this?

"In the wrong hands, that information could put me away."

"I'm not gonna let that happen."

"I don't see how. This is my problem. My fight. My fucking prison sentence."

"Lex." I push off the couch and go to her. "You're not going to prison."

She looks between my eyes. "If I do—"

"You won't."

Her fingers cover my lips. "But *if* I do, I need you to promise me… My mom…"

I catch her wrist and pull her hand down.

"It's you. Cyrus knew where your mom lives, right? That means he's been tracking you."

"Then how did he find us here? I left all my personal belongings at the resort."

"Not all of them."

I run back out to the Explorer to retrieve Lex's keyring from the center console. After getting Lex contained Friday night, I picked it up off the asphalt and chucked it in here.

Heading back inside, I meet her at the counter and pull her key fob apart. The only thing in it is a battery.

She shakes her head. "It has to be you. You're the one he has access to. At The Playground, he could've put a tracker on any of your belongings. Your car, your…"

404 | **A. MARIE**

The only items I have on me from my real life, and not James Jones's, is my laptop and…

We look at each other, both of us saying, "Phone," at the same time.

"Whose idea was it for you to go to The Playground?" I ask despite already knowing the answer.

"His."

"In Lost and Found specifically?" Because phones aren't allowed in the Lost and Found rooms, everyone has to leave them with the key girl, no exceptions.

"Yes."

"That's where he did it." But I wonder…

I get my phone from the bedroom and bring it back out. As soon as I pry the case off, a thin, quarter-sized tracking device falls out. Fucker.

"Your phone has a case on it, too?"

"Yes."

"He's been tracking both of us." While he's only had access to Lex's whereabouts the last three weeks, I don't know how long he's been tracking me. Sometime after I upgraded my phone, which still doesn't narrow it down really, considering I've spent a lot of time in Lost and Found.

Lex reaches for the tracker, but I shoot my hand out, blocking her.

"Hold on. Let's think this through first."

"Reece, he's fucking tracking us."

"That might work in our favor."

She crosses her arms. "Explain."

"If you go back to working for Cyrus, what are you going to do about Kordin?"

"I don't know. Kill him?"

I start to smile before remembering Lex doesn't joke. I've wanted to kill Kordin since I laid eyes on him, but that won't actually solve anything…in this instance.

"Killing him doesn't get rid of the evidence showing you're committing fraud."

"Well, I can't turn him in. It'd just be my word against his with no evidence to back it up. I'd need an actual witness to Kordin incriminating me for anyone to believe I didn't do it."

An accomplice. That would make things easier. But since we don't know if Kordin's ever used one, we have to assume he didn't.

"We don't have time to explore every option. We only really have one."

"What's that?"

"We run. Together."

She's already shaking her head. "Are you listening to yourself? We're not even together—"

"We're together."

"—and you want to take me, a presumed felon, away to…what? Live off grid somewhere outside of Cyrus's reach? Outside of the law? The fucking law, rookie? We'd be looking over our shoulders for the rest of our lives. I'm not doing that. Not to you. Not to my mom. And not to yours."

The rest of our lives. Even if she's not technically divorced from Kordin, even if she's being hunted by the FBI, I'd still want Lex.

But she's right. She doesn't deserve that kind of life and neither do our families. Running from Cyrus is one thing. He's the devil of Fox Hollow, not the entire world. But the police… They're everywhere.

I've wanted to get my family out of here for years. I have to figure out a way to do it without implicating them in the process.

If only there was a fucking accomplice.

What if…there was?

It's not like anybody would come forward and say there wasn't. Kordin will be too busy denying every aspect of his involvement to disprove who helped him.

"Cyrus's reach doesn't extend as far as he makes it seem," I assure Lex. "As for Kordin…if he turns you in, the account he's funneling money into gets seized. He's not going to risk that, no matter how pissed he gets that you're not around anymore. The only way he's rolling over on you is if he gets caught and is forced to in order to save his own ass."

"Which could happen at any time."

Yes, it could, especially with Kordin's dumbass brother involved.

"Not if there isn't evidence tying you to the embezzlement. We have to get rid of all traces of wrongdoing with your name attached before we leave."

Lex is quiet for a minute, and I think she's going to fight me about leaving again. Instead she points at the coffee table, and asks, "How many other copies did you make?"

She's considering it.

She's considering leaving. With me.

The numbness in my hands spreads to the rest of my body as I make myself continue on. "That's the only one."

"So it's the two flash drives, Kaisin's email records, and…"

"The invoices themselves. I can get those," I say before she has a chance.

"That's *if* Kaisin still has them."

"If he does, I'll find them." And if I can't, I'll make them.

"What about Kaisin?"

"He won't know I'm there."

"No, but he'll know about the work orders."

That's what I'm banking on.

"Like you said, it'd just be his word."

"We'll need money. A lot of it. More than either of us has."

There's only one person I can think of with that kind of cash on hand, and lucky for us, I have the code to his safe. It's—

"Your birthdate."

"What about it?"

"The combination to Cyrus's safe. It's your birthdate." I didn't realize it until just now.

Her eyes narrow. "Did you have your phone on you in the warehouse?"

"No, I left it in the Mustang."

"So did I."

"You think that's why he came home? Because he knew we were in there?"

"He doesn't know we were inside."

"How can you be sure?"

"I used to sneak out all the time through that air duct and he never caught me. Also…you're still alive."

Cyrus has my address, my real address. He has my mom's. He could've—

"But he knows we were there somewhere." Lex's voice pulls me from the bleakest of oblivions imagining all the things Cyrus could've done with those addresses.

There's another long silence where Lex stares at the floor and I stare at her.

I have to sell her on this. I have to.

"Our futures can be ours, Snow. Finally."

"Okay," she whispers, lifting her gaze to mine, her eyes green like the underside of Eucalyptus leaves.

I pull her to me, my arms tightening around her back as I breathe in her wintry-mix scent.

"Yeah?"

"Yeah. Let's write our own happily ever after."

It doesn't fucking matter what happens next, as long as we're together at the end and our families are safe leading up to it, then it'll be worth it.

It'll *all* be worth it.

Thirty-Nine

Lex

"REMEMBER, DON'T DO ANYTHING OUT OF THE ordinary." Reece tears his eyes off the road to glance at me. "We don't want to tip Cyrus off that we found how he's tracking us. Tomorrow—"

"I'll arrive at work at normal time, then at noon, I'll tell Kordin I'm taking a long lunch to run errands. I'll stop at multiple banks, staying at each one for at least twenty minutes before returning to work," I finish for him, reciting the plan we spent all morning coming up with.

In order to prevent Cyrus from growing suspicious, I'm supposed to carry on with my regular life today, doing everything I would've anyway. Then tomorrow I'm going on a midday bank crawl, so it seems like I'm attempting to assemble some sort of payoff for him.

"I know, rook. I've got my part down."

Reece has his own itinerary. Tonight he'll go on the hunt for the forged work orders at Kaisin's house and office, then get new identifications for all of us, both his family and mine.

"I was gonna say I'll meet you fifteen minutes 'til midnight."

"Outside his warehouse?"

He nods. "Same place we parked when you took me there."

Tomorrow night while Cyrus is busy waiting at The Playground for me to deliver his money, Reece and I are supposed to meet at the warehouse, sans tracking devices, where we'll clean out Cyrus's safe, getting the flash drive along with enough cash to start our new lives on the run.

It's a good plan. It'd work, too.

If I was sticking to it.

Pulling around to the back of the resort, Reece parks near the dumpsters, then rotates in his seat to regard me. He's going to say it again. I can tell. But just like before, I still don't know how to respond. When I say I love you to Kordin, it's a lie. I'm fluent in lies. If I tried reciprocating Reece's heartfelt declaration, it'd be like trying to speak a different language, one I'm practically ignorant to.

That doesn't mean I don't…

That doesn't mean I don't feel that way about him. I wouldn't be preparing myself for what I'm about to do if I didn't.

"I love you," he says, his obsidian eyes holding that same ferocity some men get when they ejaculate, a gratifying discharge in three small words instead of one to two tablespoons of semen.

A three-syllable release is too simple to express what's inside me. Whatever's at the center of the storm brewing in there, it's much bigger, much stronger than three words could ever portray.

"I…" I swallow thickly, the sound thunderous in my ears.

"I'm not expecting you to say it. I just… You should know."

So should he.

"Reece," I start again. "I would kill for you." Five words. Five words that encapsulate my love entirely, the only kind I've ever known. The only kind I've ever trusted.

His is buttered popcorn under the veil of darkness and whispered vows in a lover's embrace. Mine is methodical silence in the face of peril and gasped last breaths of an enemy. One is sweet, the other bitter, neither fiercer than the other. Like Honeysuckle and Lily of the Valley—both hold the same meaning, but in very, very different ways.

Reece's black eyebrows pull together, an unreadable expression on his chiseled face.

"You're fucking perfect."

We meet each other over the center console, our lips clashing into one another's as our hands grip anything they can—hair, ears, cheeks, necks—until there is no space, no time, no him, no me. Only us, together.

Our foreheads still connected, Reece tells me, "Don't kill anyone for me, Snow. Just breathe. Okay? Can you do that? Can you keep existing? Please?"

Opening my eyes, I gaze into his. My efficiency in lies didn't used to have any parameters. Now I'm finding it does. In this moment, I could lie. I just don't want to.

"I've made it this long." I pull away, hoping the distance will hide my evasion. "What's another thirty-seven hours?"

Reece nods, repeating, "Thirty-seven hours."

"I'll see you tomorrow."

Reece is the one to stay quiet. Does he sense my deception? This one out of all the others?

I don't look back at him after I get out. In my bikini and bathrobe again, I enter the resort with the superiority of a hollow in her natural habitat. I don't know how but my keycard stayed in the robe's pocket during Friday night's altercation, so I head straight for my room and let myself in to shower and pack the few items I unloaded before my unexpected departure.

Everything ready to return to my previous life, I sit on the bed and make a call. Luckily, Cat answers just before the voicemail kicks on, her voice groggy.

"I'm moving."

After a hesitation, she says, "Lexi? Are you fucking for real?"

"Yes."

"After all this time?"

I nod even though she can't see it. "I have to." I've put it off long enough.

"When?"

"Tonight."

"Tonight? Fuck, girl." A dense sigh rattles the speaker. "What can I do?"

"Spread the word."

I hang up, knowing she will.

I do everything Reece and I talked about. I go home to Kordin, where I stay until after dinner when I leave in my Range Rover to get my mom groceries. I drive them over to her, spending a couple quality hours with her before returning home and settling in for the night.

Except a few hours after Kordin falls asleep, I take a sharp deviation from the plan as I slip out of bed, go to my closet to retrieve the two cheap duffle bags I bought at the grocery store, then take off again, this time in Kordin's Porsche because I don't know whether Cyrus put a tracker on my Range Rover or not, and I'm not taking any chances. This *has* to go off without a hitch.

Driving to the exact location Reece and I are supposed to meet in less than twenty-four hours, I park and survey the land surrounding Cyrus's warehouse. By now Reece will be at either the firm or Kaisin's house, and Cyrus should be at The Playground, neither of them the wiser.

All alone, I empty one of the duffel bags into the passenger seat. Once I'm changed into my stealth outfit, I cut out the bottom of that same bag, taking the canvas-and-polyester flap with me as well as the other, still intact duffel bag.

Using the same air duct I showed Reece, I carefully make my way into the warehouse, stopping at Cyrus's bedroom first. His closet is full of all kinds of weapons, some not even the government can get ahold of, but I focus on the guns, making sure I grab one with a silencer and that each one is loaded before placing as many as I can fit into the duffel bag in a single layer. With a needle and a thread, I hand-sew the second bag's flap over the top of the guns in the other, concealing the guns entirely.

The safe is next. I put in my own birthdate as the combination and the door pops open to reveal…less money than there was in here last time. Significantly less. Is that the real reason why Cyrus wants me working for him so bad? Did he take a financial hit recently?

Hopefully. It's the *least* of what that man deserves.

On the top shelf sits a flash drive. I'm just releasing a sigh of relief when I notice it's black and red, not black and orange. Was it orange? It was dark but there was enough light for me to make out…

I could've sworn the flash drive Cyrus was holding was black with orange accents.

Shit. I didn't even think to double-check with Reece either.

It's not like I can ask him now.

I grab the flash drive, then start loading stacks of cash into the bag, on top of the hidden guns. As soon as the bag's full, I go out the same way I came in.

After another outfit change in the Porsche, I head toward the final destination, praying to God it's not my final destination.

Forty

Lex

THE BOUNCERS MAKE ME SET THE DUFFLE BAG BY MY FEET. While one unzips it, inspecting the contents, the other pats me down, the cold from his hands seeping through my turtleneck bodycon dress, causing me to shiver. The ribbed black material stops a few inches above my knees with only a slice of skin showing between the hem and my over-the-knee boots.

"Boss was expecting you tomorrow night," the bouncer spending too much time checking the curve of my ass says.

My body begs to physically recoil away from any touch other than Reece's.

Gritting my teeth, I wait until he circles back around to my front to arch an eyebrow at him. Is he really going to risk turning me and my bag of cash away just because I'm a day early? How well would Cyrus take that?

"How 'bout I give you a hand with that?" He tilts his head toward the bag. The other bouncer's still poking around inside, his face screwed up in thought. If he pokes too deep, too hard…

My heart speeds up as I fight to keep my breathing under control.

"Ever been in an airport?" I ask him, my words slurred.

Both men stop to exchange looks.

Keeping my face arrogantly stoic, I ignore the taste of copper as

414 | A. MARIE

I flip the sharp blade from under my tongue to above it, pushing the metal over to the side, between my teeth and cheek.

More blood fills my mouth and I unfortunately have to swallow it down to say much clearer, "Same rules apply. Never let a stranger handle your bag."

I bend down and grip the handles together, effectively cutting the search short.

"We know who you are."

The bag in my hold, I straighten my spine and neck, saying, "Then quit wasting my time and open the *fucking* door."

Another silent exchange between them before they let me in.

"What a pleasant surprise to see you again," Adie greets loudly the moment I sashay my way inside. Brushing her temple with two fingers, she mouths, "Lost."

I give no reaction whatsoever before entering the dark stairwell. Halfway down, I stop and balance the bag on the handrail using my hip.

Retrieving the blade from my mouth, I blindly saw at the new stitches until I get an entire side cut, then I give the flap a couple quick tugs, loosening the others. Once I feel the gun with the silencer, I relocate it to the top, with the money. Money stinks in general, but this much reeks.

I descend the rest of the steps with sweat coating my hairline, armpits, and back.

Out on the Merry-Go-Round, all five poles have dancers on them, and they're each spinning simultaneously to "Hayloft II" by Mother Mother, every customer in the place mesmerized by the show of staggering synchronicity of the many different kinds of spins from knee hooks to carousels to one very impressive doubles genie by the two on the middle pole.

Some of the newer girls working the floor eye me as I pass, the vets doing it inconspicuously, but I don't make eye contact with any of them. I just continue on to Lost and Found.

Cat's already at the key girl's station with Promise, both women appearing bored. Back when I worked here, I couldn't offer what they sought from each other. I was sick and grieving and I couldn't fathom joining their family while having my own to worry about. But we still helped one another. I showed them how to depend on their sense of smell to tell when someone's coming or to gauge how much someone's worth, and they taught me the tricks of the trade. No lotion, ever, because it's a major pole hazard. If you want soft skin, use Epsom salt in a bath. Shave with oil, not cream. Natural makeup only. Heat to get plastic shoes to stay on; baby powder to get them off. Baby wipes are essential, especially between clients. Don't exert yourself before midnight; if the drinks haven't kicked in yet, neither have the tips. And most importantly, no matter how much you want to, never call out while you're menstruating because without them realizing it, the barest hint of blood sends men into a frenzy. My biggest paydays were always when I was on my period. *Sharks.*

While Cat's five years older than me, Promise is only three, but they had more experience than I did and were gracious enough to impart their pearls of wisdom on me. As much as I want to resent Promise for helping Cyrus track my phone, I can't. She was under orders, and in her position, I would've had to do the same thing. I would've done the same thing. When you're drowning and someone sticks an oar in your face, you don't stop to consider if the wood'll give you, or anyone else, splinters. You just grab hold. She does what she has to survive the same way we all do.

I don't fault her. The blame lies where it always has, with Cyrus.

After removing the gun tucked between two stacks, I hand the bag off to Cat. She takes one look in it, her jaw dropping. I dig deep inside, showing her the hidden flap beneath the money, and she spins around and disappears into the dressing room.

"In This Moment?" Promise asks.

She must've been the one to put on "Sex Metal Barbie" last time I was here. I used to always dance to their songs. Their lyrics are the only ones I've ever been able to relate to.

Twitching my cheek several times to scrape against the edge of the blade, I nod, then carefully pull the metal out through my lips, hiding it in my bun.

I let the blood pool in my mouth before lifting my chin to say, "'The Blood Legion,'" pushing some of the liquid back between my lips when it tries to dribble out.

Promise's look of disgust is the last thing I see before I turn toward two Lost.

Twisting the knob, I open the door, mentally repeating po trupach do celu to myself. *Whatever it takes.*

Cyrus is seated, his head back, eyes closed as a woman kneels between his legs, her head bobbing over his lap.

There's a second woman by the loveseat, poised to blow on Cyrus's ear, and I tilt my head when she turns to look at me, silently telling her to leave. Just as the song changes over, we switch places. I angle my body sideways to sit next to Cyrus, my arm stretched out along the back so the gun's behind his head, and I stare at his pasty face, those canines of his gleaming from under his parted lips.

Moisture builds behind my eyelids. I've dreamed about this for so long, and now that I'm here, it doesn't seem real. I don't even feel like I'm in my body.

One hand gripped tightly on his cane, the other's tangled in his pleasurer's tresses until he relocates his hold to my thigh. Memory upon memory surfaces like bubbles in a hot spring—relentlessly overpowering and unnecessarily violent—bringing me right back into my physical form with sharp focus.

Cyrus's hand roots around, making every one of his touches play out like a montage, the reel going on and on and *on* until my stomach rolls.

Not feeling nearly as much skin as he was expecting, his eyes open and he wrenches his head up, spewing, "What the fuck are—

"Oh," he says when he finds me beside him, his demeanor softening a fraction. "Lexi. You're early. Impatient to take your place?"

Impatient? I've waited years for this.

Despite the goose bumps from his skin finding mine—his skin stroking mine—I lower my head in a placating nod.

"Smile," he says, his lips spreading.

There wasn't a day in Cyrus's presence that'd go by without him telling me to smile, forever perverting the gesture for me.

If only I'd discovered this next move sooner, I could've ruined it for him, too.

My mouth mimics his, warm blood oozing out between my stretched lips.

His expression morphs to one I've never seen him wear before, and his grip on my thigh tightens painfully. Despite his hold, I press the tip of my stiletto to the shoulder of the woman sucking him off and kick, causing her to release his cock with a gasp.

Instantly, she scuttles backward like a crab.

Cyrus chokes up on his cane, preparing to use it, but with his focus still on my mouth, I manage to bring his own gun up, the tip just behind his temple, and pull the trigger, sending brains out the other side of his head before he can so much as get a single swing in. Blood and chunks spray from both holes as his body slumps, his smarmy face drooping into eternal oblivion.

He's dead. The terror of my life, of Reece's life, of Fox Hollow is dead.

I could've killed him at the warehouse, in his sleep, but I wanted this moment to mean something. I wanted his last thoughts on this earth to be filled with fear, treachery, confusion, and above all, the knowledge that it was me who robbed him of everything—even his pleasure—just like he did to me as well as so many others.

My nose stings from the overwhelming smell of burnt flesh.

"That…" A voice pulls my attention away from the husk Cyrus Andeno now is, reminding me I'm not alone, and I look over to see Cia gaping up at me from the floor. "…was poetic."

For a second longer than I should, I consider turning the gun on her and shooting her, too. Not for what she just witnessed but for going out on a date with Reece.

Remembering my purpose, I rein it back in before I can.

I have Reece Souza to thank for that new emotion. I was never a jealous person…until I met him.

Is this how he feels all the time? His entire genetic makeup hijacked and contorted by jealousy?

"Sorry about the kick."

"Don't worry about it. I've endured worse…" She doesn't finish that thought, nor does she need to because I'm well-acquainted with what she's been through. Cyrus abused my body in all different ways as well, not all of them sexual.

The door swings open to Promise already clapping.

"Congratulations, Lexi. You just gave me my first O in Lost and Found."

"First and last," I tell her before wiping the gun's handle down and fitting it in Cyrus's limp hand. "It's over."

Her elation dies quicker than her former boss just did. "Until the next one comes along."

Cyrus Andeno was the main plague on this town but every virus mutates.

Fortunately, variants are mere branches, and I just chopped down the entire fucking tree.

There doesn't have to be a next one.

Rubbing my mouth with my sleeve as I push to my feet, I ask, "Have either of you ever heard of a matriarchal society?"

"No."

"Never. What is it?"

"It's where females are in charge," I tell them.

Promise gives an incredulous laugh. "Like that'd ever happen."

"It does happen. There are several matriarchal communities around the world. In animals, too. Orcas do it."

"Aren't those like killer whales?" Cia questions.

"Same animal, just different names." *Like me.*

I think about that for a moment.

"How does it work out for them?" Promise asks with a heavy dose of cynicism.

"They're apex predators." I pick up Cyrus's cane and study the fox head handle, before saying, "Come on. We've got work to do."

Out in the main area, Cat and several other dancers are stationed around the room, hands hidden behind their backs as they watch for my signal.

I twirl the cane and they all pull out their guns, a few pointing them directly at bouncers, others just letting it be known they hold the power now. *We* hold the power.

I climb on to the bar to shout, "Can I have everybody's attention, please?"

The music cuts off, amplifying the sharp inhales produced as more and more people notice Cyrus's cane in my hand. I won't openly admit to killing Cyrus, but I'm not going to hide the fact that he's dead either.

"The Playground is officially closed!"

"For how long?" a customer calls out to me.

"Indefinitely."

Another man speaks up, grousing, "Where are we supposed to get—"

"Somewhere else. Anywhere else. Settle your tabs, leave generous tips for the services you were provided, then get the fuck out." I scan every dancer's face, promising each one of them, "Fox Hollow is now under construction."

Breckyn saw what I couldn't. Change is possible, even in Fox Hollow…as long as someone's willing to lead it. I never considered being that person until Cyrus threatened them right in front of me. She shouldn't have to move away to survive. Nobody should. Reece and his family don't deserve to pay for my sins or my husband's, and now they won't have to. Should I wind up in prison, the Souza women will be safe. My mother will be safe. Reece will be safe.

Their fates are more important to me than my own.

The two bouncers from out front appear, Adie behind them, brandishing a gun at their backs as she prods them forward.

I have to deal with them. I have to deal with all of them. Cyrus employed a lot of people. While most will be happy with this turn of events, some might not be.

The entire community will feel Cyrus's death. Yes, the evil crime lord is gone but so are the incomes he was providing. However mea-sly those paychecks may have been, they were still paychecks.

Since Cyrus was clearly keeping most of the profits for himself, once I dispense that money to the people who rightfully earned it, hopefully that'll help until I can figure out what the next step in Fox Hollow's rehabilitation is.

I'll—

My stomach clenches painfully, causing me to involuntarily bend at the waist. Getting to me knees, I'm asking one of the bartenders for water when I start to heave.

Cat rushes over and shoves a bowl under my face, catching the bile my body's suddenly hellbent on expelling.

"Don't tell me it's guilt," she grumbles.

Scoffing, I assure her, "It's not."

"Well, you got something to share then? Did that hollow finally get around to knocking you up?"

I squeeze my eyes shut. I never took the pill. I was so caught up with everything else going on, I never actually took it.

"Lexi?" She nudges my shoulder, but I shake my head, doing the math in my head.

It could be the cuts in my mouth from the blade.

It could be the lack of sleep over the past couple days.

It could be the return of my anxiety.

It could be—

Vomit surges out of me.

Back in my pajamas, I'm walking into my house when a hand latches on to my wrist, tugging me downward so I'm face to face with… Kordin?

"Kordin, what's wrong—"

"Where the fuck have you been?"

"My mother's. She called me, upset about a—"

ABOVE | 421

He smacks me in the jaw with his cast, the abrasive plaster breaking my skin and causing an intense burning sensation.

The shock that Kordin just hit me stuns me into paralysis.

Kordin Debrosse hit me.

Tonight I murdered the most feared fox in all of Fox Hollow, and I just got slapped by a hollow in a cast. Two casts.

"Who is he?" he seethes.

Twisting my wrist out of his hold, his nails leave a myriad of scratches behind.

"Who's who?"

Dragging his wheelchair forward with his foot, he corners me against the wall. "The man you spent the weekend with."

"Excuse me? I didn't—"

He raises his arm in the cast and my reaction is instant. Instead of blocking, or preparing a counter blow, all I do is double over, cradling my midsection.

Still poised to strike, Kordin uses his left hand to snatch a paper off his lap and push it in my face. I assume it's going to be one of his forged work orders, but it's a receipt from the resort in the Catskills. One suite for two nights, charged to his credit card.

"I don't understand. This is exactly where I was. All weekend long."

"What did you eat while you were there? Not one single charge for food or beverage?"

He's never inspected my expenses this closely. Or if he has, he's never confronted me about them.

Because I've never given him a reason to before.

"Their selection was limited, so I went out for meals."

"There's nothing on the card."

I shrug. "I paid cash."

"Where are those receipts?"

"I'd have to check my bag."

"I already took the liberty."

I have to steady my breathing as I consider my next move.

When Kordin's out of answers, he always reverts to his favorite method of evasion—gaslighting. I decide to use one of man's top go-to lines when dealing with women, telling him, "You're acting crazy."

"How about the spa? What services did you have done?"

Before I can even try to lie, he swats the receipt from my hands, shouting, "You didn't!"

"I spent most of my time in the pool."

"Most of your time? You were there once. Friday night. After that, you disappeared until you magically reemerged for checkout."

I feel all my usual composure unravelling and squeeze my eyes shut. I'm so fucking tired of being tracked, stalked, hunted like a goddamn prey.

I'm not a prey, nor will I behave like one. Not for him. Not for any man.

My eyes snap open, narrowing on Kordin as I advance on him, my knees pushing on his wheelchair and forcing it to roll backward.

"You've been spying on me?"

"You were all alone, miles away from home. Of course I had someone on staff keep an eye on you," he tries to justify. "Which was warranted considering your inexplicable whereabouts tonight."

"How dare you," I spit before walking away, my steps brisk but light. "I explained where I was."

"You weren't at Yetta's."

I don't stop to acknowledge that. How would he know? It's not like he can drive himself anywhere.

"When I woke to you missing, the first call I made was to my good friend. You remember Matthew Hull? *The* police force?"

My feet grow ten times heavier as my steps slow.

"He went by your mom's. The Rover was nowhere in sight."

"I took your car," I say without turning around. "It's faster."

"I had him check for that, too. Why wasn't it there, Lenox?"

"I'm not sure, Kordin. Somehow we must've missed each other."

"That was an hour and a half ago."

I come to a stop. "There was—"

"Do you know what the chief of police can do? He can find

people. *Lose* people. If I find out who it is you're fucking, I'll make sure he's never seen again."

A wave of dizziness overtakes me, the floor under me spinning as I send a hand out to the side, catching myself against the aquarium, the vibrant activity inside my only solace.

That's why I chose to protect Reece's future, because mine's set in stone. With or without those work orders, I still have to be Lenox Debrosse, and now, it seems I'm going to have to find a way to be her without him.

I will movement back into my legs, ignoring their trembling to continue down the hall, bypassing our bedroom altogether.

Close behind me, Kordin demands, "Where are you going?"

"I'm sleeping upstairs tonight."

"No, you're not. You are my wife, and as such—"

"Try and stop me," I tell him as I ascend the stairs. He could hobble himself up here if he really wanted to but I doubt he will. His dignity won't allow it.

I lock myself in one of our spare bedrooms, then collapse on the floor, everything from the last few days catching up with me at once. This time I have to cover my mouth with both hands to keep the scream from escaping.

Forty-One

Lex

I STARE AT THE WHITE STICK WITH THE TWO PINK LINES FOR several minutes before looking up at my blurry reflection and wipe under my eyes, mindful of my mascara. Truthfully, I'd given up hope I'd ever have kids. I didn't think I was worthy and I know Kordin didn't either. Now that I am pregnant, in this impossibly fucked-up situation, I pray I get to.

My mind wanders back a few hours, when Kordin raised his hand to me. My body's first instinct was to protect my stomach, my baby.

It knew before I even did.

For the first time in years, I don't consider my body the broken traitor I've accused and convicted it of being. I see it as an ally.

Coming out of the bathroom, somebody standing inside my office's doorway startles me, and I quickly hide the pregnancy test behind my wrist. After getting a better look at who it is, I tuck it up my sleeve.

"God, Ree—" I remember myself, my surroundings, my…situation. Why is he here right now? I thought I had more time to figure out what to say to him. I *need* more time to figure out what to say to him. "Mr. Souza, I wasn't expecting you."

He frowns. "Are you okay?"

"Hmm." I avoid his questioning stare to glance at my desk, a bunch of flowers already awaiting me. Sweet Peas. I don't know much about them other than they're my birth month flower. "Why are you here? The plan was to meet up tonight."

Shooting a look over his shoulder, he says, "This can't wait. We have to talk before then."

I follow his gaze. "Not here. Not now."

"Here and now's all I got."

"Mr. Souza—"

"Why are you calling me that again?"

"I have a meeting that I need to prepare for. If you'd just—"

"Lex, what's going on? Why are you acting like this? And what..." His gaze sharpening on my chin, he takes a step forward.

Unfortunately, I tilt my head too late to hide the scrape from Kordin's cast, and with vitriol lacing his tone, he grinds out, "What happened to your face?"

"Mr. Souza, I don't want to have to call security, but I will."

Another step in my direction, then, "Did Kordin do that to you?"

"I was in a car accident yesterday."

"Liar."

One eye out the glass wall, I continue like I'm reading from a script, "A minor fender bender causing my chin to hit the steering wheel and—"

"Is that the story he told you to say? Why are you covering for him?"

"I'm not covering for anyone. I was in a car accident."

"Lex. Tell me what really happened or I'll go beat it out of him myself. They can't arrest me twice."

This brings my full attention back to him. "What do you mean by that?"

"That's what I came to tell you. I'm heading upstate for a while."

Upstate. Not the upstate we live in, or the further north upstate that Reece wants to live in, but prison. It's a more dignified way of saying "I'm going to prison."

"For what?"

"Forgery." Reaching behind his back, he pulls out a stack of papers and drops them on my desk, the force causing them to slide across the glossy surface to me.

I recognize them instantly as the work orders he was supposed to get from Kaisin last night. The work orders Kordin either forged himself or had someone else forge for him…

I meet Reece's obsidian eyes. They're bloodshot with bags under them. While I can't smell his cologne, I am picking up a faint char odor.

"What'd you do?" I demand.

He answers like he's going off his own script, saying, "I was hired by Kordin Debrosse to create fraudulent invoices with the intent to defraud Debrosse Investment Properties Group, while making it look like his wife, Lenox Debrosse, was the one responsible."

"No you weren't."

"Lex."

"No…you weren't."

"You needed a firsthand witness."

He's taking the fall for a crime he didn't commit. For me.

The earth tilts so suddenly I almost tip sideways. Pressing my thighs against the edge of my desk, I fight to remain upright.

"Everything we talked about getting, I already got. The IDs, the cash, the—"

"The cash? From Cyrus?" He robbed Cyrus before I did?

"Yeah." He gestures to the papers. "I went last night after I found those."

The flash drive. That's why it was a different color. He switched it while he was there.

"It's all in your mom's window boxes."

"My mom's what? You went to her house?" I can hear my voice growing more and more frenetic. "How?"

"Her address was on the tracking device… Look, that's not important right now. We're running out of time. The police will be here any minute."

"How do you know that?"

"Because I called them and confessed before coming here. They know about Kordin's embezzlement. They know he's framing you. They know about my involvement. They're coming to arrest us both."

"Why would you do that?"

"So Cyrus wouldn't have anything over you anymore and so Kordin wouldn't either. But my mom and sisters…"

He doesn't know Cyrus is dead. Nobody told him yet.

"Just get to the boxes and get them out of town. For me. Please."

Behind Reece, I see someone pass by, their curiosity watching us palpable.

"When I get out—"

"Mr. Souza." I paste on a concerned expression as I wave at the chair he usually sits in. "Mr. Souza, please have a seat. If you'd calm down, I'm sure we can figure all this out."

Reece rears back. "Figure what out? It's already done. I'm—"

"You're an idiot!" I whisper-shout while thrusting my other hand out at him…the hand also concealing the pregnancy test.

The stick flies from my hold and goes spinning across my desk, stopping closest to Reece, the two pink lines facing up.

The world oscillates the other way, and this time instead of fighting it, I close my eyes, hoping it takes me with.

"Is that…"

I force my eyes open only to find Kordin wheeling himself toward my door with purpose.

Reece's body is blocking the contents of my desk from Kordin's view, but if he comes in here… And sees… Or hears…

Fuck, fuck, fuck.

"Take a seat," I beg through unmoving lips, praying that he listens.

Reece doesn't move an inch, just asks, "You're pregnant?"

"My husband and I—"

"Didn't do that." Reece points at the positive test, then motions between us, his custom band still on his ring finger. "We did."

At the last minute, something pulls Kordin's focus further down the hall, and he changes direction, heading that way instead.

The elevators.

"Um, you know, Mr. Souza? If you were to take the stairs, you might be able to avoid anyone coming up the elevator, and you could even make use of those window boxes yourself. Move somewhere remote, without any people around."

428 | A. MARIE

"Snow?"

"You would have to leave now though. Right now." Swiveling my head, I keep my eyes locked on Kordin until he disappears out of my line of vision. They're here.

Are they here? Who exactly are "they"?

"Reece, go."

"You got my baby in you?"

Through gritted teeth, I tell him, "Kordin's. I have Kordin's baby in me."

"Stop lying."

I wish I could.

"Does he know? Is that why he hit you?"

"I was in a fucking car wreck," I snap.

Reece slams his hands on my desk, making me jump.

"I'm going to fucking prison! Tell me the *truth*!"

"The truth is…"

A man in uniform slowly comes into view before spinning around to laugh at someone behind him, his behavior telling…and terrifying.

If I tell Reece the actual truth, he's going to go ballistic on Kordin the second that door opens, and Kordin won't need to call his friend because Chief Hull's already here.

My heart's never beat faster or louder as I look back at Reece.

"I also robbed Cyrus last night. After you."

His face takes on more shadows than he walked in here with. "For…us?"

Shaking my head, I click my tongue.

"No, no, no. Don't do that."

"There is no us, rookie. There never was."

"Lex, don't do that shit."

I have to.

"I've been working you since moment one."

"On God, you better be fucking lying right now."

"Don't you get it? All I've been doing is lying. Those symptoms you noticed? I was already pregnant."

"No."

"It's true. Soon after I found out Kordin was using my name to pocket extra earnings for himself, I discovered I was carrying his baby. I didn't want him to have access to any child of mine, and I wasn't going to risk giving birth in a jail cell, so I hired Cyrus to get me Kordin's hard drive. I was planning on stealing that money to start over somewhere else."

Scowling, his head rotates side to side. "Your mom though…"

I ignore him, distracting him from the glaring truth by placing blame on him.

"But you went and fucked everything up, making me have to change my target to Cyrus. All I needed was the code to his safe and I could finally be free. Yesterday, you—"

"I gave you the code. I cracked the fucking safe for you, then gave you the code to do it yourself."

I nod.

"And you were going to take off today? Without me? Without even *telling* me?"

I nod again. "I just needed to get a few of my personal items, including the pregnancy test I took weeks ago and stored here, and then—"

"And then you were going to fucking disappear off the face of the planet and let me wonder for the rest of my goddamn motherfucking life what happened to you!"

It's not even a question. The story's that believable because I'm that untrustworthy.

I've been that untrustworthy. I don't want to be that anymore. I don't want to be…me anymore.

But that's exactly who I have to be. For him.

I raise my voice, too. "You knew I was playing you all along! You knew! You just didn't mind. Except…" I wave a hand at him. "…apparently you did. You shouldn't have fallen in love with your mark, rook. It made flipping you a breeze."

"You were never my mark, Snow. You were my world."

The look of utter treachery on Reece's face brings real tears to my eyes as I murmur, "A world too crooked for someone so sweet."

Reece's fill with water, too.

430 | A. MARIE

"You're not crooked, Lex. You're heartless."

I do have a heart—his.

But I just drove a blade through it.

"I'll make sure your family gets what you hid in the window boxes before I leave." If he is going to jail, I need him focused on his own safety, not his family's.

Thankfully, the door to my office swings open before I make more promises, putting Reece's life in danger all over again.

As police officers swarm my office like it's a buy-one-get-one sale on donuts, I rush forward and surreptitiously tuck the pregnancy test into the Sweet Peas.

Using the raw emotion clogging my throat, I transition from act one to act two seamlessly, rasping out, "Kordin, is what Mr. Souza said true? Are you stealing from the firm?"

"Reece Souza, you're under arrest…"

While one officer reads Reece his rights, two others grab his arms, shoving him down on top of my desk to handcuff him. One even digs his elbow into the back of Reece's neck.

Reece doesn't so much as make a sound.

Kordin smiles at the unusually tall man beside him before addressing me, saying, "Darling, don't give any credibility to this con artist by repeating his unfounded allegations." He says it so calmly he might as well be ordering a niçoise salad from the building café, but then his voice hardens as do his features when he adds, "To me or to anybody else."

I don't miss the threat in his words. I just don't acknowledge it, instead injecting a healthy dose of fear into my voice to see if I can evoke any in his while asking, "Are you going to jail?"

Sadly, I get none as Kordin and the man chuckle before the latter steps forward, allowing me to read his name tag. Hull.

Am I going to jail? Is this the moment Kordin throws me under the bus, revealing his true intentions for marrying me?

After a leering perusal of my appearance I feel all the way down to my marrow, Chief Hull only says, "Apologies for the disturbance,

Mrs. Debrosse, but this is routine procedure when we receive tips of this nature."

Chief Hull has a script, too, and it includes another routine procedure that favors the rich but fucks everybody else.

Kordin's the one actually embezzling millions while Reece is only allegedly guilty of forging documents, yet these pigs are acting like it's the opposite. The hollow's cracking jokes and the fox is being manhandled.

This is not at all what I was expecting. I assumed it'd be a full-blown witch hunt, with Kordin's finger pointed in my direction and Chief Hull and his men gleefully stringing me up. Even with a firsthand witness, saying it was Kordin, why isn't he at least trying to pin this on me? That was his whole objective from the start.

Unless he doesn't need to. If Chief Hull can make individuals disappear, what are "unfounded allegations" to him? Child's play probably.

They're going to make this go away.

After all, if I'm investigated, any accounts with my name on them will be, too, and there goes Kordin's secret reserve.

Reece is yanked off my desk, revealing the work orders he set there.

I gather the sheets and thrust them toward Kordin.

"These have my name on them, but they're not mine. Why did you put my name on them?"

Kordin's humor evaporates quicker than a lightning strike, and no longer concerned with keeping up the kind-husband act, he snarls, "Shut your mouth, Lenox,"

There's a scuffle on my left that I ignore to press, "Were you trying to make it look like I was the one misappropriating funds?"

"Not another word."

"Does Kaisin know what you've been doing? I want to talk to him and—"

I get cut off as I'm hauled back by my elbow.

"No need for that, ma'am. We'll just be in and out. But we will be taking these." Snatching the documents out of my hand, the cop passes them over to Chief Hull without letting me go.

Chief Hull rolls them up and taps one end against a thigh, not handling them with the care one would expect a professional to treat evidence.

Reece appears next to us—still handcuffed, still silent—and head-butts the pig restraining me, causing him to release me in order to cup his now leaking nose.

Reece's turbulent gaze connects with mine for a split second, the rest of the world exploding into utter oblivion around us until it's just the two of us. One of his eyebrows is split open, causing a thin stream of blood to flow down his nose and lips, dripping off his chin to the carpet. He's terrifyingly beautiful, and…I love him. Despite my best efforts, I fell in love with Reece. There's nobody else I'd rather get jealous over, fight against, stay up all night fucking, laughing at, listening to, admiring his every feature while he's fast asleep, gaze at the moon with, kiss amid the snow with, learn from, teach, kill for.

Even after I impaled his heart, twisted the knife, and pulled it back out, leaving him with nothing but fallacies to staunch the wound with, he's *still* willing to take on anyone and everyone to protect me. I questioned his ability to do it using only one hand, but he just showed he could do it with none.

Suddenly, one equally bloody cop tackles him to the floor, bringing our surroundings back into focus.

The gasp that leaves me as two more pile on top of Reece is real. The agony I feel when all three officers proceed to elbow and knee Reece is real.

I watch Reece thrash from the simultaneous beatings, the sickening chaos a physical representation of my own internal struggle.

I tried to protect him, too. I eliminated Reece's tormentor and he eliminated mine. Yet neither of us are free.

Kordin's scrutinizing stare scrapes my skin worse than his cast did.

Making myself look away, I focus on my husband instead. Did he see what passed between us? Does he understand Reece's actions?

I can't let him suspect anything's happening between us. I will not allow Reece's jealousy to be the literal death of him. According to him, that responsibility lies solely with me. My hands hold his fate. No one else's.

I'm still trying to protect him.

Disgust dripping from my tone, I say, "If you can't control your pet," as if Reece belongs to him and not me, "can you at least take this somewhere else? He's soiling my carpet." Because clearly *I'm* the victim in all this for having *my* office bombarded, *my* carpet stained. So very *fucking* hollow of me.

After eight years of being Lenox Debrosse, I don't want to spend another second in her skin. If I could shed it like a snake right now, I would.

I'm not a snake though. I'm bigger, stronger, faster, and smarter.

Kordin studies me for a minute longer before glancing at his friend who gives a faint headshake, silently advising him not to engage.

Chief Hull booms, "Get him up." To Kordin, he gestures to the doorway, letting him go first.

While a perfectly composed Kordin leads the brigade down the hall, Reece gets dragged out, sweaty, bloody, and winded, neither of them so much as sparing me a glance. In a matter of seconds, my office is as empty as the hole in my chest I could've swore didn't have a heart either. Then Reece left, making me realize it did.

He took my heart with him and I don't know if I'll ever get it back.

Jumping on my laptop, I send out a company-wide email, informing every employee of Debrosse Investment Properties Group our CEO was just taken into custody by FHPD, as well as what he was arrested for. I also suggest anybody with information regarding the situation come forward immediately. If the police aren't going to open a proper investigation, I'll conduct one myself.

Next, I send a similar email to a few of the biggest news outlets in New York. Friend or not, with every journalist in the state breathing down his neck, Chief Hull will have no choice but to arrest Kordin.

Then, with hands so shaky I actually drop my phone twice trying to pick it up, I search the meaning of Sweet Peas.

Goodbye.

I hurry from my office, walking as fast as my stilettos can handle to the stairwell. As soon as I hear the door close behind me, I double over and I do it. I finally fucking do it. I scream. My hands on my ears, I let it all out, screaming at the top of my lungs. Even when my legs give out, and I fall to my knees and forearms, my nose an inch from the concrete as my mouth gapes open, I keep screaming. I scream until I feel hands on me. They're pulling and rubbing and shaking and trying to get me to stop but I don't want to.

I don't fucking want to.

But I never get what I want, and eventually, my throat runs dry. My eyes, however, keep leaking long after I'm forced back into silence.

"It's okay. It's okay," Phil soothes next to me.

Another man mumbles something, and surprised, I look over to find Kaisin on my other side. I only felt two hands but between the both of them, they only have two in working order. Because of Reece.

My throat yearns to scream all over again.

"Shouldn't you be with your brother?" I ask Kaisin, my voice hoarse.

"He wanted me to be, but..." His head shakes.

This is what I've been preparing for—the stomach, the liver, the testicles.

Now it's time to go in for the kill.

Using my lack of volume to my advantage, I croak out, "Did you know?"

Both men say, "No," Phil's more fervent than Kaisin's. Whether he believed it was me or suspected it was Kordin, Kaisin must've had an inkling something was amiss or he wouldn't have taken those photos and emailed them to himself.

Wiping my eyelashes—not under this time, but actually *on* the mascara-coated hairs to smear the black around—I sniffle and sit up, saying as miserably as I can, "He's been framing me. All along. Since just after our honeymoon. I feel like such an idiot."

"No, no. He had all of us fooled, Lenox."

Since Phil replies first, I focus on him, asking, "You don't believe I had anything to do with it, do you?"

"What? No, of course not. It's just... Look, speaking for myself, I regret not questioning Kordin's rules sooner. Maybe we could've prevented things getting this far if we'd just been able to talk to you."

"Rules?"

Kaisin answers. "We weren't allowed to talk to you. If we even tried, Kordin would intervene. He was always worried about you becoming overwhelmed."

"Always," Phil adds. "He blamed your fragile state."

My fragile state? Did Kordin use my illness to further his objective?

"Now we know it was just a way to…"

"Isolate me," I say, reflecting back on the past eight years of feeling like an outcast in this building.

They both nod.

"I've known for a while Kordin's not who he says he is. He… Well…" I expose my wrist, showing the scratches, then brush a finger over the mark on my chin.

"Kordin gave you those?"

I scrunch my face on a whimper.

"You need to file a police report."

"I will."

"Lenox?"

I turn my face toward Kaisin.

"That won't be enough. The chances of him seeing the inside of a jail cell today, or any day, are slim."

"I wouldn't be too sure."

"Even if he does get arrested, he'll make bond and be right back out. The police chief… The judge… They're all…close."

I wasn't aware Kordin had a judge in his back pocket as well.

"For your safety, you should consider—"

"No, I can't run scared. That's what he wants. That's what he expects, for me to cower so he can continue to get away with the bad things he does. I have to stand up to him. I just…" Trailing off, I glance at them both.

"What is it?" Kaisin prompts.

"I don't know if I can do it alone." After saying the words aloud, I realize I actually can't. I need help. A lot of it.

"You won't have to," Phil promises. "You have our full support."

Got 'em.

"Is everything all right up there?" someone from below calls up.

Kaisin answers him, saying, "Sorry about the interruption. We're all right."

The man continues climbing until he's on our level, giving both Kaisin and Phil scrutinizing sort of glares from under a pair of wiry white eyebrows.

Speaking to me directly, he asks, "Are you okay, miss? Are these two bothering you?"

"Oh. No, they're not. They're actually trying to help me through a very difficult time." I punctuate that statement with another loud sniff.

"It must be pretty painful."

"Excruciating," I tell him honestly.

"I can believe it. I heard you from inside my studio."

"Yoga studio?" Kaisin questions the older man. "You hiked thirty-five flights?"

With his chest puffed, the man gives a nod. "Yoga does wonders for the mind *and* body."

Thirty-five flights. That puts him on the seventh floor.

"Are you right above the vision center?" I ask.

"There's a vision center here? Seems this place is bringing in a new company every month." He shakes his head. "Don't quote me, but last I checked, six was still doing graphic design."

Summit Enhancements. Graphic design. Kordin's real accomplice.

Rookie, rookie, rookie. Always so *impatient.*

It's been discovered that some orcas, not many, intentionally beach themselves while on the hunt.

But they almost never get stranded permanently.

The man turns to leave and I push myself up off the floor, ignoring Phil's and Kaisin's attempts to help.

"Actually, would you care if I accompanied you downstairs for a tour of your studio? My mind is in desperate need of some healing right now."

Forty-Two

Lex

SEVEN HOURS LATER, I'M SITTING FRONT ROW IN A courtroom. While the only movement on my top half is my hand repetitively dabbing my eyes with a tissue, under the bench, my feet are carefully working together to slowly lay my purse on its side.

The audience section is packed, but I don't have to look around to know four other pairs of legs are doing the exact same thing.

As soon as the purse is horizontal, I toe the latch open, then flip the top over.

Almost immediately, two winged insects scuttle out from under the bench, a chorus of buzzing breaking out as well. Luckily, the constant thrum of murmurs covers it.

Keeping my focus on the front, I wait until Kordin's rolled in. Thanks to the pressure from the media, as well as the DV report I filed with the police department, Kordin was arrested after all.

He and the judge exchange glances, conspicuous to me after the tip from Kaisin, but probably imperceptible to everyone else in here. Joining his team of lawyers at their table, he flashes them a smirk accompanied by a self-confident shake of his head.

I give the purse a hard kick before shoving to my feet, plunging my upper body over the railing and yelling, "How could you do this to me, Kordin?"

"Remove her!" the judge orders.

I'm already upright again, walking backward toward the middle aisle as I point at Kordin, repeating, "How could you? I trusted you! I loved you!"

Just as there's a crunch beneath my shoe, several people in the audience jump up on the benches, screaming.

Dozens of cicadas take flight from all directions, the air filled with them as they search for wood.

One female voice above the others shouts, "They're cockroaches!" causing the entire courtroom to erupt into hellish chaos. Even the administrators begin darting around frantically.

"Roaches fly?"

"Oh my God, it's in my hair!"

"Their eyes," someone says before gagging.

"They're all over my purse!" a familiar voice cries.

"That's a cicada!"

Barely above the cicadas' horrific squawking, I hear the judge bellow, "All court hearings are adjourned until further notice!"

The strike of his gavel sends goose bumps along my skin.

Kordin's not making bond today. Hopefully not at all. The less time he's out and free to alter the case, the better.

It'll take at least a day to fumigate, then another three for the toxins to clear. By the time it's safe for humans to enter the building again, he'll get a different judge, one he's not friends with.

All around me spectators pour into the aisle, but making sure I keep Kordin's gaze, I calmly purse my lips together and blow him the last kiss he'll ever get from me.

Blinking, I spin on my heel and let the surge carry me away from the thousands of cicadas we unleashed on a system that's been infested long before today.

Two blocks away, I reconvene with Cat and the others. Everyone's still dusting themselves off, making sure no cicadas hitched a ride on our clothing.

"That was disgusting," Promise says with a shiver.

"Really?" Cia says. "I thought it was kind of beautiful."

"Did you get the file onto the prosecutor's table?" I ask Cat.

"You know I did."

Now the prosecutor has everything I managed to find at Summit Enhancements. After touring the yoga studio on the seventh floor, I pulled a fire alarm, then wandered down a floor to do some digging. What will happen to Reece going forward, I don't know.

We start walking down the sidewalk toward my Range Rover.

"Who do we know doing time upstate?"

"Upstate?" Cia asks.

"The clink," Promise answers for me before saying, "And *we* know lots. Jailbirds love sending me letters, so many the post office made me rent a bigger PO box."

"I have my fair share of exes serving time," Adie adds. "Why?"

"I'm just thinking ahead. He might need protection in there."

Even with the new evidence—the correct evidence—Reece may very well be facing time behind bars, and if I can find out which facility he'll be at, I'll do everything I can to ensure he's protected in there.

"For the hollow?" Cat asks, heavy on the condescension.

I shake my head. "For Reece."

"Our Reece?" Cia asks, making a laugh knock around in my chest.

"Not your Reece. *My* Reece." *If he'll still have me.*

Cat snorts while Promise tells me, "We can make that happen. Just need approval for a conjugal visit—"

"No." I pull up short, making the others stop, too. "We're no longer in the trade business. If we find someone who can help us, we pay them with cash. Our bodies are not our currency anymore."

With a knowing smile, Cat asks, "What are they?"

"Ours," I answer, a shiver that has nothing to do with nerves or hormones or men in general runs up my spine.

"Hell yeah."

"We can still fuck men, right?" Adie asks after a moment, and this laugh I let out.

Our minds have always been our strongest assets—not our pussies like men would have us believe—and if we put them together, we can be unstoppable.

We will be unstoppable.

"We're fucking *all* the men."

Forty-Three

Reece

THROUGH A KITCHEN WINDOW, I SPY A KEYPAD ON THE WALL, all of its lights green. She put in a security system, but doesn't even activate it at night? She doesn't use drapes or blinds on the main-floor windows either, making the entire first floor of the house visible from the outside. She was born a fox, became a hollow, and in the two and a half years I've been gone, she's now what?

Fucking cocky. Cockier than Kordin ever was.

This early May weather has a damp chill trying to creep in through my clothes, but I can't feel anything other than white-hot adrenaline as I ease away from the house, the sound of nearby rushing water behind me in the woods somewhere while I scan the entire backside for any new lights. Off, all of them. If it wasn't for the quarter moon above, it'd be pitch black out here.

Every window on the second floor has blinds pulled down, so her bedroom must be up there.

That's one. One single security measure she's taken by not sleeping on the ground level.

Shit, Lex, I thought you were smarter than this.

Kneeling in front of the side door, I start picking the lock, the motions coming back to me like riding a bike. With each click of another tumbler, more adrenaline pumps through my body and I have to pause for a minute to calm my heart, steady my hands.

It's been a long time since I heard that sound.

It's been a long time since I saw Lex.

It's been a long time since…everything.

I get the door unlocked, then twist the handle and let myself in.

Aside from another smaller house on the property that looked vacant, her other neighbors are too far away to see, or hear, anything, so I don't worry about that as I make my way through the kitchen. This area isn't Fox Hollow but it definitely isn't the Catskills either. It's somewhere in between.

I pass an island with a vase of blue Forget-me-nots and have to keep from snorting. Forget-me-nots? The symbol for loyalty, trust, and unwavering love? This bitch doesn't know shit about any of those.

After doing a quick count in my head, I backtrack and pluck two stems out, crumbling the blooms in my palm. Odd numbers only, except thirteen.

I recount to make sure it's actually eleven stems in there, then continue on.

On God, being a florist's son has never been more of a pain in the ass than this moment.

Thinking of my mom makes me miss her and the twins and Silvy's and—

No. Lex is first. She owes me an apology and I want to look in her face when she gives it. I went to prison for her. Fucking prison. Two and a half years of my life I'll never get back.

The rest of the house blurs in my vision as I spot the stairs. At the top of them, there's a blue glow coming from one of the rooms, so that's where I head first. She must've brought the fish tank with her. It's not set in the wall of the hallway like her last house, but it's obviously still in the room. Her room.

I stop just before the threshold to pull in a breath.

Fuck. I can smell her from out here. When we were at that cabin, she told me what it was. Hand soap scented like whipped vanilla, amber woods, and iced Jasmine. The only kind she didn't hate. Even after being without it for that entire weekend, I could still smell it on her. These past couple years my nights have been plagued by nightmares of vanilla icicles piercing my arms, stomach, face, everywhere but the back—where Lex actually stabbed me.

"Did you even shower before you came here?" I hear from inside the room and scoff.

Never caught off guard, always a raging bitch. She hasn't changed a bit.

But I have.

I fill the doorway, letting her see just how much.

Curled up in an oversized chair in the far corner with a throw blanket draped over her lap is Lex, the woman I sacrificed *everything* for. And she looks…amazing. Her hair's still that white blonde, like Morning Glow Camellia, but she's put on a little weight, giving her a healthier look, like she's not constantly battling demons, both emotional and physical.

She wasn't anxious. She was pregnant.

Still—fucking *still*—I have to remind myself what was real and what wasn't. What I thought was going on was just a smokescreen.

Her eyes, the color of blue Milkweed flowers, travel my new body, too. Even from across the room I can feel their exploration as if she's right here in front of me, using her fingers instead of her eyes.

Goose bumps break out across my skin, spreading like Ivy.

Lex moves a book from her lap over to a table.

Images of me using that same lap as a book holder fill my head before I can stop them and my heart picks up speed.

"How'd you find me?" she asks first.

"I made friends."

She lifts her eyebrows like she's impressed.

Or unconvinced.

"Me, too."

My gaze immediately goes to the bed. It's big enough for two people but there's no one in it. I study the attached bathroom next. The light's off. I don't know why that makes me happy.

It doesn't mean she's not with somebody. She could be.

My heart beats even harder, thrashing violently against my ribs.

444 | A. MARIE

Lex is watching me, those blue eyes seeming to pick up on my every thought.

I focus on the tank next to her chair. It's smaller than her last one, and from what I can tell, doesn't contain a shark.

I didn't even realize she liked her old fish tank enough to get herself a new one. *Another thing I failed to pick up on.*

"No more shark?"

Her head shakes in my periphery. "No more sharks."

Right. Sharks. The men she worked with. The man she had a baby with.

"Where's your kid?"

"Not here right now."

I meet her stare.

Why isn't her kid here? Because she was expecting me? Expecting this? She knew I'd be pissed. She knew I'd come looking for answers.

She knew me so fucking well. She just didn't love me.

"Are those for me?" Keeping eye contact, she nods down at the flowers in my hand.

My fist tightens around the stems. I forgot I had them. I forgot everything…except her. I could never forget her. No matter how hard I tried, she was all I thought about.

Lex gets up from her chair, the blanket falling soundlessly to the floor, and wanders right up to me, taking the Lilies from my hold without touching any of my skin with hers.

A lump forms in my throat and I fight to swallow it down.

It's been over two years since I've even laid eyes on a woman. Being this close to one again, being this close to *this* woman, all I want to do is see what she feels like.

"Lilies?" she guesses correctly, inspecting the orange petals. "What do they mean?"

"Contempt."

Her gaze stops roaming, and we stand silently for several seconds until she turns around, goes over to her chair, lifts the blinds behind it, opens the window, then tosses the flowers outside.

At least she's upgraded from a garbage can.

Not bothering to close the window, she asks, "What happened to your ring?"

"Are you fucking kidding me?"

She faces me again, hands on her hips. "Am I ever?"

"My ring? The ring you gave me just to fuck with my head, to make me believe in you, in us? That ring? I threw it into the Hudson. It's the first thing I did when I got out."

"Yeah?"

"Yeah."

The sleep set she's wearing isn't as expensive as the ones she used to wear with the hollow. It's cotton and her top doesn't match the bottoms. They're both still black, but while the shorts are loose and flowy, the top is a tighter material that accentuates her tits. Tits that got bigger, not by much, but enough for me to notice. Enough for me to want to see them closer. Feel them. Taste them.

Shit! I roll my empty hands into tight fists, squeezing until my nails sting my palms.

She has changed. And not just physically. Lex looks like she's home. In Kordin's house, she never looked like she belonged. Or that she even wanted to be there. Here, she does. Here, she likes it, I can tell.

She's still her, but a different version. A new one.

I hate that I don't know this version. I hate that I don't love this version more. I loved every version of her. I understood them. Understood her.

But that was before. Before she told me it was all fake, including her, including us.

Lex crosses the room again, not stopping until she's directly under me and I have to look down my nose at her. The scar at her hairline is what draws my attention first because I always knew her flaws and I loved her, not despite them, but *with* them. She never had to hide any part of herself from me, yet she hid every part of herself from me.

She reaches up to brush my hair off my forehead. "Your hair—"

I catch her wrist, air pouring through my nose loudly.

Just as quickly, Lex's other hand comes up, the ring in question balancing on the tip of her trigger finger.

I should've expected her to pickpocket me.

I should've thrown the ring in the river. After I got released and they handed me the belongings I got arrested carrying, I tried putting it back on, but it didn't fit. I've put on weight, too. I hit the weights as often as I was allowed. That and fighting were the only things that distracted me. Distracted me…from Lex.

Plucking the ring off her fingertip, I shove past her, aiming for the same window, but before I even reach the chair, she wrenches my arm back, chopping me right in the Adam's apple and making me fucking gasp for air.

"*Don't* do that," she warns with so much authority I want to laugh in her face. Who the fuck does she think she is?

"Why not? It doesn't mean anything. It never did."

Releasing my arm, she shakes her head. I get the feeling she's going to turn away, and panic seeps into my every cell, so I grab her bicep, making sure she can't go anywhere. Not until she explains why she—

Lex's fist collides with my nose, forcing my head to rotate back. I right it instantly though, pushing into her space.

"What the fuck? You punched me? Do you know how many hardened criminals I've fought?"

"Thirteen."

"Wha—"

"Had you showed an ounce of fucking restraint in there, you would've been out sooner, but you couldn't, could you? You had to fight. You had to make trouble. You had to lose good time that would've shaved off some of your sentence. Just like always, you made things so much harder than they needed to be."

"How the fuck do you know that?"

"A friend."

"Same friend that told me where I could find you?" I ask, already knowing the answer. She fucking set this up like she sets up everything. Lex never needed a tracker to know my moves, she orchestrated them all on her own. "You bribed another inmate to keep tabs on me? To feed me information?"

"Not just one," she surprises me by saying. "Out of those thirteen fights, how many were you the agitator in?" She answers for me. "Thirteen. Do you want to know why nobody started fights with you? Why nobody retaliated against you after you attacked them or a member of their crew?"

"Because I—"

"No, because *I* made it so. I threatened retaliation against anyone who laid a finger on you and I had the numbers to enforce it."

"You don't know what it was like in there. Just because I was the first to throw a punch doesn't mean I wasn't constantly provoked. You can't show weakness in lockup. None. Day one some asshole sat down next to me and took my roll. I brought my tray down on top of his head, then ate what was left of my disgusting brick of bread while making eye contact with anyone watching. Nobody touched my fucking food again, but I got into two more fights before the end of that day for similar shit. They test all the fresh meat, and I was no different." While the other inmates might not have fucked with me physically, they fucked with me mentally.

Her voice sounds broken when she says, "I tried my fucking best."

"Best at what?"

She pounds my chest. "Protecting you."

Why the fuck would she do that? She has no reason. No one fucked me up more than Lex.

I bend down so I'm in her face to tell her, "You're a fucking liar. Dishonesty and betrayal, remember?" And because I know the bed's right behind her, I push her.

Her ass bounces onto the mattress as she glares up at me.

My eyes briefly lift to the skylight above the bed before I turn to leave. The first step I take touches the carpet, but the second one hits something much higher, and I tumble to the floor like a stack of bricks, my hands out in front of me catching the brunt of my weight.

Bitch tripped me.

Flipping over to my back, Lex is already coming down on top of me to straddle my stomach. We scramble with each other, neither of us getting a good grip on the other's arms to gain the upper hand, then she leans down and kisses me. It's just a quick peck, but it paralyzes the rest of my body. Except my cock. That's been on the rise since she punched me and now it's fucking throbbing at full mast.

"Stop fighting."

I close my eyes and admit, "I can't."

"Then give me the chance to explain everything. Just...wait."

Opening my eyes, I shout back, "I've been waiting! I've been fucking waiting!"

She continues peering down at me, her head cocked. "Whose fault is that?"

We both say, "Yours," at the same time.

"You chose to act all by yourself. I didn't tell you to send yourself to prison. I never would've told you to do that."

"It was the only way to get Cyrus—"

"I killed Cyrus."

Time stands still for at least a fucking minute. Over the years, there've been a number of rumors about how Cyrus Andeno died, ranging from suicide to execution by a rival to an FBI raid. In the back of my mind, I always wondered if it was Lex who took him out. Out of all the people that had reasons to, she had the most.

"You did?"

"Yes."

"When?"

"Same night you robbed him."

"For you—"

"No, for *you*. Everything I've done...has been to protect *you*, rookie."

My old nickname sounds better than I remember.

I don't believe her reasoning, but I do believe she killed Cyrus. If anyone could've, it's her.

"How'd you do it?"

She describes using the money she stole from his safe as a way to sneak in weapons, then shooting him in the head while he was getting his dick sucked.

"He didn't see it coming?"

"He saw," she says cryptically, before adding, "I was never going to let him near you or your family."

"We weren't yours to protect."

Our eyes search each other's until Lex whispers, "You were. You are."

I shake my head. She never claimed me. Not once. She doesn't claim anybody.

"You said—"

"I *said* what I had to in order to keep you safe. I *did* what I had to in order to keep you safe."

"Safe? Lex, I went to motherfucking prison!"

"For nothing!"

"For you!" I roar. "For *your* protection!"

She tries to get up, and that same feeling takes over my body, making me grip her hips, keeping her where she is. I like having her near me. I like having her on me. I like having her.

"I did what I had to…" I stop myself. After I was already in custody, new evidence magically surfaced, leading to Kordin's real accomplice, which was the woman I saw him talking to at Summit Enhancements, a goddamn graphic design company, not a vision clinic. They still got me on a slew of other bullshit though, including tampering with evidence, resisting arrest, disorderly conduct, and assaulting multiple officers.

I start again, this time with the truth. "I did what I *thought* I had to do to keep you safe. And I did it because I *thought* you were mine to protect."

I loosen my hold on her because I don't have her. I never did.

"I was. I am."

"Everything that comes out of your mouth is a lie. I can't trust anything you say."

Determination in her features, she leans down, her hips gliding back to just above my cock.

Before her pussy can make contact, I catch her waist and hold her in place.

"Then trust my body. That's what you used to do."

I roll us over, but using my palms flat on the floor by her head, I keep myself suspended above her by several inches.

"Your body pulled off the worst betrayal of all." I push to my feet

450 | **A. MARIE**

in one smooth motion, then tower over her. She was fucking pregnant the whole time we were together and she didn't tell me. She could've. I would've loved her even with that hollow's baby in her. I would've loved...

Fuck this. I'm out of here. I don't know what I thought I'd gain by coming here. It doesn't matter what she says, how she tries to justify her actions or her words, I can never trust her again.

"Reece?"

Fuck. My name. My actual fucking name on her lips. I remember when she would moan it, and at the cabin, when she screamed it.

"I'm sorry. I'm *sorry*. I know what I did to you seems unforgivable."

Tapping the side of my fist on the doorjamb, I shake my head, and grit, "You don't have a goddamn clue what you did to me."

"I do. I know what I did to you because I did it to myself. It killed me to push you away. It fucking killed me, Reece. And now, I'm asking you... I'm begging you to stay, just a little bit longer, just until you hear why I had to anyway. After that, if you still want to leave... I'll let you."

Let me? Like she has that kind of power over me.

She does.

She did.

An entire war within me between past and present rages as I consider what to do.

Slowly, I turn around. Lex is on her knees now, her eyes pleading up at me.

She still does.

"Kordin had connections I knew nothing about until it was too late. The kind of connections that can make people disappear without a trace. Chief Matthew Hull, do you remember him? He was there when you got arrested."

I give her a tense nod and she gets to her feet.

"Do you remember how Kordin was treated that day? How familiar the two of them seemed? How friendly they were with each other?"

Yeah, it pissed me off. What pissed me off more was how Kordin spoke to Lex.

Because she was always my main concern.

When that cop grabbed her, I lost it. I hit him with the fury I felt toward Kordin, toward everyone, toward everything.

Even while hating Lex I loved her enough to fuck anyone up that touched her.

Lex takes a couple hesitant steps toward me. "That night, after I shot Cyrus, Kordin caught me coming back into the house and became apoplectic. He…"

I almost take her in my arms, but make myself cross them over my chest instead. This is what Lex is best at, creating empathy. She's a sculptor and her medium is other people's emotions. She molds them to her own whims.

Straightening her spine, she says, "He got physical."

My frown is instant and painful. The mark on her face. I knew it was from that motherfucker.

Goddamn it. Goddamn it! That piece of shit's lucky he's still locked up. I want to bury him alive.

"From the lack of charges at the Catskills' hotel to me sneaking off in the middle of the night, he was convinced I was cheating on him."

"He threatened to have Chief Hull do something to you."

Her shoulders slump all over again. "Haven't you been paying attention? He threatened to do something to *you*. He threatened to make you disappear."

I think about that. I think about everything, all the shit that went down back then.

"The cop outside your house while Kordin was in the hospital. That was his buddy's doing, wasn't it?"

She nods.

"So it was all a lie?"

"All of it. Everything…but us."

"Not everything, Lex. You were pregnant with that—"

"With our baby," she rushes to say. "With our daughter."

I uncross my arms, the feeling in them suddenly gone. "Our?"

"Our. Mine and yours."

"Lex," I warn.

Closing the distance between us, she grips my chin and pulls my head down to hers, our faces a breath apart.

"I'm sorry I lied. I'm sorry I was untrustworthy, but that's not who I am anymore."

"Don't. Don't get my fucking hopes up when I've spent years fighting to keep them down."

Her lips brush mine, then against them she whispers, "Too late." And it's like the last two and a half years never happened as I give in, taking her face between my hands and kissing her full on the mouth. My tongue sweeps in to lick hers, making us both moan. During the entire length of my sentence, I didn't know where I'd be going home to because I no longer had one, but this, this feels like home.

She feels like home.

It hurts to do it, it fucking hurts, but I end the kiss early to ask, "Where is she? Where's my daughter?" My daughter. My. Daughter.

"She's away for the night."

"I don't care. I want to meet her right now."

"You want the first time your daughter meets you to be while you're still wearing the stench of prison?"

"I'll clean up. After that, take me to her."

"She'll be here in the morning, rook. You can meet her then."

In the morning. She's letting me stay the night. Is she letting me stay the night?

"What's her name?"

Grabbing my hand, Lex pulls me out into the hall, past a couple doors to one that's already open. She flicks the light on, revealing my daughter's room.

There's a circular crib in the middle, a custom dresser off to one side that has a 3D feature of flowers growing up the fronts of the drawers, a rocking chair in the corner, and a couple chests overflowing with toys. The walls are mostly black, the unconventional nursery color broken up by hand-painted Primroses in all different shades and sizes. Primroses symbolize safety, protection…

And love.

"She's loved."

I'd be lying if I said I hadn't considered the possibility that Lex would be a detached mom. She couldn't even say the word love and mean it before. But just being in this room, in this house, I can tell she's far from detached.

"So loved." She says it so easily I look over at her. She's smiling. The first one of the night. And it's real.

"I should've behaved better. I would've got out sooner. I should've—"

"We've both made a lot of mistakes, but Primrose isn't one of them. We get to spend the rest of our lives making sure she knows that."

"You named her Primrose?"

"Primrose." She roams along the walls, trailing her fingers over the paintings. "A sign of renewal. A symbol of love. And a sincere confession."

"Confession?" I haven't heard that one before.

Stopping, she says softly, "'I can't live without you,'" then, "It killed me, Reece. It *killed* me. I didn't know what broken was until you left."

"I'm sorry," leaves my mouth even though I never, ever planned on apologizing for my part in what happened. I did what I had to *for her*.

But she did what she had to *for me*.

"You were right. We're so goddamn alike, we actually did destroy each other."

"Sometimes you have to hit the bottom to see what's above you."

"And? What was above you?"

"That's a conversation for tomorrow."

When she leaves the room, I follow her out into the hall again, hesitating. She's talking about tomorrow like I'll still be here. Am I sleeping here? With her? In another room? Should I offer to take the couch? Go somewhere else? I don't want the couch. I don't want to go anywhere else. I want to stay right next to her, forever.

Before I can decide what to do, Lex starts in the direction of her room, saying over her shoulder, "You can use my shower."

Forty-Four

Reece

THE PRIVATE SHOWER IS NICE. THE HOT WATER'S NICER. Even though I have the bathroom all to myself, I still keep my back to the wall. It'll be a long time before I see myself breaking that habit. I have to get used to being in the free world again. Getting released from prison is like crash-landing on Earth after traveling through space. Everything you learned in your initial and somewhat gradual adaption, you have to unlearn in an instant. Your entire way of living changes as soon as you leave the confines of that barb-wired, patrol-guarded fencing. You're incarcerated one minute, then the next you're not, and you're expected to know how to behave, not like the animal you were just treated as, and usually behaved as, but like the person you practically forgot you once were.

After scrubbing every inch of my body twice, I wrap the towel around my waist since I don't have any clean clothes, and go out to Lex's bedroom. She's fast asleep though, on her side, facing me, with a leg sticking out of the covers, almost identical to the first time I saw her. And just like I did then, I stand over her, letting my gaze run wild over all the porcelain skin on display.

She's not wearing an eye mask and she's not sweating, so I take that as a good sign. We didn't get to talk about her health yet but she seems better than she ever did. She seems...happy. She seems free.

She is free.

I trace her jaw with my middle finger. Luckily, Kordin didn't leave a scar on her face. On her heart though? I'm sure he left a lot of damage there. Him and Cyrus both.

Both men are gone from our lives now. One in prison temporarily, the other in hell for eternity. Lex and I had to sacrifice a lot to get them there, but we did it. We did it for each other. We did it for our future.

Lex's lips pull to one side as she murmurs, "Stalker."

"Only to you," I say, my gaze falling down the rest of her body.

Her fingers have more dainty tattoos now—a new one on her right trigger finger, another on her left ring finger; both of them flowers.

I have new ink, too; a few of them flowers as well. They're not great tattoos, having gotten them while on the inside, but each one holds a special meaning, the biggest one being the Snow White Hibiscus on my back, right where Lex stabbed me.

Right where I *thought* Lex stabbed me.

I touch the tat where Lex's wedding ring used to be.

"What happened with you and Kordin?" I know he was found guilty and charged for what he did, but I don't know how that affected Lex. Is she still stuck in a legal marriage with him?

"I divorced him."

"Is the flower for him?"

"No, rookie. It's for you."

"What flower is it?"

"Petunia."

Petunia. Part of the Nightshade family, but not poisonous.

"Why's it for me, Snow?"

"Because of its meaning. 'Your presence soothes me.'"

It does? Her presence soothes me, too.

"What about this one?" I brush the star-shaped flower on her trigger finger.

"Also for you. A Balloon flower, meaning—"

"Endless love," I finish for her, mesmerized as her smile grows.

Who the fuck was I kidding thinking I'd be able to walk away from Lex? I'm just as obsessed with her now as I was before.

I give her another once-over, wishing she'd undressed before lying down.

"I'm obsessed with you," I tell her quietly.

Her eyes flutter open, and meeting mine, she says, "I would kill for you."

She did.

Focusing on my towel, she pulls the corner from where I tucked it in the top, making it fall off my body and down to the floor. Her gaze touches every part of my front. My muscles are bigger, harder; my face is leaner, paler; I have more tats, more scars. Outside, I'm not the same man I was. Inside…I don't even know. I want to be myself again. I just don't have a fucking clue how yet.

"I'm different," I confess with a husky voice.

She reaches her hand out to grip my stiff cock and I almost fucking come on the spot. Mine is the only hand that's touched my cock in two and a half years.

Scooting her head and shoulders forward, she licks the precum off my slit.

I fucking shudder trying to control myself. I could coat her face in cum right now *easily*. "You're perfect," she tells me, making me want to believe her. She adds, "For me," then takes my head into her mouth, sucking it all the way to the back of her goddamn throat.

"Jesus Christ." I grasp the crown of her head for balance.

Lex's mouth is so warm and so wet and so fucking tight as she hollows out her cheeks that my ass clenches up, and then—

"Fuuuck," I groan as I explode in her mouth, her throat closing around my tip with every swallow she takes.

"That was fucking embarrassing," I say, out of breath even though I did absolutely jack shit.

"I loved it."

"Yeah? How much?"

"I'll show you."

Seeing her other hand lower past her stomach, I snatch her wrist before she even gets to her waistband and growl, "Mine."

In prison, I had to be territorial. If you let one person touch you or your belongings, every person thinks they can, and they'll never stop. Nothing with you or on you is safe, so you have to be on guard at all times.

But with Lex, the need to claim her isn't just about safety. It's involuntary. It's instinctual. She is mine, every fucking part of her, outside and in.

Releasing her wrist, I stick my own hand down the front of her sleep shorts, finding her fucking drenched, allowing me to slip two fingers right in.

I get caught up pumping slowly in and out of her, just to feel the inside of a motherfucking pussy again—*her* motherfucking pussy— that I almost forget about getting her an orgasm.

While pressing my thumb down on her clit, I tell her, "Fuck, you feel so good. So tight."

"I haven't been fucked in two and a half years."

All movement in my hand comes to a halt.

"You haven't been with anyone else since…"

Of all the scenarios I imagined, Lex being celibate while I was away never made the list. Lex could get dick outside an erectile dysfunction clinic.

She shakes her head, a fair amount of sweat gathering along her hairline. "You're not the only one who's been waiting."

I resume movement, adding a swirl to my thumb for my good little Snow White Hibiscus.

"Reece," she moans, sending a fresh shot of blood to my cock.

My first round didn't last long, but at least I can still get hard immediately after a nut with her.

"I want to see all of you."

One-handed, I help her get her shirt off. While I continue finger-fucking her, she pushes her shorts down, and kicks them off her feet.

"I'm different, too," she says, not in a self-conscious way, just stating. Warning.

The glow from the moon wedge above us drips down through the skylight, highlighting every inch of Lex's new body for me. Her tits are still on the small side, only slightly fuller than they were; her areolas are darker; her nipples more prominent; her ribs and collarbone don't stick out as much as they used to; and her stomach and thighs have thin stretch marks that are somehow lighter than her already pale skin, making the wavy indents shimmer like the top layer of freshly fallen snow.

"You know what makes the moon so beautiful?"

"The sun's reflection?" she drawls sarcastically.

In addition to the finger tattoos, she also got the one on her sternum covered up with a small black sun. While the moon is feminine energy, the sun is masculine. I don't know why she would've put it on her body. She fucking hates all things men. Except me, thank fucking God.

"Its craters. Its mountains. Its dark spots. Its bright spots." I tell her honestly, "You're more beautiful now than you've ever been, Lex." I only wish I could've seen the changes in real time.

It's not long before Lex's thighs clamp around my wrist, her pussy walls contracting as she moans, "Mm, mm, mm," while she rides out the orgasm.

There's nothing like feeling my girl come. Nothing.

Using her pussy milk as lube, I pump my cock until I'm ready to go again, then reposition Lex's pliant body on the mattress, dragging her ass to the edge.

"Legs up, Snow White."

She extends her legs along my torso, one of her feet colliding with my chin, causing me to bite my tongue. The taste of copper floods my mouth as I peer down at her, that devious little smirk telling me she did it purposely.

I nip the arch of that same foot, marking her with the blood. Lex laughs, not just in her chest, but an actual laugh that escapes her mouth and transforms her entire face.

Kick to the jaw or not, I'm definitely doing that again. Every time I'm with Lex, I swear I unlock a new kink.

"Why do you always gotta be so violent with me?" I tease.

"Because you like it."

"You like it, too." I know she does.

"But I like you more," she says, quoting me from years ago.

That answer deserves another reward.

I wonder if she keeps her sex toys in the same place.

Trapping her heels to my chest, I reach over and open her nightstand drawer. *She does.* I scan her vibrators, instantly overwhelmed with the selection. Her pussy wasn't stretched by another person recently, but some of these dildos are bigger than my cock, so...

I swing my gaze to Lex, my molars grinding together to keep from asking her which ones she's been using, so I can—

"You throw out my toys, I throw out yours," she says, reading my mind.

"I don't have any toys—"

"You would've seen them if you weren't so impatient."

"—other than you."

She just rolls her eyes, and tells me to grab the pink one.

"What's it do?" I ask as I hand the toy that resembles a Rose to her. There's no way it's supposed to fit up her pussy. It's wider than a fist.

"Sucks my clit until I squirt."

Feeling my face muscles relax, I let out a chuckle. She better have flood insurance because there's about to be a fucking geyser in here.

Gripping her ankles, I spread her legs into a wide V, appreciating the view down below. Shit, have I missed that. Fuck sunsets. This is what I want to see every night.

"Condoms are—"

I'm already shaking my head. "There's no fucking way I'm wearing a condom tonight." I doubt I'll ever wear one again.

"If you get me pregnant again, you're not going anywhere."

My eyes snap back to hers. "Snow, the only way I'm leaving you is in the back of a hearse."

"Dead or alive?" she asks, her tone the same it is whenever she's joking but pretending she isn't.

"Depends on the size of the casket. If I'm still alive, you better be in there with me, fucking every last bit of life out of me. That's the only way I want to go."

"I thought you wanted to die from my scratches."

Bending over her, I lean down and say, "Your nails cut deepest while I'm inside you." Then, I kiss the fuck out of her, all tongue and teeth, just the way we like it.

Fuck, marry, kill was one of the many games we used to play inside to pass the time, except I always struggled with my answers. Now I understand why. I choose Lex to do all three to me.

Her nails score the skin down my pecs and abs when I pull away to my full height, the deep chasms instantly sprouting cherry-red drops.

"I need lube for this," she says, jiggling her Rose-shaped toy.

Without hesitation, I spit on her clit, my saliva a glistening puddle spreading over the swollen peak.

She gets the vibrator suctioned to her clit, then hits the power button, her back bowing off the bed like a possession straight out of the movies.

I line my cock up at her entrance, watching as I nudge myself in between her tight walls just enough to feel the vibration traveling down those fat pink lips, tickling my head.

"I love you," I tell her before driving the rest of the way inside her pussy because I have to. In this moment no other words will do.

I don't withdraw right away, instead staying completely buried as our bodies get reacquainted.

I hear, "I love you, too," and drag my gaze up her torso to meet Lex's stare.

"Say it again."

After licking her lips, briefly biting on her bottom one, she says, "I love you."

Grinning ear to ear, I circle my hips, my balls in her ass cheeks, then pick up the pace.

It was worth the wait.

She was worth the wait.

Forty-Five

Reece

STAY ON THE STAIRS, MY BODY A FUCKING STATUE AS I LISTEN to their voices. After waking up to an empty bed, I threw on the shirt and pair of sweatpants Lex left out for me, then came to see where she was, and immediately heard her—my daughter. Primrose. That was several minutes ago. As much as I want to see Primrose with my own eyes, I like hearing Lex with her. She's…soft. She's still very much Lex, just a bit softer.

Eventually, I descend the rest of the steps and follow the noise to the kitchen where Lex is a streak of black and white as she glides around the room gathering stuff for breakfast, all with a dark-haired little girl on her hip.

Primrose is playing with Lex's hair, wrapping it around her fingers and clenching her fist with the strands. Lex's head tilts toward our daughter, but she doesn't react otherwise to her hair being pulled.

Before she even sees me, Lex says, "Glad to see you found the courage to finally join us."

Smirking, I shake my head. "You could've woken me up."

At my voice, Primrose twists her head over Lex's shoulder, meeting my eyes with a deep frown, her black eyebrows puckered to almost touching.

"Who's that?" Lex asks her with a gentle tone. "Who's that, Prim?"

All at once, Primrose's features transform into one of the purest expressions I've ever seen as she breaks into a smile, breathing, "Dada."

My knee goes weak. Before this moment I didn't think it was possible to fall in love twice in one lifetime.

Still focused on mixing something together, Lex says, "Dada. That's right."

I approach the two slowly, clearing my throat to tell Primrose, "Hi, happy girl."

When she doesn't shy away from me, only smiles bigger, I take her chunky hand, and unwrap the hair from it. Just because Lex's pain tolerance is higher than most doesn't mean my tolerance for her pain is.

Wrapping my arms around both girls, I hold them. Neither of them squirms or rushes to end the embrace, giving me the time I need to wrap my head around this. Yesterday I had nothing. Absolutely nothing. Now I have them, which feels like everything. For the first time in years I feel like crying.

But I also feel okay. Incredibly fucking okay.

I press a long kiss to the back of Lex's head before pulling back to say, "Good morning, Snow."

"Morning, rookie."

"Mummy," Primrose says, smacking Lex's shoulder.

"Yeah. Your mommy," I tell her before asking Lex, "How does she know who I am?"

Lex spins around and sidesteps me. "Because we told her. We've been showing her pictures of you since she came home from the hospital."

Pictures? Where'd Lex get pictures of me? And who's "we"?

"When was that?"

"She was born July twentieth and she came home with me a couple days later."

That means Primrose will be two in a couple months.

A robotic voice from somewhere in the house announces, "Motion detected door one," just before the front door opens, then another voice—one I grew up with and would know anywhere—calls out, "Found the sippy cup!"

My mom? My fucking mom?

"It fell under the seat, so I had to really get—" My mom comes around the corner holding up a lidded cup, but stops when she sees me. "Hey, Reece."

"Hey, Ma."

"You made it." Her eyes fill with tears as she rushes over to wrap her arms around me. I hug her just as tightly, rubbing her back as she sobs.

"I made it…"

Lex breezes past us, saying, "Home." She puts Primrose in some sort of kid chair, and our little girl immediately starts spooning the… mush—I don't know what else to call it but it looks like fucking mush—into her mouth.

Releasing me, my mom asks Lex, "Did she recognize him?"

I hear, "Motion detected door one," again before the front door opens and closes.

Lex nods. "At first glance."

My mom clasps her hands together, saying, "It worked."

"What worked?" Breckyn asks, rounding the same corner my mom just did. "Holy shit, you actually made it out."

We hug, not as tight or as long as my mom and I did. It's almost overwhelming, the sensation of touch again. Thankfully, it wasn't last night with Lex. All we fucking did was touch. Once I started, I couldn't stop.

"And huge," my sister adds after we separate. "What were they feeding you in there?"

I gesture to the bowl in front of Primrose, telling her, "Not much better than that."

"Must've been all those jailhouse fights." Breck laughs. "We thought you'd never get out. Charlie and I even had a bet going."

"They did not," my mom says, opening the fridge to take out a bottle of apple juice and pouring some into the sippy cup.

What the fuck is happening right now?

"So…you all…"

Everybody stops to stare at me.

"He doesn't know?" Breck asks Lex, who just shakes her head.

"Maybe if you'd called and checked in on your family," my mom says with a hint of disapproval.

"Those calls would've cost you money." I wouldn't even see them the times they tried to visit. I couldn't. In my mind, I failed them. In my mind, I became my father. I risked their lives for an obsession.

Breck scoffs. "We got loads of that now."

Do they? How? Did Lex give them all the money I stashed at her mom's?

"I heard about Silvy's closing."

TV was a luxury I rarely earned. If we were lucky enough to get newspapers, we'd get them two or three months, sometimes longer, after publication, and we didn't always get Fox Hollow's, so most of the news I got was from word of mouth—mouths that were apparently only repeating what Lex wanted me to hear.

Finally, Lex speaks, saying, "Yeah. We closed it down."

Lex obviously got the contract back from Cyrus's safe, but again, who's "we"?

"Why? What happened?" My mom loved Silvy's.

She shrugs. "Nothing. It was named after a man. We opened Gwen's Florals the next day. No business was lost."

I look to my mom. She's smiling so big her eyes crinkle at the corners. "Can you believe it? It's back in the family."

Breck says, "Perfect timing, too, with property values on the rise."

"So you did end up going into real estate?"

Breck ignores me to ask Lex, "You didn't tell him anything?" To me, she says, "I work for Lex."

She calls her Lex now, too. I thought I was the only one.

"*For* Lex?"

"Yeah, at Apex Realty."

"You own it?" I ask Lex, but Breckyn answers me again.

"Lex owns all of Fox Hollow."

"I don't own Fox Hollow," Lex argues weakly.

"She runs it," Breck amends before wordlessly switching places with her to supervise Primrose trying to feed herself.

"Your sister's exaggerating." Lex rolls her eyes as she passes me, but then adds, "It's a group effort."

Before I can ask what kind of group, that same voice from before alerts, "Motion detected door three." Another door opens, this one from the rear of the house.

"My mom—"

"Aleksandra? Why are there—"

At Lex's mom's voice, I shut my eyes.

"Oh, a stranger," Yetta says.

"Mum, this is Reece. Do you remember seeing his face in the pictures we show Prim?"

Before Yetta has a chance to get flustered, I step in the direction I think she's in and stick my hand out, reintroducing myself as, "Reece Souza, your—"

"My next son-in-law."

I smile. She remembered.

This time she takes my hand and gives it a timid shake before quickly letting go.

"Mum?" Lex asks, closer than she was a second ago.

She didn't tell her daughter about our first meeting.

"Your mom and I met before."

"And you said—"

"That I was going to marry you." I turn my head toward Lex's voice, promising, "Because I am." When I ask Lex to marry me, I'll be gazing into those color-changing eyes.

"You're exhausting," comes out on a sigh I know is her trying not to laugh.

"He should talk to your father first," Yetta says.

"Mum, that's impossible. Dad's grave was vandalized beyond repair."

I stick both hands in my pockets. "Beyond repair? It was a grave of dirt."

"Someone dug that dirt up and basically cremated my father's remains."

I bob my head along.

"And left Roses behind, perfectly intact, out of the blaze's reach," my mom adds.

My body goes still, and I get the feeling looks are being exchanged because nobody says anything for a couple minutes. Do they know?

Finally, Yetta breaks the silence, telling me, "You can look."

"Are you sure?"

After a deep breath, she says, "Yes."

I open my eyes. All the females are focused on me, even my messy-faced daughter through her long, unblinking eyelashes.

Yetta's got a hand up to her face, half covering a large eye patch. I don't see any ink, so her tattoo must be underneath.

I consider telling her how beautiful she is, because she is—she looks just like Lex but older and with darker hair—but figure it's better not to comment on her looks. There's more to everyone than meets the eye. I learned that from her daughter.

So instead, I ask, "How are your window boxes holding up?"

"Um, oh."

"My mom lives out here with us now. Her house is just a short walk away."

It must be the one I saw last night. It didn't have any window boxes.

"You didn't get her house in the divorce?"

"All of Kordin's assets were seized. I didn't bother fighting for it since my dad…"

"Well, I'll just have to put new window boxes up at your new place," I tell Yetta to get us off that topic.

Yetta lowers her hand to her collarbone, then chest before letting it fall altogether, giving me a hint of a grin. "I do like flowers."

"Yes, she does. She even works at Gwen's with me a couple days a week."

"Think you can order me some Queen of the Nights?" I ask my mom.

"For Lex?"

"For my future mother-in-law. I promised her I'd plant some for her. And stick around long enough to help her see them."

"Ah, Reece, you're so—"

"Sweet," Lex finishes for my mom with a headshake.

"Only for you," I say to her. I thought maybe I'd lost that part of me, but being around Lex again brought it back out. I love her so fucking much.

I love this, whatever the fuck is happening. I think it's always been my destiny to be surrounded by women, and after spending the last couple years of my life without any, I'm perfectly fucking at peace with it.

"What about Charlie? Where's she?"

"Oh, I forgot to tell you, but Charlie's running late," Breck reports to Lex like she's already on the clock. "She was dropping off donuts at Home Base, but she should be here any minute."

"Home Base?"

"You probably knew it as The Playground."

What the fuck?

"Lex?"

"A lot's changed, rook," is all she says.

"A *lot*," Breck agrees. "It's a community outreach center now, specializing in helping women and children in need."

My sisters have the luxury of never knowing what that building was really like.

"Charlie's one of Lex's volunteer coordinators there."

I swing my gaze back to Lex. "You own that, too?"

The only explanation she gives is, "It's a group effort."

"What is?"

All four women answer in unison, saying, "Everything."

Now I'm fucking overwhelmed. Lex runs Fox Hollow. Or she at least runs it with other…women? Yeah, she runs it with other women, including my—Including *our* family. That's why they renamed Silvy's to Gwen's.

After Charlie arrives, and we all catch up over gluten-free muffins, I join Lex in the kitchen where she's drinking from a mug of dark liquid. It's not black and it doesn't smell like coffee, but I don't think it's that disgusting tea that's for her thyroid either. She told me last night she's still in remission and isn't as strict with her diet as she was.

468 | A. MARIE

Thanks to her doctor, Charlie's also in remission. Where Lex's thyroid was overactive, Charlie's was apparently underactive.

"So your security system isn't just for looks?"

"The second you stepped on the property, I deactivated the house alarm."

"You gonna tell me you smelled me out there?" It's a big property. Several acres at least.

Over her mug, Lex's gaze touches on every person before she says, "Before Cyrus's untimely death, he had a will made, generously leaving everything to his stepdaughter."

I almost snort. No way he did that, but I'll bite.

"Everything?"

She turns her head to look at me directly. "Everything. And while most people don't know who his stepdaughter is, some have strong memories and even stronger grudges, so my house is protected with sensors on every window and door, along with motion detectors both inside and out that alert me to anyone approaching whether the alarm is set or not. I knew the moment you got here because the entire property's monitored by twenty-four-hour trail cams, but I knew you were coming because…"

"Because your spy told you?"

"Because you're loyal."

"I didn't come out of loyalty." I don't want her thinking I sought her out with a happy reunion on my mind. My thoughts were far from that when I showed up last night.

She smirks. "Yes, you did, rook. Even when you lost sight of me, you were loyal to me. I was completely gone, missing from your life, but you still found me."

"Sunflowers," I murmur, remembering that conversation.

Lex's tone changes, grows more serious as she says, "I am in a different place than the last time you saw me. I wasn't worthy of being anybody's sun then, but I've worked hard these past couple years to make myself worthy of being yours."

Her chest tattoo.

"You were always worthy to me, Lex."

"Until I believed it for myself, I wasn't able to take anyone else's word for it. I still don't do everything right, but what I do wrong, I do for the right reasons."

I think she did them for the right reasons before, too. She just didn't let anyone see it, not even herself.

"What do we do about the police chief? If he—"

"Chief Hull, along with half of the FHPD, were forced to resign after it came out that they had been taking bribes from notorious crime lord, Cyrus Andeno, for years leading up to his untimely death. They were also some of his best customers. News stations around the state were sent copies of Cyrus's personal records of meticulously detailed receipts listing every transaction, including any and all services they were provided at The Playground."

"How long ago was that?"

"I can't remember the specific date, but a little over two years ago."

Jesus. She is a goddamn apex predator. That's what's above her. Absolutely nothing.

As Breck's preparing to leave to go look at possible locations for a new domestic violence shelter, she asks, "Can anyone take Primrose to her Mommy and Me swim lessons this weekend for me? I'm in my luteal phase and unwilling to wear a swimsuit in public during this difficult and confusing time."

I have to laugh. I never thought I'd miss hearing about period cycles.

"What kind of witch are you?" I ask Lex since I know my family would've educated her on the different types by now.

She answers without pause. "Red."

"You bleed on the full moon?"

She nods.

That means she'll be ovulating soon.

I'll have her pregnant in no time.

Charlie, sitting on the floor and getting her hair "brushed" by Primrose, raises her hand, saying she's available. Next to her is a punching bag, not right in the middle of the living room, but off to the side. Lex was right. If I hadn't been in such a hurry to find her last night, I would've noticed this place is exactly what we talked about. I haven't seen the shelves of smut yet but I know they're here somewhere. And they better not be wrapped up in paper.

Lex tells them both, "We'll do it."

"Lex."

She arches an eyebrow at me.

"I don't know how to…"

"Swim? I'll teach you."

"No, not swim. Be…" Primrose's dad. A Mommy and Me participant. Out in the free world.

My skin itches and I feel hot trying to explain it.

"I'll teach you that, too," Lex promises.

"You don't know what I was gonna say."

"I don't need to. I'll teach you anything you need me to."

I used to be the one willing to take on the world for her just so I could show it to her. Now the roles have reversed and she's the one offering me unconditional support.

"I don't know. I'm a…convict." I have a lot of shit I have to unlearn, including walking, talking, and behaving like someone serving time.

Lex moves around the counter, positions herself in front of me, and drapes her arms around my neck.

"I don't want to hide you. Not here. Not anywhere. In private or public, in the dark or light, I want to treat you the same. Like you're mine." She seals the same vow I once gave her by brushing my lips with hers, then pulls back and adds, "Because you are."

This is exactly what I wanted—to touch her, gaze at her, openly flirt with her, *love* her—and it's better than I ever could've imagined.

Staring into eyes like Snow in Summer foliage, I realize what it is that affects Lex's eye color. It's not the lighting. It's her moods.

"What's that term that means better than happy? The one my sister used?" She never told me.

Those silver eyes break from mine to glance at Breckyn, then they return, an easy smile both in them and under them.

"Nothing above."

Bonus Scene

Reece

The night before/morning of his arrest

AFTER DISARMING THE ALARM, I FLIP ON THE LIGHTS, instantly illuminating the back room of Silvy's. Floral arrangements cover every available surface, some even on the floor. My mom's busy on a consistent basis. She has no slow times.

With no one in here to make noise or cause distractions, I can hear it—the gunshot that left me fatherless. The blast rings through my ears just like it did that day, except this time, I welcome the closure it brings.

Lex and I have that in common, too. We both had disgraces for dads.

Unlike Lex though, I've never visited my dad's grave. Tonight I'll get my final message across without even needing to.

I pass the wall of ribbons and decorative picks, stopping by the large counter-height table where my mom does most of her work to inspect the row of buckets stuffed with flowers; none of them what I'm looking for.

Turning for the cooler, I walk inside, careful to keep the door propped open so I don't accidentally lock myself in here. My parents used to scare the shit out of me about that when I was a kid, and to this day, I think about it every time I set foot in the walk-in.

I scan each shelf. *Black, black, black.*

Finally, I find them in a bucket on the floor. Since there's no such thing as real black Roses, they have to be made. The Black Baccara Rose, which has black-tinged burgundy petals comes closest, otherwise florists create black Roses by putting white ones in water mixed with black floral dye. The colored water gets absorbed through the stalk, turning the petals black. I was hoping for thirteen since it's the unluckiest omen, but my mom doesn't have enough on hand. Instead, I take out four long-stems, a nice even number—the standard for funerals—and leave the rest in case she gets an order. She must not have had time to pluck off the thorns yet because they're all still intact. Thorns are a sign of evil, so my mom typically dethorns every Rose upon getting it in. I'm glad these ones weren't. Four thorny black Roses—it doesn't get any more spiteful.

Once I get the lights off and set the alarm again, I drive to the cemetery Lex's dad is buried. I don't know if Cyrus is tracking my car and I don't have the time to check it over, so after dumping the Explorer, I stole a gray Honda Pilot, the back just large enough for all my supplies.

I get everything unloaded next to Aleksander Obuchowski's grave, the moon bathing the graveyard in an eerie glow, giving it an entirely different feel from the last time I was here with Lex. That was like a dream. This feels more like a nightmare.

Not for me though.

For him.

Unzipping my pants, I pull out my dick and aim right at his engraved name. My piss hits each letter, creating a steaming waterfall down the marble facade. When I'm done, I tuck myself away and zip back up, then I get started digging.

Luckily, the snowstorm missed Fox Hollow entirely, making it *slightly* easier than if there was snow, too. The ground is still pretty damn solid. It takes longer than I was hoping, but my shovel hits the casket after only four feet. I clear the top of dirt, then bring my shovel down through the lid several times, making sure to breathe through my mouth. I don't even want to *imagine* what this mother-fucker smells like, let alone experience it firsthand.

After climbing out, I switch my shovel for a gas can, emptying it out over the grave.

Next I prop the black Roses on the top of the headstone. Black Roses are associated with death, mourning, revenge, and hatred. Even though I've never met this man, I fucking hate him. I hate him for what he did to Lex and her mom. Before Lex even had a chance to pull that trigger, Aleksander'd already killed parts of both his wife and daughter—their futures, their lives; they might as well be buried alongside him. He fucking robbed the Obuchowski women of any happiness.

And for once in my life, I want to return what's stolen.

Looming over Lex's father, I pull a box of matches out of my pocket, and say down to him, "You failed. You failed your wife. You failed your daughter. Just like my dad, you failed everyone that depended on you."

I strike a single match and let it burn in front of my face for a moment before dropping it down into the hole. The entire grave ignites into an inferno, the flames hot and angry as they eat through the gasoline, wood, and whatever the fuck Aleksander Obuchowski is. He's not a man any more than Kordin Debrosse is or Silvino Souza was.

Good fucking riddance to them all.

"I'm gonna take care of both of them, better than you ever could," I promise Aleksander, the universe, myself.

Aleksander's body being here is what's been keeping Yetta here. Now, if Lex needs to leave, she can without breaking her mom's heart. She said she was willing to at the cabin, but I'd never make her. Breaking her mom's heart would break hers, and whether or not she'll admit to giving it to me, Lex's heart is mine to protect. That's exactly what I'm gonna do, tonight, tomorrow, and every moment after.

"Oh," I say before I leave. "Tell my dad about the Roses." Because I know wherever Lex's dad ended up, my dad landed, too. "They're as much for him as they are for you."

The moment the taillights from a passing car disappear down the street, I come out from the side of the house and return to the window box out front, topping it off. Using my hands, I spread the dirt around and pack it down so it doesn't look new. I move on to the next window box, repeating the same process of scooping out the soil that's already in there, layering the bottom with the bags I brought, then pouring the dirt back over top.

Along with the money I stole from Cyrus's safe earlier, the bags also hold fake IDs for all the women in my life, smutty books for the ones over eighteen, and both flash drives, even though I already erased everything on them. I don't know how much time I'll have to talk to Lex tomorrow, but I'd rather they be in her possession than have her worry where they might turn up. She'll have enough going on.

"Aleksandra's already got a date to homecoming," I hear somewhere beside me, and freeze.

The bags in the second window box have a thin layer of dirt covering them, so I shut my eyes tight, and tell Lex's mom, "I know," wondering if that's a homecoming Lex ever made it to.

"Then what are you doing?"

I start to turn around.

"Don't."

"My eyes are closed." I hold my hands up, too. "I can't see anything."

Yetta waits until I'm fully facing her to ask, "Why are you out here in the middle of the night?"

"I wanted to surprise, um, Aleksandra with flowers." I point in the direction I last saw the window box.

"She won't like them unless they're unscented, otherwise it'll overwhelm her sensitive nose."

I grin. So it wasn't something she picked up working at The Playground. She's always had a strong sense of smell.

"You're better off planting flowers for another girl. I told you, Aleksandra's taken."

ABOVE | 475

I shake my head, a sliver of light slipping through my eyelids, allowing me to make out Yetta's form peeking around the corner of her front porch. She has a hand up to her face. I'm assuming to cover her tattoo.

"I can't do that," I tell her.

"Why not?"

"Because he's the wrong guy for her."

"And you're the right one?"

"I'm the only one."

There's no sound for a solid minute, then a quiet, "Are you her husband?"

She must've figured out what year it is. On her own, too, because I didn't correct her once.

Lowering my hands, I say, "Not yet." I stick one out toward her and tell her, "I'm Reece Souza, your future son-in-law."

Somehow, someway…someday…I'm gonna marry Lex.

Yetta's laugh is the opposite of her daughter's. It's completely untamed.

I wish I could hear more of it.

I will.

Eventually.

She doesn't shake my hand, just asks, "What flowers did you plant?"

I lower my hand and turn my head like I can actually see my work.

"Um." I didn't plant any.

I can plant flowers for her. Not tonight, but one night I will.

I turn back to Yetta. Lex told me her mom never leaves her house unless she has to, but here she is, outside, under the veil of night.

"Queen of the Night flower," I tell her. "It's a Cereus flower in the cactus family. It blooms one time a year, only at night."

"Sounds special."

I nod. "It is. It's a symbol for enjoying the little moments." *Because they don't last,* I think, keeping the rest of the meaning to myself. "It's said whoever sees one will have good luck." Even though I'm not technically seeing Yetta, I'm still hoping that's true.

After a long pause, she whispers, "I might miss it."

"They take at least four or five years to bloom." By then, I should already be out and have planted one for her.

Five years…it shouldn't be that long. It better not be that long.

My dirt-coated fingers itch to claw at my prickly throat.

I promise her anyway, "I won't let you miss it."

"Well…" Yetta sighs and shifts. "If you're serious about marrying Aleksandra, you'll need to talk to her father, let him know your intentions."

My lips curve into a smile. Whether she forgot her husband's dead, or she's so damn old school she expects me to go get permission from a fucking ghost, that asshole's been made well aware of my intentions.

"Consider it done."

Books by
A. MARIE

Creekwood Series
Detour
Changing Lanes
Blind Spot
Roundabout

Standalones
Let The Light Shine Through
The Comedown
Nothing Above

For more playlists, inspiration boards, and bonus scenes, be sure to check out my website amarieauthor.com.

Acknowledgements

Huge thank you to my team on this one—Samantha, Shanna, Brandi, Judy, and Stacey. This book is so beautiful, inside and out, and I have you all to thank for helping make that happen.

Thank you an infinite amount of times to Stephanie Rinaldi for being infinitely smarter than I am and helping me every single time I come to you. Thank your hubby for me, too. You both were a tremendous help.

Thank you to Joanna Krawczyk for helping me with the Polish. And Kat Noelle for making that happen.

Finally, thank you to my family for once again giving me allllll the patience. I'm so lucky to have you four in my corner cheering me on.